Dedication

I dedicate this to the family that I built because without you I would still be lost. To all the dreamers and those who believe in true love between souls. Last but certainly not least I dedicate this to you Alexander because you are my inspiration and will always have a part of me.

Chapter 1

Every fall semester brings with it an indescribable feeling of renewed hope in the air of a university. It's as if the hopes and dreams brought by each student can be felt flowing through the campus. With faces in a comical state of confusion, distress, and excitement they march onto campus willing to take on the challenges ahead. Every incoming class brings with it the bittersweet reality that success and happiness is not a guarantee. Some will graduate with honors, some will eventually drop out, and some will go on to do great things, but unfortunately some will never see past their first year. The common factor is that they all begin with a clean slate and the potential to take their lives wherever they want to go.

Prior to the start of class most schools host a welcome week with a n orientation aimed at getting the new students acquainted with and possibly involved on campus. This is where people might meet their best friends, while some find their life's partner. For most, it is just a time where they are tested by the trials of life and are expected to take the necessary steps to building a better future, though most are unaware of this. The first few weeks can be very taxing on the spirit of the new students who have no idea what's in store for them. While it is frightening, it is also very exciting.

The story begins at the State University where thousands of excited freshmen roamed the campus while coordinators ensured that the school's *Welcome Week* proceeded smoothly. They did their best to direct the crowds towards the organization fair and check in stations. The tables all aligned through the designated area served as introductions to the different organizations ranging from Political Activist Club to Television Club. It would seem that school was already in session because the campus was buzzing with activity but this was only a fraction of the total student body. By now many lost newcomers had formed groups at the information tables as they searched for the check in areas. Some of the foreign students could be seen quickly making friends with other foreign students who shared their nervous excitement. It's fascinating how a simple smile can be welcoming enough to create new relationships with people during a time of chaos.

Near the edge of the academic campus, at the heart of the residential campus stood a lonely sign that read: *Welcome New Students!* This was clearly the idea of a person who had never actually been present for the welcoming of the new students because it was way too small for people to see and it was posted onto a tree that provided shade for the check in tables but blocked the sign's visibility. Whether or not people could read the sign didn't pose much of a problem because the long line of students made it pretty obvious that this was where the check in station was. It is here where a young man sporting a backpack with only one strap over his shoulder stood waiting to check in. He hid nervously behind his dark sunglasses.

It was a hot Midwestern summer day, which meant high humidity and an uncomfortably sticky afternoon. Of course being that it was the Midwest it could be warm in the morning and cold by the afternoon. He could hear the check in process as the other students ahead of him went through it. *State name, state year, state hall* and the person at the table would hand over the welcome package, it all seemed pretty simple. The never-ending line caused some of the people to become impatient while the young man maintained a cool attitude. He understood that there were worse things than the line he was in so he shrugged off the unpleasant environment and instead took out his headphones so that he could listen to some music. He selected one of his new favorite songs from the short list of music he had accumulated over the summer. As he listened to the music he smiled at the lyrics of the song. He was in good spirits and filled with excitement. He bobbed his head to the beat without worrying about what the people around him would think. To him this was a safe place to act as silly as he wanted to. As he enjoyed the music he thought about how great it was to not worry about the Christian school teachers or pastors seeing him. This was part of the anxiety faced when you attended a Christian school where the appearance of the person was more important than the actual person.

"Rhian Alexander Pierce." The young man announced with excitement as he finally reached the front of the line. He pulled off his sunglasses revealing two brilliant emerald green eyes, which carried a kindness that was both comforting and warm. The girl behind the table was so distracted by his eyes that she stared for longer than was necessary. Rhian realized her apparent distraction and responded with a smile while he repeated his name.

"Rhian…" Of course his smile just added to the mounting tension that the poor girl faced. She was brought back to what she was doing when he repeated his name but she was now blushing with embarrassment.

"I'm sorry… Let me check…" She glanced up at him a few times as she searched for his name. "I don't see that name."

"It sounds like Ryan but it is spelled R-h-i-a-n." He responded with a chipper smile. She was now more nervous than before. Rhian's smile was disarming and inspiring, showcasing a set of perfectly straight pearly whites. Rhian had very attractive features including a symmetrically slender face, high cheekbones and a sharp jaw line. His brow rose gently upwards to a full head of hair. While his strong features gave him a very masculine appearance his button nose coupled with his full but slightly feminine lips gave him a boyish contrast that was uniquely beautiful.

Rhian stood about average height at five-foot eleven-inches tall with an average frame. He didn't have a toned figure but he didn't care, he was content that his body was naturally balanced. For most, his face was more than enough to label him as attractive but he didn't think that he was anything special, though he did admit that his eyes were his best feature.

"Are you a freshman or a transfer?" The girl asked nervously.

"I'm a freshman, my apologies for not saying so. That is a beautiful necklace by the way." Rhian figured he would charm the girl.

"Oh, no not a problem at all… Thank you. Here you are, I found you." She replied with a smile as she handed him his orientation packet.

"Thank you… Tami." He said as looking at her nametag. The girl must have forgotten that she was wearing it because she seemed startled when he said her name.

"Have a great day!" She awkwardly called out as Rhian walked away.

"You too!" Rhian replied with a wink. Rhian had always been a spirited person, never afraid talk about what was on his mind, barring a few taboo topics. He was the one to start a conversation and likely the one to finish it. Rhian's personality was magnetic, attracting all kinds of people.

Rhian walked away from the check-in table with more excitement than he had ever felt before because this was the journey that he had waited so long for and it was finally here. There was no way to describe how happy he was. It was the perfect opportunity to start over after such a dark period in his life and he wasn't going to waste a single minute. He walked to his car, which was parked in front of his residence hall and new home. As he approached the vehicle he noticed the many parents helping their kids move into their new homes. It made him a bit sad that he was here alone but he knew it was better this way so he banished any thoughts of jealousy. He found Bella, his old yet faithful bright red SUV, parked in front of Washington Hall. Bella was filled with most of Rhian's earthly possessions, which included all of two large suitcases, a few boxes, a set of bed sheets and his art supplies. He looked through the welcome package for the map to where his room was. As luck would have it he was at the right spot just a few feet away from his door.

Rhian opened the back door and pulled out a smaller box so that he could find his room without wasting a trip. Just then a group of people that came out of nowhere, walked up to his car and asked if he needed help, Rhian happily accepted. It didn't take very much help to get his things into his dorm room because he didn't have much to bring. While others were bringing in boxes of the most unnecessary things carried by overbearing parents, Rhian had arrived alone with few belongings but fewer attachments to the life he used to know. It was a miracle that he was able to go to school and if not for a last minute grant he would still be sitting at home with his parents and wondering *What if?* He was very happy that his dreams were starting to come true so he didn't mind sacrificing fancy gadgets now for a better future. Once he had all of his things put away he breathed in a sigh of relief because for the first time in his life, he was on exactly where he wanted to be. For the first time in his life, the demons of his past weren't going to follow him and he could finally be happy.

Across the street in Jefferson Hall, commonly known as Jeff, another young man by the name of Alexander was struggling to get his things through the side door of the building. The bulky refrigerator wasn't too heavy, but its awkward shape made it a challenge to maneuver. He struggled for only a few moments but being the prideful athletic guy that he was, there was no way he would let the refrigerator win this battle. After a few attempts he was finally able to pass the threshold and was soon setting it down in his room. He stepped back to observe the amount of space in the room and created a mental picture of how he wanted the room to look. He moved the fridge to the corner of the room so that it was out of the way.

Alexander, at six-foot-three, had broad shoulders, strong arms and a trim waist that gave him the physique of a swimmer. A square face, strong jaw, and straight yet flawless nose created a masculinity that was irresistible to ignore. Alexander's shy upward smile was cute while his captivating eccentric blue eyes gave him a dreamer's demeanor. He had the true All-American appeal that could melt even the coldest of hearts. While he appeared to be a stereotype, Alexander was nothing like the typical jock. As an intellectual individual, he kept mostly to himself interacting with others only out of necessity. He was a star lacrosse player on his high school's team but he rarely hung out with the other guys.

"Are you going to stand around and make your mother and I carry everything or are you going to help?" Alexander's planning was disrupted by his father who walked into the room with a heavy box.

"Sorry dad. I was just trying to figure out how I wanted to arrange the room."

"You can do that once all of the stuff is in the room. We still have a long drive home and we want to get back before five."

"Alright, I'll figure it out later. Thank you for your help."

"That's what parents are for, Son." He must have realized that he sounded cold so he forced a smile.

"I love you dad." Alexander appreciated his father's attempt.

"I love you too." His father turned around and headed back to the car. There wasn't much else that was said between Alexander and his parents. They quickly unloaded the car.

"Ok, is there anything else we could help you with?" Alexander's mother asked.

"He is fine." His father immediately added.

"Well I'm just making sure that he is completely set."

"I'm fine Mom… Thanks." She looked at him and smiled as she held back tears. She hugged him and then he hugged his father. They quickly left the room and were on their way home. Alexander looked around for somewhere to sit down but couldn't find a single place to settle down and rest. Unable to leave the room in shambles, he began to unpack some of his things and came across an envelope that he didn't remember packing. Inside he found a few hundred dollars and a short note.

Alexander,

> *Please use this money wisely. Call often. Study hard and have a wonderful time.*

> *Love Mom*

Alexander couldn't help but break out into a smile. She always knew what to say at the right moment. He hadn't really had time to think about how nervous he was because he was so focused on making sure that his parents were back on the road quickly since his dad didn't do well with deviations from his schedule. But after reading the encouraging note, he felt at peace with everything. He sighed as he considered putting up his posters on the baron walls but there was still so much to unpack that the posters would have to wait. He liked to keep things organized but he did allow a bit of a mess so that he wouldn't obsess over minute details. As long as everything was clean, he was content. The long drive from home and the unloading made him want to lie down for a minute so he cleared his bed and put some of the boxes underneath. Just as he was about to lie down he remembered that he hadn't set up his gaming system. Alexander popped up and began putting together his TV and gaming system. By the time he finished setting it up he was feeling hungry so he figured it was a good time to get some food and explore the campus.

He took a second to gather his thoughts and plan a route. He didn't like to go anywhere without a plan, probably a quirk passed down from his dad. Alexander closed his eyes and slowly counted to ten. As a boy he used this technique to escape the torment he faced in the abusive environment of the foster care system. Now he used it when he felt nervous. In this case his nerves were a direct result of the unknown that was outside of his building. But Alexander realized the privilege he was given by attending college and he wasn't going to let his nerves get in the way of the new world ahead of him.

He toured the campus by himself while collecting bits of information from passing parents who had once attended. He joined in on a tour unannounced and followed them the rest of the way. Alexander usually took an academic approach towards new experiences and researched all he could before his involvement. As expected, he had already looked through campus maps, memorized the names of all the buildings, and scouted out potential study and hangout spots. After the tour Alexander found himself at the activities fair surrounded by other wide-eyed freshmen and their equally confused parents.

There were clubs for every interest! One of the first tables he noticed was the video game club, nestled between chess club and cycling club. He would have approached them but they were ironically too involved with the game they had set up for potential recruits to recruit. He passed baking club, reading club, hookah club, and tight-rope walking club, gathering pamphlets and whatever free things they had to offer. Nothing stood out to him until he passed lacrosse club. He played in high school so it made sense that he would continue in college.

"Do you play?" The young man in bright pink gym shoes and a *Lacrosse Club* shirt caught his attention.

"Yeah, I played in high school."

"I can tell. I'm John by the way." The jockish young man reached out to shake Alexander's hand.

"I'm Alexander. Nice to meet you."

"Likewise. You should check us out. We meet every day from five to seven in the field across from Jeff. Everyone is welcome so don't worry if your skill level isn't up to par." John was challenging him.

"I was captain of my high school team. I think my skill level is alright."

"We'll see."

"I'll come by tomorrow."

"Awesome. We look forward to seeing you there." John kept his cocky smile as Alexander walked away.

"Thanks." Alexander thought the exchange was a bit short but he loved playing lacrosse and he couldn't stand down now that John had challenged him. He continued walking the aisles of the fair, until he saw another group that interested him. There were about ten guys gathered around a model airplane and a model helicopter. As he approached one of the guys called him.

"Hey man! Come on over and join us."

"Ok… What club is this?"

"Model Airplane Club!" Several of the group members responded with enthusiasm. Alexander was intrigued by the toys as he picked up the helicopter from the table and examined its parts.

"Do you want to try it?" The one who called him over asked with a big smile.

"Sure!" Alexander listened closely to the instructions he was given on how to fly it properly. He caught on quickly and was flying it around the table. He was having fun flying the toy helicopter and he was laughing like a kid at Christmas. As he continued playing with the toy he didn't realize that he had walked towards the aisle of moving people and accidentally ran into someone.

"Sorry about that! I wasn't looking!" Alexander said with a goofy smile still excited about the airplane.

"I'd say so… It's alright." The young man sarcastically yet warmly joked with a light-hearted laugh.

He didn't get a good look at the young man that he had accidentally bumped into but he noticed that his shirt was an awkward shade of orange. Before he could say anything else the young man had already put his headphones back on and was off in his own world. Alexander found him peculiar but didn't think anything else of it so he quickly made his way to the helicopter that had landed on the table.

"Ok dude, you're going to have to give that back… Maybe *next* time you can fly it." The club member suggested as he nervously reached for the remote.

"Sorry about that… Thanks for letting me try it." Alexander handed the remote over with embarrassment.

"No problem." With that unfortunate occurrence he ended his remote control helicopter flying career. He picked up a few more pamphlets before leaving the fair. He had socialized enough for now so he went back to his room and finished putting it together. Once everything was set up the way he wanted it he settled down and began playing video games.

A few hours later he noticed that he had wasted away much of the afternoon playing the game so he turned it off and pulled out the welcome packet. He glanced through the scheduled events and noticed that there was a welcome dinner that evening. Free food was his favorite food so it didn't take much for him to commit to going. He thought about the new friends he might make and was excited but it also meant explaining who he was and where he came from. The picture of his family sat on his dresser as a reminder of his unusual upbringing. He knew that his home life had been anything but normal but he also knew that he was greatly loved. The tumultuous time he spent in abusive foster homes forced him to develop a rough exterior. His adoption was finalized years ago before he was a teen but things were much different now. Though his childhood was no longer a problem he still hid behind a contagious smile and a warm personality, when he wasn't being shy of course.

The welcome dinner was scheduled for that evening in one of the dining halls on campus. The dining area was decorated in the University's colors and there were programs at each seat. Contrary to his desire for discretion he chose a spot near the center of the room and waited for others to join. Though most of the students had spent the better part of the day becoming acquainted with the campus, they all maintained the nervous freshmen look.

For the first time since he was adopted, Alexander was by himself in a new world. It all began to sink in once he realized that no one had joined him at the table. He began to wonder why nobody had sat with him. Maybe he smelled bad. No, that wasn't it. Maybe he was underdressed. No, most college students wear jeans and a t-shirt to… everywhere. Maybe he gave off a bad vibe. No, everyone said he had a kind demeanor. Maybe it was the fact that he was sitting at the center table and the people around him assumed he had reserved the best table. A few had looked at the empty seats but when they made eye contact with him they turned away and kept looking. *Maybe I'm so attractive that the people around me are intimidated.* He laughed quietly at the thought.

"Is there something funny going on? Or are you just weird?" Alexander snapped out of his trance and noticed that there was a young man standing next to him. He stared awkwardly for a second still confused why this guy was looking at him kind of funny.

"I'm Rhian, what's your name?" the young man again spoke up.

"I'm Alexander… nice to meet you!" Alexander said quickly standing up to shake the young man's hand. He had a firm handshake; something that Alexander appreciated.

"A firm handshake is the sign of security, that's a good thing to know when meeting someone for the first time." Rhian responded to the firm handshake. Alexander immediately felt comfortable. "I take it you're not going to tackle me this time?"

"I'm so sorry about that! I wasn't paying attention and… I'm sorry." He felt bad for accidentally running into him earlier while flying the toy helicopter. "It was really embarrassing. I'm not usually that careless."

"I hope that's true. It's alright, at least I know someone here."

"I feel bad about it… it was really embarrassing. Again, I'm sorry. Will you please sit with me so I don't look so pathetic?"

"Of course! No harm done, the distraction proved useful because I found the club I was looking for." Alexander smiled awkwardly knowing that Rhian was just trying to make him feel better about it.

"So are you planning on joining the model airplane club or were you just trying to have an excuse for tackling people?" Rhian jokingly sassed.

"I don't know if they'll ever actually let me back but I'd like to. How about you? What clubs were you considering joining?"

"I am strongly considering the Sailing Club… I love the water and I've always wanted to try that."

"That sounds like a lot of fun. I like the water too, although I prefer water at the beach as I'm chillin' with a hot girl or something."

"Oh, you have a girlfriend?"

"No… Now that I'm starting school I promised my parents that I would focus on school for now. But a guy can dream right? What about you?" Alexander laughed at Rhian's question.

"I… don't have a girlfriend." The cheerfulness was suddenly drained from his face and Rhian became withdrawn. Alexander, sensing the awkwardness, thought it strange how quickly Rhian's mood changed.

"Well then we are going to have to find some girls to talk to." He did his best to mend the situation. Rhian's eyes perked up and his smile was back with full force. Alexander found it questionable that he could go from such a positive state of emotion to such a negative one and then right back to positive in such a short amount of time. He could tell that Rhian was holding back and that he forced the smile to make the situation less awkward. He didn't linger on this thought because he understood that if his new friend was hesitant to talk about something it was best to let him talk about it when he was ready. "So, what's your major?"

"I'm not completely married to the idea but I'm considering something in business or maybe political science… I haven't actually declared a major yet." Rhian shrugged.

"That's cool, I haven't either. My parents told me to wait until after the first semester to decide what I wanted to do. I have to join at least three clubs that interest me and get involved so that I find what it is that I want to do. I think I want to study math, but I also really like the idea of studying business so I may try to do both. We'll see! For now I'll be taking a few intro courses."

"Same here. I can't wait to start. Moving here was a good first step." Rhian added with a smile.

The two sat pausing only for a moment before the conversation again began and continued naturally until the dinner was over. They discovered that they lived across the street from each other so they walked back together and continued their conversation. They talked about everything under the sun and found that they disagreed on almost nothing.

"I understand that peanut butter is good, but Reese's doesn't compare to Twix… I'm sorry that's just a fact of life." Rhian arrogantly stated

"Twix is like silver, it's a good consolation prize. Reese's is like gold. Everybody wants Reese's." They bantered back and forth, about which candy was superior but eventually ended up changing the subject. Alexander told Rhian all about his high school and the things he did. Rhian learned that Alexander was a natural athlete and loved playing any sport. Rhian didn't have very many stories he was willing to share just yet so he kept asking questions to avoid being asked. He listened intently to what Alexander was saying and he felt confident that they were going to be good friends. He did notice that Alexander didn't mention his parents much and wondered why that was. But then again, he hadn't really opened up either.

"Ok, so I don't know if you're a gamer but if you are I have this new video game… Wanna come over and play?" Alexander's enthusiasm was undeniable.

"I've never played it before but I'll give it a try." Rhian wasn't one to shy away from an opportunity. Besides he had already made his first friend. He was excited to get to know him better. They shared a few good laughs and continued learning about each other. As the sun began peeking in through the windows, they became aware that they had lost track of time hanging out. Rhian decided it was time to get some sleep at least for a few hours before the day began. He walked back to his room, taking his time as he reflected on the great day he had and the new friend he had made. When he finally made it to his room he sprawled out on his bed over the sheets and buried his face in the pillow before falling asleep.

Between move-in and the first day of school, Rhian explored the campus, applied for a few campus jobs, and decorated his room. He wanted his room to feel like it was his so he put up posters of his favorite bands on the walls. He didn't decorate too extravagantly, as he preferred elegance in simplicity and he didn't have the money to decorate beyond a few pictures on the walls. His bed sheets were grey with two black stripes that ran the length of the sheet. It was simple, mature, and stylish, much like Rhian thought of himself. He didn't want to be seen as an extravagant guy. Perhaps it was because back home, flamboyance was rewarded with punishment, though it wasn't in his nature anyway.

As the first day of school approached Rhian jumped into a consistent daily routine. After returning to high school from his summer at therapy, he followed a very inconsistent eating and sleeping schedule. To keep from going back to the camp, he had to make sure that no one suspected that he hadn't changed. He was a shell refusing to let anyone in for fear of going back. Rhian spent his remaining high school days as an example of successful reformation and his nights as a deeply troubled soul. As a result he didn't sleep much at night because of the night terrors and his weight dramatically fluctuated. It was the only thing at his control so he controlled it. He liked seeing the results that came from his eating decisions because it reminded him that he was still in control and kept him focused on the future. But that period was over and he was now free to do what he wanted.

Rhian's plan was to get his body into good shape, this time without the fluctuations in eating habits. He was excited about spending the next four years in his new home building a better person one day at a time. He was determined to find happiness and he knew that the key to making this happen began with changing his habits and unhealthy lifestyle choices. He began by waking up early every morning and going for a run, this way he was tired enough at night to sleep.

On the morning of the first day of class Rhian's alarm rang for five minutes before there were any signs of life in his room. He got out of bed, yawned and wiped the sleep from his eyes before looking around his room for his running shoes. He put them on, grabbed his phone and headphones and made his way outside. The warm summer air was quite welcoming on his tired face. The warm breeze gently caressed his cheeks reminding him to be thankful for another day of life. He looked up and admired the beautiful sky. He had to find the perfect song to start his run with so that it was more enjoyable. He finally settled on something upbeat and began running.

Rhian ran towards the main campus area. Nearing the academic part of campus he saw a path that he wanted to check out so he headed in that direction. As he ran, a young woman in all pink passed him. Pink sports bra under her white shirt and pink running shorts with matching pink shoes and socks. This girl looked like she just ran out of a Victoria's Secret commercial. Her hair was even flowing just like you would expect to see. She had a slightly round face and soft demeanor. Her cheekbones were perfectly placed giving her a never ceasing smile. Rhian noticed that she was beautiful, even in her work out gear.

She's so pretty... She doesn't look like any of the girls from home. She's probably a model. Rhian thought to himself. He wondered what her story was, where she came from and who she was. *Mom and dad would be proud if I ended up with a girl that looked like her...* He joked to himself. He noticed that by now she had passed him but he didn't want to let her beat him. Where was he going? It didn't matter; he just had to catch up to her. As he pushed himself to run faster he began to catch up to her but she continued unchallenged by Rhian's attempt to compete. It was in his nature to compete, though he would never admit it, so he pressed on. *I'm not letting this chick beat me…* he thought to himself.

When he finally caught up to her he tried to keep speeding up but he was really starting to feel just how out of shape he was. He looked over at her and gave her a sarcastic smile. She saw him and raised an eyebrow in protest of his smile. The words *"what are you doing?"* clearly on her mind. Feeling confident that he had beaten her at this pretend race, Rhian looked over at a car that was off in the distance and didn't see the giant rock that was ahead of him. He turned just in time to see the giant rock, but not in time to avoid it entirely. He jumped out of its way but somehow still hit the rock with less force causing him to fall down.

"Oh my gosh! Are you alright sweetie?" The girl in pink asked Rhian as he realized what had happened.

"Um… yeah I think so... Yeah I'm fine..." Rhian said now blushing from the embarrassment. *Who are you Rhian?* He questioned his sudden impulse to race.

"Did you hurt anything or are you ok? It looked bad but sometimes these falls look worse than they really. Although, if my dad were here he would say 'put some ice on it and walk it off' hah! Story of my life…" She began on her own tangent. Rhian looked at her curiously

"Hah, well ice would probably help but I think I'm alright… You're a fast runner!"

"You're quick too… unless there's a rock in the way…" She laughed unapologetically. "Too soon?" Rhian smiled and began laughing.

"That rock jumped out at me!"

"How did you not see that?"

"I was looking around… I didn't expect it. I don't know!" Rhian was still on the ground trying to make sense of what had happened. "I'm sorry I didn't get your name, I'm Rhian" He reached out to shake her hand.

"I'm Leena, nice to meet you!" She said as she grabbed his hand and pulled him up to his feet without him expecting it.

"I was trying to shake your hand… You are strong!" Rhian was fascinated by the way she lifted his weight without much effort.

"I know, but I figured I'd help you up while I shook your hand. There is something familiar about you Rhian…"

"My ability to fall?"

"I'm not sure what it is but something about you makes me want to talk to you." Leena was drawn in by Rhian's soothing smile but there was something more to it. Perhaps she recognized the dark backstory he hid behind the happy smile.

"I'm open to talking …" Rhian was a bit thrown off by the comment and Leena's candidness.

"Let's be friends."

"People aren't usually that direct when it comes to making friends. I like that."

"Well I'm pretty direct. You'll learn that about me." She said with a smile. "I'm heading back to my place, how about you? Where do you live?"

"I'm at Washington Hall… You?"

"I have an off-campus apartment. It's close to Washington, come on I'll race you to your building." She took off suddenly, leaving Rhian behind. He took off after her and continued until they reached his building.

"Let's do this again soon. I like having someone to push me." Rhian suggested

"Alright, same time tomorrow at this corner. But next time don't kick the rocks please." She replied with a wink before taking off.

He returned to his room and went to take a shower. By the time he was done getting ready he still had about 45 minutes until his first class. He decided that he would eat a breakfast bar and check his emails. *Nothing yet?* He impatiently wondered. *Well that didn't take long… I guess I'll go to class now… It's too early. Eh, this way I can take my time.* The walk was relatively short compared to his run. He was amused when he crossed paths with his nemesis, the large rock that he tripped over. He imagined that he would go running every day now that he had a running buddy to keep him encouraged. He walked into the empty lecture hall feeling excited for his first real college class and sat in the front row. The class was an intro to Psychology course, which he was interested in taking.

As usual with every intro course, the syllabus was read and students are tricked into thinking that by the end of the course they will be experts in the field. Luckily the professor was enthusiastic and spoke briefly on each point in the syllabus. Rhian was intrigued but overall the first class was less than memorable and he was soon out. He had a short break in between classes so he decided to sit near one of the fountains and get ahead on his readings for Psychology.

"Hey Rhian! What are you reading?"

"Oh, hey Leena! I'm just being a nerd and reading ahead for my psych course. What are you up to?"

"Just headed to class. I'm actually running kind of late so I'll talk to you later!"

"Ok, good luck!" Rhian waved as she walked off.

He continued reading until it was almost time for class. When it was finally time for class he headed to the building a bit more excited now that he was more awake. Rhian accidentally pulled open the door with more force than needed, expecting to find an empty classroom and a good seat. Instead, he was greeted by the cold stares of an entire classroom of people and a professor who had stopped the lecture to stare at the person who had just interrupted the lecture with his overzealous entrance. Rhian looked down at his schedule thinking that he maybe had seen the wrong time and looked at his watch but there was no mistake. He looked at the blackboard and saw the words 'Quantum Mechanics' written on the board and realized that he was early for his class. He turned bright red and headed out the door. As he left the lecture hall he heard the professor sarcastically yell "freshman" and then the room burst into laughter. He was so embarrassed that he almost left the building to go back to his room when but a familiar voice stopped him.

"Hey Rhian!" It was Alexander.

"Hey…" Rhian was clearly upset.

"What's wrong? Is everything alright?"

"Yeah, I'm fine, I just walked into a lecture hall while a lecture was going on… I feel so embarrassed, the professor called me a freshman and then the whole class laughed as I walked out."

"But you are a freshman…" Alexander realized after speaking that it probably wasn't the nicest thing to say. Just before Rhian could run off in tears he added, "Awe it's not as bad as you think. I'm sure it wasn't a big deal. They probably forgot about it already. You're not the first one to do that and you won't be the last… Just watch." Alexander quickly pushed open the door to the big lecture hall and with the dumbest voice he could muster he stupidly looked around and made his presence known by asking the professor, "I guess this isn't Art Appreciation class?" To which the professor responded with sarcasm. This was completely out of character for Alexander but there was no way he was going to let his new friend be embarrassed like that. "See, I told you there would be others." He said with a reassuring smile.

"I can't believe you just did that… I feel a lot better but I still can't believe you did that. What are you doing here anyway?" Rhian felt better.

"This is my next class… it's…" Alexander looked at his schedule. "*Intro to Politics.*"

"No way! That's the class I have too! Let's sit together!" Rhian shouted with excitement.

"Of course, we can study together too."

The boys sat around and talked some more about their days. During the class the two took notes and paid attention, for the most part and afterwards found out that they had a break so they decided to get lunch afterwards.

"Hey, do you think this guy is color blind? I think he is wearing two different colored shoes…" Alexander point out to Rhian who was trying not to laugh. After class the boys had lunch together at one of the dining halls and sat around for a few hours just hanging out. Rhian had lost track of time and was late for his Chemistry course so he quickly made plans to meet up with Alexander and study. He invited Leena to join in their study group, which gave them all an excuse to talk and continue to get to know each other. As it turned out Alexander didn't have much in common with Leena but their personalities made it easy for them to get along. Leena's good looks also made it easy to hold anyone's attention. The study session proved to be more of a hangout than a *study session* but they had a great time and quickly realized that they would all be great friends. As the semester commenced, they continued to meet as a study group. They kept each other motivated and it was a great way to productively hang out.

Chapter 2

Two weeks into the semester had gone by. Rhian and Alexander had met up every day to study while Leena and Rhian had made it a habit to get coffee after their morning run. "Rhian, I've never clicked with someone like this before. Growing up I always wanted a brother or a sister but it was just me. I know we just met but I feel like I can trust you. It's like I know you will be there for me. I'm really glad you tripped on that rock!" She laughed out loud amidst the noise of the café that had quickly become their spot.

"I know what you mean." Rhian said with a smile. "You are like the sister I never had." He hugged her and kissed her on the cheek.

"Can I tell you something?"

"Anything, you know I don't judge."

"I'm going to tell you a secret."

"I'm intrigued now." He tried to sound playful but she was now too serious for the lighthearted banter.

"I haven't told you about my past and the only thing I've mentioned in regards to home is my dad."

"I figured you would tell me when you were ready. I don't believe in forcing trust and connection."

"I appreciate that. I grew up in Los Angeles. I don't remember my mom; she died when I was very young. I have pictures of her holding me as a baby but I never knew her. My dad was very wealthy and as a result I had a lot of opportunities that most people only dream of."

"That sounds exciting." Rhian smiled.

"It was a blessing and a curse. Just like every Hollywood cliché I began hanging around the wrong crowd and I got into trouble."

"We all make mistakes when we are in high school. I got into trouble for painting a caricature of the principle with devil horns." Leena smiled politely.

"I was arrested for drunk driving at thirteen and possession of cocaine at fourteen. My dad got me off the hook both times. He was never there and thought it was his fault. The truth is that I was just bored but I let him carry the burden."

"Wow… Was he absent?"

"It doesn't matter. I wasn't taking responsibility for my actions and I let him blame himself. Maybe it was his absence or maybe I was just a spoiled brat. Either way it was wrong."

"But you learned your lesson?" She looked down. Rhian remained silent.

"After getting caught with the coke, I stayed away from it for a while but by my fifteenth birthday it was becoming a bad habit. On my birthday I was allowed to go out with some of my older friends. My friend Robbie picked me and a few friends up to take us to his family's beach house. We drank for a few hours there and hung out. It was late but my dad thought I was sleeping over. Robbie got a call and told me to wait while he went to get ready to give me my present. He went outside for a few minutes and then came back inside. He said we had to go pick it up so we got back in the car and drove to a different part of the city. We finally arrived at a house that looked abandoned. He told us to stay in the car and. We were all really drunk and were passing a bottle of something strong around. No one noticed that Robbie had opened up the trunk. When he closed it I noticed that there was someone with him. It was a little girl. He walked her up to the front door with only the dim streetlight glow to guide them. For the second it took her to pass the threshold I could see her face. She was filthy, covered in blood and what looked like dirt. I could feel her pain. I could feel the fear. She couldn't have been older than eleven years old. She looked right at me with big eyes. *Save me,* her face screamed. Sobriety never hit so hard. In my heart I prayed to whatever god would listen that she was just being delivered to her family who paid to have her cross over the border… but…" She paused.

"What happened?"

"The little girl would most likely die without anyone knowing her story."

"What do you mean?"

"I saw Robbie reach out as someone handed him a brown bag. He stuffed it in his pocket and made his way back to the car. No one else saw it. I stayed quiet and we left. Later I realized that the bag was coke. It was the coke I had asked for. I realized that Robbie had traded the life of a little girl for a bag of drugs. Her life was only worth a few thousand dollars. She was gone, forever and no one would ever know. She was probably sold into slavery or killed for her organs. I'll never know."

"There was nothing you could have done."

"That night I couldn't get her tearful eyes out of my mind. I could have told someone but I didn't. I took a few hits, hoping it would bring up my mood, thinking that the girl couldn't die for nothing. In a messed up kind of way, I got fucked up to commemorate her and forget but there was no way I could forget her. I was young and becoming an addict. I woke up hoping it was a bad dream and for a few days I really thought it was but when I tried to talk to Robbie about it he refused to say anything. He got really mad and told me to *just forget about it*."

"Leena it wasn't your fault."

"It was my birthday and I wanted to party. I told him that if he could score some I would sleep with him. I don't even remember if I slept with him or not. After that night my *habit* got worse. I couldn't sleep. I couldn't eat. I stopped living. My dad realized that something was wrong but when I told him what had happened he decided enough was enough and sent me to rehab first and then New York for a fresh start. He did a lot of business out there so he could keep a closer eye on me. I was able to finish high school but I wasn't the same. Rehab, the time I spent alone, it was all very comforting. I felt safe. That's why I decided to come to college in the Midwest. Dad wanted me to stay out east since we could spend more time together but I needed to reinvent myself again. I left L.A. to change my image. I left New York to change myself. Nobody else knows that story."

"If you could get justice for that little girl, would you?"

"Without a doubt but that's in the past. I can't change what happened."

"I saw something horrible too and I stayed quiet."

"Really?"

"Yeah… I don't know her name but I would recognize her if I saw a picture of her. The look in her eyes told me everything. It lingers and it doesn't go away. Some nights I wake up in a cold sweat from a nightmare about her. She could have been a good friend. She might have changed the world. I let them get away with it."

"What happened? Why didn't you tell?" Feeling overwhelmed by the sudden memory Rhian didn't feel comfortable sharing in the café.

"This isn't a café conversation. Perhaps we could go back to my room or your apartment?"

"That would be fine." Leena gathered her things and the two were on their way. They settled on Leena's couch. Rhian considered telling Leena a different story, but he felt obligated to share the truth. She had just told him her deepest darkest secret and now it was his turn. But he wasn't ready.

"So why did you tell me that story?"

"I trust you and I couldn't keep it to myself anymore. I know it sounds stupid but it had been eating away at my conscience for years.

Last night I had a dream about the girl. I had forgotten about it for the first time in a long time until the dream."

"I see. You know it wasn't your fault, right?"

"I feel responsible."

"That girl was already in trouble. However it was that she got there had nothing to do with you. She was not your responsibility." Leena had never been able to think like that about the girl. She began cry. Rhian didn't say a word. He sat down next to her and held her as the years of pent up emotion came rushing out. It was not the right time for him to share his past.

The first few weeks of the semester had gone by and Rhian was doing well in all of his classes. His adjustment to college life was quick and he made several friends in the process. So far everything was working out better than he expected. Going away to college was not an option he thought he had, but after his time at the camp he decided that going away to college was his only option.

For the first time in a long time, Rhian felt he was around people he could trust. Until now, none of his friends knew about the camp. They only knew that he was trying to reinvent himself by shedding his fundamentalist background and embracing new ideas. Rhian was fascinated by the way others were kind to him without making judgmental comments. His new support system was just what he needed.

What began as a study group with Leena and Alexander had eventually grown to include several others. Rhian, having such a magnetic personality, attracted people of all sorts. When it came to making new friends he was thriving. Rhian was a well-intentioned charmer with a good-hearted nature. He didn't stand for the rejection of others and was inclusive to all when it came to socializing. If he met someone, he immediately considered the person his friend. This rapid connection that he made with people wasn't always reciprocated, but through time people would warm up to him. This new group of friends now included a mixture of males and females from all walks of life. Not only did Rhian have a way of connecting with people quickly, but he also had a way of connecting people to each other. He was able to help people create friendships with others who otherwise probably would have never considered being friends. It was because of his caring nature that people gravitated towards him. This allowed them to connect with him and the people around him using a non-prejudicial lens. His method of making friends was almost an art form.

The group of friends that Rhian started had grown to include a total of seven people who he considered close friends. Of course he had made many acquaintances but he spent most of his time with the seven. The group was made up of Leena, Alexander, Nikolaus, Kala, Gianna, Sophie, and Sebastian. Alexander's friend John would sometimes be around but he was kind of illusive. This new group of friends celebrated their unique backgrounds and respected individual expression. The point of college was to broaden perspective by interacting and being exposed to a diversified student body. Rhian quickly realized that most of his peers were only interested in meeting people who were exactly like themselves. He disliked that idea so he put a lot of effort into appreciating the diversity of his core group of friends.

Rhian awkwardly met Nikolaus at lunch one day when he noticed the young man reading a physics textbook similar to his. The boy's book was slightly different so Rhian was naturally intrigued. He approached Nikolaus who was quietly reading and asked if he could sit with him and talk about the class. Nikolaus was a bit put off by this at first, but after a few minutes of not saying much he finally began to talk to Rhian. Nikolaus was a foreign student, which was given away by his strong accent. He was definitely the athletic type as he was wearing an F.C. Barcelona jersey and built like a soccer player. Nikolaus and Rhian bonded over their distaste for the material in their shared course. They made it a routine to have lunch together and work on their physics homework together.

Kala and Gianna were friends from high school who decided to go to the same school. Not because they followed each other, but for similar reasons. Neither wanted to live too far from home and they were in the same program. Rhian had met the two of them one day while studying in his spot near the fountain. The girls were talking about purchasing tickets to see Maroon 5 in concert. Rhian didn't know that they would be performing nearby and was immediately intrigued. He turned to them and began to ask them about the concert. The girls were more than happy to talk about Maroon 5. They chattered about Adam Levine's amazing vocals as well as his striking good looks. Rhian didn't give his opinion about Adam's good looks, but he loved the band and wanted to see them live. The girls seemed to click with Rhian and they ended up exchanging information. After an hour-long conversation about Maroon 5 and other bands they were talking like they had known each other for years.

Rhian got a job at the school bookstore to make some money while in school. It was here where he met Sophie. She was another exchange student but she was from China. At five-foot five inches and naturally slender, Sophie had a gracefulness about the way she carried herself. She and Rhian got along really well because they could have deep well thought-out conversations, as well as lighthearted joking. She was a hard working student who was at school on scholarship. She had to work in order to pay for other expenses. She made just enough money to survive so she was content. She was quite simple, which was refreshing since there were a lot of stuck up people around. Similarly he had to work in order to pay for his extra expenses while the rest of his tuition was covered through scholarship and loan. His work money allowed him to have some kind of a social life.

Leena and Rhian were having lunch one afternoon when they met a young man who was working as a waiter. He was tall and lanky, the kind of guy that probably ran track in high school. The young man seemed to be very intelligent but limited by his current state as a server. Nevertheless he was one of the most polite and friendly waiters that Leena or Rhian had ever encountered. They talked about how friendly he was and decided to talk to him.

"What's your name?" Leena boldly asked.

"Sebastian… and you are?"

"I'm Leena."

"And I'm Rhian."

"It's very nice to meet you both." He responded with a kind smile. That was the extent of their conversation that day because he was busy. Leena paid the entire bill but told Rhian to leave a tip. Rhian expected to spend about twenty dollars so he left the money as a tip. Yes it was a lot for him but the service was great and the server was very friendly so he didn't mind. When they were walking out Sebastian came running out to let him know that he had left a big bill on the table. Rhian reassured him that it was his tip. Sebastian was so grateful that the next time they came in he wrote them a *thank you* note on a menu and handed it to them.

After that they began to talk to him and found out that he had a daughter. Sebastian had been raising his daughter on his own since she was one year old. Her mother lasted a year with Sebastian before she was out of the picture. Without the second income it had become difficult to pay the bills and support his daughter but he had found a way to make it work. He knew that the day would come where he would have to start making more money, so he had started taking classes in an effort to someday provide a better life for his daughter. He was a brilliant young man with less than ideal circumstances, but he loved his daughter more than anything else in the world and he wouldn't trade having her for anything.

Meeting Sebastian and learning more about his struggle to raise a daughter on his own left Rhian with the urge to reach out and help those in need. It also served as a form of therapy for him because he was able to see that everyone has their struggles, for him it was his past, while for Sebastian it was the challenge of raising a daughter without her mother. It wasn't like he was well-off himself, he was struggling too, but if he could help someone even a little bit it could make all the difference in their lives. He hoped that if he was ever in a tough spot that someone would do the same for him though he understood that he shouldn't expect it. He began volunteering at a homeless shelter on Fridays. He also volunteered to babysit Sebastian's daughter on the weekends in order to let him pick up a few extra shifts so that he could make some extra money. Rhian made a personal pact to live by four standards: love everyone, live honestly, care for others, and maintain integrity.

Over the course of the first few weeks Rhian and Alexander had become very close. They shared a special chemistry that neither one had experienced before. They weren't just comfortable; they were drawn to each other the way lifelong friends are. The boys agreed on most things but the one thing they passionately disagreed on was which candy was the best. Alexander believed Reese's was the obvious choice while Rhian disagreed and argued that Twix was the best. Either way, Rhian made sure to bring a Reese's candy with him to Monday morning Poly Sci with Alexander; at least when he could afford to. It was a silly thing to do but it made Alexander feel special so Rhian enjoyed making the effort.

"Here you go." Rhian said as he handed the candy to Alexander.

"Awe, thanks!" Alexander said as he opened up the candy.

"You didn't get one this week?"

"No… I um… I didn't feel like it." Alexander raised an eyebrow.

"Didn't feel like it? You like these things almost as much as I do…"

"I couldn't afford two this week. But that's ok. I'll get one next week." Rhian responded with a smile. He was genuinely happy to give up the candy this week so that Alexander could have it. But Alexander wasn't about to let Rhian go without. He split the candy and the boys shared.

"No friend of mine will go candyless!" He proudly stated. "You didn't have to get me the candy. But I'm really glad you did." Alexander laughed.

One afternoon as the boys studied in the common room of Rhian's building, the TV was on louder than usual. The boys were reviewing notes for an upcoming quiz when Rhian's attention was drawn to the television. That night a special report was on about the alarming number of teen suicides related to bullying. Rhian looked down at his wrist to see the three scars that were obvious to no one but himself. He sighed deeply as he drifted into a memory of how and why the scars were there. Rhian's attention was soon redirected when Alexander responded to the story with disgust.

"I don't get why anyone would want to hurt themselves. It seems pointless to me." Without much thought he returned to his work. Rhian couldn't react to him right away. He looked up at Alexander and then back down at his wrist. Alexander must have realized that Rhian was still thinking about the report.

"Are you alright?"

"I'm… fine." Rhian's pause made Alexander suspicious. But he was worried to discuss such a delicate topic.

"What's bothering you? What is it? You know you can tell me anything."

"Those kids in that news story… It's so sad."

"Yeah, it's sad. But it's ridiculous. It's so selfish. Those kids needed to become stronger. They gave up too quickly."

"Have you ever been suicidal?"

"No, I haven't. But I've been alone, completely abandoned and I didn't try to kill myself."

"Then consider yourself lucky. I was like them. I tried to but I didn't have the guts to do it."

"No, you got some sense and realized it was stupid." Alexander quickly interjected.

"I had the blade in my hand, at my wrist, but I couldn't do it. I was scared and lonely. But I did have a moment of clarity where I saw my possible future. It was better than I could have planned. I saw that before I could end my life."

"Well I'm glad you didn't. But what made you want to kill yourself in the first place?"

"I was afraid of rejection. I was very lonely. But what drove me to that point was the possibility of finding relief. Up to that point my life was all a lie. I had paid a huge price just for being myself and I didn't see the point in living."

"What price was that?"

"I lost my innocence. I felt powerful with the blade in my hand but as soon as I cut the first time I felt weak. Luckily I hadn't cut deep enough and I was ok."

"Shit, Rhian… I had no idea. I'm sorry for being an insensitive ass."

"Don't apologize. That is part of getting to know each other." Rhian's tone was somber.

"It was still uncalled for. Now I know that you say it was because of loneliness and a general hopelessness but people don't just magically become suicidal."

"I come from a very conservative, religious background. I was raised in an extremely strict church that preyed on the innocence and ignorance of its members. It was a place that had me brainwashed to believe that no matter what I did, I would never be good enough to love. We were conditioned to fear anything that we didn't understand or couldn't define using the narrow lens that they used. Through guilt they instilled something so terrible that I still have nightmares. We were taught that the only way that we were living right was if we felt guilty for the things that we did because they were *sinful*. This was a place that taught abstinent morality instead of moderation. It was a dangerous place where the people loved to hate and the hatred fueled the destruction of many. We wore smiles like masks, removing them once we were out of view because a true smile meant that we were 'doing something wrong.'"

"This just sounds like a typical church to me…" Alexander interjected.

"As terrible as it sounds you're probably right, but here is where it gets bad. They found always found new ways to infiltrate our personal lives. They manipulated and lied to get us to reveal dark secrets about ourselves that we never meant to share and then use those secrets against us for their own sick personal agenda. Alexander I'm gay." Rhian paused for a moment to allow Alexander a chance to react.

"Ok."

"Well, I am attracted to both sexes but I connect better with men and therefore by societal terms I'm gay…"

"Ok…" Alexander clearly wanted to say or do something in this moment because he knew that what Rhian was telling him wasn't easy. But he remained unmoved to allow Rhian to continue.

"I trusted someone with my secret… I asked for prayer but they told my parents and then everyone around me became hateful. The people I used to talk to stopped talking to me. My *friends* wouldn't even look at me anymore. It was like a wall was suddenly put up around me and I no longer existed. They were all so cold."

"That's messed up… I don't think they were really your friends… Continue though."

"Like I said I trusted someone with my secret and instead of praying for me or with me, they told some of the church leaders." Rhian nervously tensed up.

"Rhian are you ok? What's wrong? You don't have to tell me if you don't feel comfortable talking about it."

"I need to talk about it… It's just that… you are the first person I'm telling." Alexander looked down at the ground in preparation of the story. "One night, while I was in bed sleeping I was awakened by a loud knock on my bedroom door. I slowly turned the knob and just as I began to pull, the door swung open and I fell on the floor. I looked up and saw two men dressed in black with masks covering their faces." Rhian again paused, closing his eyes before continuing. "One of the men grabbed my arms and pulled me up while the other one grabbed my legs. I was paralyzed with fear, unable to scream, unable to fight; I was powerless to save myself. I thought I was having a nightmare but that was only the beginning." A chill ran down his spine as the memories of this haunting night came back to him. "They took me to a place somewhere in the desert. There was no one around for miles. I wasn't the only one there. I only saw the others once, though I could sometimes hear them screaming."

"Rhian, what did they do to you?"

"They took my innocence." He was brought back to the smell of burning flesh and stale blood.

"My church sells the idea of discrimination by promoting certain television shows, churches, and *outstanding* members of the church community. The leaders are very intelligent people that play on the ignorance of others by using fear to drive their agendas. The unwillingly ignorant follow religiously because the people in charge are so damn charismatic. They convince these people that they are not in control and that God will take care of them. It is the most powerful high in existence; it is the feeling of security."

"I call my church Kalumnia, a Latin word that loosely translates to mean *fraud*. In Kalumnia, the addiction to that feeling of security is sold in exchange for blind following. I believe that if the radicals of Kalumnia had it their way they would exterminate people of different beliefs and you would have a world like Hitler's fantasy except instead of calling him Fuehrer, you would call him Pastor."

"That sounds extreme… I understand that people can get out of hand but I don't think a church would ever promote that kind of ideology…" Alexander challenged.

"Extremism has no church…"

"But you really think that they would kill to spread their message?"

"Christians already did that…"

"Good point."

"It wasn't easy for anyone to be involved in Kalumnia because of the ridiculous rules, yet almost everyone put on a face and pretended to be compliant. The leaders understood that if they could get their members to pretend to be perfect, sooner or later people would simply follow the rules without question. There was no place for people that didn't conform so people were either exiled or, if you were gay, sent to this place called White Horse Ranch. This was one of Kalumnia's darker secrets; the Ranch was a horrible place. Very few people knew about its existence and even fewer knew where it was…" Rhian stayed quiet for a moment.

"You don't have to talk about it anymore if you don't want to." Alexander put his hand on Rhian's shoulder for comfort.

"We suffered from the moment the sun came up until it was dark. Everything was intended to break us. If Hell is real, I think it was there."

"Day one: we were taken from our beds in the middle of the night, blindfolded, handcuffed, put on a bus and not allowed to say anything."

"Where did they take you?"

"Well… they didn't want us to know obviously…"

"Oh… I guess that's why you mentioned the blindfold, handcuffs, and silence."

"I figured it out."

"How did you do that?"

"I kind of have a really good sense of direction and time. I think of a song and let it play in my head. I knew which direction we started in when we left my house and I remembered all of the turns and about how long we drove in each direction. The hard part was figuring out where I was after we got off the plane."

"How did they sneak you onto a plane when you all looked like inmates?"

"We flew in and out of a private field. It wasn't hard to figure out where we flew out of, it was only about twenty minutes from home. I tried to figure out which direction the plane was headed but that was a lot harder. I know we were in the air for several hours. When we landed I figured out which direction we were going because the sun began to rise and my eye was partially uncovered. I tracked the rest of the trip and when we arrived I wrote my calculations under the bed. I coded them so that they couldn't figure it out. Something told me to remember where they had taken me."

"Is that something you always do?"

"What? Track my location?"

"Yeah…"

"Kind of. I don't always do it but I do when I feel something is important."

"It sounds exhausting."

"You would think so but it's honestly not that bad. The songs help me keep track of time, that's pretty natural, and the positioning I figure out by the motion of the car. Turns are easy, it's the long stretches that are challenging because it's hard to tell the speed, but I've done it since I was young, watching the speedometer so it's pretty much second nature to me."

"Wow."

"Once we arrived the horror began. The place, White Horse Ranch, was a conversion therapy camp that aimed at breaking us and making us straight. Of course it was based on outdated or made up *science*. Before getting off the bus they recited some Bible verses and said a prayer, then they explained why we were there. 'The root of sinful lifestyles can be traced to excess in one of the seven deadly sins, where all sins come from. The first phase of the program will serve as an opportunity to identify which of the seven you tend towards. You will have time to meditate over the ways this sin has damaged your relationship with God.' Phase one was unique to each individual because different people will resonate with different sins therefore some will be done after the first week and others might continue till the fifth."

"Why not lie?"

"I'll explain in a second. 'Phase two can begin one week after phase one is finished. Phase two is the healing process by which individuals grow spiritually.'"

"For week One we dealt with envy. They believe that envy breeds *lustful desires*. I was strapped to a bed and immobile for six days straight because I needed to learn to 'appreciate the ability to move around freely.' The second week the focus was sloth. They told us that slothfulness was the result of not being taught the value of hard work. They took us out into the desert and made us dig. We dug holes for six days straight. My hands were bleeding and I had to wrap them in my shirt. It was so painful."

"Why did you do it? Why didn't you just refuse."

"Alexander, we were in the desert surrounded by miles of nothing. The only people who knew we were even there were the people in charge. They guarded us like caged animals. They didn't keep guns, but they did have batons just in case anyone got too rowdy. Again silence was crucial. I wasn't allowed to say anything. That was probably the hardest part because I had to stay trapped inside of my head."

"Rhian, I don't know if I can continue listening to this… I hope you are making it up… I really hope this isn't true." Alexander gave Rhian a very sad look. He felt overwhelmed with horror and sadness for his friend. He looked him in the eyes to try to read his friend's emotional state but he could tell Rhian was still lost in the story.

"I wish I were making it up. The third week dealt with gluttony. 'Indulgence in food will lead to gluttonous habits' they would say. Six days of fasting with nothing but a Bible to read and water to drink. This was the only week we were allowed to drink as much water as we wanted. But we were already almost starving on the little amount of food that they were feeding us. Week four *treated* a problem with greed. Simply put we were water boarded. They had a mechanical bed that could position itself over a water tank and vertically dip the person. I remember my face being covered with a towel or cloth and then I was dunked in for a few seconds at a time. Sometimes it was as long as twenty seconds. I couldn't flinch or anything when I was strapped in because they had us securely strapped in order to keep us from breaking free."

"Rhian, that's horrible. Isn't that illegal?"

"This place wasn't concerned with the law… trust me. Week five was when we worked on lust. They basically used electrocution therapy to create an aversion to gay images and propaganda but they also used it to form an aversion to things that stood against the church. Not all of the torture was consistent. Sometimes they would throw me back into my room for a few hours and then start again. It didn't really feel consistent."

"It seems like they were pushing you to the point of almost killing you."

"Yeah, it felt that way. Week six, pride. They tied me to a cross, dropped me off in the desert and made me walk several miles back to camp. The cross was larger than me so that it was guaranteed to be painful to walk because I couldn't stand up straight. It hurt really badly when I would fall because I hit the hot ground face first. The whole time I was out there I didn't see any helicopters or small airplanes. We were really secluded. I broke after this week. I couldn't go any further. Six weeks of silence and physical torture was too much for me. I was seventeen and I honestly didn't understand why I was there."

"What would have happened during the last week?"

"That was the week of anger. I don't know exactly what they did. But I remember seeing a girl briefly who had made it to week six. She looked at me like she was looking into me and she mouthed the words *don't break*. The next time I saw here she was dead… I looked out the window and I could see that they put a body wrapped in a tarp into a truck. Before they closed the door a wind blew and I could see that it was the girl. They had killed her."

"Oh my god!"

"When we arrived to the place we were told that if we tried to run we would be hunted and killed. They said that our loved ones would be told that we ran away and that we didn't want anything to do with them anymore. I thought it was a scare tactic but I am assuming that's what they told her mom because no one ever looked for her."

"That seems unbelievable."

"You don't understand how powerful the name of Jesus is until you've been in a place that has so many people brainwashed. It's all true. When I came back I knew I had to get out so I said and did exactly what they wanted. It took ten weeks until I was considered rehabilitated after which they sent me home. At the end of summer I went back to the Christian school and lived the lie. I dated a girl and pretended that it had all gone away. My stubbornness got me through camp but when I got home I was alone again and that's when the darkness really hit me. I fell into a deep depression. I had been depressed in the past because I was raised by guilt and learned to never be happy with myself. I was completely alone… I almost took my life. I began cutting myself as a way to deal with the pain but eventually that wasn't enough. I needed to be free of it all."

"I'm so sorry for being insensitive… I shouldn't have said all that. I was being a jerk."

"It's ok, you didn't know."

"So what stopped you?"

"Just before I dug the knife into my wrist severing my chance at a future, I had a flash of hope. It was a moment of serenity. I saw a happy family, my happy family and that was all I needed to see to believe in myself. You're the first person I've told. I left home for school because I wanted to be free. Now I'm sitting here sharing all of this for the first time with my new friend who probably thinks I'm insane…" Rhian's somber voice suddenly went back to its usual lighthearted tone. Alexander had to give him a hug. He felt compelled to not because he thought Rhian needed security, but because it helped him grasp the reality of it all.

"I'm really glad you didn't kill yourself…"

"Yeah, I can't help but wonder how different things would have been for those kids that killed themselves if they would have had someone to tell them that they were beautiful souls who meant the world to someone. I wish everyone could see his or her worth. Everyone is beautiful in his or her own, unique way. I have these small scars from the blade that remind me to believe this with all of my heart. I learned that I had no one but myself to blame for the scars because I didn't see myself for what I am worth. I only saw myself worth as much as I thought the people around me valued me. I hope someday I will be able to help someone see things the way I do." Rhian trailed off as if drifting back into his daydreaming state.

"But I still feel guilty about the girl dying. I feel like I shouldn't have broken in week six. Maybe I could have helped her. Maybe we could have gotten through it together. She might still be alive if I hadn't cracked."

"Rhian, it wasn't your fault and you shouldn't feel guilty about anything. They hurt you and you were afraid. No one can blame you. But everything will be alright. I promise." Alexander hugged Rhian tightly. Rhian cried tears of relief into his shoulder as Alexander simply held him. Rhian was relieved to finally tell someone.

It was almost time for fall break, which meant Rhian would be going back home soon for the first time since he left. He was nervous about seeing his family because they weren't fully supportive of his decision to go away and he wasn't sure how they would react to having him back. He also wasn't sure if he could stand to be around them after being released from their overbearing rules. Judging by the conversations that Rhian and his parents had, it seemed that the distance was good for them. He had a tumultuous relationship with them before going away to that camp but afterwards he just existed in their home. He held resentment towards them but it was easier to ignore his feelings than to deal with the potential of speaking up. Rhian knew his parents would never accept him for being gay so keeping peace would be the only thing he could do to prevent them from meddling in his life. He loved his parents even after everything that had happened between them but he was also still hurt and fearful of what they might do so he preferred to remain silent.

Rhian didn't want to go home alone so he asked Leena and Alexander to join. Leena had made plans for the break already, but she wanted to meet Rhian's family and being that the break was on a Monday and Tuesday, she decided to come along for the weekend and resume her plans after that. Alexander didn't really have plans so he agreed to come with as well. At this point, Leena didn't know anything about the camp, but Alexander did and he wasn't too excited to meet the people that sent his new best friend to that horrible place. Alexander felt that he had to go find out what kind of people Rhian's parents were and to be there in case Rhian needed to be protected from them.

"Hello kids!" Rhian's mother came out to greet them as they pulled up to the house. Her hair was perfectly in place, her outfit neatly complimenting the rest of her carefully put-together ensemble. Mrs. Pierce looked like she had walked out of a nineteen-fifty's edition of a homemaker magazine.

"Hi, you must be Rhian's mother… Nice to meet you, I'm Alexander." He shook her hand.

"Hi! I'm Leena! I love your outfit, you look so… proper." Leena almost sounded sarcastic. Mrs. Pierce didn't seem to notice and graciously accepted the compliment.

"And you must be Rhian's dad, nice to meet you sir." Alexander shook his hand.

"Nice to meet you too, it's about time Rhian found a friend with manners." There was a moment of awkwardness.

"Thank you, sir…" Alexander answered uncomfortably. He was thrown off by how friendly they were. He expected more anger or suspicion from both of them but was disappointed by the sense of normalcy they gave off.

"Hello." Leena said to his dad.

"Nice to meet you young lady."

"Wow you are very pretty. She is very pretty Rhian." Rhian's mom announced to the room.

"Mom…"

"Yeah, this one's a keeper Rhian, just look at her!" Rhian's dad loudly followed

"Do you have to be so rude? Come on guys I'll show you where you can put your stuff." Rhian told his friends as he walked towards his room in embarrassment followed by the two.

"Oh we're just trying to be funny…" his mother called out "The food is ready when you kids are."

Although Leena and Alexander were put off by Mr. Pierce's behavior, their hunger distracted them when they entered the kitchen. The smells were almost intoxicating and they couldn't wait to begin eating. They all sat down together at the table when Rhian's dad insisted that they pray. Everyone ate quietly savoring every bite of the delicious food and exchanging awkward stares and awkward smiles. After dinner Rhian's mom brewed some coffee and brought out the desert, an apple pie she made from scratch. She divided the pie into even slices and distributed them to each person. By now they had migrated into the living room and were finally starting to interact a bit.

"So Rhian, how are all of your classes going so far?" His mother asked.

"They are going well so far. I love my psychology class but I'm not too happy about the physics class that I have to take. It's so pointless. I hate that class."

"Well you need to learn a little bit of everything so that you can handle the real world. How about you Leena?" She quickly moved on from Rhian.

"Well… I am taking four classes… Calculus, German, English Lit, and Philosophy. I like all of them. My professors are all really interesting and they definitely know how to teach… Except the calculus professor… He is old and kind of just tells us to figure it out on our own…"

"Well that seems kind of useless. You pay all that money for a professor to tell you to teach yourself… what a waste." Rhian's dad chimed in, making everyone feel awkward again.

"Well I'm sure you are a smart girl and you'll do just fine." His mom broke the silence.

"Thanks." Leena said with a smile.

"What about you Alexander? How are your classes going?"

"Well I like most of them. I am in a few easy classes but none of them really capture my interest."

"I'm sure you'll find your niche, son." Rhian's dad said to Alexander.

"Yeah, I have to or else I'm wasting money…" Alexander paused before looking up at him, waiting for his reaction.

Rhian's dad started laughing and then everyone else joined in. After they had broken the ice, they sat around and talked about some of their experiences. They made sure to keep it PG because Rhian's parents weren't very open-minded. They also avoided talking about Rhian's sexuality. All in all the time that they spent there was quite enjoyable. They played a few games of Scrabble that night before going to bed.

Later that night Rhian went to say his goodnight to his parents.

"Rhian, sweetie, you know we love you… I just wish that you would listen to us about getting involved with the Christian organizations on campus. They offer a lot of support for your *confusions*." His mother said, making sure to quietly whisper the word 'confusions' so that no one could hear her.

"Ok, I'll check one out."

"We only want what is best for you."

"These friends of yours seem like good people, you should hang around more people like them." His dad added.

"They are great people Dad. I'm glad you like them."

"Come here sweetie." His mom said before planting a kiss on his forehead, "We love you very much, nothing can change that. Just make sure you are doing what God wants you to do." With that Rhian left their room and joined his friends. The three stayed up to talk. Although he had played the part very well, Alexander was not too happy about being near the monsters that sent his friend to that horrible camp. He knew it wasn't entirely their fault, because they didn't know what went on there, but it was still their fault.

Leena left after the weekend feeling very welcomed into Rhian's family. She loved Rhian's mom and was warming up to his dad. Rhian couldn't shake the feeling of discomfort but it wasn't anything he hadn't felt before. When it was time to go, the boys left with clean laundry and a car full of groceries that his parents had bought for the two of them. It was hard for Alexander to smile and not think about the terrible things Rhian told him about going through the conversion therapy, but it was also hard to believe that the warm loving people who had just opened their home up were capable of such things. What he did gain was a better understanding of why Rhian was so caring; he had been trained to be.

Feeling obligated to, Rhian decided to find a group of Christian young people that he got along with in order to get his parents to stop nagging him about it. Alexander agreed to go with him for support. The boys searched for organizations online but seeing a website is very different than attending a meeting. The first organization they visited claimed to be about 'Christ's Love.' Rhian thought it sounded promising so they made plans to attend their meeting. When they arrived, two men who seemed overly dressed for an informal meeting greeted them. Soon after their meeting began, Alexander noticed that the men stared at them uncomfortably. There was an emptiness that hid behind their eyes. These men reminded Rhian of the people from his church. They were manipulative in their choice of words and it seemed that they had an answer for everything. Alexander felt very out of place and Rhian began to feel an intense anxiety take over.

"So I hope you fellas enjoyed visiting with us. We would love to have you join our group."

"Thanks… We really enjoyed it… We will be back next week; we kind of have to meet our friend…"

"Yeah, she is… cooking… dinner for us! And we are already late. We'll see you next week!"

"Excellent! I am very excited!" The well-dressed men were all smiles.

"Goodbye." The two boys said in unison without turning around.

After a few more visits to different organizations, Rhian began to feel completely conflicted about his beliefs. He wondered if there was even a place for him in Christianity anymore.

"You look terrible!" Alexander said one day as they were eating their lunch. "Still trying to make your religion fit you?"

"Hah! Thanks buddy, I love you too." Rhian returned sarcastically.

"You look really tired…. are you sleeping well?"

"Yeah, I don't know how to feel about everything. My beliefs are a big deal to me but I feel like I don't belong in any of those groups. It's like I am slowly being forced into a cage that I will never be able to get out of. My biggest fear in life is to wake up one day in a life I hate that was set up for me by some list of requirements. I struggled for a long time because I thought I would someday be forced to marry a girl just because that was what was *right* in the eyes of the church."

"So you're still trying to fit into your religion… You don't have to fit into a life that they set out for you… Have you ever thought that perhaps you don't need a religion? I mean, why is one right and another wrong? Isn't it possible that both are right?"

"What do you mean?"

"Well, what makes each religion different? Their moral beliefs…. but if that's what makes the difference in getting you to heaven, don't you think it's a bit silly to believe in it? I mean think about it… You will never be able to be perfect and you don't always know when you do something wrong because what's wrong to you may not be wrong to someone else… A God who allows each individual to see right and wrong differently is a God who either has a sick twisted sense of humor, or one who thinks you are perfect just the way you are and loves you regardless of what other people try to tell you. I gave up believing in religion a long time ago because there is no possible way to appease everyone and that's what religion tries to do. But it has caused more problems for everyone than anything else." Alexander realized that seeing his parents after being away probably served as a trigger for Rhian.

"Wow… When did you get so smart?"

"A few minutes ago when you weren't looking." Alexander replied while winking at Rhian.

"Well I guess I have a lot to think about. I agree I just wish there was a sign that I was doing the right thing… I am working hard and I give back to society… I don't think I'm a bad person."

"You aren't."

"I guess I will have to learn to believe that I'm ok…"

"You'll be alright. I think your answers will come soon enough."

"I hope so."

Chapter 3

As the cool of fall made its timely arrival in the small college town, Mother Nature was busy painting her canvas with brilliant shades of yellow, orange, and brown. Each leaf was meticulously decorated to remind her children that the time of carefree summer was now gone and the tender coolness of autumn was upon them. For the Midwest, autumn served as a reminder of the upcoming winter freeze. It can be a time of peace and tranquility for the world that was winding down to welcome the deep sleep. It was during this time that the campus was at its most beautiful with the colors of the changing landscape elegantly complimenting the brick of old buildings and creating a picturesque scene.

Fall break had passed along with the stress of midterms. Rhian had done well on all of the exams, primarily because he had spent most of his free time with Alexander studying. He went running that Saturday morning without much stress to distract him, which gave him time to begin to confront some of the dark thoughts that had been lurking in the back of his mind. As a firm believer in the idea that *everything happens for a reason* he fiercely believed that his experiences were meant to strengthen him and teach him something, but what and why? Up to this point there was no explanation and although he wanted so badly to find the good, his memories only inspired pain.

He never ran without his headphones but he had left them at Alexander's so he decided to go running anyway. Today there was enough noise in his head to keep him going. He ran, in particular direction, following the path wherever it took him. What seemed like only a few minutes of wrestling with his thoughts had actually turned into an hour and several miles. In fact he had gone farther than he had ever gone before and all without the aid of his music.

Rhian was haunted by the face of the girl killed at camp. He couldn't get the thought of her lifeless body being thrown into the back of a truck, to be thrown out like garbage. He put himself in her place and felt her fear, felt her pain. He felt the intolerable weight of guilt on his conscience. Why didn't he tell anyone? Why didn't he hold out? Why? Why? Why?

The camp left him damaged by teaching him to hate himself for something that wasn't his choice. At camp he learned that his value was dependent on the perception others had of him. For most of his life Rhian was aware of and at peace with his attractions to both sexes. He considered himself to be sexually fluid until the camp taught him differently. Now that Rhian had time to reexamine his thoughts, he felt more overwhelmed by the guilt of watching the girl die and not doing anything.

"Hey what's up?" Alexander called out to him as they arrived to the same street corner. Alexander was walking back to his room from early lacrosse practice.

"I'm just out for a run, trying to clear my head. I've got a lot going on." Rhian tried to make it obvious that he wanted some private time but he was the one who approached Alexander.

"Do you want to have dinner and talk? We can meet up at 7pm, pick up some food and hang out in the garden?" The garden was exactly where Rhian needed to go.

"I'll see you then." He said with a smile before continuing his run. It occurred to him that he had run a twelve-mile circle, more than he had ever run at one time. He thought about what he would say to Alexander; he wasn't sure if he was ready to verbalize his fears just yet. By now he had learned that Alexander was a very inquisitive individual. Just because he hadn't stopped right then and there to find out what was going on didn't mean he wouldn't ask later on. In fact, Rhian knew to expect a series of questions that he probably didn't want to answer, but that was just the way Alexander was. He cared about

Rhian and wasn't afraid to make it known. Rhian didn't really understand why Alexander functioned the way he did. The break in trust by close friends left him with little faith in people. Though he was no longer involved in the church or exposed to that corrosive environment anymore and things were different, he still feared being hurt again.

"God…" Rhian called out, alone in the communal showering area. His mind flooded with the words of his teachers and the preacher. He began to think about the many times he was told that he was sinful and disgusting and that he was wrong. There were so many conflicts that he was facing all at once that it become too much to handle. He didn't want to think about it anymore. He wasn't even sure what it was that was bothering him because it was so much.

"Please show me the right way. I can't live in this confusion anymore and I don't want to walk away from you because I don't know if I can stop believing in you, but you have to show me that you are here with me and that you still love me." Rhian's quick prayer allowed him to forget about it all for now.

A few hours later Rhian and Alexander got dinner at a nearby fast-food place before heading up to the garden. The garden wasn't really much of a garden. While it contained a few decorative flowerpots and a bush or two it was more of an outdoor patio located on the roof of one of the academic buildings on campus with a few tables that students could study at. Few people were ever there, so it was the perfect place to just get away and escape the troubles of student life. It was definitely a best-kept secret.

"So what's got your thinker box all catawampus today?" Rhian looked at Alexander stupidly wondering why anyone would use that phrase.

"I don't know about this whole *God* thing…I don't understand how a god could make people suffer so much. I don't understand how he can let people follow a religion that uses his name in vain and he never does anything about it. If I believe what my religion has taught me then it means that my entire life is wrong… But deep down inside I don't believe I'm wrong. I believe with all of my heart that I am exactly how God wanted me to be. Why do I feel like I'm going to be punished? Like I was punished by going to that place? I can't help but feel like I'm at a loss… like I have to make everyone but me happy."

"Because you are a good hearted person who doesn't like to hurt people and you are afraid that if you go with what your heart is telling you, that you will hurt the people you love." Alexander shot back quickly.

"Wow… I guess I hadn't thought about it that way." Rhian was taken by Alexander's enlightened words.

"Who is to say that they are correct? You are human and so are they. Shouldn't you be allowed to feel the same things that they feel if it comes naturally?

"My attraction to guys feels natural to me. I never felt like it was wrong."

"Well then it sounds to me like you know that there is nothing wrong with you and that God still loves you, right?"

"Yeah, but everything I feel conflicts with everything I have been taught." Alexander stared blankly.

"I think you are perfect the way you are. What you are experiencing is the conflict that happens when you leave home for the first time. It is partly tied to your religious background because that stuff was so deeply engrained that you are having trouble getting it out of your mind. With enough time you will begin to think clearly."

"Thanks for caring. I really appreciate it." Rhian said with a quick smile.

"I know this may sound a bit difficult to believe but have you also considered that you really have no reason to question God? I mean you are here, in a college you chose, living a life you want… He technically allowed you to leave your past for greener pastures didn't He?"

"I hadn't considered that…"

"Looks like you have some thinking to do…" Alexander responded with a raised eyebrow and a smile. Rhian remained silent for a moment as he was still trying to digest Alexander's enlightening words. Perhaps there was something to the theory but he was now uncomfortable thinking about it all so he changed the subject.

"Well here I am talking about myself and my problems and I haven't even asked how you are doing."

"I'm alright just ready to get out of this place for a bit."

"I know what you mean. I don't want to think about exams or homework!"

"Yeah same here… Though I'm not looking forward to the holiday argument." Alexander looked down in retreat from the coming question.

"Why is that?" Alexander sighed before answering.

"Well it's kind of complicated but to make a long story short, my biological father showed up a few years ago and demanded that I spend the holiday with him because I'm his only son. I think he feels bad that he didn't know I existed for most of my life. Either way he isn't much of a dad because he only talks to me like twice a year and he fights with my parents to get me to come with him."

"That's uncomfortable… For you I mean."

"Yeah, tell me about it. He throws this stupid Christmas Eve party for his employees and most of them show up. The few who don't usually don't last in the company. I don't think they come because they like him… I think they come because they fear him. He insists that I come to the party and says it's because he wants to spend time with me but really it's because he wants to look like a good parent. He'll call me up a few days before and ask me all about how life has been, just enough so that he can come up with a story about how incredible his son is. The man doesn't even know that I'm allergic to soy. He'll go around and brag to his coworkers that I'm doing really well in school and that I am such an athlete and he'll go on and on but once I go home he forgets I exist until he calls me again. I don't like it but he is still my dad"

"I'm sorry to hear that. He doesn't sound like a much of a dad. What about your mom? Your biological mom?"

"She's was pretty much just an egg donor."

"That's a heartbreaking idea I hope it's not a sore subject. I didn't mean to prod."

"No it's not a problem." He returned with a smile. "It's just a really long story. In any case, I want to spend Christmas Eve with my parents but my biological dad will inevitably convince me otherwise."

"So he wasn't always a part of your life?"

"Not really. Actually he didn't know I existed until I found him. I decided that I wanted to find my biological parents by the time I graduated high school because I wanted to invite them to my graduation so that they could see that I had accomplished something. I know it was just high school and I know 'why would I care now after all of these years?'" Alexander mocked.

"Not at all. I would probably do the same thing if I were in your shoes."

"Well my parents didn't have much information about my biological parents since I was passed around in foster care for several years so we weren't sure if we were going to be able to find them. I started looking for them in my sophomore year of high school. After a few weeks we were finally able to get their names. My dad was a successful businessman who was completely shocked to find out I existed. He came to the graduation and was around for about a month but then stopped contacting me. I think he felt guilty for not knowing I existed but his selfish nature eventually got the better of him and he just lost interest in getting to know me any better. As for my mom… I found her in a rehab center. It turns out she spent most of her life between jail and rehab. When I met her she didn't really understand what was happening. She felt bad for leaving me. She told me that she wished she could have been there for me when I was growing up. I don't think she really knows what is going on around her because she would talk about taking me back someday and raising me on her own."

"You mean she thought you were still young?"

"Yeah, she kept saying 'Mommy is going to take care of you baby… as soon as she can get the money that they owe me, Mommy is going to take you to Florida and give you the life you deserve.' I don't think she knows where she is most days. It was really sad when she showed up at my parents' house and asked to see me. She told me about her dream to be a singer and how she would take care of me the way she should have done years ago. The next day she stole some money and disappeared. I haven't heard from her since then."

"Wow… I'm really sorry to hear that Alexander! Here I am complaining about my problem as if it's the end of the world."

"It's ok. Your problems are yours and mine are mine. What bothers you may not bother me or vice versa." Alexander didn't see his life as a sad story because he was very much loved and taken care of by his parents.

"It's amazing to me how you turned out to be such a great person. You really are amazing! I'm glad I have a friend like you." Rhian put his arm around Alexander's shoulder and smiled.

"Likewise and for the record I could not have survived what you did at that camp. Most people wouldn't have." Alexander said with a smile as he embraced his friend. He had never fully told anyone the story of his past. He did leave out the troubled times he had as a child going from home to home and the long adjustment that he had undergone when he finally settled down with a family, but he had opened up for the first time. Rhian was the first person that he felt he could connect with on such a level. He trusted him more than anyone he had ever encountered and although he didn't understand why, it was nice to have someone like him. The boys continued to talk for a bit longer before going their separate ways for the evening.

Walking away from the conversation, Alexander couldn't help but think about being abandoned. The conversation reminded him of the lonely Christmas Eve's when he saw movies about children who were loved, learning a lesson in selfishness, or the 'true meaning of Christmas.' He never understood those movies because he didn't have any of those things. The thing that made Alexander such a warm soul was the fact that he had learned from a young age what it meant to be alone and what it meant to appreciate the few things he had. Even though he was now grown and his life completely different, deep down he was still that little boy whose breath would fog up the window on a cold December night, as he stared out the window waiting for a mom or dad that would never come. A childhood without loving parents created in him the desire to connect with people and allowed him to greatly empathize with others. Telling Rhian about his past was a big deal to Alexander because he didn't talk about it.

Alexander had helped Rhian settle some of the conflicts he had with his religion but he still carried the guilt of remaining silent about the girl. He cried himself to sleep most nights and it was starting to take a toll on his studies because he lacked focus and began falling behind. He became quiet and withdrawn, which was not like him at all. His friends grew concerned when they noticed that he wasn't interested in the usual stuff so they confronted him about it. He wasn't looking for pity he just needed to be alone. He could talk to them about losing his religion, about his restrictive upbringing but he couldn't tell anyone about the girl. If he told the truth about her they might come after him.

"Those are some pretty heavy things to be dealing with… there is obviously a lot about your past that you haven't dealt with. I think that for your own sake you should try to focus on your studies so that you don't lose your chance at a good future." Nikolaus logically stated.

"Babe, I know this all seems like the only thing that matters right now… but Nikolaus is right. If you let this get the best of you, there may not be a second chance for a good future. And I think if there is one thing that we can all surmise it's that you need to get a good job so that you never have to go back to life under your parents' rule." Leena had a way about her, perhaps it was the ability to make her voice softer and sweeter, but she would say exactly what needed to be said. "I know it sounds kind of cold but we care about you sweetie and we want you to succeed. We can see that thinking about your past is going to keep you from that so we all hope that you take our advice because we love you."

"I know you all do… Thank you." It wasn't the answer that Rhian wanted but it was good advice.

The advice his friends gave him forced him to reexamine what he was doing. Over the next couple of weeks he dedicated his time and energy to his schoolwork. This was the way it should have been all along but when a student is experiencing turmoil in their personal life, studying effectively becomes almost impossible for some. With the holiday season fast approaching he knew he couldn't stay at school so he had to accept the fact that he would be going home. He wanted guidance from his parents but he didn't want to go back to the camp and he wasn't sure if he could trust them. Nevertheless he had to be brave enough to at least try. In his mind, it was possible that they would empathize with his pain and have a change of heart.

Alexander had worked very hard to throughout the semester so when it came time for final exams he was more than prepared. He confidently took each exam, expecting nothing less than an A for each class. He had packed his things so that he could leave immediately after his last exam. Winter break had begun and it was going to be a good one. He was excited to catch up with his friends from home and just forget about school.

The usual drama that his biological father caused wasn't a problem this year. In fact, he didn't even try to contact him this time. His disinterest, while unsettling, was exactly what Alexander wanted. He was relieved that he wouldn't have to spend his holiday in a tug-of-war game between his biological father and his parents. He spent most of the break at home with his video games. It was the well-deserved break he needed before continuing with the stress of school.

For Rhian, the break was more stressful than all of the exams and homework assignments he had in school. Ever since fall break, he was weighed down with guilt over death of the girl at camp. His dreams were full of violent scenes from the camp all of which concluded the same way. Night after night he woke up in a panic, covered in sweat and breathless. This trip home began giving him anxiety from the time he got into his car. As he neared the house he grew up in the sense of calm that should have eased his nerves was replaced with greater anxiety.

Rhian arrived just before it was time for dinner. He had rehearsed the words in his head over and over again in the car. He stretched as he got out of the car and walked up to the front door. As he entered the familiar home he was greeted by the familiar smell of his mother's cooking. Suddenly he was welcomed by the feeling of *home*; his anxiety dissipated. Soon after arriving he was greeting his parents with hugs and kisses before sitting down for dinner and catching up on the latest family gossip.

"What's on your mind?"

"Girl problems?" His mother asked with false hope. Where was he going to begin? He knew he had to tell them the truth about the camp. It was so long ago but they didn't know what had happened. They had no idea where they had sent their son to. Maybe, by being honest, they would realize how horrible it was and he could get help for his nightmares. He took a deep breath, closed his eyes, and seriously considered running out of the room. When he opened his eyes he looked up at the two concerned individuals in front of him and thought about the responsibility they had to accept him and how they hadn't lived up to that expectation. This was their chance to do the right thing. He was giving them the opportunity to make things right. Rhian was giving his parents a gift and they should appreciate it. With this bit of inspiration and a little bit of courage, he began.

"Mom… Dad… you probably won't like what I'm about to say." He waited for them to recognize what he was talking about, but he should have guessed that they would be blindsided. The last time they had discussed it was a few nights before he was sequestered and robbed of his innocence. "I have been experiencing very vivid nightmares… night terrors… I don't really know what to call them."

"What are they about?" Mrs. Pierce asked with concern.

"Well, the dreams are related to my past and I am really depressed. This is probably the worse bout of depression I've ever had."

"Is this about your confusions?" His father's eyes narrowed and he was no longer concerned. He was threatened. The genuine concern that they wore was quickly dismantled.

"I thought we dealt with that already? What is going on, Rhian?" Rhian began to regret his honesty. He had to think quickly because his plan was falling apart. They weren't going to take him seriously. They weren't going to continue listening.

"I think I saw someone die while I was at camp that summer!" Shocked by his words, Mr. and Mrs. Pierce remained silent. "I keep seeing her die in my dreams and it's haunting me. I never told anyone because I was afraid of what they might do to me."

"I knew we shouldn't have ever let you go away to school."

"Honey, you are stressed and we understand that you have been working very hard. We are very proud of you for going to school and trying to make a better life for yourself. Maybe you have been working too hard?"

"You don't believe me?"

"This is a very stressful time in your life. A lot is expected of you. Perhaps those dreams are your mind's way of letting you know it's time to relax." She was completely serious. Rhian realized that they weren't going to believe him. He knew that denial was a solution in their book. They didn't believe that he was gay until someone else came and told them, but by now they had repressed that too.

"You're probably right… I don't know what I was thinking. I'm sorry." They didn't say another word about it.

Thanksgiving went by without any more talk of the girl. Once Sunday afternoon came Rhian couldn't wait to get in the car and leave. As he packed his things into the car his mother came out of the house with a compassionate smile on her face.

"Although we didn't think it was a good idea at first we are proud of you for going out there and taking on school. Do your best on those finals and bring back those A's. I love you." She spoke from her heart.

"Thanks… I know you do. Goodbye, Mom." He tried to believe her.

Theresa Pierce wasn't the kind of woman who was easily moved by the emotions of others. While she played the role of a caring housewife and concerned member of her church community, she was more concerned with her image. She grew up on the Northside of Chicago in a conservative catholic home. She aspired to be a doctor but her father didn't support those ideas. He believed that she should find a man to settle down with and raise a family. When she got to high school, she met a senior named Thomas, or Tom. She was only a freshman when they began dating and he was a senior, which she knew would upset her father. In the year that they dated they caused a lot of trouble together but after Tom graduated, he disappeared and Theresa refocused on her studies.

Thomas didn't come back into her life until she was in college. A night of heavy drinking and lowered inhibitions led to an unplanned pregnancy. Theresa dropped out of college and was forced to marry Tom by her parents. He committed to her as soon as he found out about the baby but she wasn't so certain. When she found out the baby was going to be a girl, Theresa insisted on the name Rhiannon, like the song by Fleetwood Mac. This baby would replace her aspirations with responsibilities preventing her from ever achieving her dreams. "Dreams unwind, love's a state of mind" replayed in her head as she thought about her baby girl. She couldn't be a good mother if she hated her child. This lyric reminded her that she could someday love her daughter like she deserved, though for now she couldn't. Her resentment grew with every doctor's visit as her hatred for the girl intensified. She prayed that it would all go away though she would never tell Tom nor explain the reason for the name.

On a warm morning in July, Theresa gave birth to a healthy baby boy. Tom liked the name Ryan but in an effort to combine his wife's choice of Rhiannon, he decided that the spelling should be Rhian for uniqueness. Theresa couldn't refute the name since Rhiannon was her first choice so she agreed. As she looked into her son's eyes her pent up anger faded away and all she could feel was love for the boy. She cried, not because she was happy, but because she felt guilty that she hated her own baby for so long. The resentment had been replaced with guilt. When he cried, she was there right away. She set out to become the perfect mother and housewife in an attempt to get over her guilt. This eventually became too much and she needed someone to talk to. She began going to a church, a Baptist church, since Catholicism hadn't worked out for her. Tom began joining her and the two decided to raise Rhian in the church.

So much had changed since she and Thomas first brought Rhian home from the hospital. Theresa had always been very close to her son but after that summer he went to camp something had changed. He wasn't the same and she knew it but she didn't want to talk about it because she feared it would cause trouble between her and Tom. The relationship with her son had been damaged but it was still there and she would do her best to keep it. Rhian's confession about the girl made her wonder if it were true. She approached the pastor one day after Sunday service.

"Pastor, I wanted to talk to you about my son." She held eye contact for a few seconds before becoming distracted by the many pieces of art in his office. She hadn't spent much time there so she immediately noticed a Monet. "That's a beautiful painting. Where did you buy that?"

"Oh, I didn't buy that. It was a gift. Now what is going on with Rhian? He hasn't been experiencing any of those *confusions* has he?" Monet, it was definitely a Monet. But it couldn't be real.

"No… Who painted this? It's beautiful. I've never seen anything like it." Theresa was distracted by the painting. But she was curious how a pastor could afford a true Monet.

"It was a gift from a friend. I believe it was painted by a European guy many years ago. If you would like a picture of it you may take one after we talk but right now I need to know what is going on with Rhian." Theresa was now uncomfortable. There was something demanding in his voice. Or perhaps it was the look of wrath in his eyes. He was good at playing a role. Just like she was good at being a *good housewife*, he was good at being a *good pastor*. Something was not right about it all. She had never felt unsafe being in the church until that moment. The hair on the back of her neck stood up. She felt threatened and she needed to leave.

"Well, he was just telling me that he had been experiencing some nightmares. Perhaps it's just his imagination but I wasn't sure if that was common in young men his age." She wasn't lying.

"What kind of nightmares?"

"He claims to be seeing demons in his dreams. They torture him and they mock him. I told my husband it was probably because he watches too much television."

"That is more common in children, when fear is irrational."

"Are you saying that demons are irrational?" She challenged. Where did the courage come from?

"I am saying that at his age, fear is more focused on things that can actually hurt him. Not things that go bump in the night." He spat back.

"So what should I do?" Pastor stood up and walked to the window. He looked out for a moment while stroking his chin. It eased the tension a bit, at least for him.

"He will outgrow these fears. Dreams of demonic entities suggest a problem with his heart; guilt perhaps. Let me ask you, has he given you more trouble lately?"

"No, he is very well behaved."

"Why haven't I seen him in the service lately?" His emotionless eyes burned through her.

"He is… working. He has a job and it requires him to work on Sundays. I was against it but he is old enough to make his own decisions." The empathy suddenly returned to Pastor's countenance.

"I understand how boys are. Give him time and he will be alright. A mother is right to worry about her child but know that everything will be alright. Rhian is a good kid and you have done a great job of raising him."

"Thank you, Pastor." Theresa couldn't escape fast enough. Her intuition convinced her that Rhian was telling the truth. If it was true that the girl was murdered and he saw, then he might be in danger. She would do whatever it took to protect him.

Theresa prepared dinner just as she always had, with exhaustive precision. She didn't want Thomas to know how much she had on her mind. Rhian was coming home for winter break that night and she hadn't talked to him since the Sunday after Thanksgiving. He walked in just as she finished placing the last fork on the table.

"Hello sweetie!" Theresa planted a kiss on his cheek. "Did you have a good drive back?"

"Yeah… The drive was alright…" He hesitated to continue as the heaviness of his thoughts weighed down his mood. Theresa immediately felt the knot in her stomach tighten up.

"That's good. Dinner will be ready soon so you should go get ready." She knew he wanted to say more but she wanted to avoid it.

Her son had a darkness that surrounded him. He wasn't smiling and happy the way he had been before. The heavy air filled the house for the rest of the time Rhian was there. Christmas had become Theresa's favorite holiday because she found a great deal of fulfillment when she saw Rhian's face as he opened his gifts. Being an only child meant that he was spoiled when it came to the gift giving. But he was never a bad kid. In fact, he would save up any little bit of money he had to buy his parents something nice as a sign of his appreciation.

This year, Theresa reflected on all of the happy years that they had spent together. There was an obvious change in Rhian's level of happiness but Christmas morning it all subsided. Theresa saw her son smile again for the first time in a long time. She didn't see the dark cloud. To her, he seemed happy again for the first time in what felt like years.

Later that night, Theresa passed by Rhian's room when she heard him talking to someone on the phone.

"Hey Leena, I miss you." Theresa was about to walk away when she heard him say, "I have to tell you something." For the next twenty minutes she listened to the gruesome details of the camp that she and her husband had sent their son to. She heard about the way he was tortured and the guilt he felt for not saying anything about the girl. She heard everything she didn't want to believe. Yet deep down she knew he was telling the truth. She could feel it. The conversation left her shaken. She didn't sleep much after that. This is how the rest of the time with Rhian went. She couldn't talk to anyone about it. She felt alone with this secret.

"Mom… Dad?" Rhian asked for their attention just before he walked out of the house to back to campus.

"Yes?" His father answered.

"I need to talk to you about something. It has been bothering me and I need to tell you." The familiar look of disapproval was all over his father's face.

"Not again." Realizing that it wasn't going to get their attention, he panicked.

"I have a boyfriend… Had a boyfriend. But he left me. I've been losing sleep over it and that is why I have been having the nightmares." Theresa knew her son was lying.

"You lied to us?" His father responded without missing a beat.

"I didn't lie… I just…"

"You lied." Theresa added. It wasn't what she expected to say but she couldn't defy her husband.

"I've been having a difficult time ever since we broke up. I'm not telling you to upset you. I just feel like I need my parents to tell me that everything is going to be ok." He held back emotion as best as he could by clenching his fists.

"It's not going to be alright. I thought we went through this already. You made your choice!" Mr. Pierce was not moved by Rhian's plea.

"Dad, it's not a choice! Why don't you understand that?"

"I would rather see you dead than with another man. Get out of my house and don't come back."

"Thomas…" Theresa never expected such a fierce reaction.

"…Dad… You don't mean that."

"Get out before I call the police."

"I'm going! You'll never see me again." Rhian slammed the door behind him.

"You are disgusting. I didn't raise a daughter, you faggot!" Tom yelled out as he watched his son get in the car. Rhian turned back one more time before turning away. It was not supposed to go this way but the damage was done.

Rhian struggled to catch his breath as he drove away from the house. He couldn't believe what had just happened. This wasn't his life. This couldn't have been what happened. He had good parents, they weren't bad people. It hadn't happened. It was too quick. But it had happened. He was driving back to school for the last time. There was no more *home*. There was no more *family*. Everything had changed over the exchange of a few words. This was real. This was now his life. He picked up his phone and dialed Leena but there was no answer. He scrolled to the next call and it was Alexander.

"Hey, do you have time to talk?"

"Absolutely! I feel like we haven't talked in days. How's it going?"

"I… I…" The tears poured down his face. "I don't even know where to begin. I just got kicked out of my house."

"What!? Why? Rhian, what happened?" Alexander sensed something terrible.

"I don't know why but I told them I had a boyfriend that I broke up with and that the breakup was the reason that I kept having the nightmares."

"Is that why you haven't been sleeping, because of the nightmares?"

"Yeah, but it's not the point."

"Why didn't you just tell them that you were having nightmares?"

"I did; at Thanksgiving dinner but they didn't take me seriously."

"So just tell them the truth."

"I can't. They will send me away again. I can't go back!" Alexander felt Rhian's distress through the phone.

"Rhian calm down. Where are you?"

"I'm driving back to school."

"I'll be waiting for you when you get here. In the meantime please concentrate on driving. Be careful."

"Thank you."

"You're not alone. I'm here."

Rhian arrived at his door to find Alexander waiting for him. Without saying anything Alexander briskly approached him and enveloped him in his arms. He held Rhian as he began to cry. At first Rhian cried quietly but as Alexander tightened up his grip he sobbed uncontrollably.

"Shhhh, it's ok. You are ok. You are safe now." Why those words? Alexander didn't really know but it used to work for him. He knew that the word *safe* was comforting when in a state of such distress. After a he was able to sooth Rhian enough to get him to come into the room they sat down on the bed. Alexander kept his arm around Rhian.

"I don't understand why they can't just love me for who I am." He was now a bit more audible than before.

"Sometimes these things don't make sense. The truth is that it doesn't have to. You can ask *why* until you're blue in the face and it won't make a difference because it will never make sense. Take comfort in the fact that you aren't alone, and the fact that everything will be ok."

"How can you be so sure? I feel like my world is falling apart…"

"Your world is not falling apart… It only feels that way. Everything will be ok."

"I feel worthless… like I am not good enough. I honestly feel like I am not worthy of being loved and without love why is life worth living…" He said letting the last statement slip quietly.

"Wow… Rhian, you've got to stay away from those thoughts. Ok, here's the thing, you are not worthless. You are most definitely worthy of being loved and I think that they are just scared because they don't know how to help you become better since you are already perfect just the way you are."

"You're just saying that because you're my friend and you are trying to make me feel better." Rhian said out of frustration.

"Well duh!" Alexander returned. Rhian gently turned away unsure whether to take it as a good thing that his friend cared or just a rude comment.

"Rhian, you are… amazing. You are intelligent, kind, caring, hilarious, good-looking and a genuinely great guy. Anyone would be lucky to have you in their life. I'm lucky to have you in my life. . And

I'm not just saying that. It's true. If I were gay, I don't think I'd be good enough for you…" He lightened the mood.

"That's the gayest thing you ever said to me." Rhian returned with a crooked grin.

"Shut up Nancy and come over here so I can hug you to make you feel better."

"Watch it straight boy! You're sweet but don't push it." Rhian jokingly barked back as he went in to hug Alexander. The boys embraced for a bit longer than a standard hug. Rhian needed the physical comfort of his friend's presence. To his surprise it was the first time he had really noticed Alexander's physically comforting presence. Maybe it was because he never needed it as badly as he did now.

"Everything will work itself out… you just have to give it time. I know you are strong enough to make it through this."

"I feel so alone… and unsafe… It scares me. I feel sad…" And with that he began to cry softly. Alexander put his arm around him and hugged him tightly. Rhian simply cried into Alexander's chest again. They didn't say a word but it was exactly what Rhian needed at that moment.

"Lie down."

"What? Why?" Rhian was thrown off by his command.

"Just do it." Alexander said with a snicker.

"Are you tucking me into bed…?" Rhian asked innocently with mild chuckle as he lay down. "Are you leaving me now?" He added with a more serious tone.

"No. I'm going to stay with you if that's alright. I figured you needed someone to cuddle with and I am comfortable enough to do that for you."

"Isn't that what girls do? Like… lesbians…"

"Shut up and go to sleep, I doubt any other straight man would offer to cuddle with you to make you feel better." He said smacking Rhian in the head playfully.

"Alexander?"

"Yeah?"

"I don't think I can sleep?"

"Close your eyes."

"But…"

"Close them. What do you see?"

"Darkness…" Rhian answered with sadness. Alexander unexpectedly wrapped his arms around him and held him closely.

"Now what do you see?" Rhian remained silent for another moment.

"City lights."

"You always like the city lights don't you? What else do you see?"

"The beach. It's really warm and I can feel the sand between my toes. I hear the water nearby. It's beautiful, Alexander! The skyline, the ocean, the mountains I've never seen anything like it! Where am I?"

"It's San Diego."

"Yeah! That's it! It's San Diego. Can we go there?"

"Someday."

"We could learn to surf and open up a restaurant, right on the beach!"

"We'd have to save up a lot of money."

"Leena could help."

"I'd rather keep this between you and me."

"Then we'd have to put our house up as collateral for the bank to give us a loan. But if you go to law school then it may have to wait until you make enough to pay back your loans. So I'll have to put the loan on my name."

"Well, perhaps. But what if I go into politics?"

"Then you could pay for the restaurant with your huge salary!"

"It's settled. We'll have the restaurant by the time we are thirty and by forty it will be a nationwide chain. You will be the king of…. whatever it is that we serve."

"I like that." Rhian sighed with relief. The distraction had worked. "San Diego." He repeated with excitement before falling asleep.

"San Diego." Alexander said with a smile as he fell asleep.

The new semester began and Rhian's moods were very inconsistent. His grades from the first semester qualified him for another scholarship which allowed him to have more freedom with his money. It also meant he didn't need to contact his parents for any reason. Most days he was able to forget about them and avoid thinking about his lack of a home. But there was still a change in his mood. One afternoon Rhian met up with Leena and Sophie to study. They had originally agreed to study in the library, but Sebastian had recently been promoted and needed someone to take care of his daughter, Lilly. Rhian had taken care of her several times so he was willing to help Sebastian. As stressful as the schoolwork was, the three found that spending time with Lilly was like therapy. Her adorable laugh and playful nature made all problems go away. Once Sebastian came home the girls left but Rhian stayed to help get her ready for bed. He and Lilly shared a special bond. He kissed her goodnight on his way out.

"You're her best friend Rhi." Sebastian was the only one who was allowed to call him that.

"Well that's good because she's mine." Rhian responded with a laugh.

"You're going to make a great dad someday." Sebastian laughed. He patted his friend on the shoulder as Rhian was leaving. On the walk home he couldn't stop thinking about the time he spent with Lilly. He loved children but he was so afraid of being a parent. He could easily spend hours with playing with her but at the end of the day, his mistakes didn't affect her like Sebastian's did. He thought about the way his parents had hurt him and he knew that he never wanted to hurt his children that way.

Rhian returned to find Alexander waiting in his room. Alexander had been sleeping in his friend's room almost every night since they came back from the break. He kept a sleeping bag in the room and was able to sneak in his mattress in. They stayed up every night talking about whatever was on their minds. It was the escape Rhian needed. San Diego was a major focus for both of them although it was all just an idea. Rhian needed to those talks and in a way so did Alexander.

Being away from home was now easier for Rhian because he didn't feel wanted there, but Alexander was becoming homesick. Rhian had a way of making Alexander feel like he was at home. This semester Alexander did go home a few times over the weekend. During those weekends Rhian was noticeably sad.

"Are we going to any concerts this summer?" Kala asked Rhian.

"I don't know… I don't think I can afford to go."

"That's too bad! There are some pretty awesome shows this summer in Chicago. I figured you would want to maybe check them out. We could go to Lolopalooza!"

"Maybe… I'll let you know."

"What's wrong, Sweetie? You're acting like someone kicked your puppy. What's got you in a funk?" Leena could tell there was something he wasn't saying.

"I don't really want to talk about it."

"I'm one of your best friends. You can talk to me about it."

"Alexander is gone for the weekend so I've been sleeping alone… and I don't like being alone with my thoughts." Rhian realized how odd that sounded. He hadn't told anyone else that they had been illegally rooming together for entire semester now.

"What?" Leena was shocked.

"It's not what it sounds like!" Rhian laughed loudly.

"Well then you should probably explain what you mean because I'm confused."

"I didn't want to tell anyone because I don't want pity."

"What aren't you telling us?" Leena suddenly became worried. "You spent the first part of the semester in a hazy depression and now you're telling me that Alexander has been staying with you? I'm getting worried. You aren't a danger to yourself are you?"

"No! At least I don't think so..." Rhian wasn't really sure now. But he didn't want to be doing this in front of everyone.

"Rhian, what aren't you telling us?"

"My parents kicked me out of their house. I'm not allowed to go back home."

"Why are you barely telling us this?" Sophie was annoyed.

"I was worried about school and I didn't want to think about it. I figured it would blow over but I haven't heard from my family. I was going to try and figure it out after the semester."

"I don't believe this!" Leena pulled out her phone and walked away from the group. She immediately called Sebastian. "Hey, Rhian's parents kicked him out of their house. If I help you out with some of the bills will you let him stay with you?" Her mothering instincts kicked in.

"Leena, you know he can. You don't have to pay me anything."

"I'll let him know. I would bring him with me if I wasn't going to be in New York for the whole summer."

"I'll make sure he stays out of trouble."

"Thank you. I owe you one!" Leena hung up the phone and took a deep breath. She made her way back to where the others were and explained to Rhian that Sebastian was willing to take him in for the summer.

"I'll be fine. I just need to find a better paying job."

"Rhian, I love you but you need help and right now the only one that isn't going to be across the country or around the world is Sebastian. Please just stay with him. You'll be able to spend time with Lilly and it would be a big help to him.

"I guess you're right… Ok." It hadn't occurred to him until that moment that he was going to be homeless at the beginning of the summer. For now, Leena had solved the problem, but he would have to find a place after the summer. This was going to be difficult to navigate through but he would have to worry about it later.

The realization that he was now completely on his own became too much for Rhian to keep ignoring. The hardest part about it all was the feeling of loneliness that overcame him each time he thought about his parents. The semester had gone by quickly and it was rapidly approaching the end but it seemed like Rhian's motivation had been drained. While he tried to keep it a secret from his friends, Alexander was keenly aware of the changes in his friend's mood.

"Hey… what's up?"

"Nothing… what's new with you?" Rhian forced a smile. Alexander tilted his head to the side, which he did more often than he realized, and cracked a smile. He turned around and grabbed Rhian's arm, gently pulling him towards the door.

"Come on."

"Where are we going? I'm not even ready!"

"You look gorgeous as ever darling! Now come on."

"Well let me at least get my shoes on."

"Ugh, women."

Alexander led him down to the car that was waiting for them in front of the building. Alexander was lucky that they hadn't towed it since it was a no parking zone. Katy Perry's song *The One That Got Away* was playing just as he started the car. "Oh, turn the volume up!" Rhian shouted with a big smile.

"Slow down crazy!" Alexander said laughing as he turned up the volume. He liked a lot of Katy Perry's music but this song had a bittersweet feel to it. It starts as a cute story about love then turns into a song about regret and the *what if* path that life hands us. This wasn't something Alexander was particularly fond of thinking about but Rhian liked it so he didn't object.

They made their way through campus driving past one of the places that Rhian liked to read at. He noticed someone sitting in his favorite spot. It was surprising how quickly a college campus can change over the course of a few days. He had barely been going to class because he was busy sulking alone in his room. They were soon far from campus as they drove in the direction of the mall. He noticed that Alexander kept looking down at his phone.

"Keep your eyes on the road! I'll check your phone if it's that important! Sheesh!"

"No, no… it's not a big deal, just a *hello* message. I'll check it later." He seemed nervous.

"Ok… Where are we going by the way?"

"Well, you've been a bitter crab the past few days so I thought it would be a nice treat to get some sweetness in you. So we are going to get a Cinnabon, my treat." Alexander was proud of himself for knowing Rhian's true kryptonite, sugar covered bread.

"Well… if you insist. Thank you, Alexander. It means a lot that you are trying to make me feel better."

From the moment the boys crossed the threshold of the mall's front entrance the smell of warm bread coated with cinnamon and the creamy icing permeated the air. Its welcoming brilliance was more captivating than the aroma of the other businesses in that food court. Rhian quickly walked up to the counter and ordered the small Cinnabon with a cup of water. Alexander followed and ordered his as well. He pulled out his wallet and paid for their treat. When they received their scrumptious morsels, the boys looked for a spot and sat down.

As Rhian took his first bite, he was suddenly lost to the world. He could only hear, taste, feel, smell, and see Cinnabon! While Rhian was distracted Alexander took the time to check his phone. There was one message from Leena.

Where are you now?

We are at Cinnabon. We will be there at 5pm sharp. Alexander quickly replied.

"New lady friend?"

"What? No… I mean, it was just Leena, she needed something."

"Oh ok, is everything alright?"

"Oh um… she needed light… A light… for her car. You know how she is, can't do anything for herself." Alexander said with a fake laugh. Leena knew how to change her car's oil, which Rhian knew, so he found it strange that Alexander was lying, but he didn't question it. He figured Alexander was just being weird. The boys sat and finished their sweets while chatting about their weeks.

"Hey, let's go to the sports store. I wanna check out some shoes."

“Sure.”

The boys spent about an hour at the mall searching through the different shops for whatever caught their attention. The two had lost track of time just goofing around. Suddenly Alexander looked down at his phone and realized that it was now 5:25pm. He had ten missed calls and several angry messages.

“Uh, let’s go!”

“What’s the rush? I just found a shirt that looks good on me and I want it.” He pouted.

“That does look good on you. Here I’ll buy it for you but we have to go now.”

“Ok… Is everything ok?”

“We have to go pick up Leena, she said she needs a ride…”

Rhian felt uneasy about Alexander’s strange behavior. He quietly followed him back to the car. Alexander was usually a cautious driver, but today caution was thrown to the wind. He made the trip from the mall to Leena’s house in record time. He quickly got out of the car and walked to the door. He knocked on the door and saw an angry Leena through the window. The lights were off so that Rhian couldn’t tell what was going on. Leena unlocked the door and remained hidden. Alexander walked in closing the door behind him.

“I’m so sorry! I lost track…”

“You closed the door on him!”

The doorknob turned and everyone was again quiet. Rhian walked unsure of where Alexander had disappeared to. Suddenly the lights went on and his friends popped out from their hiding places.

“Surprise!”

“Aww… Thank you…?” He wasn’t sure what was going on.

"It's your coming out party, Sweetie!" Leena yelled out in excitement. She pointed to a rainbow banner that hung above the table with the words *It's a queen!* written on it. Rhian could only laugh.

"It's a celebration of YOU! We wanted to remind you that you are important to us and that we are your family." Alexander said with a big smile. It was good to see Rhian in good spirits for the first time in months.

"This big goof here put this all together for you, well with the help of my planning expertise, of course. I asked him if there was some way to show you that we appreciated you and after some talking we figured it out. Even though your blood relatives don't support you, we do and we love you very much. Because we are your family too!" With that Leena gave Rhian a hug followed by Alexander. The rest of the group came over one by one showing their appreciation for him.

This was exactly what Rhian needed to get him back to being his usual cheerful self. He was surrounded by love and he couldn't have asked for a better group of friends. As they partied the night away, they all had a blast dancing, singing karaoke, and eating the delicious food. It was a well-planned out party for being on such short notice. Of course, when Leena was involved everything was always done to impress.

As the night came to a close, the music was softer and a few people were dancing with their significant other. Alexander was sitting at the table talking to John about a few events for the coming week when he noticed Rhian sitting alone while watching the couples. He could tell that Rhian was feeling a bit jealous he didn't have a boy to dance with so he walked over to him and held his hand out.

"No guy should be sitting alone during a cheesy slow song at his own coming out party! May I have this dance?" Alexander asked with a goofy smile.

"Why, how could I turn down such a handsome prince like you?" Rhian sarcastically returned.

"You forgot to mention my huge… ego…" He said with a wink, which made Rhian laugh out loud as he grabbed his hand. They both knew how to do a basic waltz and decided to go for it. The other couples stopped dancing to allow the two enough space to show off. They danced around the room proudly displaying their skill. Rhian followed Alexander's lead gracefully and at the end of it even bowed properly. The room broke out into clapping as the boys laughed their way back to their seats. The night came to an end once everyone had already left Leena's apartment. Alexander walked Rhian back to his dorm room.

"Alexander, you are the most amazing friend anyone could ever ask for… You all are! I can't begin to express how happy I am that I have people in my life who love me so much. Thank you. I love you!" He gave Alexander a big hug and a kiss on the cheek, which Alexander wasn't expecting but welcomed. Rhian was able to fall right to sleep right away without any tears, but Alexander stayed with him out of habit.

That night Alexander thought about his own life and how he had faced some interesting challenges while growing up. He hadn't revisited those feelings since he was very young and he wasn't sure that he wanted to. He was quite happy with the way his life was turning out so why ruin the good thing he had. Watching Rhian *come out* at his party was somewhat inspiring. He saw how well received it was by all of the people that loved him. He figured that he hadn't made much effort to open up to people but it was out of fear of rejection or possibly getting hurt. He wasn't like Rhian. He didn't have to come out sexually; he had to come out as… someone who didn't really know who he was. Being a kid who grew up in several abusive households made it difficult for him to open up. But this was different. He had found a loving family both at home and at school. There was no longer a need to protect himself.

Life continued for the group of friends and they continued to spend their afternoons studying at Sebastian's place while taking care of Lilly. She loved the attention that she received from all of these smiling faces. Alexander had been quiet the entire time, which was normal for him when he was around people he didn't know. But this was the family.

"I hate my chin… And I used to suck my thumb until I was about fourteen. My mother is a drug addict who probably doesn't know that she has a son anymore and my father is a selfish ass who only talks to me when he feels it will benefit him. The truth is that I think of him as a sperm donor and her as an egg donor. I have no idea who I am, nor where I'm going. You all are the first people besides my parents that I feel like I can trust. I am not as self-assured as Rhian. I am not as smart as Nikolaus. I am not as organized as Leena…"

"But you are our Alexander… and that's all that matters." Leena shouted back at him with authority. "There is no other person quite like you and we love you for that. Now, I'm sorry if you felt it necessary to tell us these things because we didn't make you feel accepted but know that we accept you regardless of anything because you are family. And that goes for anyone of you."

"Leena, I know you all do. But I have always had trouble opening up and getting close to people. I'm sorry if I made it seem like I was complaining. I wasn't. I am trying to open up. It feels good." Alexander smiled warmly.

"What about me?" Sophie inquired.

"What do you mean?" Alexander was puzzled.

"You started to say things that the others did better than you according to what you think. What do you like about me that I do better than you?"

"Sophie, you have one of the most beautiful voices I have ever heard. I wish I could sing as well as you." He winked at her. She hugged him and then began singing a song, purposefully out of tune.

Later that night, while Rhian was lying in his bed and Alexander in his sleeping bag, Rhian asked how his friend was doing.

"Are you alright? What was that about earlier? Is there something going on?"

"What do you mean?"

"Alexander, you blurted out a bunch of facts about yourself. I understand what you were saying, but are you sure you are alright?"

"I guess I just forgot about a lot of the things that used to bother me when I was younger. I don't know why but seeing you at your party inspired me to try and open up to people. To work towards not feeling so guarded around everyone. But it also reminded me that I was abandoned. It's like I always knew that both of my parents walked out on me, but it wasn't until now that my heart realized it. It's upsetting." Tears rolled down his cheeks. He had stopped talking so Rhian figured he was done.

"Alexander, you are an incredible human being. I honestly wish I could take away all of the pain that you endured growing up and the pain that you feel right now. Unfortunately I can't, but I can say that I will always be here for you because I love you. And I know that your real parents, not the donors, will never abandon you no matter what happens."

"Thank you." Alexander was proud of himself. He had been completely open with someone other than his parents and he even felt comfortable enough to cry in front of his friend. He wiped the tears from his eyes and tried to lighten the mood by talking about going fishing.

"I think we should this weekend." Rhian sounded excited.

"I agree. I can't wait"

"Me either! I used to go all the time with my dad when I was younger, but we stopped doing things together after…" Alexander sensed that this was a sensitive topic so he decided to change the subject.

The semester had passed a lot faster than anyone expected, but that was the life of a college student. Finals were only a week away but Leena felt that she needed to get away so she Gianna, Kala, and Sophie took a last minute trip to Chicago. The promise of exams overwhelmed Alexander, so he decided to get away for the weekend as well. He drove home as soon as his last class was done. Rhian was the only one who had stayed that weekend. He was so focused on his review sheets that he jumped when his phone began ringing.

"Hello?" Rhian answered.

"Are you planning on coming home in a few weeks?"

"No. Why would you ask…" Before he could finish the sentence Theresa cut him off.

"Your father and I have been talking about what happened. He agreed to give you another chance but there will be conditions. We don't appreciate that you lied to us about having a boyfriend. We don't support the lifestyle you are choosing and have therefore decided that you must make a choice. At the end of the semester you are to come home and go to the camp again, to treat your disease. If you choose to come home at the end of the semester we will know you made the right decision. You will go to camp and we will not talk about this issue again. But if you choose to continue in your immoral lifestyle then you are not welcome here. We have been paying your phone bill but that will stop if you don't come home." She paused for a moment. "We will also remove our contribution to your tuition. You will not likely be able to afford the tuition if we do so I hope you choose wisely. You have till the end of the semester to decide. If you don't come home we will know the choice you made. We love you."

Chapter 4

With finals now over, most of the campus had emptied out. The only people ones left were graduate students and the townies. Leena had an internship that began immediately after finals. Nikolaus had returned to Germany and Sophie back to China. The rest had also gone back home. Alexander would be back in a few weeks for summer classes but for now only Rhian and Sebastian remained. Leena got Rhian a job at the café she worked at for the extra money. It didn't pay much but if he worked at both the bookstore and the café, he would be able to pay for his own apartment.

The first few days behind the espresso bar were rough but it wasn't long before he was a pro.

"You're pretty smart, man!" A coworker of Rhian's named Matt praised.

"Thanks, this stuff is tricky but once you get the hang of it, it's not too bad."

"Yeah man! Hey, what are you doing after work?"

"I hadn't made any plans yet… I was just going to go play with Lilly."

"Who's Lilly?"

"Oh, she's Sebastian's daughter."

"Who is Sebastian?"

"You really don't pay attention do you? Sebastian is my friend."

"Your boyfriend?"

"Sebastian is the friend who is letting me live with him since I can't go home."

"Why can't you go home?"

"I don't really like talking about it."

"Rhian, I know we aren't close but you can tell me."

"My parents kicked me out because they didn't want a gay son."

"That's insane! I hope I have a gay son! That way I won't have to worry about grandkids before I'm old."

"Thanks for the compliment?"

"I'm just trying to lighten the mood. Look, let's just hang out after work and we can bond."

"Alright, I'm ok with that."

"I'll meet you right here." As promised, Matt showed up right as Rhian was leaving the café for the evening.

"So what's the plan?" Rhian was curious.

"Well I think you need to loosen up so I figured we could go back to my place for some drinks and then we could go out and howl at the moon."

"Are we wolves or something?"

"Yeah kind of!"

The boys did exactly as Matt had planned, finishing off a bottle of cheap liquor and then going out to one of the piers at the river. Rhian walked out reluctantly as he felt the flimsy structure wobble beneath him.

"Are we safe here?"

"Perfectly."

"It doesn't feel like it."

"You are always safe, because you are always where you want to be. And if you are going to die, where better to die than exactly where you want to be."

"That's kind of deep."

"A bit. Here try this." Matt pulled out and ingested one small tablet and then handed Rhian the second one.

"What's that?"

"E."

"Ecstasy?" Rhian was shocked. Until now he had never done anything more illegal than underage drinking.

"It will mellow you out. Just take it."

"I don't know…" Just then Matt pulled him in and kissed him on the lips. Rhian accepted the kiss and closed his eyes. Matt carefully slipped the pill into Rhian's mouth and Rhian swallowed it. He pretended to protest, but the truth was that he was curious about the drug, hoping that it would perhaps give him an escape from the painful truth.

"There, now you know."

"Did you just…?"

"Yep!" Matt began laughing playfully as he proceeded to lie down with his feet dangling over the pier and into the water. Rhian joined him, feet in the water as the two enjoyed a peaceful evening under the stars.

"So what's it like? To be gay?"

"What's it like to be straight?"

"I don't know because people have never treated me like I was anything but human."

"Good point… Well, to be honest I don't see myself as anything less than people who are straight. The problem that I have is being tolerant of intolerance. It can be really frustrating to hear people constantly judge me or even *accept* me for something that I didn't choose nor can I change. Imagine waking up one morning and going online. You find that all of a sudden there are hundreds of hits on why people with your particular hair color were inferior to the rest of the world. And that there were studies proving it. Now imagine that those same people start saying that people with your hair color are hated by God, or somehow not accepted because of their hair color… Sure you could dye your hair and cover it up but you can't change your natural hair color. That is only scratching the surface." Matt leaned over and kissed Rhian on the head. He was more affectionate than any other man Rhian had ever encountered. Then again it could have been the drug.

"Wow… I guess I've never thought of it that way. Well buddy… I accept you."

Matt laughed as he put his arm around Rhian and brought him in for a hug. Rhian sighed and smiled as he closed his eyes and pictured himself flying. He knew that Matt understood and felt relieved. And so the summer of firsts began, blurry by the mind altering high of experimentation. Rhian felt extremely relaxed that night, unconcerned with the fact that his parents had kicked him out of their lives.

Heavy drinking and ecstasy provoked relaxation by the pier became the norm for Matt and Rhian. They would share a bottle or liquor by the water and swap stories of their childhoods. Matt was particularly interested in the church that Rhian was from. He was raised in a very liberal home that was accepting of everyone. Rhian loved to hear about life as a child without the restrictions he grew up with. He was fascinated by the thought that going to see a movie in theaters was a weekly occurrence. These nights allowed Rhian to recognize the repression he experienced and he was able to release some of the guilt that had haunted him.

At the beginning of the summer, Alexander returned home expecting to reconnect with old friends and to pass the warm nights near a bonfire. But until now, he had only seen his close friend Jake once in passing at the grocery store. He quickly realized that things were never going to be like they were in high school. He couldn't wait to get back to school where his new life was.

Alexander returned to school after being away for one month. He was so relieved to be back because he was starting to get bored but he also missed being around his friends.

"Hey, I just got back into town. What are you up to?"

"I'm taking care of Lilly… You should come over. I want to see you."

"I'll be right over." Alexander was excited to see Rhian again. They had kept in contact through text messages but it wasn't the same as hearing that other person's voice. As soon as Alexander walked through the threshold, Rhian jumped up and hugged him.

"I missed you!"

"I can see that! I missed you too!" Alexander noticed something different about Rhian, but he wasn't sure what it was.

"Lilly and I were just playing with some of her toys." Rhian picked her up and made a waving motion at Alexander with her hand. She was all smiles. Alexander walked over and gave her a kiss and talked to her. Somewhere along the line, he became keenly aware of the fact that Rhian was going to make an amazing father someday. He chuckled to himself because of the irony of the situation. Here was a young man who had been kicked out of his own home by his parents who thought that he was such a terrible person, and he would probably be the parent of the year.

Rhian's nights of debauchery with Matt came to a halt as soon as Alexander returned. The three hung out a few times, but Rhian made sure that Matt didn't bring any of his *party supplies* when Alexander was around. They still returned to the pier almost every night but instead of getting high, or *low* as Matt called it, they simply drank and danced around some nights literally howling at the moon.

The boys had more fun that summer than they had had all year. Rhian and Alexander discovered that they both really enjoyed fishing on the pier when they weren't busy working, in class, or taking care of Lilly. Although Alexander was supposed to be staying in a dorm he preferred to stay at Sebastian's, right next to Rhian. In fact, he didn't spend a single night in his dorm room.

We regret to inform you that due to your poor academic performance during the most recent semester, you have been placed on probation. Please meet with your academic advisor. If you have any questions you may contact the Office of the Dean of Students.

Rhian had never received any kind of corrective action for poor performance at school before!

"I knew I shouldn't have opened this email!"

"What's wrong?"

"I think I'm in trouble…" Rhian read the rest of the letter, which was filled with unapologetic apologies.

"What do you mean?"

"I got this email a few weeks ago, but I just opened it. It says I'm on probation… I guess I wasn't doing as well as I thought I was."

"You went through a lot last semester, especially at the end. It's not really shocking that you didn't do well. I'm sure you will be alright. Why don't you just go talk to your advisor?"

"Yeah I should do that." Rhian couldn't believe that along with the added stress of his finances, he now had to worry about getting his grades up. He immediately made an appointment with his advisor. It was the first time in several months that he had seen her. She looked at him with a puzzled expression.

"Well, I'm not really sure what happened because it looks like you were doing really well your first semester. Is everything ok?"

"Not exactly." Rhian proceeded to explain his situation to her. She empathized with him.

"Why didn't you come talk to me about this?"

"I guess I didn't understand how badly it had affected me."

"I see, well my honest opinion would be to make sure you are equipped to focus all of your energy into your schooling. This is a difficult time for you and the most important thing is to make sure you find a strong support system to get you through so that you don't end up getting kicked out of school."

"I could get kicked out?"

"If you don't improve, yes it is possible to get kicked out."

"Ok… I will do better."

"Control what you can control." Rhian began to walk out. "And Rhian?"

"Yes?"

"There is nothing wrong with taking some time off."

"I'll keep that in mind. Thank you."

"No problem."

Rhian felt relieved that he was not in any immediate trouble. He was aware that he would have to work a lot more in order to bring his GPA up, but it was still summer time and he had a few weeks left to enjoy himself. He went right back to his summer of enjoyment. That weekend he and Matt planned to visit some of Matt's friends in Chicago.

"You're going to love my friends! They are awesome people!"

"I can't wait! Could I invite Alexander?"

"You can… But I doubt he would enjoy being around them… They are really open-minded."

"What do you mean? Alexander is one of the most open-minded individuals I know. He accepts anyone."

"My friends are recreational partiers."

"Oh! That kind of open-minded. Yeah, I don't know if he would want to join. I'll ask just in case. But I'll let him know."

"Ok." Later that day Rhian invited Alexander to tag along on the adventure in the city. He reluctantly agreed to go. He was growing concerned that Rhian was masking his feelings with partying. He wanted to make sure that his friend was going to be ok.

Matt led the boys to an obscure location several blocks away from the train. He knew where he was going, but the others had no idea. Finally, after what felt like miles of walking, they came up to a brick house surrounded by a rod-iron fence. They could hear music coming from inside the house. They walked around to the back, Matt still leading the way. He didn't knock; just opened the door and the three were now surrounded by unknown faces. Matt asked one of the guests if his friends were around. The pointed him to the living room. Once Matt found his friends, there was no taking him away from them. Rhian and Alexander sat quietly in a corner watching the party. The people were all very sociable, with each other. Not one person greeted them or even inquired about their presence. They were simply two random guests.

Rhian felt uncomfortable after a few minutes and diced that he didn't want to stay in that room much longer. He poked Alexander on his arm and motioned for him to follow. He walked past kitchen and out the door they came from. They stood out back for a few minutes until one of the other party guests came out and started talking to them. He asked if they wanted to smoke with him. Of course Rhian, in his naivety assumed that he meant cigarettes. He was mistaken. Upon realizing what the guy meant, he made up an excuse and the two left the party.

"Where are we headed?"

"I'm not sure… You know, Los Angeles is the city of angels. New York is the city that never sleeps… But what is Chicago?"

"Chi-raq." Alexander sarcastically responded."

"I'm being serious!"

"I don't know, but I'm sure you do…" He smiled.

"What about… *The Dreamer's Oasis.*"

"That sounds refreshing." Again Alexander was making fun. "Why *Oasis*?"

"Because people around here, the Midwest I mean, are so narrow-minded. They stare at you and refuse to accept what they don't understand. It's like they are stuck in the 1950's."

"Gas was cheaper back then."

"Alexander, be serious with me for a second!" Rhian was pretending to sound frustrated.

"Ok! So you see it as a type of oasis because it's like an oasis in a land void of tolerance?"

"That's exactly what it is. I mean look at this place. People from all around this area flock here to find themselves because moving to New York is way too expensive and moving to Los Angeles is too risky."

"I've never really thought of it that way. I guess people do stay here because it's kind of safe."

"Exactly! I don't want to be safe! I want to fly!"

"Easy there peacock, remember you have to learn to fly first."

"I know, but I'll get there. I'm not worried about that. Right now I want to enjoy the *Oasis* with my best friend."

"Well what do you suppose we do?"

"I'm kind of hungry… Let's find some food!" It was now getting really late, but they continued to walk around. They finally found a place that was open and decided to check it out before calling

Matt and finding out where they were staying. When they walked in, they were surprised to see Kala sitting in a booth with a group of people.

"Rhian? Alexander?" She jumped up and hugged both of them. "What are you two doing here? Are you following me around?"

"Not quite." Alexander laughed.

"We came up with a coworker because he wanted us to come meet his friends but we left the party early. It wasn't really our scene."

"What does that even mean?" She mocked. "Well, since you both are here and without anyone to take care of you I think you should come back with me and my friends. We are staying at a hotel. We just got back from an amazing concert and we are going to see another one tomorrow! You two should come with!"

"We would love to but I don't think either one of us has the money." Rhian reminded her.

"What is the concert?"

"Coldplay!" Kala screamed.

"Are there still tickets available?"

"I can get two tickets…"

"We'll take them."

"Alexander… I don't know if that's a good idea."

"I'll pay for your ticket. I owe you one."

"Really?"

"They are one of your favorite bands… we are going!"

The next day they went to the concert with Kala. They had a great time and almost forgot about Matt. Rhian called him but there was no answer. Eventually they got a hold of him and arranged to go back to school.

Later that week Rhian and Alexander decided to go fishing on the pier. It was the epitome of what an evening of fishing should be.

The sun had almost completely set as they sat with their lines in the water. Suddenly, Alexander's line started to move. He struggled to reel it in, and then suddenly was pulled into the water with a big splash. Rhian waited for him to resurface but when he didn't he jumped right in without giving it a second thought. The water was cold but the adrenaline made it negligible as he frantically searched for his friend. He dove down but without the help of any light it was impossible to see anything. When Rhian surfaced, he could hear movement nearby. As he approached the now clearer figure, he could see a smile on Alexander's face.

"Are you ok?" Rhian asked in a panic.

"Hahaha I'm fine! Are you ok?" Rhian stared at him in disbelief.

"Why do you like to scare me like that? You knew I would jump!" He splashed water at his friend.

Alexander shrugged his shoulders and again smiled. Something in the reflection of the moonlight on the water caused Alexander's face to light up as if there were a spot light on him. It brought out a side of him that Rhian had never really noticed until now. There was care, concern, love, passion, confusion, and a general appreciation for the soul that just tried to rescue him and it was all written on Alexander's face. The look he gave Rhian was powerful. There was a great deal of trust and connection shared between the two boys and although he wasn't really drowning, Alexander knew that he could count on Rhian to always jump in and save him. Now that they were wet, and unsure of what might be lurking in the murky waters below, the boys quickly dried off before making their way to Sebastian's.

Throughout the summer the boys continued to become close by sharing intimate details of their lives unlike either one had ever done before. Some might have said it was strange to see two grown men acting like children around each other, but that's who they were, Rhian and Alexander. Most nights, Rhian would talk about his parents and how he missed them. It would usually result in a nearly inconsolable Rhian turning into a mess of emotions. Alexander did his best to comfort his friend but there was only so much he could do. He couldn't make the pain go away, but he could try to make things better for his friend. The others kept in contact by regularly video chatting. Nikolaus, while happy to be home, missed his group of friends, as did Sophie. Gianna and Kala hung out often, but Gianna had gotten a job so she was busy most of the time. Leena's internship in New York City kept her busy and almost unreachable. She was very mysterious about her adventure in the concrete jungle. The summer was a long but much needed break for everyone.

Towards the end of the summer, it became clear that they would have to move out. Based on their good chemistry and the fact that they did well, living together for the past few months, the boys decided that sharing an apartment would be the best option for both of them. Rhian looked around for the best price because his budget was limited. They settled on a two bedroom apartment close enough to campus that walking was feasible but far enough that it was relatively inexpensive.

They moved in two weeks before school started and Rhian began decorating the place the way he wanted. Ever since he had returned to campus, Alexander hadn't been home for longer than a few hours. He was afraid to leave Rhian alone with his thoughts. Alexander had never felt so close to anyone else before, and while he didn't understand it completely, he liked the feeling of security that he got from making sure Rhian was ok. He felt it was his duty as Rhian's friend to make sure that he was all right because he couldn't stand the thought of him hurting or worse, losing him. He made great efforts to make him feel loved. Alexander had a good heart. Nevertheless, he decided that he had to spend a week at home with his family so he went back right before school started again.

Rhian curiously noticed the students arriving on campus for a new semester. He was excited for his friends to return but he was also reminded of the situation he was in. He observed countless families arriving together with children high on aspirations and dreams. It was a lot for him to take in and without any support from his parents, the only thing he felt was abandonment. He didn't talk about these feelings because he didn't want to become consumed by them. Rather than deal with his depression, Rhian avoided it once more by going out with Matt for the week that Alexander was gone.

The first day of classes began just like the previous year, but this time the boys were both late for class. Alexander got back in really late the night before, and Rhian was up crying as usual. He wiped the tears from his eyes when he heard the door unlock so that Alexander wouldn't notice that he was crying. Alexander came in to Rhian's room to check on his friend and then went straight to bed. He didn't get much time to talk to him but he could tell that something was wrong. He knew Rhian needed to talk it out so they made plans to go out for dinner the next night.

Rhian told Alexander about how it affected him to see the loving parents on campus. After talking I out he was in a much better mood and the boys spent the rest of the night cutting up and joking around. As usual they lost track of time and ended up spending three hours sitting and talking.

"I'm glad we accidentally became friends. I knew my charm was too much for you to resist." Alexander coolly stated.

"Hah! If anything it was my relaxed temperament that allowed us to become friends since you attacked me while flying a toy."

"Yeah, yeah, yeah!" Alexander returned. After they had dinner, the boys headed back home calling it a night.

Alexander continued to keep an eye on Rhian. They did their homework together and hung out together almost every day. It was a good escape for both of them and they shared that special chemistry. The others joked that they were like newlyweds; one never without the other. It was to the point that when one was invited somewhere, it was assumed that they were both invited. They worked out together and walked to class together.

Alexander continued to play lacrosse on an intramural team. He barely saw the guys last semester because he was always with Rhian, which they teased him about. Though they had only met him one or two times they had no problem when Alexander brought him along.

Alexander and his lacrosse buddies threw a party at John's house one weekend because it was still early enough in the semester that they weren't all overloaded with homework and studying. John lived with three other guys in a four bedroom party house. Rhian walked into the unfamiliar house and recognized one of the guys he had met before. He greeted him and some of the other people in the room that he didn't know before awkwardly going into the next room. He saw John grabbing a beer out of the fridge.

"Hey man, how are you?" John was clearly drunk.

"I'm good, how are you?"

"I'm good man, just here drinking, ya know! Well let me know if you need anything alright. I'm going to talk to some of the ladies haha!" Just as quickly as Rhian had found him, John was gone. He felt uncomfortable by the comment about finding some *ladies* because he became aware that he was probably the only guy in the house who was not looking for the *ladies*. He continued to make his way through the house until he finally found Alexander relaxing in the back corner of a room talking to a girl. She didn't seem too interested in what he was saying but Alexander seemed really interested in her. Rhian was kind of irritated after his conversation with John but he wasn't going to let that ruin his evening so he put on a smile before walking up to Alexander and greeting him.

"Hey! What's up?"

"Hey! Not much, just hanging out. Join us. Rhian, this is Meagan. Meagan, this is my best friend Rhian." Rhian shook her hand.

"Hi Rhian, nice to meet you." Meagan seemed kind of distracted but she was friendly, probably because of the alcohol. Rhian began to analyze her like every good friend to make sure she was good enough for his *best* friend. Somewhere over the course of his analysis he realized that she was probably just a hookup waiting to happen, which again annoyed him and made him feel uncomfortable. Alexander ignored Rhian's mood change and kept the conversation going. Rhian felt the effects of the alcohol pretty quickly and forgot about being annoyed.

The three congregated for a few hours before Rhian got up to go to the bathroom. He didn't realize how much he had been drinking until he stood up and almost fell back down. When he came back the other two were gone. He looked around but they were nowhere to be found. By this time the room was filled with people he didn't know and in his drunken state he felt awkward so he left. He stumbled through the streets, trying to find his way but he was lost. With everything spinning Rhian lost his balance and fell down into some bushes where he passed out.

"Whoa man!" John found a blacked out Rhian lying in the bushes. He was returning from one of his many conquests and while he had been drunk earlier, he was fairly sober at that point. He tried to wake Rhian but he knew that he wasn't going to get up and walk away by himself. He checked Rhian for a pulse. As a summer lifeguard, he was trained to handle life or death situations. Rhian was clearly in bad shape but he could tell that he was going to be ok. John picked him up with ease, swung him over his shoulder and headed towards his house. Rhian's place was pretty far and he figured it was futile to try and make it there at this point.

He thought about what a sight this must be with him a dark-skinned jock carrying this scrawny white guy who was obviously drunk. As a local, he was keenly aware of the way people made prejudicial remarks, even though they *didn't* mean to. It was something that he was self-conscious about because he grew up hearing his father talk about the way people perceived them. It was a learned insecurity but it was deep rooted at home and reinforced by society. Nevertheless he had to get his friend to a safe place. This was one of those times when he was glad that he was into so many sports because he spent a lot of time working his body out and was able to easily carry Rhian. He stood 5'11" with broad shoulders and muscular arms. His body looked like a football player's that had been made lean by swimming.

John was a good guy with a bad boy personality. In fact, many wrote him off as a typical jock who didn't care about anyone else but himself and was run solely by hormonal impulses. But John was much more than a stereotype. A true introvert with a strong front, John used this mask to protect his good-hearted nature from people who would take advantage of him. He cared a great deal about the people that were close to him. The judgments came when he would meet someone for the first time and be as direct with them as his close friends. He was a straight shooter and would tell you what he saw. If he thought someone was lying or avoiding a subject, he would point it out and clearly state his opinion. It was a strength that he had yet to fully master. This incident demonstrated his good nature; Rhian wasn't going to be easy to carry but he had to make sure that he was safe.

"Hey, who are you?" Rhian asked as they arrived to John's house.

"It's John, Alexander's friend. You're safe man I'm just taking you to my place 'cause you are really drunk and I found you in a bush near an alley."

"You're John? Oh ok… I remember," he said almost throwing up "You're the cute guy with the jokes…. Hah! Well as long as you don't try to do anything funny 'cause I'm a virgin!"

"Ha ha ok buddy, you'll be alright. Let's get you somewhere safe." With that John continued down the street and to his apartment. When they got there, he helped Rhian up the stairs and into his bed. Rhian fell asleep right away and being that there was nowhere else to sleep, John lied down next to him.

Rhian woke up in a panic the next morning when he realized that he had no idea where he was or how he had gotten there. He looked over and was relieved to see John sleeping next to him, but was worried because he didn't know why he was there. He gathered his things and quietly tiptoed out of the room. As he made his way through the house he could see people sleeping on couches and on the floor. There was no indication why he was there other than the fact that he had too much to drink and might have slept with John. He made the walk home in record time, making sure to avoid any major streets so that no one would see him making the walk of shame.

I can't tell Alexander… I can't tell him that I slept with John. He was overwhelmed with guilt and shame. When he got home, he lied down on the couch and cried. He couldn't remember ever feeling so out of control and he didn't like it. He couldn't stand the thought that something had happened with John, and he had no idea what it was.

Rhian pushed that night to the back of his mind for as long as he could. He considered talking to Leena about it all but there was nothing she could do to make the ambiguity go away. The night with John triggered memories of the camp along with more recurring nightmares. One night, Alexander was woken by the sound of Rhian's restlessness.

"Hey, hey… It's ok. You're safe." Alexander gently calmed Rhian as he woke up from the nightmare.

"What happened?"

"You were yelling in your sleep and kicking the wall… Is it the nightmares again?" Rhian could still feel a ghost pressure on his neck from the hands that were holding him down. It wasn't just a dream, it was a memory.

"I was held down… by a man. I couldn't see his face because he was wearing a mask. I remember him saying 'This is for your own good.' I never understood it. None of it made sense to me." Rhian paused for a moment in an attempt to keep his composure. "The man… or men… tied me to the bed so that I couldn't move and then one by one they… they beat me." Rhian lost control of his emotions and was sobbing uncontrollably. "He held me down by the neck in order to keep me from screaming. I eventually passed out and woke up in a pool of blood." Alexander wanted to comfort his friend.

"Rhian… I… I don't know what to say."

"You don't have to say anything. I'm sorry for sharing that because I know it isn't something that's easy to hear." Rhian lowered his head and cried into his hands. Alexander seized the opportunity to sit down next to his friend and hold him. Neither one said a word; the only sound in the room was whimpering.

"After last night, I've decided that I'm going to move my bed into your room if that's ok. We can use my room as the study room as long as it's ok with you, of course."

"I'll be ok. You don't have to go through the trouble." He found it really strange that Alexander didn't care to have his own space. He had almost spent the past year sleeping next to him and finally had a room of his own but that's not what he wanted. Rhian wasn't opposed to the idea; it was just a bit unusual.

"It's really no trouble at all. I feel comfortable and safe around you. It would help me sleep easy at night. There is something comforting about your presence. I don't know what it is but it makes me feel at home."

"Likewise…" He hesitated. "I feel happier around you."

"Well good. You deserve to be happy."

"You're such a good friend, Alexander… There is something else I have to tell you about… I don't know if you've noticed but I've been kind of distant with you."

"I wish you would just tell me when you're mad at me."

"I'm not mad… I was just kind of upset…"

"So, mad." Alexander cut in.

"Ok. Mad."

"Why were you mad?"

"Do you remember that party that we went to and I showed up and we were drinking with that girl?"

"Yeah…"

"Well, to be honest it upset me that you ditched me to go have sex with some girl you don't even know…"

"Oh I see what's going on here…" Alexander said with a goofy grin. "Look it is ok if you have a crush on me, I would too if I were you but you don't have to get all distant and weird. I wish you would have just told…"

"What? No! I don't have a crush on you!" Surprisingly, the thought had never crossed his mind. "I didn't really know any of the people there and it upset me that you ditched me without notice."

"Oh, I'm sorry. I didn't' mean to ditch you. It's just that she was kind of hot and I really wanted to… well you know what it's like."

"No, I don't know *what it's like*. Doesn't sex mean anything to you? I mean, don't you even want to care about the person that you are having sex with?" Rhian was getting worked up.

"I'm sorry for ditching you. I really didn't mean to. In fact, I came back for you a bit later but you were gone. John told me that you had some crazy night."

"John told you? Does anyone have an ounce of dignity?"

"Whoa, relax. No one is judging you. We've all partied too hard at some point in our lives." Rhian remained silent as he processed the situation.

"I never wanted to do anything with him… I… I wasn't ready to be intimate with anyone. I am still dealing with the nightmare of the camp. I didn't want to do it." Rhian began to weep softly.

"Wait, what happen? John told me that he helped you home and that you both fell asleep on his bed. Did he do something?" Alexander's anger began kicking in.

"He said that?"

"Yeah, he said that you were really drunk and he didn't want you to sleep on the floor so he didn't see any harm in sharing his bed. Did he try anything? Do I have to go beat the shit out of him?"

"I don't know… I don't remember what happened. I assumed that something had happened because I woke up in his bed. I was really confused and really upset. I don't remember any part of that night after you left."

"I think we should talk to John together, in case he was lying to me. I'm usually good at telling when people are lying."

"No, if he said nothing happened then nothing happened… There were no signs that we had done anything other than sleep… I guess I just rushed to a terrible conclusion."

"Are you sure? If he did something to you I want you to tell me."

"I'm fine, just please don't ditch me again."

"I promise."

"You don't have to stay with me. I will be alright."

"No, I want to make sure that you're alright." Alexander insisted on staying in Rhian's room. The demons that were haunting Rhian weren't going away and the situation with John might have caused the nightmares to return.

The boys rearranged the room and spent the rest of the day talking about anything and everything. Their conversations might have seemed like nonsense to anyone else but to them each one they were much needed stimulation. Rhian was usually misunderstood by people and preferred not to share his intellectual side with others for fear of rejection. Alexander loved this type of conversation because he felt challenged by Rhian's ideas and it made him really exercise his brain in a way that his classes couldn't. Alexander referred to those conversations as *brain sex,* which Rhian found odd but went along with it anyway.

After moving his bed into the room Alexander felt close to Rhian again. He figured that disconnect he had been feeling was due to their sleeping arrangements. Luckily staying in the same room would fix that for them and they could be the same friends that they had been before. Alexander had several close friends throughout his lifetime, but none like Rhian who somehow made him feel safer than anyone else could have done. He had never been *this* close to anyone. He thought for a moment about how all of this could be perceived but he reminded himself that he was straight so it didn't matter what anyone else thought about it. The thing that did concern him a bit was that Rhian might start getting the wrong idea, but he needed the security for the time being. He would eventually change things but Rhian knew that he was straight and that they could never be anything more than friends so it was ok. Alexander rationalized that if Rhian did get the wrong idea, it wouldn't be his fault because he had made it clear that he was straight.

During the night, Rhian woke up to go to the bathroom. He walked to the kitchen to get himself a glass of water. As he walked back to his room he felt something different about it. He was used to sleeping in the same room as Alexander but there was something different about it this time. It felt like a special moment for him to walk into the room as Alexander slept. He was quiet to avoid waking him, and closed the door. He looked over at the sleeping giant and smiled as he thought about how intimate the moment really was. It felt like he was sharing the room with a lover because there was a level of trust and closeness that is required to sleep with someone like they were experiencing. It was more than just a friend sleeping next to a friend. This was a certain soul who connected with another soul. This moment was pure and beautiful, and Rhian was thankful that he recognized it. Alexander had claimed that he didn't like sleeping in the dark yet he closed the door behind him when he came into the room and fell asleep. Rhian began to try and grasp what was happening to his emotions. Was he appreciating the closeness and trust of a real friendship or was he feeling something else? He was too tired to deal with these complicated thoughts for the time being so he fell asleep.

Alexander became more attached to Rhian in the proceeding days after moving his bed. As the weeks pressed on it seemed that wherever Rhian went so did Alexander. In fact, he had begun to change his schedule to spend more time with him. He didn't mean to, it just happened so Rhian embraced Alexander's clingy behavior. Eventually the boys had stopped hanging out with their other friends because they preferred to stay home and hang out with each other. It was becoming more and more unusual to see one out without the other.

The semester was flying faster than it seemed and Leena hadn't seen her friends in a while so she threw a party since she was the only one over 21 and with a big enough apartment. The music was great with a good mix of dance and hip-hop, Rhian and the others were in the mood to dance away their stress. He pulled Leena into an open space so that they could dance. It wasn't long before everyone else joined in. Time became irrelevant under the glow of the strobe lights Leena had going. Rhian lost track of how much he was drinking but he was feeling great. He didn't feel nervous or out of place because he was with his friends and there was little to no danger here, unlike at the other party.

There was a sudden moment of clarity that came over Rhian. It was one of those moments in life that stick with you. *Certainty.* Alexander was coming out of the bathroom, contemplating another drink even though he was approaching his limit. He looked over at the half empty bottles of liquor as if deciding which one he would take from. They made eye contact and Alexander smiled lovingly. Rhian waved for Alexander to join him in dancing so he did. As he made his way over, Rhian noticed something that, until this moment, he had never really noticed before; Alexander's smile was beautiful. He knew that his friend had good teeth but in the dim light they luminesced. They complemented Alexander's eyes magically as the bright white glow demanded focus. His eyes, so vibrant and deep kept Rhian mystified by their hypnotic sapphire hue. This moment of clarity brought an overwhelming sense of peace that made him feel complete.

"Are you ok?" Alexander disrupted Rhian's moment.

"Oh, yeah! Why?"

"Well you were just smiling… and now you're blushing."

"Let's dance!" He pulled Alexander in close and danced with him.

Rhian had danced with Alexander long enough to make his awkward smile irrelevant so he stepped outside for a breath of air. He noticed a good-looking guy sitting on the sidewalk, watching people go by. Thinking that he was disrupting this guy's alone time he tried to walk away.

"Hey, how's it going?" He was caught.

"There is great music and I'm surrounded by great people so it's a great night. How is your night going?"

"It was boring until now. I'm Chase by the way. What's your name?

"I'm Rhian." He said with a smile. Chase was very attractive with a chiseled facial structure and a scruffy beard, giving him a lumberjack-like appearance. There was kindness in his big brown eyes but something said *danger* and that was intriguing.

"Would you like to sit with me, Rhian?"

"I would."

"So tell me, are you a whiskey person?"

"I'm not really sure. I guess I'd have to say I really like vodka."

"I take it you're not 21 yet?"

"I am!"

"Sure you are."

"What does it matter to you?"

"Just checking to see if we have anything in common."

"How'm I doing?"

"Not very well… but you get three strikes."

"Favorite book?"

"I don't read." He slowly leaned in close to Rhian's face.

"I don't either."

"Strike two. Paper or plastic?"

"Plastic, it's easier to carry."

"Strike three." Chase pulled Rhian in and kissed him firmly. The door was thrown open and Alexander stumbled out.

"What are you two doing?"

"Nothing." Rhian jumped up and dusted off his shirt as if he had just been caught doing something wrong.

"It didn't look like *nothing*. I wish I got *nothing*…" Alexander mumbled in his drunken state.

"Chase, it was nice meeting you. I'll see you around. I have to get him home. Good night."

"Good night." Chase turned around and continued watching people walk by. The boys stumbled off into the night as Rhian tried to help the drunken Alexander get home.

The next morning Alexander apologized for ruining Rhian's moment and offered to make it up to him.

"Let's have a man-date… in the city! I haven't been there since the summer and I want to go back. We could get your favorite pizza!" Rhian loved the idea.

"When do we leave?"

"Are you free for the rest of the afternoon?"

"Yeah… for once I actually am!"

"Then… Right now."

In the distance, Rhian could see the beautiful skyline of Chicago. His heart began to race and thoughts of possibilities ran through his mind. He had never lived in the city itself but every time he went, he felt like he had arrived home. He had always been curious about the West Coast, and perhaps he would someday live there, but this was home. This city was where he knew he would always feel safest. The irony of it all was that its reputation would beg to differ, but Rhian didn't fear death like most people. Rhian feared loneliness. In the city, he was anything but lonely.

"Look Alexander! I see it!" He called out like a child on Christmas. Rhian smiled like never before.

"I see it. It's like… It's like home." Alexander quietly said to himself. He hadn't talked about the city much before, but since they had gone in the summer he couldn't get the idea of living there out of his mind. Growing up in a small town left him curious about the world and while he loved his hometown, he felt that there was more for him in life.

They got through traffic quickly and parked the car in a pay-by-the-hour lot. Alexander wasn't too happy about spending the money to park his car, but it was for Rhian and he wasn't going to make a fuss. He wanted to make his friend happy.

"Where to first?"

"I want to go to Navy Pier, and I want to walk down the Magnificent Mile. I love looking at all of the things in the windows."

"We are a bit of a walk from Navy Pier…" Alexander saw the disappointment in Rhian's eyes. "… So we should walk up the Mag. Mile on our way to Navy Pier." He said with a smile.

"Ok!" Rhian's face lit up with childlike excitement. He grabbed Alexander by the wrist and led him down the street, pulling him into the Ralph Lauren store. Alexander felt out of place in that store but he was there for Rhian. He had never really seen this side of him before. Rhian began to try some things on. He knew he couldn't afford them but he wanted to know what he looked like in the outfits.

"You look good in that one." Rhian tried on a pair of white jeans, accented with a brown leather belt. The shirt was blue and red plaid covered by a shawl-collard classic blue sweater. He looked like he belonged on display.

"I really like this sweater… I just wish I could afford it."

"Well maybe if you're good Santa will bring it to you." Alexander winked. The boys had a few more laughs in the dressing room before they left the store without buying anything. As they continued down Michigan Avenue, Alexander noticed a well-dressed man, who looked like him. He noticed the man's briefcase and his beautiful watch. The man smiled at him and nodded so he returned the gesture. Rhian didn't notice anything that was going on, but for Alexander this was an important moment. He could see his future.

"Rhian, do you think I could live here someday?"

"In Chicago? Of course… Why not."

"I mean, do you think I could make it here? Become financially successful." Rhian paused for a moment.

"Why do you ask?"

"I think I just saw my future and I think I have a new dream. I want this to be my home."

"Alexander, listen to me closely. You are one of the most amazing human beings I know; from your passionate heart to your seemingly limitless brilliance. You will do great things no matter where you are. I whole-heartedly believe you can make it anywhere." Alexander pulled him into an unexpected embrace.

"Thank you. That really means a lot." He kept his arm around his friend's shoulder and they continued walking. The boys checked out a few more stores and a few more outfits but they eventually made their way to Navy Pier.

"I love this city!" Alexander shouted from the end of the pier.

"I do too…" Rhian sounded disappointed.

"Why does it sound like you're not convinced?"

"It's not that. I would love to live here too… In fact, I want this to be our pit stop for a few years before we move to San Diego."

"I'm more than ok with that. We live here, become financially successful and then open up our restaurant. I like that plan… It's more secure."

"Yeah… The problem is that I can't live here."

"Why not?"

"Pastor."

"What are you talking about?"

"If I move up here, the Pastor will find me and I don't think that would be good."

"Why would it matter?"

"I… I just don't want to be sucked back into the church life." Something wasn't right.

"You won't. I won't let that happen."

"Thanks." Once the awkwardness of the church conversation faded Alexander took several pictures of the skyline and of Rhian and himself. He was filled with joy over the fact that he had discovered a new goal in life. He not only wanted to find a job, but he wanted a job in Chicago, the Windy City, the place where he felt at home. After spending some time at the pier the boys made their way to the pizza place.

"This was exactly the escape I needed. Thanks for being spontaneous." Rhian took a bite of his pizza slice.

"Not a problem. I needed to get away from school for a few hours. Although I still can't wait to go home and relax. I miss my bed!" Rhian stayed quiet. "…Rhian, I'm so sorry. I didn't mean to throw that in your face." Alexander quickly apologized.

"Don't apologize, it's not your fault that my parents are like that." Rhian said with a crooked smile. Of course Alexander still felt guilty.

"Yeah but I didn't have to throw that in your face. How about you come home with me next break!" Alexander was really excited. "I would love for you to meet my family! We could hang out and I could show you my hometown. It'll be fun!"

"Well, I was going to stay and sleep but…"

"You can sleep when you die." Alexander plainly said.

"Well I guess I can't argue with that logic!" Rhian mockingly answered.

"I think we have an extra mattress, but if not my bed is more than big enough for both of us."

"Ok." Rhian said with a slightly uncomfortable chuckle and a raised eyebrow.

"But you're not getting into these pants… I'm not that kind of guy." Alexander quickly added to lighten the mood after realizing the implications of his proposal. After they finished eating, they decided to take a nighttime walk along the lakeshore. It was a peaceful night, the moon reflecting off the glassy lake, dancing in the waves. The only sound was the water crashing against the rocks and the few cars on the road behind them.

"I can't wait to live here…" Alexander said, breaking the silence of the night.

"Why is that?" Rhian asked, genuinely curious.

"Because I feel like I'm held back… I want to fly but something holds me back. I feel scared. Scared to succeed in life. Scared to make a difference in the world. But right here, right now, I feel fearless. I feel invincible. Rhian, I feel like I really can do anything I want!"

"And you can! Like I said before, you will do great things.

"I hope you're right… no I know you're right!" He said with excitement. "I also hope I find a good girl to love and care about me. I don't want to feel alone. I want someone to love me and look at me like… like I'm the most amazing man in the world. I want someone to see me and say, *'that's my man, the most caring, sensitive, strongest, and amazing man.'*"

"I'm sure you will find her…" Rhian paused to think. "We will find you a good girl who appreciates you for the amazing man that you are." He hugged Alexander for reassurance.

"Thanks."

"I can't wait to get out of this place. I can't wait to be far from home… Some wounds don't heal as easily as others and unfortunately I don't think I'll be able to move on with life until I can start over somewhere far from here. I know I am surrounded by love, but I think about my past every damn day. I can't understand it, I don't think I ever will, but maybe it won't always haunt me. Who knows, maybe someday I'll meet a guy who will make me forget the pain and I'll just be happy." Rhian sounded defeated.

"Am I not good enough for you?" Alexander asked with an exaggerated mocked shock.

"Shut up! I mean a good guy, not a fool like you!"

"Ouch! Right here… That stings right here." Alexander pointed to his heart. The boys continued enjoying their nighttime stroll along the water, while poking fun at each other. This was what they did back at school only here the dramatic scene painted on the waves was *Starry*

Night picturesque. They drove back soon after their night out. It was a comfortable drive back with Alexander at the wheel and Rhian asleep at the dash. Alexander looked over at Rhian and noticed that he was curled up as much as possible in the confines of his seat. It was a chilly night and the car was at a cool temperature so that he wouldn't fall asleep at the wheel. He grabbed his jacket from the back seat and covered Rhian up to keep him warm. Rhian continued to sleep comfortably. When they got back Alexander insisted that Rhian wear the jacket to stay warm from the car to their building. Rhian didn't argue since it was such a cool night. They went straight to bed.

It was almost time for fall break again and the girls were tired of the gloom brought on by school so they decided to spend some time far away from the college town. They made plans to go to Leena's beach house in Los Angeles. Of course Rhian didn't have the money to go, but Leena being Leena took care of the trip for him. Alexander had planned on bringing Rhian back home with him for the break but Leena insisted that they share custody of Rhian. He would go home with Alexander for the first two days and then he would fly out to Los Angeles for the rest of the week.

Leena offered Alexander a ticket to as well, knowing that he didn't have the money to fly out but still willing to bring him, but he declined. He wanted to spend some time with his friends from home and his family. He agreed to the terms and was excited to bring Rhian home with him. The boys planned on leaving the weekend before the break started so that they could spend a little bit extra time away. Rhian missed two classes while Alexander missed three. They packed their things quickly and left early on Friday afternoon arriving in Alexander's hometown soon after. It was a beautiful night so the boys got in the hot tub for some much needed relaxation. They talked about school and the academic progress they had made.

"I want to meet a really good looking guy who is smart and will treat me well. I want to raise kids with him and grow old. I want to be happy." Alexander smiled noticing the dreamy look on Rhian's face as he shared his dream

"I want almost the same thing except with a woman. A supportive, smart, gorgeous woman who wants children and will love me for me." Alexander and Rhian both sighed as they thought about their dreams. After being in the hot tub for almost a half hour, Alexander wanted to show Rhian his hometown. He drove around telling Rhian stories about his childhood going from foster home to foster home until his parents adopted him.

"Sometimes when I come home I drive around and revisit these places. They used to scare me… Especially this one." He said, pointing to the house they had parked in front of. "The last time I was here I began hyperventilating."

"How do you feel now?"

"I feel happy. I guess I finally outgrew the fear."

"What made this place so scary?"

"He used to beat me. My foster dad would come home after getting high with his buddies and he would beat me." He remained quiet for a few moments.

"You know, it's ok if you're not…"

"I think I'm still really angry at the people that hurt me when I was a kid. It makes me mad to think that I was abandoned and had to go through all of that garbage. But without all of that hurt, I wouldn't be the person I am today. I wouldn't be as fulfilled in life."

Alexander carried so many feelings about his hometown that he never really realized. It held a lot of bad memories, and after seeing the way Rhian's parents had treated their own son he was reminded of how lonely his childhood was. This moment would remain ingrained in his mind for a very long time.

He continued the tour to include his high school, and his church. They followed the road past a hill that Alexander became excited about. "I would go sledding here in the winter time when I was a kid. This hill seemed a lot bigger when I was younger…" He said with a laugh. "Oh, you have to try this ice cream! This place has the best ice cream!" As they walked in, the man behind the counter recognized Alexander.

"Buthy! How are you? Getting the usual? Mint Chocolate Chip if I remember correctly." The friendly old man said as he reached in to get Alexander his ice cream.

"Don, you never forget do you?"

"And who is this young fella' next to you?"

"This is my best friend, Rhian. He came home with me for break. He likes Rocky Road." Alexander proudly stated. Rhian snickered at the way he knew exactly what he wanted. "Oh but could you add some caramel on top, he really likes his caramel." Alexander added. Don let out a hearty laugh

"Of course!" Don replied as he prepared the two cups of ice cream. Alexander talked to Don for a few moments while Rhian stood by and smiled out of courtesy.

"So why did he call you Buthy?" Rhian curiously asked as they walked back to the car.

"When I was younger I couldn't pronounce the word 'buddy,' so instead I pronounced it 'buthy' and since then that's been my name."

"That's cute…" They both laughed.

When they got back to Alexander's house the boys were both ready for bed. Alexander had forgotten to set up the air mattress so he suggested that they simply share the bed.

"I don't feel like setting the mattress up… You can just stay up here with me. Don't worry I don't bite. I fart, but I don't bite." The boys shared a laugh Rhian got into the bed and they settled in for the night. They continued talking about Alexander's lonely childhood, which made Rhian feel close to his friend, but also thankful that he didn't have to go through what Alexander went through. For having such a rough childhood, he turned out to be an honorable man. Perhaps it was the support of his parents that made him who he was. Whatever the reason was, Rhian felt safe and at home, a feeling he had lost with his own parents.

After spending a few more days with Alexander and getting to meet some of his friends from home, it was time for Rhian to meet up with Leena in Los Angeles. He had learned a lot about his friend and had a better understanding of his background. Alexander dropped him off at the airport and said goodbye with a bear hug. During his flight, Rhian reflected on some of Alexander's stories as well as some of his own. While learning of Alexander's past, he found himself reliving some of his own painful memories. Rhian had never realized just how alone he was as a kid. Keenly aware of who he was and the fact that he was different. Rhian was predisposed to being a lonely person, but what really pulled at his heart was the fact that he had never been truly honest with anyone but Alexander. He acted his way through a cult-like Christian upbringing and he was good at pretending to be something he wasn't. Now that life didn't require him to try so hard to hide, he was suddenly faced with a very different understanding of reality.

Rhian arrived in the early afternoon expecting to tour the city before going back to Leena's. Unfortunately, Leena had gotten stuck in traffic and there was little time to go exploring on the first day. She was late to pick him up, which was very unlike her, but that's the nature of traffic in the City of Angels. Leena was a very down-to-earth kind of girl. She worked hard at school and even at her job. She never talked about Los Angeles as being a major part of her life, but in fact it was her home. Rhian was completely shocked when they pulled up to the house. He knew that her family was well-off, but he never imagined that she came from such a glamourous place.

"Don't judge me… But welcome to my humble abode…" She said as she before laughing loudly. "This house is so over-the-top that I won't pretend like it's not impressive. Come in! I'll help you with your bags." She said with a smile. "Daddy is inside waiting. I hope you're hungry because he prepared a lot of food. Daddy likes to spoil our guests." She said with another hearty laugh. If it were anyone else, Rhian would have been bothered by the sarcastic and almost egotistical arrogance, but it was Leena. He knew she was mocking her father's obsession with the extravagant and expensive.

"Where are the others?" He asked curiously.

"Well, they apparently decided to go to Vegas for the weekend. Random? Yes, but let's be honest here… It's Kala and Gianna… They are capable of showing up in Mexico tomorrow." The other girls were rarely around anymore because they were both always so busy, though Sophie still enjoyed her random lunches with Rhian.

"What about Sophie?"

"She actually is with them… Can you imagine poor Sophie trying to keep up with them? Imagine Gianna gambling all of her savings away while Kala is trying to pressure them into going to see some magic show and poor Sophie as the buffer just tagging along for the ride." They laughed about the situation as they made their way to the kitchen. Rhian felt out of place with his cargo shorts and non-designer t-shirt; total retail value of fifty dollars but he got his stuff second hand.

"This is an amazing home Leena! I love it!" He said.

"Why thank you." A masculine voice responded, which startled Rhian from his star struck gaze.

"You must be Rhian, nice to meet you, I'm Paul."

"He likes being called by his first name by everyone because he says it makes him feel young… D-E-N-I-A-L!"

"Hey now!" Leena's dad said with a laugh as he hugged his daughter. "Sit down, Rhian. I hope your flight wasn't too long. I've prepared plenty of food so I hope you're hungry." Paul, just like his daughter, was an excellent host. This must be where Leena got her ability to throw together so many impromptu parties. Paul was very welcoming and made Rhian feel comfortable

"Well Rhian, I just wanted to say that Leena has told me about the situation between you and your parents. Sometimes parents don't understand their children no matter how hard they may try…" Paul said looking over at Leena who simply rolled her eyes "…But you are always welcome here. There is always enough love in this family for one more."

"Thank you." Rhian said with a big smile. It was funny how he thought that he had lost everything and yet somehow he had found so much more love than he ever expected to find. The meal continued and Rhian learned a great deal about Leena and her background. They had bonded before and he was aware that her mother died young but he didn't realize how close she was to her dad. She called him every night to say goodnight. Rhian learned that Paul would take a lot of time off of work to take care of his daughter. She was usually away at private school throughout her education, but once a month and on every break, they would both fly out to the house in L.A. and spend time together. It was a non-traditional upbringing, and yet it created a bond between parent and child that he had never before seen.

Of course Leena wasn't handed everything on a silver platter like many might think. Instead, her father made sure to make her work for everything she had. She would get straight A's in school and in exchange she was allowed one expensive purchase. This was never more than a purse or a new shirt, but it was special for her because she got to go with shopping with her dad and his attention was all on her. The other major thing that Rhian noticed was that Paul's attention was completely on them. He didn't use his phone when Leena was around. It was a small gesture, but it made his daughter feel important to him and that's what he wanted.

The three spent the rest of the break sightseeing in L.A. and experiencing the simplicities of life. Rhian was impressed that this father-daughter duo seemed to have more fun doing everyday normal things than most people with a traditional family. He really enjoyed this time getting to see what it really meant to find a loving family. He couldn't help but question and compare his upbringing. He always thought he had a great childhood but everything was suddenly changed. While he was reminded of the pain his parents had caused him, he had to smile at the thought of his mom frolicking in the waves at the beach or his dad helping him build a sand castle. The break came and went too quickly for them but it was time to back to their busy lives. Paul had left before Leena and Rhian did but he called her right before she boarded her plane.

"Have a good trip. I love you dear. Make me proud."

"I love you too dad! I will, and the same goes to you!"

"Thanks baby doll. Let me say goodbye to Rhian."

"Ok. Bye, I love you!" She said with a warm smile as she handed the phone over to Rhian. "He wants to talk to you," she whispered.

"Hello?" Rhian curiously spoke into the phone.

"Hello, Rhian? Hey, it's Paul. I just wanted to say it was a pleasure to have you for the few days that we were together. I wanted to remind you that my offer is always good. You are welcome in our home whenever or wherever that may be. Take care!"

"Thank you Paul, that means a lot..."

"Don't mention it. Just take care of my baby." Rhian could hear the smile in Paul's voice.

"I promise."

"Good man." And with that Paul ended the call. The two boarded the plane and returned to school.

Chapter 5

Shortly after returning from the break, the group got together at the club for a night of fun. They had all made other friends and some of them decided to tag along. One of Kala's new friends, Chloe, was very interested in Alexander though he was more interested in hanging out with his friends. After he spent the night dancing with him and trying to keep his attention but he was more interested in having fun with his friends. Chloe ended up following the boys home hoping to get some time alone with Alexander. Rhian made his way to bed while Alexander and Chloe stayed out in the living room talking.

"So he's gay and you don't mind living with him?" Rhian could hear her asking from his room. She probably had no idea that he was still awake or she wouldn't be speaking so loudly. Of course, based on what she was saying it was possible that she just didn't care if he heard. He could tell that she was from a conservative background like too many people they went to school with. The kind that fear people they don't understand and intend to keep their neighborhoods ethnically uniform with a hint of diversity.

"Well yeah I chose to live with him, he's my best friend… what's the problem?"

"Well it's just… I don't know… Being gay is so wrong. It's weird and unnatural. I mean I don't judge anyone who is… I just don't agree…" Rhian wasn't shocked. She fit the profile. She was just like the people he was surrounded by at home. Her ignorance made him cringe but he was thankful that he was sitting in the other room because he probably would have caused a scene by walking out.

"What do you mean agree with? You are straight… what the hell do you have to agree with?" He whispered to himself as if he was a part of the conversation. Alexander must have had the same thought that Rhian did.

"What do you mean? What do YOU have to agree with? Why should you even have an opinion about someone else's life like that?" Sarcastically implying that it wasn't her business. Rhian laughed quietly.

"Well, what I meant was isn't it strange that you two live together? I mean what if he tries to turn you gay? They can do that you know?"

"Oh my, you're right! He must have trained his unicorn to bite me and infect me with the gay. Oh, cover me in glitter! Do you realize how ridiculous you sound?"

"All I'm saying is that it's weird… What if he likes you and isn't telling you… He lives with you so he can check you out whenever he wants and he could try to turn you and he would know all of your weaknesses…"

"Ok now you are going too far… Look, he is my best friend and I love and trust him. He isn't going to try to turn me. He and I are friends. I don't have to explain my friendships to you. He knows we are just friends and I know that. Period. I'm straight and secure in my sexuality."

"But what if he came up to you one day and professed his love to you… then what?"

"Then I handle it when it comes. But it won't because it's not like that. Besides if he did I would just reassure him that I was straight and that I don't want that kind of relationship with him. It's that simple. I don't think I could handle being gay… Why would you bring this up anyway?"

"Because you're living situation is bazaar. I mean you are straight and he is gay, most straight men would never live with a gay roommate. I don't know it's just strange to me… Plus the way that he looks at you is just odd."

"What do you mean?"

"You know, he has that star-struck *in love* look in his eyes when he looks at you. And he seems to hang on your words. It's kind of pathetic."

"Enough, you need to go." Alexander felt uncomfortable with the accusation she was making. Rhian was the only person who made him feel completely comfortable about himself, but that's what friends do; they accept you for who you are. That doesn't mean that they are *in love* with you. His friendship with Rhian was never unusual because it felt so natural to him. Chloe's words provoked Alexander to consider the possibility that she was right but he didn't let that uncomfortable thought linger for too long.

"I don't look at him like I'm in love with him…" Rhian repeated to himself. He loved his friend and was happy he had found someone like Alexander who he connected with on such a deep level, but *in* love? No. At least, that wasn't what he would call it. He greatly appreciated how caring Alexander was with him and how not matter where they were or what they were doing, they could just be together and no problem in the world mattered. He thought about his coming out party and how sweet Alexander's thoughtful planning was. He remembered how Alexander would stay close to him when he was going through a rough time just to make him feel safe. Like Alexander felt, the thoughts were much too uncomfortable to take seriously.

"Have I been in love with him this whole time? Have I really been acting like I have a crush on him? Maybe that's why he did all of those things for me. She says I look at him like I'm in love but I don't… At least I don't think I do."

Chloe's suggestions made Alexander question his relationship with Rhian, though he didn't make it obvious. He was very confused because he knew Rhian was gay, and he had never had a problem with it, but he was straight. There was no way anyone could get the wrong idea, especially Rhian. He thought of Rhian as friend and only that. He loved him, there was no doubt of that but he had never thought of him as anything else than a friend. For a moment, he entertained the idea of being in a relationship with his friend; everything was basically the same, but when it came to the sex, Alexander found it too awkward to continue. He dismissed those thoughts and did his best to forget.

The conversation between Chloe and Alexander seemed to spark enough discomfort between the boys that they subtly avoided each other. Alexander had not said much to Rhian in the few days afterward, while Rhian kept himself busy and away from the apartment. Although each one wanted some space, it made both feel uneasy that the other had also withdrawn. Rhian wondered if Chloe's comments hadn't gotten the best of Alexander because he usually found a reason to talk to him or hang out with him daily. But after that conversation there was something different about their interactions so he decided to take matters into his own hands.

"Hey, so do you want to go to the store with me? I have to pick some things up."

"Sure, I have nothing better to do." The boys got into Rhian's car and headed to the store for what they needed. It was an awkwardly quite ride, which was very uncharacteristic of them. Rhian turned on the radio to dampen the awkward mood. Alexander was in his own world thinking about how much he wanted to go away for a vacation. They passed one of their favorite places to eat, which they hadn't been to in a while because they lived together and the opportunity to eat together was always there, even though they didn't always take it.

"Do you want to stop and get some food after we are done shopping?"

"I'm not really hungry… Maybe next time." Alexander stated without thinking too much about it.

"Ok…" Rhian was disappointed because he wanted to attempt to act normal around Alexander but he couldn't act normal around him if he wasn't willing to be around him. *Maybe he does think that I look at him like I'm in love with him. But I don't mean to. At least I don't think I do. He is my friend and that's all, right?*

"Well if you wanted to get something to eat we would stop somewhere but I'm not really that hungry."

"I just wanted to chill and talk since we haven't done that in a few days. It's no big deal."

"Oh… well we can talk now… What's up?"

"That's not what I meant. I just wanted to catch up see how everything was going."

"Like what?"

"Never mind."

"Ok." The rest of the trip was pretty silent for the boys. It was the first time that they had been together and not had something to talk about. It was quite the awkward experience for both of them. When they got back to their place each one went into their rooms and closed the door. Rhian was only in his room for a few minutes pacing his floor when he decided that he should make dinner for them so that they could talk. He walked up to Alexander's door and was ready to knock when he heard the doorknob move and immediately walked into the living room. He sat on the couch and turned on the TV. Alexander walked out the door without saying much. Rhian refrained from saying anything even though he usually would have wished him a good time wherever he was going.

That was an awkward trip. I wonder why he was being so quiet. Alexander thought to himself. He and Rhian always had something to talk about so it was shocking when their conversation ended before getting to the store. The thought of Rhian being in love with him hadn't crossed his mind for a few days, since he had avoided him and everything seemed to be the same. *Maybe he is in love with me...* He thought to himself. *He probably was just feeling off today. I can't let Chloe's stupid words get to me.*

Shit! Shit! Shit! He probably thinks I'm insane. Why did I make that so weird? Why did I suggest catching up when we live together! He probably thinks I'm in love with him and now he is going to be awkward around me. Rhian was starting to over think things as usual and began to get worked up over nothing. He settled in on the couch for a lonely movie night until he fell asleep.

Alexander stumbled in drunk after a late night of partying with John. He saw Rhian sleeping on the couch and stared at his friend for a second noticing that he had no blanket so he went to the other room to retrieve one. He brought it out for Rhian and covered Rhian up with the blanket before going to the kitchen for some water. Once in his recliner his attention was pulled to the movie that Rhian had probably fallen asleep watching. It was late and he was tired so it wasn't long before he was asleep.

When Rhian woke up he saw that Alexander had put the blanket on him but had fallen asleep on the recliner without the blanket. He took the blanket covered Alexander with it before going to get ready for the day. He didn't have much to do since it was a Sunday but he wanted to be ready in case his friends wanted to meet up for whatever reason. He looked over at Alexander who was still asleep and thought about how thankful he was for him. It wasn't just the little things that he did, like covering him with a blanket or knowing his favorite foods and activities, After getting ready, Rhian walked in on Alexander making breakfast.

"Do you want some pancakes?" Alexander asked

"Sure, and some bacon." Rhian answered with a wink.

"Ah, my specialty. Coming right up!" He called out. The boys had breakfast together and talked about whatever came to mind. It was as if there had been no pause in their friendship. They decided to go for a Sunday walk through the campus and town. Rhian being the romantic type loved walking around and appreciating the livelihood of the college campus and nearby town.

The boys were walking through campus together towards a café nearby. It was pretty busy that evening but Rhian insisted on getting his vanilla latte so Alexander gave in as usual. They waited in line, ordered their drinks, and then waited for them. While waiting, Rhian noticed that Leena was behind the counter so he waved at her but she didn't respond. He tried a little bit harder to get her attention but she wasn't responding to any of his actions. He started to become frustrated until he realized that it wasn't her. He was so embarrassed that he asked Alexander to grab his drink when it was called out. Alexander came out of the café with Rhian's drink in hand. He looked around and saw Rhian sitting at a bench staring off into the distance so he walked over and joined him.

"What do you see here?"

"I see people... grass... I don't know, buildings too I guess."

"I see happiness. I feel comfort and I am discovering joy. It's all around us, but we rarely notice it."

"What are you talking about?"

"Look at how vibrant the colors are in this park. It's beautiful and the impressive part about it all is the fact that the blades of grass just grow. They don't judge each other and refuse to grow next to a certain blade of grass just because they don't like it or because they don't get along. No they just grow and accommodate for each other. It is almost as if the grass is happy to grow next to a fellow blade of grass."

"And the buildings stand strong, protecting people from the elements?" Alexander added.

"Yeah, exactly it gives them comfort but they don't really realize it. But the thing that I see most is the people who walk around enjoying their lives and being true to themselves. It is refreshing to see people interacting and appreciating the life that they have and the people in their lives. How many times do you walk past someone you know but don't acknowledge them because you don't feel like talking to them?"

"I don't do that… Ok well I don't always do that."

"It doesn't matter if you do or don't my point is that how amazing it is to have people you connect with in a way that they are so close they become your family. It is truly beautiful to see that happening in front of me. I've noticed several people sit down to chat with friends who they were passing by and took the time to talk to them. It makes me feel joy that my life has been enriched with so many good people." Alexander smiled at him and looked at the scene in front of him.

"You are a different kind of guy aren't you, Rhian?

"That I am. Let's go and meet up with the others." The boys continued to walk around the campus for a few minutes before heading to their friends place. This conversation put Rhian's mind at ease about Alexander thinking that he looked at him like he loved him. He felt like things would be all right between the two of them.

The boys headed to Nikolaus' apartment to watch a movie they had all agreed on. Nikolaus was a fanatic about his electronics. He had the latest big screen television with a state of the art surround sound system set up in his living room. He was always inviting his friends over to hang out. It had become a Sunday night tradition since he bought the television at the beginning of the semester. Alexander remembered how heavy all of the boxes were when he helped Nikolaus bring home the setup from the store. The setup was probably harder than the physical labor it took to carry the equipment up the stairs but fortunately Nikolaus was brilliant when it came to wiring and electronics.

Nikolaus had invited everyone over to watch a newly released action movie. He was quite the host, as he had prepared a traditional German dish for his friends and had plenty of snacks to go around. He had taken some time to adjust to his new environment but was very thankful to have found a new group of friends that were very welcoming. He loved being around this group because there was a liveliness that no other group he associated with had. After the movie was over everyone helped clean his place up and thanked him for everything before leaving. Rhian and Alexander walked back slowly, talking about the movie they had just seen. Without notice, Rhian jumped on Alexander's back and made him carry him all the way home.

Rhian found himself confused by the sudden rush of unexplained feelings he began experiencing due to the lack of boundaries. There were many details about their friendship that, until now, had gone unnoticed as potentially romantic in nature. His feelings for Alexander were changing rapidly and he grew fearful of what it meant, but more fearful of what it didn't mean. Rhian didn't understand why or how he was suddenly confused after so long. It wasn't like he had intended on falling for his friend. On the contrary, he was just happy to have a friend that was so supportive. They had a special chemistry, but until now it was never confusing.

Of course, there were certain hallmarks about their relationship that set them apart from the typical friendship. The first peculiarity of their friendship was the way Alexander was affectionate with him. Rhian was touchy with Alexander, but that was just because he was Rhian. While many guys would find it off-putting, Alexander welcomed it. In fact, it was he who cuddled with Rhian whenever he was having a bad day. It was also Alexander who suggested that they sleep in the same room. It was obvious he had no problem being physically close to Rhian, no one else, just him. The second defining trait of their relationship was the ferocity with which Alexander protected Rhian. Alexander was always quick to silence anyone that had anything bad to say about his friend. There was a passionate loyalty to him that everyone noticed. Rhian depended on him to save the day and be his knight in shining armor. When Rhian told Alexander about his night with John, Alexander almost went into a blind rage because he thought that John had tried to hurt Rhian. He had never been so protective of anyone like that before. The other key characteristic was Alexander's attachment to Rhian. They shared a room to be close, Alexander refused to leave Rhian alone for too long after his parents abandoned him, and they had even made plans to move away together after graduation. It was obvious that Alexander needed Rhian just as much as Rhian needed Alexander.

He knew that Alexander was comfortable enough around him to be his true self, but that was just the effect that Rhian had on people. He was generally quiet, but Rhian brought out the unapologetic joy in him and Alexander's spirit luminesced with life. Yet, Alexander's true self seemed to *only* come out when Rhian was around. Rhian relied on Alexander for physical safety and protection from ending up in a situation like the camp again. Alexander relied on Rhian for moral support, protection from the loneliness of his misunderstood past, and the promise of immeasurable solace.

"Hey, I need to talk to you about something." Rhian's lip trembled slightly.

"Sure, what's on your mind?" Alexander turned his face toward Rhian but kept his gaze on the TV.

"Well, I just wanted to say that I think you are amazing friend and I really appreciate you. You are caring, fun, intelligent, accepting, and the list can go on."

"Are you breaking up with me?" He still kept his eyes directed at the TV. "Thank you for that. I really appreciate you too!"

"Well I was thinking that we have gotten very close lately and I really like spending time with you…" Rhian paused nervously. The tension began to rise. "Alexander I think I'm developing stronger feelings for you…" Alexander's smile faded to a more serious face. He turned to look at Rhian to see if he was joking. Rhian waited for him to say something.

"Oh… I'm really flattered. Thank you for your honesty." He finally responded after what felt like an eternity to Rhian.

"It's just that we are so intimate with each other. I mean, we pretty much sleep together. I feel like I've been getting closer and closer to you. Everything that you've done for me has made me feel like I matter… Like I'm important. I love spending all the time in the world with you, talking to you, and being close to you. You make every day feel like it's an adventure that I can't wait to wake up for. Alexander, around you I feel safe, secure, loved, and complete. You've said it yourself that we have a special chemistry. I think we would make a great couple." Alexander dodged Rhian's piercing gaze by looking down at his feet.

"I agree we do have a special kind of chemistry Rhian, but as friends. I love you like my friend, I love spending time with you like a friend, and we make a great couple… of friends. I'm sorry if it hurts but I don't feel the same way about you." Alexander didn't want to hurt Rhian's feelings but he knew that no matter his intention, the rejection was going to be painful.

"So you're telling me that you don't feel anything special even though we share an amazing connection that some married couples can only dream of having? What about all of the times we were there for each other and the times we spent together or the way you seem to accommodate your life around mine… friends don't just plan the rest of their lives around each other. That's what couples do! That's what people who are in love do." These false accusations were making Alexander mad.

"Look Rhian, I didn't mean to lead you on if that's what you are implying. I like spending time and of course I'm always there for you because you are my friend but that doesn't mean that I want something more than friendship with you. I care deeply about you and I would love to continue my life with you in it but that doesn't mean I want to be with you like that." Alexander said with obvious frustration in his voice.

"But it's not fair… How can you say that you didn't feel a thing? What about San Diego?" Rhian was confused.

"San Diego was a nice idea but it's never going to happen so just get over it." Alexander stormed off angrily slamming the door as he left the apartment. There was always risk that Rhian would fall for him and he had purposed to handle it as maturely as possible but something inside of him snapped. He felt attacked and rather than subjecting himself to more accusations and a possible argument, Alexander chose to leave rather than say something else that might be hurtful.

Rhian sat alone in the apartment embarrassed by Alexander's rejection. He was beyond confused about the entire situation. He wasn't sure what he expected to come from his confession, but he didn't expect to feel so terrible. Rhian wanted to talk to someone but the only person that he really wanted to talk to was Alexander. For the first time in a long time he pulled out his paints and began to transfer his feelings over to the easel. He painted a forest during the winter, covered in snow and baron. He worked tirelessly for what seemed like hours, using an actual twig to create a realistic flawed perfection. His trees were so life-like with sharp edges and attention given to the smallest detail. He was pleased with this for the time being and eventually went to bed before Alexander returned home.

Alexander walked into the room they shared and quietly sat down next to Rhian. He regretted storming out earlier but he was now calm. Rhian woke up to Alexander sitting next to him, which put a smile on his face. Rhian looked up with excitement at his friend waiting for him to say what he wanted to hear.

"Hey, I'm sorry for freaking out like that earlier. It was completely unnecessary and I am jerk for doing that."

"It's ok. I understand. I kind of dropped a bomb on you so I get it." Rhian chuckled in an attempt to dissipate the lingering awkwardness.

"Yeah, I am honestly flattered, I mean you are an amazing person and any guy would be lucky to have you. I am lucky to have you." Rhian hugged Alexander before letting him continue. "You really are. You are caring, loving, smart, and a good-looking guy. Any guy would be lucky to be with you. And if I weren't straight I wouldn't even question it because you would be the guy I would want to be with." Alexander's words tore through Rhian's heart bringing back the sting of his earlier rejection. He didn't know what to expect, though he hoped Alexander had come around, he was still heartbroken. Alexander was reaffirming his rejection in a more gentile way, which Rhian appreciated. He simply smiled to make Alexander think that he was alright.

"I appreciate the complement. I'm kind of tired so I'm going to go back to bed." Rhian said as he lied back down.

"Ok. I love you Rhian. Everything will be ok. I promise." He smiled and looked down for a moment. "Hey Rhian?"

"Yeah?"

"You are really brave… to tell me the truth. I know it wasn't easy and I appreciate your honesty. This really won't change anything between us."

"Thanks." Rhian rolled over and tried to sleep.

There was nothing Alexander could say or do that would remedy the situation. Rhian was again hurt but this time, he was the source of the problem. He decided not to change the sleeping arrangements in order to keep life as normal as possible for the two of them. As much as he wanted to do what he always did and coddle Rhian, he thought it best to give his friend some space.

Rhian spent the days moping around. He noticed a drastic difference in the way Alexander treated him. He didn't look for him like he was used to and they barely spoke to each other. He understood that Alexander was straight and tried with all that was in him to remember that fact every day. Rhian didn't mean to develop feelings for his friend; in fact he took pride in the fact that he never allowed himself to see more than what was real. But it was too much to handle. Up to this point his friend was only aware that he had developed some feelings for him that were more than just friendly. They were closer than most friends will ever be so it was only natural that they would feel that they shared a special bond. But the thought lingered that they were much more than friends, and it killed Rhian to know that it would never be more.

"You look like someone stepped on your kitten." Nikolaus said to Rhian as they sat in his apartment watching television. Rhian preferred the company of another friend over the silent awkwardness that lingered in the apartment after his confession. Rhian didn't plan on telling Nikolaus anything. He hadn't even planned on telling Leena, but Nikolaus noticed his despondent demeanor and wasn't going to let it go until Rhian told him what was wrong. He considered making something up, but he was a terrible liar. It made sense to talk to Nikolaus because he was always so logical about things. There was no questioning his answers because when it came down to it, he pointed out the reality with such precision it was scary.

"I did something."

"What did you do?"

"I…"

"I'm not going to play the guessing game."

"I think I fell for Alexander… and I told him."

"That is *something,* isn't it? What did he say?"

"He said that he was flattered and that it didn't change anything between us but he didn't feel that way about me. Then he told me that if he were gay, I would be the guy he would want to be with. I think he thought it would make me feel better."

"I'd agree with that."

"Nikolaus, he has done so much for me and I don't want to lose him as a friend but I'm afraid that this changes things between us."

"Why?"

"Because things have been really awkward between us. He has been avoiding me and we barely talk to each other. I feel like I did something really wrong. Like I shouldn't have developed feelings for him. I almost feel guilty… even dirty."

"That's interesting… and a bit dramatic." Rhian channeled his frustration into it in the form of a loud sigh into a nearby pillow.

"You're right. I'm probably being a bit more dramatic than I should be but it really bothers me that things feel weird now."

"Well you have to give it time to go back to normal. But it probably never will go completely back."

"I don't want to hear that."

"It's the truth!"

"But why?"

"Because you have feelings for him and he doesn't feel the same way. He will have to decide if he can continue to be your friend and keep things truly normal. You did your part by telling him how you feel. If he made you feel that way, but didn't mean to then you two have to establish some boundaries because god knows you two have few if any in place."

"That does make sense. So it's not up to me if we can stay friends the way we were. I didn't do anything wrong, did I?"

"Besides letting your emotions get to you, no."

"I can't help the way I feel. I can't help that he makes me feel safe. I can't help that he makes me feel like I am important and gives me confidence in myself. I can't help that he makes me feel at home and safe with him. It's not my fault that he makes me breathe a sigh of relief when things get rough. There is something about him that makes me want to make him happy. His smile melts me and makes me forget all of the problems of my life. When I'm with him I feel complete…" He realized that the confusing things he felt were out of his control. But this realization also prompted him to think differently about Alexander. Nikolaus could see the wheels turning in Rhian's head and he knew Rhian would have to figure it all out for himself. "…Maybe he is in love with me but hasn't figured it out yet…" He whispered to himself.

"What did you say?" Nikolaus asked pointlessly.

"Oh, nothing. I was just thinking out loud."

"I don't want you to get your hopes up and continue to linger on this. He gave you his answer and that's just the way it has to be. I'll agree, he does sometimes treat you like his girlfriend, but keep in mind that you sometimes treat him like your boyfriend too. My best advice is to establish some boundaries and you two will be fine." They didn't say anything else about the situation and went back to the television. Nikolaus was uncomfortable with what Rhian was saying because he knew he couldn't get through to him.

Later that afternoon, Rhian met up with Sophie for coffee.

"How are you? I heard you had some troubles with Alexander. Is everything alright?"

"I'm… sad… But hopefully things work out. I found the one person in the world who makes me feel safe no matter what, the person that I am so attracted to and I connect with on the most intimate of levels and it's never going to happen… I'm tired of being broken-hearted. First the camp, then my parents, and now this… is there a *reset* option?"

"You need to relax, or else the stress will make that pretty face grow old. You are strong and you will be alright. Give it time and you'll see that everything will work out for you."

"Thanks Sophie, you're the best. So what's going on with you?"

"First of all, the boys on this campus are idiots. They act like dating a Chinese is some strange!"

"I can understand that." Rhian added with a laugh.

"I guess you do…" She joined in with a chuckle. "I understand that I look different because I'm not from here but back home I was hot… Here, some of the boys won't even look at me… Maybe I'm just being too sensitive."

"What happened?"

"Well I was texting this guy for a few days. His name is Kyle and he is a friend of a friend. We clicked so well and we'd text all day. It was kind of a blind date thing so it was very exciting. We exchanged pictures and I sent him one but after he sent me his first. I thought he was really cute so I was really excited about sending my picture. It was a picture I had of me wearing my favorite hat and sunglasses. He told me I was really hot and that he wanted to take me out for coffee. We decided to meet up at this café but when I got there and saw him he got up and walked out without saying a word. Then the asshole decides to text me and says *Sorry, I don't date Asian girls.* Not a single word more from him since… How do I even respond to that?"

"What the hell? I can't believe he was such a jerk! Well there are plenty of stupid backward people for him in this world. You are WAY too good for a fool like that. You are beautiful, smart and you have an amazing personality. Not to mention the most amazing person in the world sitting next to you right now." Rhian said with a wink.

"I'd say so! I'm tired of talking about stupid men. Let's go back to my place and watch some TV."

The two returned to Sophie's for TV and cookies. To say that she was obsessive about the level of cleanliness and organization of her apartment would be an understatement. The girl had her things arranged in a particular order and didn't like things out of place. The genius behind it all was that the arrangement she had was perfect in her eyes but seemed casually chaotic to everyone else. To her it was anything but casual. It was organized by some secret system that she followed religiously.

The two settled down in the living room in front of her television and watched a movie. The movie was poorly made, or at least Rhian thought so, but there was one thing that stood out to him. The male character was not that attractive. In fact, it seemed that the director intended the guy to be downright unattractive. But the character had fallen in love with a beautiful girl. Of course the girl wanted nothing to do with the guy at the beginning of the movie, but after the story continued she began to see past the exterior and fell in love with the male character by the end of the movie and they ended up together. Rhian was bothered by that idea. Alexander's words *if I were gay I would be with you*, replayed in his head. He sat there for a moment and thought about the implication that the movie was making. It was essentially saying that if you try hard enough, you could get the girl you wanted… the problem was that he was in love with a man.

He sat quietly watching the next movie Sophie picked but of course by now he was completely lost in the thought of the guy working hard to get the girl and the girl eventually falling for him. He thought about all of the times that he had connected with people in the past and about how he had done it. Connecting with someone is something that isn't forced; there are some people who he will never connect with because they just don't click. But that wasn't the case for Alexander, no; they connected deeply and were quite the pairing. He tried to understand how it could work. It brought him back to the fundamental idea that connection can occur between any two people. He always believed that love was limitless and that anyone could fall in love with anyone regardless of his or her sex. He was open to love from a male or a female and he had always been that way. Not everyone was as enlightened as he was of course, so he couldn't come out and just give his heart away to someone who didn't want it. He could only offer his love and hope for the best. He could understand why the girl said yes to the guy that at first she wouldn't even consider talking to. It was because she looked beyond the physical. She saw beyond the façade of a lesser attractive person and instead saw the amazing, loving, beautiful soul under the exterior. It was what was inside the man that made her fall in love. But that would not have been possible if the man had not put so much effort into proving himself.

This made perfect sense to Rhian, who by now had gone from hating the ending to loving it. In fact, he began to think about his own situation with Alexander. He knew that they would be a great couple, because they already were. But he had to find a way to make Alexander see beyond the exterior. He had to show Alexander who was on the inside by demonstrating that he loved him, he had to prove that he would give anything to be his. It wouldn't be easy, but in that moment Rhian finally saw a ray of hope. His new mission would be to show Alexander the beautiful soul behind the façade. Rhian got up and began to get ready to leave. He had to prove to Alexander that they were meant to be and there was no time to waste. He said his good byes and headed home. He was going to start doing more for Alexander and show him that they were meant to be.

Rhian did more and more things to win Alexander's heart over. He made extra efforts to keep things in the apartment the way Alexander liked. Though he put much energy into making it a happy home for the two of them, Alexander had become more distant than before. He was avoiding Rhian, talking to him only when absolutely necessary usually giving one-word responses. Rhian didn't want to let things get worse, so he planned to make dinner for the two of them as a surprise for Alexander. He began to cook. An hour later he was setting the table when the door opened. Alexander walked in; he looked like he had been at the gym. He walked in, looked at the table and then at Rhian who had been eagerly awaiting his return.

"Special dinner?" Alexander questioned.

"Kind of, I made it for you… I was hoping we could talk." Rhian responded nervously. "I feel like we've been distant from each other."

"Sorry, I have plans with John. Maybe next time." With no other explanation, Alexander walked into the bathroom and closed the door, making a point to lock it. He never locked the door. Almost immediately, Rhian became overwhelmed with a clash of sadness and anger. There was so much he wanted to say but No words to say it. He was hurt and he was annoyed all at once. He wanted Alexander to stop pushing him away. He wanted him to go back to being his best friend. But it was obvious that he wasn't going to be the same Alexander he used to be any time soon.

Rhian stood in the dining room feeling stupid. He walked into his room and closed the door leaving the food on the table. He fell onto his bed and let out a quivering sigh. He couldn't take it in anymore. He couldn't handle Alexander's evasive attitude. Rhian lied in his bed silently releasing emotion through doleful tears until he heard a knock at the door. He wasn't sure who it could be so he approached the door slowly. He could still hear the water running in the bathroom from Alexander taking a shower. As he got to the front door he remembered that he had let his classmate Christian borrow his book, which meant that this was probably the guy returning it. He wiped his eyes and put on his signature smile.

"Hey, how are you?" The young man asked from outside the door.

"I'm alright. How are you?" Rhian said, worried that the young man would see that he had just been crying.

"That's good to hear" The young man said with a big smile. "What are you up to this evening? It seems like a nice day for a walk in the park don't you think?"

Rhian politely laughed at the reference to a sarcastic use of the phrase in class to describe training for a marathon. "Yeah, it is nice outside…" He paused for a moment to think about the dinner that he had failed to share with Alexander. If he didn't eat the food, it would just go to waste. "Are you hungry?"

"Why, yes I am! How did you know? Are you a mind reader? I knew it!" Christian lightheartedly responded.

"Why don't you join me for dinner? I made too much food and my roommate is not going to be joining… I don't really want to eat alone, sooo…"

"Sure, why not! I honestly have nothing else to do and I never turn down a free meal." Christian responded with a charming smile.

The two sat down to eat just as Alexander was getting out of the shower. He quickly went into his room and closed the door.

"Are you talking to yourself?" Alexander asked, as he emerged with a different outfit, clean and ready to meet up with John.

"No…" Rhian sounded irritated.

"Oh… See you later." Alexander walked out as fast as he could, feeling awkward.

John was outside waiting for him in. When he got into the car, John noticed the confused look on his face.

"What's wrong?"

"Huh? Oh, nothing… let's go."

"Alright dude. Whatever you say."

Later that evening Alexander returned to find Rhian and Christian sitting on the couch, so involved in their conversation that they didn't even notice him walk in. Alexander felt a tinge of jealousy towards Christian, the guy that he didn't even know and Rhian barely knew. He didn't let them see that it bothered him and simply went to bed.

After observing Alexander awkwardly return, Rhian realized that he had spent the entire night hanging out with Christian. Sensing the tension between the two boys, Christian got up off the couch and tanked Rhian for dinner before heading out. While walking Christian out, Rhian no longer felt guilty about his feelings toward Alexander, which was a relief. He looked out through the window at the cool night, noticing the people walking back from a late night of studying. He was curious about them and wondered what their lives were like. What made them smile; what it was that made them unique. It was fascinating to him to think about those people and then to consider their loved ones. He surmised that one person is more than just one. There were many loved ones that went into making those people who they were. He started to think about his own loved ones. Not the parents that had abandoned him, but rather the friends that had helped him get through the tough times. He wanted to something nice for them so he baked some cookies and delivered them to Leena's apartment.

"Hey! How are you?" Leena and the girls greeted him as he walked in with the plate of fresh baked cookies in hand. Rhian thought for a moment before answering.

"I'm… great!" He returned, replacing the undecided look on his face with a big smile. In that moment he decided to answer with *I'm great* from then on when asked how he was doing. He had learned that sometimes when things aren't going the way he expected, faking would often times lead him to end up in a better mood. The way he saw it, if he could fake it enough times, eventually it would be true.

He continued to do things like this for his close friends and soon found himself distracted from his feelings for Alexander by the relationships that he had strengthened over the few short weeks. He felt much better about himself, but there was still something missing in is life. It was time to start investing more into himself than into thoughts of the past and Alexander.

One of the things that Rhian began doing in an effort to improve himself was to work out every day at the gym. While there one afternoon, he noticed a young man who seemed to be checking him out. He didn't pay much attention to it because he thought the guy was probably just checking his form and judging. For the next few days they exchanged looks instead of words. On the fourth day of seeing the guy and noticing him stare at him while he worked out, Rhian felt obligated to go and talk to the guy, but just as he was about to make his move another guy who was just as good looking as his potential stalker walked up to the guy and took his attention away. The rest of the day Rhian went without another look from him.

The next day he was in the gym doing his usual routine when he felt a tap on his back, it was his admirer! Rhian look surprised quickly removing his headphones before saying:

"Hi, can I help you?"

"Well, I noticed you left your water bottle at the bench press so I thought I'd bring it to you."

"Oh, thanks… I don't know where my mind is today…" Rhian responded with a light chuckle and his signature smile.

"Not a problem. Hey do you need a spotter?" The guy asked, not paying attention to the fact that he was lifting light weights not to mention he was working on biceps, so there was minimal safety concern.

Rhian laughed in his head and decided to humor his admirer. "Sure, why not? But first, what's your name?"

"Dimi!" The man responded quickly

"Demi? Isn't that a chick's name?" Rhian jokingly asked.

"It's Dimi not Demi, and it's short for Dmitri." He answered with a false arrogance, mockingly stressing the *e* in Demi. "It's what my friends started calling me when I got to college." returning back to his friendly tone.

The pair worked out for a few minutes longer before leaving the gym. As they were leaving, Rhian was pleasantly surprised when he tried to ask Dimi to dinner.

"I've had a great time working out, are you perhaps hungry? Maybe we can grab a bite to eat?"

"Oh…" Dimi hesitated slightly

"I'm sorry, I didn't mean to make you uncomfortable, forget I said anything." Rhian quickly babbled out not letting Dimi answer.

"Well what I was going to say was that I had already made plans with my sister to meet up for dinner, but I am free tomorrow if the offer still stands. We can go after we work out." Dimi answered confidently.

"Oh, so you think I'm going to work out with you again?"

"Well I sure hope so..." Dimi responded with a wink.

"I guess we will have to see if I work out tomorrow then…"

"I guess so…"

Rhian walked home that night feeling optimistic. His new admirer had turned out to be a really nice guy and it seemed like he had just made plans for a second date… but had they already had the first one? It didn't matter at that point, he felt very good about himself. He was happy and no one could change that. He went to bed that night without saying a word to Alexander.

Rhian woke up inches away from Alexander's face. He was by Alexander who was watching him and smiling. He sat up quickly, confusion written all over his face. Alexander reached for his hand gently as if trying to comfort him.

"Are you ok?" Alexander was obviously concerned.

"What are you doing in my bed?" Rhian snapped back at him. Alexander got up and started laughing.

"You're ridiculous sometimes…" he replied as he patted Rhian on the shoulder and walked towards the bathroom. Rhian blushed when he realized that Alexander was completely naked, but he couldn't look away. Alexander smiled a naughty smile as he walked back towards the bed and touched Rhian's nose with his.

"Mmmm, somebody likes what they see." He said with a wink, staring deeply into Rhian's eyes. He kissed him on the nape of his neck and wrapped his arms around him. Rhian instantly felt safe, at ease, and in a state of complete bliss. Alexander went into the bathroom to shower and get ready for the day. Rhian was shocked by what had just happened but more so he was confused about his whereabouts. He had no idea where he was but it felt like home.

He left the confines of the small bedroom for what appeared to be the living room, which was a mess of clothes and toys. *Whose stuff was it?* He thought to himself. He didn't know where he was. He thought that perhaps some time in the middle of the night Alexander had somehow moved him somewhere and was trying to pull a prank on him. He started to get angry, marching his way back to the room as he heard the water in the bathroom stop. Suddenly a door behind him opened up and a little boy came out followed closely by a little girl. The girl was wearing a diaper and her booties along with a shirt that read *Daddy's little princess*. Rhian was now completely lost. *Who are these kids and why are they here? What is going on?* He noticed how beautiful the children were. They were perfect in his eyes. He didn't fully understand why there were children there but he was too excited by their presence to question it.

The children ran up to him and he scooped them up in his arms. Kisses for everyone as they kissed the sides of his cheeks. These children were clearly well taken care of and happy.

"What are you making for breakfast daddy?" The little girl asked.

"I want biscuits and gravy!" The little boy said wiping the sleep from his eyes and yawning.

"Um… " Rhian stood with a blank look on his face. Luckily Alexander walked in, this time fully dressed. He threw the towel and opened his arms.

"Good morning my little munchkins!" He said extending his arms expecting the kids to run and greet him. They did as expected, leaping from Rhian's arms and into Alexander's. Rhian jolted as they flew from his arms over to Alexander. He watched them as they grabbed hold of each one of his legs. Such an unexpected sight after such a strange wake up.

"Good morning Papa!" the children said in unison.

"Let's get you some breakfast… What do you say?" Alexander stated while smiling at Rhian. *There it was*, Rhian thought to himself. *There's the look that he gives me, the one that disarms me, moves me, and torments me…* Rhian was brought back from his daydreaming when the children ran past him. Alexander walked by and as he did he put his arm around Rhian's lower back and pulled him in for a kiss. Rhian instantly melted and kissed back very passionately. Alexander looked at him in the eyes once more and then turned to head towards the kitchen. Rhian followed slightly confused but not questioning what had just happened.

"Alright kids, remember that today we are going for our picnic at the park, so let's get ready for that. The kids followed their Papa to the other room so that he could get them ready. He changed their clothes and brushed their teeth. The entire time Rhian observed them get ready for the picnic. Once the family was ready to go they headed out to the nearby park and picked a spot to settle down at. It was near all of the playing equipment so that the children could play. Rhian and Alexander watched the two from the blanket that they had placed on the ground. They sat there hand in hand watching the children play and waving at the people who walked by. Everything here seemed so perfect.

He blinked for a moment and suddenly he was in a living room standing in front of his daughter who was now much older.

"Why do you always say you understand me? You don't!" Makayla shouted at Rhian.

"Makayla, don't walk away from me. I know you think you're so smart and that you have all the answers but you don't! You are still young and you have to be respectful towards your father and I. Now come here and talk to us."

"No! I just want to be alone right now, no matter how much like a *female* you say you feel like, you aren't... You can't understand me!" Makayla yelled as she walked away.

She was challenging him for being a man and that was something that Rhian had feared would be a problem with her in the future, he stood for a moment until she was out of his presence before he let out a shaky sigh. Alexander who was standing in the doorway behind him walked up and wrapped his arms around him. He stood there holding him without saying a word as tears quietly rolled down the side of his cheek. Rhian felt an instant sense of relief. He kissed Alexander's arm, turned around and kissed him softly on the lips, and embraced him.

Rhian looked into Alexander's eyes, losing himself slightly. It was in these moments, looking into his eyes, where Rhian would find himself the happiest, at ease with everything in his life. When he came back to reality he was sitting in a chair next to Alexander. They were at Makayla's wedding. She stood at the altar looking beautiful and happy. Her handsome groom excitedly standing with a big smile on his face. Next to Rhian sat a happy Alexander, beaming with pride. He looked over for a moment noticing how happy Alexander was for his daughter to be getting married. It was a beautiful ceremony but the most important thing was the sense of general happiness that existed in his heart. He smiled as Alexander noticed him looking over at him and shined a big smile right back at him.

After the ceremony he hugged Makayla and shared a dance with her, then one with Alexander. He leaned in and rested his head on Alexander's chest, closing his eyes to take in the moment. The sound of his heartbeat soothed him until it began increasing rapidly.

He opened his eyes to find himself in a hospital bed holding Alexander's hand. The two were much older. He began to feel a great deal of stress and sadness on his heart. It was only a few moments before the unspeakable would happen.

"I love you, I am the luckiest man to have been given so many years with the most amazing human being I have ever had the pleasure of knowing. You truly are the reason my life was worth living. I will wait for you. I will always be with you. I love you." With that Rhian felt a great sadness and deep sorrow in his heart.

Suddenly he awoke in a cold sweat. His heart was beating faster than normal. He had fallen asleep. Rhian could only think about the wonderful feeling that he got from his acceptance of Alexander as his husband. He hadn't really thought about raising a family with another man, let alone with Alexander. The dream inspired hope in him for a happy future, which terrified him because there was always the possibility of losing that hope. Like many young gay men raised in a conservative Christian environment, the thought of a happy life with a husband and kids was simply not in the cards for them. But now, after living in fear, he found a new purpose in life that could yield the happiness he longed for and he wasn't going to let that fear keep him from it.

Chapter 6

In a few short weeks Alexander had gone from a great summer with his best friend to avoiding Rhian as much as possible. There was nothing he could do to remedy the situation since it wasn't his fault that Rhian had fallen for him. He kept telling himself that he was keeping his distance for Rhian's sake. It was for *his* own good. Once enough time had passed and Rhian could see clearly that they were just friends they could go back to the way things were. Alexander would leave the apartment before Rhian woke up and was in bed before he got home. He spent most of his time away from home either studying on campus or with other friends.

Rhian wanted to go back to the way things were before he told Alexander about his feelings. He didn't regret his honesty but he wondered if there would have been a better way of approaching the situation. For now he would have to deal with the consequences. He didn't know how long he could last without Alexander's support but he would have to learn. He began to realize how dependent they were on one another. Perhaps it wasn't the healthiest of circumstances but it was what had brought them close. Their codependence was the basis of their intimate relationship.

While Alexander missed Rhian and their closeness, he knew it was better to keep the distance. He was also very aware of their codependence ever since he began avoiding him. He realized that he didn't do anything without Rhian. He had been there for him throughout all of the rough patches of the last year and he was more than happy to do so. But this situation was different. It wasn't that Rhian made him feel uncomfortable, on the contrary, Rhian made him feel safe. The problem was that he didn't want to lead Rhian on any more than he had. But he didn't lead him on… at least, not on purpose. Either way, things were the way they were; Alexander was straight and that wouldn't change so Rhian didn't have a choice but to accept that. It wasn't completely fair and he knew it but he didn't want to deal with the complications that could arise from simply entertaining the thought of something more than a friendship with him.

One night after being out longer than expected, Alexander entered the apartment into what sounded like Rhian painting. He tried to be as inconspicuous as possible but it didn't matter because Rhian was so involved in his painting and in the music playing over his headphones that he didn't notice Alexander walk in. He quickly got ready for bed and lied down. It was unnecessary for him to try and be sneaky about being there because they had gotten used to avoiding each other by now. No matter the state of their friendship, any interaction was awkward, and Alexander hated awkwardness. As he quietly made his way out the door he noticed that Rhian had scrapped a painting in the trashcan. He looked down at it and realized it was a painting of him. Rhian had been painting Alexander's face. Wow, he's really good at this. He thought to himself. *I guess throwing my face away somehow helps him deal with everything. That's a good creative way of working out emotions...* He liked the painting though so he folded it up and put it in his pocket and went to bed.

Rhian painted, losing track of time and forgetting about what was going on between he and his friend. He began painting after splashing the canvas with random paints out of frustration. *I can take this ruined canvas and make it beautiful.* This philosophy on life was how he saw himself after the time he spent in the camp. Although his feelings for Alexander left him unable to talk to anyone about his trauma, the art allowed him to relieve his stress in a productive way. As he painted he realized that he didn't *need* Alexander the way he thought he needed him. But he began to understand that what he felt for his friend was not simple. It was more than attraction. It was more than understanding. It was more than a desire to be around him. What Rhian began to realize was that there was a genuine desire to be with him. To resonate with him in spirit, mind, and body. There was a sense of completeness that came from the very notion of Alexander's nearby presence. They may not have been speaking but it didn't matter because what was important was that Alexander could be anywhere in the world and he would still be right next to Rhian all the time.

Of course, Rhian's interpretation of what was going on between them didn't necessary coincide with Alexander's actions. This disconnect lead to varying reactions from Rhian who didn't know how to read the situation. What he understood was different than what he was experiencing. Alexander was irritable, snapping at the smallest of details and causing an argument to erupt out of nowhere. In a few short weeks they went from being the best of friends, closer than ever, to acting like roommates who couldn't stand each other. Alexander stopped responding to his attempts at communication. Rhian knew that he had to confront Alexander.

Hey are you going to be home tonight? When Alexander didn't respond to his message he tried again a few hours later.

Is everything ok?

Yeah I'm fine.

Well, are you going to be home?

Why does it matter?

I wanted to know if I should wait for you before going to the store.

If I need something I'll get it myself. Rhian waited for Alexander to get home that day.

"You promised me that things were going to stay the same; that my feelings for you didn't change anything, but you've been acting like I did something wrong!" Alexander listened angrily. "We need to clarify some things because I think we damaged our friendship, and it needs to be repaired immediately. If we don't deal with the problem now, we may lose what we had forever. I know that it all started because of my emotions. I let them get out of hand, but the truth is that we're both to blame. The scary reality for me is that what we had, or perhaps still have, is something I don't think I want to live without. I've never felt this way about anyone before and it scares me because I can see what we could have. It's so close yet miles away and my biggest fear is losing you, but I'm worried that I may have already lost you…" There was an awkward pause that Rhian let go on longer than he should have as if expecting some response from the now tense Alexander. "I hate that you have been ignoring me. It really bothers me. Can we please just talk about it?"

"What do you want me to say? It's never going to happen… get over it." Alexander responded coldly. Alexander had been dreading this conversation because he was very aware that things between the two of them had become jaded. It wasn't uncommon for him to be busy throughout the day but it was very apparent that he was avoiding all contact with Rhian, who also had a lot of his feelings to get out.

"I don't know how to live my life without you right next to me… I can't seem to get a grasp on the reality of the situation. I want so badly to just see you and talk to you. I want so badly to just be near you but I can't. I try to act normal and to just be ok with the way things are, but let's be honest, things aren't the same, and they won't be. I wish there was a way I could take all of the confusion and feelings away. I can't. I can't live like this. I damaged us and there is no going back. I wish I could just run away from here and not look back, but even this broken feeling, with all the distant thoughts of us and who we were, is better than never seeing you again. In my head I've already boarded the flight to a new life and we are no longer friends. You know deep down that it will never be the same. I can't be mad at you because it was not your fault it was mine and I can't change anything. I do not apologize for who I am or what I feel. I know that I would stand by you no matter what and you may think you can find a better match but if I honestly believed you would find someone who would be there for you more than I will and love you like I will, I would encourage you to go after them. Alexander, we are bound for life through time and space." There was Rhian's word vomit again. He immediately regretted the phrasing because he knew it would freak Alexander out.

"You sound crazy. I hope you realize that. You sound like… like you are some kind of desperate ex who is trying to hold on to the past. We were friends not lovers so get that shit out of your head. We are roommates now and nothing else." Alexander began walking away before adding; "I'll be moving my bed out of your room because I think it's better for me to have my own space." Rhian was stunned and didn't know what to say. That evening while Rhian was out Alexander moved his bed into the study room and cleared Rhian's stuff, leaving his belongings in the living room. Rhian came home to find Alexander already locked in his room with the lights on.

Rhian began losing sleep, staying up all night to work on his art. He lost track of the days, drifting from place to place like a mindless zombie. One night he felt like creating his masterpiece. The masterpiece was of Alexander, of course, which he had already painted once before. But this time the painting had a purpose; to inspire Alexander to realize that they were meant to be together.

This painting had to be perfect. It had to capture love in Alexander's expression that proved he loved Rhian as much as Rhian loved him. This facial expression was so imprinted on Rhian's heart that he was certain he could paint it and prove that they were in love.

Alexander wouldn't be able to deny what Rhian saw if he could see it himself. Rhian became obsessed with painting this piece, believing fully that Alexander was happiest when they were together. He had never connected with someone the way he did with Alexander and that expression of pure joy was all the proof he needed. He was terrified of scaring Alexander with his passion so he worked in secret. Rhian was either on the brink of obsession or inspiration.

He had to recreate this image completely from memory since there was no picture that accurately captured what Rhian could see. There was no doubt in his mind that he saw that private moment several times but he wasn't sure just how he would bring it to life. While it seemed crazy to him, he also saw it as a very romantic gesture to expose the truth and show Alexander that they were meant to be together. Whatever the motivation, it was what Rhian needed to help keep his sanity while Alexander continued to distance himself. His paintings were the expressions of his heart and they needed him, to complete them, to perfect them, to love them, and to believe in them. Most importantly, he needed them.

As he began to paint, he reminisced about some of the times that Alexander expressed his happiness with a single smile. He thought about the first time he noticed it. They went fishing at a nearby lake. Alexander loved to fish but Rhian didn't. It was a beautiful summer night; the sun had almost completely set as they sat with their lines in the water. Alexander's line tensed up and the pole became warped. He was having trouble reeling in his catch and out of nowhere he fell into the water. Rhian, taking a moment to realize what had happened, jumped right in without giving it a second thought. He hit the cold water with a harsh splash of chilled water. He frantically swam looking for Alexander, who was nowhere to be found. He dove down but without the help of any light it was impossible to see anything. When

Rhian finally surfaced, he heard movement nearby so he swam over without any hesitation. As he reached Alexander, he could see a smile on his face.

"Are you ok?" Rhian asked in a panic.

"Hahaha I'm fine! Are you ok?" Alexander gave a charming smile.

"Why do you like to scare me like that? You knew I would jump!"

Alexander shrugged his shoulders and looked at him with a look that acknowledged what he had just said. In the reflection of the moonlight, which lit up Alexander's face, his countenance changed from sarcasm to warmth. He knew and felt in that moment that Rhian really did care about him. He had never really seen anyone do that for him. The look he gave Rhian was powerful and expressed their deep connection. It was as if he was sharing part of his soul through his eyes. His face expressed care, concern, love, passion, confusion, and a general appreciation for the soul in front of him.

The next time that he remembered seeing this look on his face was the time when Alexander had woken up after having a terrible dream. The anxiety he had when he was a child seemed to show its trauma in the way Alexander slept. They had stayed together for about half a year at this point and Rhian had noticed that Alexander had a tendency to move in his sleep so much so that he would sometimes hit the walls of the room. It never bothered Rhian but it did make him aware of it. He had been concerned that there might be something neurologically wrong with Alexander but after confronting him about it, he reassured him that it was not more than simple sleep movements so Rhian dismissed it, but remained aware of it.

One night Alexander had been moving more than usual when he suddenly awoke in a panic. He had experienced a night terror and awoke in fear. Poor Alexander awoke in a cold sweat and frightened by his surroundings because he wasn't sure if he was actually awake. Rhian hadn't fallen completely asleep when he heard Alexander wake up.

"Are you ok?"

"Oh, hey… you're awake…"

"Yeah, I am… What's wrong? Why are you out of breath?"

"I just had a really bad dream. There was a woman who had a child and when she gave birth, she didn't stop to make sure the child was ok. She cut the cord, set the baby on the ground and walked away without making sure that the child was all right. I walked into a dark room and found this child lying on the ground. The dream continued in a strange way cause suddenly I was working as a bartender while holding my child in one arm, I could feel how protective I had become of him. The next part was the last part before I woke up because I was walking on the sidewalk while holding my kid's hand, he was older now so I was taking him to a park but instead of actually staying, I set him down on a park bench and walked away. I could see that there was a dark shadow coming after him, trying to hurt him and I could hear his screams but I just continued to walk away. I heard one last scream before an eerie silence fell over the park and then I heard a gunshot. Then I woke up."

Rhian was stunned by such a wild dream… he didn't know what to say so he paused for a moment.

"Do you think it could have something to do with the problems that you have had in the past with your parents?" It seemed like that was all Alexander needed to hear before he began to tear up. He looked down and wept quietly.

"Maybe… I don't know, I guess…" Rhian came over and sat next to him in his bed. He put his arm around his broad shoulders and gently rubbed his back. He didn't know what he could say, but what worked for him was a physical connection to reassure him that he was all right.

"It's going to be alright… You'll see… You are amazing, strong, beautiful person who will do great things… I love you." Rhian spoke from the heart. Alexander didn't say anything right away. Again there was the look on his face. It was the look he had when they were fishing. It was care, concern, love, passion, and a general appreciation for everything that Rhian was to him, but this time there seemed to be more clarity than confusion. Rhian simply hugged him and went to bed. These examples were only snapshots of this complex moment that he was trying to capture… There was so much more, and he had to spend some time working this out.

Alexander was doing his best to avoid any deep conversations with Rhian. It wasn't that he was mad at Rhian, he just didn't' know how to be around him anymore. The most frustrating part about it was that he didn't have anyone to talk to about the things that were going on in his mind. The only person he trusted enough to talk to about what was going on between he and Rhian, would have been Rhian. But without that option, he had no choice but to take out his frustrations at the gym. While he was happy with the results he got from going to the gym, he was still unsatisfied with the way his and Rhian's friendship had soured. The fragility of their situation was made worse by the lack of interaction that they had. It was obvious that the two longed to spend time together but Alexander couldn't simply go back to being *best buds* with Rhian, no matter how many times he told him, and himself for that matter, that he could. It was a state of limbo that wasn't magically going to change. They were broken and it would stay that way until they decided to change that.

They both knew that they had to talk and yet, neither one was willing to make the first move. Alexander noticed that Rhian seemed more affected by him. Something had changed in him and it made Alexander nervous. What he was beginning to see was that the longer he avoided Rhian, the stronger his feelings seemed to grow. He couldn't avoid his friend forever. Unbeknownst to Alexander, Rhian no longer saw him as just a simple crush, but rather as the man whom he wanted to spend his life with. It wasn't a title he was looking to give away. It wasn't that he was convinced that Alexander's heart was speaking to him and only him. It was his soul, longing for its other half. He had found the person who could make him feel the most amazing things, while also feeling the most terrible of things. For Rhian, it was not a question of *if* but rather *when,* because in the depths of his heart, there was true love, a bond that carried with it the utmost importance and could not be challenged. Alexander couldn't accept that idea. Rhian understood that some souls can be bound together regardless of time, space, or even sex and that sometimes it takes people time to accept that their other half lies in the soul of one of the same sex; but Alexander was not one of those people.

Alexander had a different perspective. He didn't want to hurt Rhian anymore. He hated when he saw him cry. He knew that this man was a genuinely good man. There was nothing he wouldn't do for him. But he didn't know how to get Rhian to abandon his feelings for him without causing hurt. He wanted to go back to the days where they would share those amazing moments as friends together. Those moments that would often force him to make time for him; the times when they would share everything without fear of judgment and feel as though they were truly in a good place. He wanted to feel the love that they had again without leading Rhian to feel those feelings.

He had thought about the possibility that he was actually in love with Rhain but the thought only lasted a moment because he wasn't *gay*, therefore he couldn't reciprocate the feelings. For Alexander there was no clear point where he went wrong in his friendship with Rhian. There was definitely a deep bond formed but it was simply friendship and nothing more. The more he thought about it the more he began to feel confused as to why Rhian had developed feelings in the first place. At times he could tell that Rhian would respond strangely to his actions but it wasn't a big deal because Rhian knew that he was straight. But as he thought more about the nature of their relationship, he began to realize how some of the things that defined *them* could be perceived as more than friendship.

All of these thoughts were too uncomfortable. He had spent enough time creating arguments about why Rhian was imagining things but he couldn't let the entire blame rest on Rhian getting his hopes up simply out of loneliness or desperation. He had to admit to himself that he had said things that could have confused Rhian. But that was not something he could take back. He would remain firm on his decision to ignore what Rhian was saying and remain true to what he decided was the only truth. He was straight, end of story. Rhian would just have to find a way to deal with it. Even though he didn't have to work hard to accept Rhian as gay, Rhian would have to find a way to accept that he was straight.

Rhian began to avoid his friends, becoming isolated and even missing class. He distanced himself from everyone except Matt, who seemed to pop up at the most opportune times. Sensing that something was up with him, Sebastian asked Rhian to meet him for lunch.

"It's been a while since I've seen you… how have you been?" Sebastian asked genuinely curious about what his friend was going through.

"I've been, alright. I'm going out and enjoying myself, trying not to focus on things that I can't change." Rhian was *going out* again like back in the summer. He assumed that Matt was the instigator.

"Well, how often are you going out? With who?" Sebastian questioned.

"Oh, just Matt…" There was hesitation.

"Oh…"

"Look, I don't need you to judge me."

"I'm not judging you. I'm just concerned."

"I'll be ok. I don't want to talk about it right now."

"Promise me that you'll take care of yourself?"

"I promise."

Rhian didn't intend on stopping his partying. He wanted to dull the pain of Alexander's rejection. To feel nothing was better than to feel the pain of being rejected by someone who you are convinced is meant to be with you. It was to the point where the certainty was set in Rhian's bones. Rhian found someone to buy him liquor so he asked for several bottles. He was set on spending his night drinking with Matt.

Heading home, Rhian sent Matt a text message letting him know that he had some liquor:

Party tonight?

On my way!

That night the two stayed in and drank. Rhian was so drunk that he couldn't see straight. Matt hadn't drunk as much as Rhian had so he wanted to go out and have some fun. He suggested that they go dancing but then decided he wanted to go swimming off of the pier. Rhian stumbled around the apartment before he and Matt took off. Alexander walked in to find Rhian looking like a mess and Matt coming out of the bathroom. He didn't like Matt because of the trouble that he had caused in the past. He didn't understand why Rhian was so sympathetic towards him. Alexander shook his head in disapproval.

"Hey… you… What are you doing tonight?" Rhian slurred

"I'm staying in. I have an exam tomorrow morning." He sounded annoyed. He was used to dealing with a drunken Rhian but this was a Tuesday, and he was more intoxicated than normal, especially for a weekday. He was concerned but elected not to say anything and dodged any further questions by going into his room.

"See Matt, I'm honest with someone and they push me away. I make the same mistake again and I'm surprised when the same thing happens. This is why people suck. Let's go, it's cold in here." Rhian said quietly to Matt but loud enough for Alexander to hear. He didn't want to acknowledge that he had heard it but he didn't want Rhian to think that he didn't care about him anymore, especially if he thought he hated him. He didn't, in fact he wanted so badly to tell Rhian that he still cared about him and never stopped loving him, but he didn't want to lead him on anymore. He sat there in his room more frustrated than when he first saw Rhian drunk. He was worried and confused about what to do but he could tell that his friend was in some serious trouble.

He changed his clothing in preparation for the night. As he walked out to the living room he noticed Rhian was leaving.

"Where are you going?"

"Swimming!" Rhian shouted just as he closed the door.

Alexander made a strange face as it took him a second to realize what Rhian had just said. He ran into his room to get his shoes on. Something was going to happen to Rhian if he didn't do something to stop it. He ran outside and looked around but there was no trace of them or Rhian's car. He knew where they were going and he would have to run to be able to catch up to them. So he did. He took off as quickly as possible. It wasn't too far form there and by the time he arrived he could see Matt sitting on the edge of the pier. Rhian was hanging from the railing shouting about how nice it was outside.

Alexander walked up carefully to the two of them trying not to startle Rhian and cause him to fall. As he got close enough to grab Rhian he reached for him but he jumped into the water. Alexander jumped over the railing looking around for Rhian to surface but he hadn't surfaced. Alexander couldn't wait any longer so ripped off his sweater and his shirt and jumped in after him.

"What are you doing bro, he's fine." Matt said after taking a puff from his joint. Alexander swam towards Rhian who had surfaced just as Alexander hit the water and was gasping for air.

"Alexander, help me! I'm sorry! I'm so sorry. Help me Alexander, I'm so scared!" Rhian cried, grasping onto Alexander as tightly as he could. In that moment where everything was dark and he felt like it was the end, Alexander appeared like a light in the darkness to rescue him. He was never happier to see anyone in his life.

"Hey, it'll be alright. Calm down, you're safe now." Alexander said as he tried to calm him down. He helped Rhian get to shore, calming him down the entire swim back. Alexander walked Rhian back to the parking lot but his car was gone. He figured Matt had taken the car, which was typical Matt. Rhian was shaking as the cool of the night and wet shirt made for a very cold walk. Alexander looked at his friend with pity and gave him his dry shirt and sweater. Rhian pulled his wet shirt off and gratefully accepted the shirt and sweater. They walked the rest of the way as quickly as possible. Alexander was more concerned with the wellbeing of his friend than the problems that they had recently encountered.

When they arrived back at the apartment, Rhian's car was in the parking lot and the keys were on the coffee table. Alexander was very upset with Matt but was too concerned with Rhian to care. He helped him get into some dry clothes before laying him down for bed. Rhian gave Alexander a hug and a kiss on the cheek, causing him to flinch slightly. Alexander didn't mean to flinch out of disgust; it was because he didn't want Rhian to get the wrong idea in his altered state of mind. But of course, Rhian only noticed that he had flinched and immediately became upset.

"Leave me alone. I'm fine." Rhian shouted angrily.

"Rhian…. I'm sorry. I…"

"Just go… don't you have to study?"

Rhian was right, Alexander didn't want to make him more upset so he walked out but made sure to leave the door slightly ajar so that he could check on him throughout the night. Alexander spent the rest of the night studying and checking in on him. He was up for most of the night studying so instead of trying to sleep he went straight to class to take his exam. Afterwards he went home to sleep.

Rhian spent the rest of the night awake, thinking about Alexander and the ordeal that he had just had. He felt stupid and he knew that he would have to apologize. The problem was that he wanted to kiss Alexander and he so badly wanted Alexander to kiss him back but he didn't. He was reminded of the fact that Alexander didn't want him, which made him feel worthless. Rhian didn't understand Alexander's point of view because he wholeheartedly believed in love between two people, not sexes.

Alexander felt bad for pulling away from Rhian's kiss, but he didn't want to do anything that would lead him on. Regardless of the situation between them, Alexander was still concerned about Rhian's wellbeing. He waited until he thought Rhian was asleep to go in and check on him. He monitored him for a few hours to make sure that he was ok. Figuring that Rhian would wake up with a headache, Alexander placed a cup of water and some aspirin next to Rhian's bed.

Rhian didn't sleep that night, contrary to what Alexander thought. He pretended to be asleep every time that Alexander came in to check on him. His friend's caring actions reminded him about the way they cared about each other and the way things were before his feelings got in the way. He knew he had to get over any feelings in order to save their friendship.

Chapter 7

The next morning Rhian woke up in a haze. He looked around for Alexander but he had already gone to take his exam. Rhian decided to work on his painting instead of letting himself sit around all day in misery.

The doorknob wiggled making Rhian nervous in anticipation of Alexander's mood.

"Hey, how did your exam go?"

"It was alright. I probably could have done better if I would have studied a bit more. Oh well."

"I'm sorry about that. I didn't mean to take away from your study time."

"It's alright. Things happen."

"That shouldn't have happened."

"There are lots of things that shouldn't have happened but they happened anyway. Sometimes it's just best to pick up and move on." While the words were harsh, Alexander added a smile to soften the impact. He also patted Rhian gently on the back as he continued to walk past him. They didn't say anything else for the rest of the day but something about the physical barrier being crossed seemed to ease the tension between the two boys.

Rhian's mood lightened up considerably since Alexander had patted him on the back. He thought a great deal about Alexander's words and the possibility of rebuilding their friendship. There were little things that had changed since Rhian admitted his feelings to Alexander. One of the most obvious things was that Alexander began locking the bathroom door when he went in to take a shower. Neither one had ever been too concerned with privacy but suddenly Alexander started locking the door and Rhian noticed. Rhian gave up on trying to use the bathroom while Alexander as in there because he knew that Alexander wouldn't change that. But since the other night he hadn't heard the door lock after Alexander got into the shower. He wondered if Alexander was comfortable again.

Rhian had to use the bathroom but Alexander was in the shower one morning. Rhian knocked on the door to see if Alexander was almost finished.

"The door is unlocked." Alexander called out.

"Thanks…" Rhian was a bit nervous. He looked down the entire time, even though he couldn't see anything through the glazed glass. He didn't want Alexander to think he was trying to sneak a peek.

"You left the door unlocked?" Rhian asked before leaving the bathroom.

"Yeah… Why?"

"Well I thought you had been locking the door ever since I told you about… well you know."

"I was… but I kind of got over it."

"Oh ok. I was going to make some biscuits and gravy do you want some?"

"Um… Sure sounds good."

"Ok, I'll get started on it right away!" Rhian said with a smile.

"Just make sure to wash your hands." Alexander said with a laugh.

"Will do." Rhian finished up and went into the kitchen to make breakfast. Maybe Alexander was coming around. He quickly prepared the food while Alexander was getting ready. Alexander emerged from the room fully dressed and with his bag ready to go.

"Hey, I'm actually running late. I can't have breakfast." Rhian's enthusiasm was gone. *He probably only agreed to have breakfast because I was in the shower with him and he was freaked out.* Rhian thought to himself.

Alexander realized that he had upset him and didn't really know what to say. He left without saying a word, but he felt guilty for ditching Rhian, who was so excited to share breakfast with him. It had been a while since he had seen his friend smile so brightly. But again, he was the cause of Rhian's disappointment. It was time to stop acting like a selfish child and talk to him. Alexander wasn't going to give up on their friendship that easily.

"Hey, so are you free for dinner tonight?" He could tell Rhian was still upset about breakfast.

"Yeah… what did you have in mind?"

"Well I wanted to treat you to dinner because I goofed on breakfast this morning… and it would give us a chance to talk. I wanted to apologize for my behavior."

"It's ok. I know it was probably weird to hear the things I said."

"…Look let's just meet for dinner at 7pm."

"Where at?"

"The burger place." Rhian could hear Alexander smiling through the phone.

"Sounds good. I'll see you then." Rhian spent the better part of the day doing homework and going to class. He tried to distract himself so that he didn't get his hopes up before the dinner but it was all he could think about. He was hopeful that things would go back to normal.

It was 6:30 when Rhian started getting ready and was out of the house in a few minutes. He planned on arriving a few minutes early. He sat in the parking lot for a few minutes before walking inside and requesting a table for two.

Hey, I'm inside at a table already. Rhian sent a text message as soon as he sat down expecting Alexander to show up a few moments later. He waited and waited but still no sign of Alexander. The waitress came and asked if he wanted to order something.

"Is your friend almost here? You could order a drink while you wait." She said with a smile.

"I'm sure he will be here soon. I will take a cherry coke while I wait." He responded.

"I'll be right back with that babe."

"Thanks." Rhian drank as slowly as possible in order to give Alexander time to get there. It wasn't like Alexander to be late, but his recent evasiveness made Rhian wondered if he would even show. He had to show. It was his idea! He thought to himself. He called him but there was no response. It was pointless to leave a message because he had already waited long enough. Rhian left the restaurant feeling empty and worthless.

"Fine! You win! I get it." He howled at the night sky. "I'll leave you alone." Rhian's heart was again broken and his hope lost.

After making plans with Rhian to meet up for dinner, Alexander went about his day without thinking about their problems. There was time to talk later so it was best to set aside the stress. On his way home after his last class, Alexander had his headphones on and was lost in his music. Without paying attention, he accidentally ran right into someone.

"I'm so sorry!" Alexander apologized just before looking up to see a dark-skinned beauty that he had never seen before. He was instantly start struck by her exotic features.

"It's alright." She calmly responded as she picked up the book she had dropped. "I guess you're a bit preoccupied." She sarcastically added.

"I'm so sorry…"

"It's ok…" Her anger was subsiding. She was taken back by Alexander's good looks. His warm eyes hypnotized her. "…You'll just have to buy me coffee sometime. Her confidence and mystery charmed him and he was hooked.

"Please, let me..." He insisted.

"Alright, here is my number and you can give me a call… What's your name?" She asked as she wrote down her number.

"Alexander. What's your name?"

"I guess you'll have to call and find out." She said with a wink as she walked away. Alexander didn't wait long before calling her. He sat around the library until the next passing period, figuring she was in class until then.

"That was quick." Her now familiar voice answered.

"I could hardly wait to call…"

"I'd say so. So where are you taking me, Alexander?"

"The coffee shop just south of campus."

"I'll be by the window in fifteen minutes. Don't make me wait."

"I won't. I promise."

"I'll see you then."

"Wait, what's your name?"

"Nadia." Without saying another word she ended the call. Alexander met her a few minutes later. They sat down and talked for several hours before Nadia suggested that they go out for drinks. She had a favorite bar with a favorite bartender that seemed to be very generous with the alcohol when she ordered. It wasn't long before they were both pretty drunk.

"Let's go back to my place." Alexander suggested.

"Only if you promise to make it a memorable night."

"Don't worry, I will." He winked. Just as they were walking into the apartment Alexander froze when he realized that he had forgotten about his dinner with Rhian. Of course, with all of the alcohol clouding his thoughts, he refocused on Nadia. He walked her over to the couch before making sure that Rhian was asleep.

"What's wrong? You look like you just saw a ghost." Nadia asked sounding annoyed.

"I… I'm fine. I just wanted to make sure my roommate wasn't here."

"Too bad… I like when people are around. It makes it hotter."

"Well it's your lucky day. He is sleeping so we have to be quiet."

"Perfect. Where is your room?" Alexander was now nervous because his bed was still in Rhian's room.

"I want to stay on the couch."

"I underestimated you." She sat him down before undressing for him and climbing onto his lap.

Rhian had been lying in silence since he had returned from the burger place. His anger kept him wide awake. Once it started to get really late, he began to worry about Alexander who had yet to even respond.

What if something happened to him? He thought to himself. He was filled with concern wondering what horrible thing could have happened to Alexander. Just as the mystery of his whereabouts became too much for Rhian, Alexander walked in with Nadia. Rhian heard them stumble in and quickly got back into bed and pretended to go to sleep.

"Do you have condoms?"

"No. I don't use them."

"You're kidding."

"I don't like the way it feels…"

"Are you sure we will be alright?"

"I've never had a problem before… We'll be alright…" Rhian could tell that Alexander was drunk by the way he was slurring his words. It became quiet for a few minutes until Nadia began moaning. Tears ran down Rhian's cheek. He didn't understand why it was so easy for Alexander to ditch him for sex with someone he didn't even know. He didn't understand why Alexander would lie to him and lead him to believe that he was actually interested in making things right. But Rhian was most bothered by something he didn't fully understand. He didn't want to admit it to himself but his heart was broken because it didn't make sense that Alexander couldn't see the potential they had as a couple yet he was easily able to be intimate with a person he didn't even know simply because of the person's body parts. In a way he envied Nadia because she didn't have to try. She didn't have to appreciate anything about Alexander. She simply had to play her cards right and he was stricken. It wasn't fair to Rhian and it made him feel completely undesirable.

Rhian was relieved when the two were done having sex. He closed his eyes and tried to fall asleep when he had the terrible urge to pee.

There is no way I'm leaving this room… I am not going out there right after they finished having sex. He thought to himself. But unfortunately for him the feeling only got worse. He didn't have a choice. He quietly got up and peaked under the door to see if there was any sign of the two of them. The coast was clear so he made his way to the bathroom. He was angry with Alexander for ditching him, he was upset because he was convinced that Alexander was now trying to mess with his head, and he was angry that he couldn't sleep.

Alexander and Nadia were in the other room. He must have heard Rhian enter the bathroom and thought it was a good idea to escort

Nadia back to her place. As soon as Rhian opened the door to exit the bathroom the two walked out of the other room.

"Wow…" Rhian said to himself with disappointment. Alexander was immediately enraged and confronted him.

"Do you have something to say? I don't have to ask for your permission to have sex with someone. You're so self-centered and obsessed. You're not in love with me like you think you are. You don't care about me… You just want to have sex with me and you're just jealous that it wasn't you tonight. IT'S NEVER GOING TO HAPPEN!"

"Dude!" Nadia shouted as she pushed his shoulder in protest of his angry words towards Rhian.

"Alexander, you are too blinded by your arrogance to realize how wrong you are. You know I would die for you if it came to that…"

"Then die and go to hell faggot… I can sleep with whoever I want… And it sure as hell isn't you! Leave me alone!" The impact of his words stung Rhian harshly. The room grew silent as disbelief set in. Alexander, still enraged, felt satisfied with what he had done. He knew that those words would trigger a reaction. Fortunately for Rhian, he was strong enough to simply clench his fists and turn away.

"Goodnight." He coldly responded as he walked back to his room.

"Stop judging me and stay out of my business you freak." Rhian stopped for a second and again clenched his fists before continuing into the bedroom. Nadia had seen enough.

"Wow… I didn't expect a guy like you to be like this… I guess I'll dodge a bullet."

"Nadia, wait! Let me walk you home." He called out to her. Seeing that Rhian was almost to his room he shouted at him. "Look what you did!"

"I don't know what is going on between you too, but whatever it is he didn't deserve that."

"Ignore him! He is just crazy."

"No Alexander, I am crazy for thinking that you were actually a good guy. You are definitely not the kind of guy I want in my life. Please do me a favor and delete my phone number."

"Nadia, let's talk about this."

"There is nothing to talk about. My brother is gay and I would hate to hear you ever say anything like that to him. Those words you just said, you can't take things like that back."

Feeling stupid and still drunk Alexander lied down on the couch and fell asleep. He woke up the next morning to an empty apartment. He couldn't remember what had happened but he knew it wasn't good. He remembered walking in with Nadia, but there was no sign of her. He pretended to forget what had happened with the hope that Rhian wouldn't be so mad at him.]

Hey, what happened last night? I don't remember…

Just leave me alone.

Why? What did I do?

It doesn't matter.

I'm so sorry, Rhian. Whatever I did, I promise that I didn't mean to hurt you. I was drunk.

You're not sorry.

What are you talking about?

I get it. You confirmed everything for me.

What are you talking about?

I get the point. You ditched me to hang out with that slut. It's clear to me now. You don't want to fix things; you just wanted to string me along because you love my attention. I get it. You want me to die and go to hell. Have a great life, Alexander. Alexander's heart skipped a beat. He forgot about Rhian because he was out with that girl. He stared at his phone as he thought about how crazy it all sounded but realized that from Rhian's perspective it made sense. He didn't plan to forget about his friend and he didn't plan to hook up with the girl, it just happened but the timing of it all couldn't have been worse. He felt bad for Rhian because he knew he had gotten his hopes up about fixing things between them but now that Rhian was upset again there was little chance of him accepting an apology. As he continued to think about it, his hurtful words came to mind.

"Then die and go to hell faggot… I can sleep with whoever I want… And it sure as hell isn't you! Leave me alone!" The words began to replay in his head, forcing the guilt to weigh heavily on his heart. It was either now or never. He had to fix things with Rhian or else they were never going to be friends again. He could only hope that it wasn't already too late.

Rhian walked into the apartment and found Alexander sleeping on the couch. He had been sleeping there since the fallout. Rhian wasn't sure if he was doing it because Alexander was trying to stay away from him or because he was giving him space. Either way it was probably for the best. If it were up to Rhian, he would have already left and never returned, but he had signed a lease and couldn't afford to get out of it or pay two places so he made due. He could smell something cooking in the slow-cooker and figured Alexander had made himself dinner. He went into his room and locked the door. Alexander was awaken by the sound of the door shutting and he jumped up. He gently knocked on Rhian's door.

"Hey, I made chili for us to have for dinner… I was hoping we could make up for the other night."

"I suppose." Rhian's sadness could be heard through the door causing Alexander to feel guilty. The boys sat across from each other at the table. Rhian's eyes piercing Alexander's soul from one side of the room. There was more than just sadness in his eyes.

"I'm sorry. I'm sorry about everything. I have been a terrible friend and a terrible person. I should never have put you through any of the shit that I put you through." Rhian didn't say a word. He had no words and though Alexander was right, he felt that it was partly his fault too. Alexander continued, "I was an idiot and I didn't know how to handle the fact that you had feelings for me. I mean I've never had a man tell me that to my face before. I was selfish and childish and I'm sorry."

"It wasn't all your fault. I didn't have to take your rejection so personally. I kept thinking that it was because there was something wrong with me and that I had done something to make you not want to be with me. But I get that you don't want that kind of relationship with me and I have to be ok with it. I'm sorry I didn't accept that."

"Rhian, you really are an amazing guy and you will find someone as good as you and he will be the luckiest guy in the world to have you." Alexander reaffirmed with a smile.

"Thanks."

"So... best friends?"

"I never saw you as anything less." Rhian returned with a rising of his eyebrow.

"Me either. I was just being an ass." There was a lingering awkwardness that could not be explained nor did either one want to acknowledge. Rhian didn't get the closure he wanted and Alexander's apology was not exactly what he expected but he was ok with it for now because he figured time would work out the problems between the two of them.

The sun was shining brightly on a beautiful summer morning. There wasn't a single cloud in the sky as the birds happily chirped their joyous song. The peaceful smell of summer coupled with the vibrant colors of life inspired tranquility and ecstasy. Amidst the heavenly warmth there lay a troubled soul on the floor of her bathroom. She had done something terrible the night before, as suggested by the empty bottle of pills lying next to her. It wasn't supposed to come to this. She was meant to do great things, yet there she was a victim of her own disappointment. No matter the circumstances surrounding her misfortune, she was alive and ready to get what she wanted. She was no longer the sweet girl she used to be. She was changed and ready to show the world who she had become.

The girl took a moment to gather herself for the day ahead before leaving the apartment. She walked through the campus with determination, ready to move anything in her way. She wore her favorite pair of sunglasses, her favorite black skirt and custom-fitted blouse, and an unwavering confidence. It was all part of the presentation from the life she would never live again. As she neared her destination she picked up the phone and dialed Rhian's number.

"Hello?"

"Hey, what are you up to?"

"Eh, nothing much just reading at home how about you?"

"I'm meeting Alexander but he said he was running late, is it ok if I come over and wait for him on your couch?" she said, the taste of disgust lingering on her lips.

"Okay..." Rhian said with hesitation. He didn't know her. So, how did she get his number?

"Cool, I will be there in five minutes!" She arrived promptly five minutes later.

Rhian opened the door and saw the unfamiliar face. Suddenly there was a loud bang and Rhian was on the ground. He looked up at her, paralyzed by fear.

"He will never love you the way he can love me." Alexander walked in; concerned by the sounds he had just heard. He stared at Rhian in disbelief. Rhian took his last breath. Alexander dropped to his knees and reached for his hand but it was too late. Rhian was already gone.

"Rhian!" Alexander woke up in a panic, covered in sweat and with his heart pounding. He looked around the room frantically searching for Rhian until he realized that it was just a dream.

"Are you ok?" Rhian asked as he burst into the living room. Alexander stared at him from the couch he had fallen asleep on. "What's wrong?"

"I had a dream about Amber…"

"The crazy girl you dream about?"

"Yeah."

"What was it about? You seem shaken…"

"She killed you… Right in front of me…"

"Oh…"

"I couldn't deal with that. I couldn't deal with losing you. I'm glad we fixed our problems." Alexander pulled Rhian down on the couch next to him for an unexpected hug. Rhian froze, unsure of what to do with his arms. Alexander had fallen asleep without a shirt on and Rhian was self-conscious about making Alexander uncomfortable. But Alexander held on longer than Rhian expected so he hugged back, contacting the palms of his hands with Alexander's warm skin. Rhian held on, lost in the physical contact. They held for a few seconds longer then Alexander began to let go but before he completely pulled away he grabbed onto Rhian's upper arms and looked into his eyes. He wanted to say something but nothing came out. Rhian waited for an explanation but Alexander silently continued staring into his soul. Overcome with instinct and a deep desire for love, Rhian gently but passionately kissed him. Alexander became paralyzed. This was the first time he had ever kissed a man before, or in this case, the first time a man ever kissed him. Instead of pushing Rhian away, like he thought he would do, Alexander closed his eyes and kissed back.

For Alexander, everything slowed down. Without realizing it, Alexander had pulled Rhian on top of him so that they were face to face. He couldn't hear anything but the sound of their breathing. He couldn't feel anything but Rhian. The surroundings fell silent as he became electrified by the burst of energy from the overwhelming emotions. He became hyperaware of the scent of Rhian's skin in a way he had never been before. It was an intoxicating combination of his shower gel, cologne and Rhian's natural masculine scent. Alexander shifted his hands to Rhian's lower back and pulled him in closer. Rhian's pelvis pushed against Alexander's stomach. He could feel Rhian's soft skin, though different than the soft and silky girls he had been with, was soft and smooth. His hand ran under Rhian's shirt and up the length of his back. While soft, there was a firmness to it that he enjoyed touching. He didn't have to be gentle and yet he wanted to be. He gently caressed Rhian's back, enjoying the soft yet firmness that seemed to ignite a passionate desire in him.

The moment was abruptly ended when Alexander tossed Rhian off of him onto the floor and wiped his mouth with disgust. Rhian hit his back on the edge of the coffee table when he fell.

"I'm not a faggot like you!" He shouted before running into his room for a shirt and storming out of the apartment. Once again Rhian was crying because of Alexander but this time it was more than just his words.

Alexander had no direction in mind when he left the apartment but he knew he had to get out. He walked to a nearby gas station and picked up a pack of cigarettes and a lighter. He wasn't a smoker but he heard it helped to calm people's nerves. It was worth a try considering his hands were shaking. At this point he needed anything to get Rhian and the kiss out of his mind. He lit the cigarette and inhaled its calming effect. This was the first time he had ever smoked and wasn't prepared for the harsh burn he got. He immediately began coughing and threw it to the ground. With the failure of the cigarette and the kiss with Rhian fresh on his mind, he decided that he needed something more than just a cigarette to calm his nerves. He walked the few blocks to the bar and found his way to the back corner. The benefit of having a fake was that he could go out if he wanted to although he never told the others that he had a fake.

Maybe Rhian was right... Maybe there is something between us. Maybe I am gay. He thought as he walked to another nearby bar. The night was still young and his melancholy wasn't going to just go away. He found a place right at the bar before drowning his loud thoughts in whiskey and Coke.

If I'm gay, why didn't I figure it out a long time ago? Isn't that something people just know...? None of it made sense to him. He took a long swig of his drink, looking down at the counter for answers.

"Hey buddy! What are you doing here?" Asked the familiar voice.

"What? Oh… Hey John."

"How's it going? You look like you're concentrating on counting bubbles in your drink."

"No, I was just thinking."

"Sure you were!" John agreed with excitement. The music was loud and there were lots of people dancing.

"Do you want to dance?" Alexander asked innocently. *Where did that come from? Rhian is getting to me.*

"You want to dance… with me?" Alexander's face turned red. *He knew. He knew what I was thinking about.*

"Of course with me!" Alexander tried to sound casual.

"I don't want to make Rhian jealous."

"Forget about him!" Not wanting to press Alexander for details at the risk of making him angrier John agreed and followed him to the dance floor. The two danced as goofy as usual, taking time to mock some of the others who were trying too hard to get attention. They shared a few laughs until a slower song came on. John got close to Alexander and put his arms around his neck.

"Does this make you uncomfortable?"

"Not really... Rhi… I mean, no. I'm comfortable enough in my sexuality to be able to dance with a guy just for fun. It is getting late though. Do you want to come over for a beer? You know, to wind down."

"Well I was just going to go home. But I'll come over for a few."

John found the invitation unusual. His curiosity made him wonder about Rhian but he knew Alexander would eventually tell him. He followed Alexander towards his apartment making small talk on the way. When they walked up to the door Alexander unlocked it. Before John knew what was going on Alexander turned around, wrapped his arms around John and pressed his lips against John's. John kissed him back, while Alexander turned him so that his back faced the door and pushed him up against it, pressing harder on his lips.

Rhian was asleep on the couch in the living room when he was awaken by noisy people walking by. He got up to go to his bed still unsure of what had happened to Alexander. As he was about to go to his room he heard someone messing with the doorknob but no one came in. Then he heard a thump on the door and went the window to investigate. There in front of his very eyes was Alexander and he was kissing John.

John sobered up quickly when he realized that he was about to make a mistake by continuing with Alexander's advances. He protested with a push to Alexander's firm chest.

"What are you doing?" John was defiant.

"I thought you liked to kiss girls *and* boys?"

"I do… But I don't think you know what you are doing?"

"Of course I do! I am trying to have a little fun."

"Look, if this is your way of getting back at Rhian for something, don't use me. I'm not like that. I like Rhian, he's a really good guy and if you hadn't already noticed, that's not something *you* should take lightly."

"Rhian has nothing to do with anything!"

"Buddy, I know this isn't really you. If you really want to kiss a guy, go in there and kiss the one that's yours."

"What are you talking about? I'm not gay…" Alexander responded increasing discomfort. John could see the confusion on his friend's face so he placed a comforting hand on Alexander's shoulder.

"You two have something special. Don't ruin it." Alexander swatted away John's hand and turned away. John quietly walked away. Alexander wanted to punch something. He didn't understand why, he just felt so overwhelmed that he needed to go punch something and scream. The night had yielded much insight but there was nothing conclusive. The only thing he was certain about was that he had become enchanted by Rhian's kiss.

That weekend he decided to visit home. He sighed with relief when he arrived to the familiar house. It had been a stressful week and he needed to forget about all of his problems. He made plans to go out later that night with some of his high school buddies. They met up at a local bar where they always talked about going when they were old enough. While sitting at the table with his friends he saw a familiar face sitting at the bar. He decided to approach her.

"Hey Cara, how are you?"

"Alexander! I'm doing well, how are you?"

"Better now. It's been too long." Alexander couldn't remember the last time he had seen her.

"It has… A lot has changed since high school. I'm engaged now."

"That's great. He is a very lucky guy."

"I feel like I'm the lucky one. He treats me like I'm his queen. He is everything I never knew I wanted."

"That's great. I'm happy for you, Cara."

"Thanks. How about you? Are you seeing anyone?" Alexander thought about Rhian's smiling face.

"No, I've been very busy with school. I'll never become President if I am distracted."

"Sometimes distraction is a good thing. I'm sure you will find someone who will sweep you off your feet."

"Shouldn't I be the one doing the sweeping?"

"Life is full of surprises, some good and some bad. Appreciate both." She winked at him. A kiss on the cheek and a firm hug and she was gone. I was hard to mask the depression he was experiencing but his friend Jake knew that something was bothering him. He knew Alexander well enough to give him the space he needed while he figured things out. Alexander went home early that night to be alone with his thoughts.

Is it unbelievable that I enjoyed the kiss? He always brags about being a good kisser. But why does it bother me? We are close and I love and care about him… as a friend… but more? I don't think it's more than that. Yeah, skin is skin and love is love right? Or did I just say that because he said that? If it's true, then what's the problem? I'm not gay! That's the problem. I didn't feel anything after that kiss with John and I wouldn't feel anything if I kissed him again. It was just the thrill of a new experience. That's all.

Chapter 8

"Do you believe that anything is possible?" Rhian lay in his bed looking up and imaging the stars.

"I do… I think that we can do anything we want, as long as it's within reason… What impossible thing are you dreaming about?" Alexander asked openly into the darkness.

"Sometimes I fear that I'll actually never achieve my dreams. It's like I need to get my head out of the clouds." Rhian confessed his despair. He felt Alexander gently place his hands on his bare shoulder. It calmed him and sent a warming sensation throughout his body.

"You are one of the most amazing people and you should never give up on your dreams, I love you too much to let you do that…" Alexander reassured with a yawn. In an attempt to get closer to Alexander Rhian turned shifted his body over toward Alexander but instead rolled over the edge, hitting the ground with a thud. It was only a dream; one of those awful dreams that let the hope stay for a moment before it is snatched away from you by the reality of consciousness.

To love is to accept and embrace all that comprises a person including past, present, and future. Though there may be disagreement, at the end of the day love is what binds two souls together. Through time and space loves warm comfort can endure the tribulations of life but it is the weakness of the heart that proves to be the true challenge of its strength. The heart whispers its true desires in the form of our dreams and when ignored it is then that love begins to die. What a waste to let a true love die an untimely death when the only thing we ever want is to be loved.

After a failed attempt at kissing John, Alexander began hanging out at the local bar after his classes. He used the fake ID he borrowed from one of the lacrosse players to get in but by the end of the week they didn't ask for ID. In a college town, the rules about drinking are often overlooked because of how loudly money talks. One night, while enjoying his fourth beer, he noticed a droplet of water that had condensed on the outer surface of the glass. He watched as it made its way down the side of the glass to the surface of the table.

I know how you feel... He thought to himself. *You feel like you are falling holding on to whatever you can, losing a part of yourself with every inch you fall you try to grab on. And you try so hard to hold on but there is no way you can stop the inevitable. You simply give up and drown among the other fallen drops before you. You are just another drop falling into a puddle where you don't matter.* He stared at the beer in the glass as he thought about the promise he had made to himself that he would never touch the stuff. He looked down at his bare forearm, remembering what it was like to worry about people seeing his bruises.

Now vulnerable to his emotions, Alexander remembered the night he was beaten for grabbing a drink from the fridge without asking. He was only five years old and had already been passed around from house to house. He had been told to stay in his room that night but he was thirsty. He walked out into the kitchen where he could hear the television in the other room. He could still smell the musty house as he remembered walking up to the fridge. He opened the door and saw the milk, sitting cold and inviting in its glass container. He reached for it with his little hands but when he had it in his grip it was too heavy for him. It fell to the ground with a loud crash, launching milk and broken glass all over the kitchen floor. He was so stunned that he didn't hear his foster dad come into the room. He felt a sudden pressure on his arm as the man grabbed him with all his strength and threw him into the next room. He then came in and began kicking Alexander who lied helplessly on the ground. The last thing he remembered from that night was looking up at his foster parent as he sat back down on the couch and continued drinking his beer as if nothing had happened. The next morning the man forced him to wear a sweater to school even though it was exceptionally hot in order to cover up his bruises.

"If you tell any of your teachers… I can do much worse." The man threatened. This was only the beginning of his horrible experience in that house.

As Alexander sat at the bar he imagined the bruises on his arms and legs. He thought about the many nights he went to bed crying from the physical abuse and helpless feeling he lived with for so many years. It was a lonely time in his life, far removed from where he was now. He remembered hiding in the cold dark basement, shaking with fear and wishing that he had a mother to come down and tell him *It's ok sweetie, Mommy is here. Everything will be alright. I love you.* He remembered sitting in school and thinking about how he wanted to hear a father tell him *Son, I'm so very proud of you. I love you.* But he didn't have that until Mr. and Mrs. Thomas adopted him, and even that was a struggle. This loneliness he felt all though his early years of life was what allowed him to relate to Rhian when his parents kicked him out of their lives. It was one of the reasons why he was so adamant about being there for him. He knew that feeling of loneliness better than anyone of Rhian's friends and although he was no longer that lonely child, a part of him still was.

Yes, it was a lifetime ago and so much had changed but he was still very aware of his past. While he felt disconnected from his parents, he really loved them. When he first came into their home he hoped that they would be warm and loving towards him because they were both genuinely good people. But they weren't quick to give him hugs and praise him for being himself. In fact, they were very strict about getting him into a regimented life, which was exactly what he needed. He was naturally a warm, loving person with a big heart but because of the abusive environments he had been in, Alexander harbored distrust towards people in authority and was considered a problematic child by most of his teachers. The Thomas' struggled with him when he first came into their home because they had to gain his trust. They had to make sure that they were setting him up for success in his future and although that required them to be more authoritative, they cared about him enough to do that. The most important thing at the time was for him to learn to have a routine. It didn't take long for him to turn around and start showing promise but their parenting methods didn't change much. Alexander wished they were more expressive of their love, but he knew they loved him.

By the time he finished drinking his emotions away, it was late and he was drunk. He found his way home, and stumbled into the apartment smelling of cigarettes and alcohol. Without putting much thought into it, Alexander stripped to his underwear and carefully climbed into bed with Rhian. He snuggled up to him gently and sighed before falling asleep.

Rhian had woken up when he heard Alexander trip over something in the living room but he remained motionless. His heart skipped a beat when Alexander began shuffling around the room and suddenly lied down next to him. Rhian fought the urge to push Alexander away until he heard Alexander quietly crying. He became confused about why Alexander was lying next to him crying but instead of turning around to comfort him, he simply lied there, melted into Alexander's warmth and faded into sleep. Rhian woke up to an empty bed the next morning. Curious where Alexander had disappeared to, Rhian looked around the apartment for any sign of him but he was gone. That night, while Rhian was lying in bed, a drunk Alexander wandered into the room again and lied down next to him. He was again confused but refused to disrupt the blissful feeling of being close to him. He knew that the first time was probably just a drunken mistake, but twice in a row?

Over the next few days Alexander continued to do the same thing as before. He walked in to Rhian's room while he was asleep and lie down next to him, holding him tightly. He first held Rhian after his parents rejected him.He couldn't exactly talk to Rhian about what was going on in his head because he didn't fully understand it yet. He was very confused about his feelings towards Rhian and the kiss. He spent his days busy with class and his nights alone with his thoughts at the bar until he was drunk enough to come home and sleep in Rhian's bed. Rhian didn't say anything about it to anyone, especially Alexander. He didn't want to make him mad but mostly he didn't want Alexander to stop. He knew there was something wrong but he would have to wait for Alexander to tell him about it.

Alexander needed comfort from the physical closeness because he couldn't put his feelings into words and he didn't trust anyone else with his emotions. Rhian made him feel safe and important to an extent that he had never experienced with anyone else besides his parents. That safety he felt didn't change just because they hadn't spoken in days. He didn't understand what was wrong but it didn't matter because it was Rhian and he knew that everything would be alright as long as he was around.

"Hey, Alexander?" Rhian cautiously approached Alexander one morning while Alexander was studying in his room.

"Yeah?" He asked with a smile that melted Rhian's heart.

"Well, I was thinking…" The tension suddenly increasing as neither one knew where the conversation was heading. Alexander was afraid that Rhian would ask about his sudden change in sleeping accommodations. Rhian was curious about his elusive behavior but he was more concerned with his inability to express his troubles. He considered asking the question they both feared but instead remained for an uncomfortable moment.

"You were thinking?" Alexander finally broke the silence.

"That we should get the group together for drinks tonight. We haven't gotten together in a few weeks." Alexander responded with a big smile of surprise.

"Sure… I would love to see everyone."

"Fantastic! Let's plan to meet for dinner at seven."

"Sounds good to me!" Rhian was put off by Alexander's bright mood. It wasn't what he expected especially after their new sleeping arrangements. He knew it was only a matter of time before Alexander opened up so he let it go but he was still angry that Alexander was sending mixed signals and was now pretending like everything was completely ok. Leena volunteered to have the gathering at her place as usual since she had the space and hosting skills.

That night Leena noticed that Rhian and Alexander weren't all over each other as usual.

"What's going on? Trouble in paradise?" She directed her question at Alexander.

"What do you mean?"

"You two haven't said a word to each other and you look like you're trying not to catch a cold from him… What's wrong?"

"Nothing… I just… I've been enjoying the music. I can't force him to dance with me. Right Rhian?" He put Rhian on the spot.

"Well I wasn't sure if I was allowed to dance with you." He snarled.

"Of course you are!" Alexander's too-good-to-be-true mood was back. Rhian, not wanting to cause the others to ask any more questions began dancing with Alexander. At first they avoided eye contact, making small talk to make the situation less awkward. The talking worked until the first few notes a familiar song began playing. It was one that they had danced to before and Rhian always got out of control. He closed his eyes becoming hypnotized by the beat, grinding slowly. Rhian was channeling his most passionate desires on the dance floor and Alexander was enjoying every move. His body pulsed with the shockwave of energy he felt from Rhian's sensual movements. Alexander hadn't noticed that he was fully aroused until Rhian began focusing his motions on gently encouraging his erection. The feeling was intensified by thrill of the setting but Alexander didn't last long before he realized exactly what was happening. He immediately pushed Rhian away and left.

Rhian almost fell down but was able to find his balance. He looked around but only saw Alexander's back as he walked towards the door. Without saying anything to the others he followed Alexander out. Exiting the club he could feel the chill of the air wake him up and heighten his senses. He could smell the fumes from the gas station nearby, he could feel the slight pain his eyes experienced from adjusting to the streetlights, and he could barely hear. There was a moment of confusion due to this overwhelming environment, but after he adjusted clarity came to him and he remembered why he had left in the first place. He walked towards the apartment and wondering what he was going to say, what he could say. He thought about what he was feeling but couldn't think of a way to verbalize it because it was much more than just disappointment. It was confusion, fear, anger, sadness, happiness, worry, desire, and passion. He walked in to find Alexander sitting on the couch. When he walked in Alexander stood up to walk away.

With his hand on his shoulder Rhian stopped Alexander from walking away again. This was his only chance to test the feelings he had been experiencing in the past few weeks. He pulled Alexander back to face him. Alexander didn't resist, instead he slowly turned towards Rhian looking down at first, and then tracing the outline of his figure with his eyes. He felt excited but nervous as their eyes locked on each other, and he began leaning in. Rhian was also nervous because he always thought of himself as being the passive lover and was now naturally assuming a role of dominance as he grabbed Alexander by the back of the head and brought him in to close the distance. That was all the control that Rhian needed. The moment Alexander's lips touched Rhian's the shockwave of emotion and pleasure they had felt a few minutes before had returned but with an increased intensity that made them lose control. Rhian's senses were heightened for the second time that night. After that Alexander took control and knew what to do. It wasn't something he had to think about, it was pure instinct. Rhian raised his hand up to grab Alexander's head with both hands but Alexander stopped him before he could get it all the way up and instead, he willingly kissed him passionately. Alexander guided Rhian to the bedroom as they continued kissing, while his hands moved up and down Rhian's body.

Alexander walked Rhian up to the door and pressed him up against it while using one hand to turn the doorknob and the other to feel Rhian's chest. The room was dark and that's how Alexander wanted it. As they kissed Alexander continued pushing Rhian towards the bed. When they reached the foot of the bed, Rhian fell back and Alexander began slowly removing his shirt. Rhian followed silently. Alexander passionately kissed Rhian on the lips and then down the length of his neck.

Without warning Alexander punched the wall and climbed off of Rhian. He had a look of disgust as he gathered his things and aggressively dressed himself without saying a word. He didn't dare look at Rhian who was still on the bed. With little light in the room it was difficult to find all of his clothes so he decided to forfeit his socks to the darkness. He didn't dare turn on the light because that would certainly mark the end of his *hetero* sexuality and the end of life as he knew it. He had to keep things hidden in the dark. It was better that way and as long as he didn't see Rhian in that room everything was going to be ok.

"Dammit! What was that?" Alexander asked himself out loud once he was able to talk again. "What did I just do?" It wasn't supposed to happen. He wasn't supposed to kiss Rhian again, much less almost have sex with him. Alexander wandered the streets, alone with his thoughts until it was late enough that he was the only one walking around.

Alexander entered the quiet apartment nervously anticipating a conversation with Rhian that would require him to explain himself. He wrestled internally about whether or not to talk to him. He knew that after his dramatic exit there was no way he could avoid talking to his friend about it; if anything he had to at least make sure that Rhian was ok. When he arrived he found Rhian sleeping in bed and sat down next to him.

"Hey Rhian, are you awake?" No response. "I'm so sorry about earlier. I'm sorry about the past few weeks; or months now. I'm sorry for my immature reactions and I'm sorry I hurt you. I'm only human and sometimes I do things without thinking… and I hurt people without meaning to," He gently stroked Rhian's shoulder with his hand. "I don't know what all these feelings I have mean but I need you to know that I never meant to hurt you. I love you. You know that… right?" He lied down with Rhian, facing him as if they were having bed talk. "I know you do. I do. I think you are an amazing person. I think you are a strong, loving, brilliant man. I just don't know how to tell you what you mean to me because I honestly don't know to what extent. I mean… my feelings for you really confuse me. You are always my best friend but at times I see you as more and I just don't know how to express that or how to tell you. I know you care about me. I don't doubt that. That's why I hate hurting you when I do. I really care about you and I want you in my life… forever, but I was never attracted to you that way… then the kiss. Does that make me gay? Where do those lines get crossed and where am I crossing them. I don't even understand what happened or how it happened. I am scared of being judged, of being hurt, of going through what you went through." Alexander sighed deeply before letting out a yawn. He couldn't keep his eyes open for much longer so he got comfortable and began to shut his eyes. "I don't think I could do what you do. I don't think I'm as strong as you are. I wish I were as brave." He drifted off into sleep.

How did we end up like this? Rhian asked himself as he turned in his bed the next morning to a sleeping Alexander. He wanted to kiss him but it was now morning and Alexander had a tendency to revert to his "straight side" once the sun came up. Rhian felt dirty and confused because just a few hours before he was convinced that Alexander finally understood what he knew but instead Alexander ran off. He felt completely undesirable and now Alexander was in his bed, again. It was all too confusing. He ignored the sleeping giant, leaving the comfort of his bed in preparation for the day ahead. As he brushed his teeth, Rhian considered the situation he was now in. What had started out as a simple friendship was now complicated beyond his comfort zone. While he still felt the special bond between them, he also felt inadequate. It was a hodgepodge of emotion that he had never experienced with anyone else. Rhian had two options: endure the turmoil until Alexander was ready to open up or confront him and risk losing the close physical contact he relished.

The boys shared a level of intimacy that crossed many traditional boundaries. It happened subtly yet neither one saw it as a problem until Rhian developed feelings for Alexander. Alexander viewed Rhian as a *girl* friend, because he was gay. But what he didn't realize was that he had treated Rhian like a *girlfriend*, and it was comfortable that way. Rhian didn't see it that way. To Rhian, love was independent of sex. It was unfair to him that Alexander would treat him like his girlfriend and then deny him the privilege of being exactly what he was to him.

I shouldn't have let myself feel the things I did... But none of it was on purpose. We accidentally fell in love and I know he feels what I feel! I can't explain it but I know with all my heart that I'm not imagining this. He kissed back and then last night... He probably just doesn't know how to process all of this. He is in love with me too... Rhian's conclusion gave him some peace of mind for the time being.

Later that day Rhian decided to go to the grocery store.

"I'm planning on going to the grocery store later... I have to pick up some things for the party this weekend. Do you want to come with me?"

"Uh... Yeah. I guess I could use some new razors and shampoo."

"I'll be going in about an hour."

"Ok." Alexander's words seemed to linger heavily. Rhian quickly sat down next to him with concern.

"What is going on with you? I'm worried."

"I don't know, Rhi. I feel like I have nothing to complain about yet it's like something is missing... I don't know how to explain it." Alexander never abbreviated his name because it was something that bothered Rhian, but this time he found it cute.

"Like your life is seemingly perfect but there's still a void? You can't ignore it, you can't hide it and you feel like everyone but you knows what's wrong. It fills your dreams and no matter what you do to numb it, the emptiness still consumes you."

"Yeah… like that… I mean is that weird…"

"No… no it's not." Rhian looked up at Alexander who was looking right at him desperate for an answer. That moment captured what Rhian was to Alexander; security. Rhian was addicted to Alexander and Alexander was addicted Rhian. He could feel the emotion building up inside of him, the words on the tip of his tongue. *I love you.* Three simple words but he kept them to himself. This wasn't the right time or place.

"I am trouble. I cause people to want to keep their distance. I screw people up. It's why my parents abandoned me. Something about me tells people to run."

"Don't you ever say that!" It was strange seeing Alexander so vulnerable but it was clear by the mention of his biological parents that he was struggling with more than just his feelings about Rhian.

"Well it's true… I'm going nowhere. All I do is hurt the people around me."

"That's ridiculous. Stop saying that. You are an amazing person who I…" He paused awkwardly. "…Care about. You are depressed not worthless. Stop bringing yourself down."

"I hurt you, I have wasted my parents' money on this school and I've wasted our friends' time. I'm not going to amount to anything. I came from nowhere, abandoned because I was nothing and that's all I'll ever be. I'll never find anyone to love me because I'm nothing!" Something in Rhian couldn't take the verbal abuse. Alexander had put him through Hell in the past few weeks and now he was trying to get Rhian to convince him that he was worth loving. Yes, he was genuinely struggling with these feelings of depression, but it was obvious that he was trying to get Rhian to defend him.

"Stop! This isn't fair. You can't make me do this!" Alexander stopped talking and stared quietly waiting for Rhian to speak. "I have told you countless times just how amazing you are. I don't need to keep doing that. You are depressed and you need to figure out how to get out of it because no one else can do that for you. You can't say that you'll never find someone because you have. It's not my fault that you can't see that but it's not fair that you want me to sit here and tell you that you will when I'm standing right here telling you that I am in love with you and I would do anything for you." Rhian was shaking with adrenaline. Alexander just maintained eye contact but refrained from saying anything. "You made it crystal clear that you don't want me as your boyfriend, so why do you expect me to act like I am? You push me away then you hold me close." Alexander's eyes widened. He knew Rhian was talking about their sleeping arrangements. "Stop breaking my heart. You either need to stop doing what you're doing or you need to come to terms with the truth. I don't know how much more I can handle. This game of emotional tug-of-war isn't fair to me. You know you could have me in a heartbeat, so why do you keep playing with my heart. You want someone who treats you the way I do… but I don't understand why you don't want to see me. You expect me to remind you of who you are because you don't even believe in yourself anymore but why am I the only one you want constantly reminding you of who you are? You can't accept that your heart calls for me. Is it because I'm not good enough for you? What do I have to do to be worthy of your love?" Rhian was out of breath.

"You sound like a desperate ex…"

"I won't let you play games with me anymore."

"Rhian wait!" Alexander shouted but it was too late. Rhian was gone and he wasn't going to stop him. "I don't care what these feelings are anymore! Everything has gotten way out of control and it's all too complicated. I'm straight and that's what I'm sticking with!" Alexander spent the rest of the night alone with his thoughts.

Rhian didn't return that night. Instead, he spent his night with Leena and Sebastian.

"I know that you think that there is something there, and you might be right, but the uncertainty that it causes is too much and you are just going to keep hurting until you stop letting him control your emotions. You are strong and you will be fine without him." Sebastian understood where Rhian was coming from but he didn't want to see his friend brought down by another situation he couldn't control especially after the grief his parents caused him.

"You're in an unhealthy relationship and you need to stay away from him. He may be depressed and need someone but he can't come to you. He needs someone who can talk to him without bias. If he talks to you, your feelings may get in the way. You will only tell him what is in your best interest." Leena explained.

"But I have tried to remove my feelings when he talks to me. Is it still wrong?"

"Yes, because if what he is feeling isn't what you think it is, you are leading him on the way he did to you even if you don't mean to. That boy loves you, there is no question about that, but you can't make him see what he doesn't want to. He has to realize everything all on his own for it to be real, which may take a long time. You should walk away. I love you sweetie and so do the rest of us."

"We care about you and we don't want to see you going through anymore. He isn't worth it." Sebastian added.

"You're right. I will walk away."

Chapter 9

Today was terrible. I thought this would get better for me but it hasn't. I wish I could take it back... but I can't. I wish that I could undo the damage that I did to our friendship. I thought that telling him how I felt would help me learn to get over him or give me some closure but it hasn't. I hate that I'm feeling so much I don't understand. I am so sad. Not depressed like before, I am just sad. I want to cry. I miss him. I don't want to lose sight of my future but I can't help but feel lost. I feel like I have ruined what we had. I told myself over and over again not to say anything because in the end it will all work out. Nothing has actually changed and yet it feels like nothing is the same. I can't explain it. I am so lost and I am broken. I love him so much. I love him; I don't just care about him. I love him. I want to be with him. He makes me feel safe and he makes me feel loved. I used to think he was just beautiful but he is so much more. While I do find him sexy beyond belief, it is his heart and soul that I'm in love with. I have never felt this way before. It feels as though I could fly when I'm with him. I feel that I can achieve any dream as long as he is there to hold my hand and tell me that I can. The sound of his voice triggers feelings that I can't explain. The look in his eye can disarm even the roughest of my exteriors. When I feel his touch it is as if all of my problems melt away. The mere thought of him sends me into an overload of emotions. It's an exciting, overwhelming, frightening feeling.

Everything about him intensifies the most powerful feelings in me. When he is present I can't think about anything but him. When he isn't here all I want to do is talk about him. He shakes me down to the core. He brings out the best and worst in me making me most vulnerable when I'm with him. Knowing all of this makes life difficult because I can't be with him; because I can't explain to him what he means to me. I know that I would stand by him no matter what. He may think that he could find a better match but I honestly believe that no one would support him, love him, and encourage him the way I would. The way I do. We are bound for life through time and space… there is no going back. This is going to be a long road. But I would wait a lifetime if that were what it took to spend even just one day in his arms as his and only his.

Alexander read the words from Rhian's journal over and over again. He had never heard anyone talk about him that way and while it made him feel uniquely important it also troubled him.

No one has ever said or thought any of this about me… especially a guy. Men don't feel like this about me. Could I feel this way about him?

Alexander was haunted by Rhian's words. It wasn't his fault that the journal was left carelessly opened to the last entry but he would have to deal with these feelings of confusion. Finals were over and he was getting ready to head back home for winter break. They hadn't spoken in a long time because they avoided each other at every opportunity. That night their friends were getting together for a party before the break. Alexander considered ditching the party and leaving early but he had a few things he had to take care of before leaving so he figured he'd just go for a little while. If he didn't feel comfortable he could always leave.

He arrived before most of the others had gotten there. The only person he knew was Matt. He hadn't seen Matt since the night Rhian jumped in the water but he wasn't going to bring that up.

"Hey Alexander!" Matt called out from the kitchen. "How's it going?"

"It's going. How are you?"

"I'm doing well. I'm about to go downstairs to hang out for a bit. Come with!" Matt didn't wait for a response. Alexander curiously followed. There were a few others gathered around a coffee table engaging in a seemingly serious discussion. They were so involved in their conversation that they didn't notice Matt and Alexander join. Matt jumped in on the conversation when he realized that they were talking about recreational drug use. Alexander was thrown off by the topic and didn't have any input so he remained silent but listened carefully.

"Rhian! How's it going?" Matt called out, breaking Alexander's concentration on the conversation. "Come sit with me dude!" Alexander could tell that Rhian was uncomfortable but he didn't show it. Rhian and Alexander locked eyes for a brief moment, igniting their hearts. Rhian broke the look and made his way to the couch with Matt and Alexander. Rhian hadn't told Matt about the ongoing troubles he had with Alexander so Matt had no idea the predicament he had just put Rhian in. They continued the discussion while Rhian and Alexander sat awkwardly trying not to touch on the terribly uncomfortable couch.

"If I were offered a hard drug and I knew I'd be ok I'd probably try it." Alexander broke his silence. Rhian looked up at him with uncertainty. He never thought Alexander would say something like that.

"You would?" Matt asked curiously.

"Sure. If I knew that I'd be ok. I would try it. I've always been curious about trying something hard."

"I'm sure Rhian could help you out with that." Matt replied without missing a beat. Rhian and Alexander both turned bright red. "Fine… put your money where your mouth is." Matt set down a bottle containing a very small amount of liquid.

"What is it?"

"This is my girl… Lucy?"

"What is… Lucy?"

"Lucy in the Sky with Diamonds…"

"Oh!" Alexander pretended to know what it was." Rhian was wide-eyed.

"So?"

"Yeah… I'll try it. How do I do it?"

"You just drop some on your eyeball. Not too much though." Matt handed him the bottle as Rhian remained silently shocked. Alexander lifted up the bottle but Rhian unexpectedly slapped the bottle out of his hand.

"Don't!" Rhian was finally able to interrupt.

"What the hell dude!" Matt looked at Rhian with confusion. Rhian ignored Matt and turned to Alexander with pleading eyes.

"Please don't do it. I don't want you to get hurt."

"I don't need your permission to do anything. Just leave already. You're making me uncomfortable." Rhian was hurt by how cold Alexander was being, but in the moment neither one was thinking clearly. They were both angry, for different reasons, and neither one would back down.

"I'm not leaving until I know you are safe. If you're going to do this I'm going to take care of you."

"No, you need to leave right now! I don't fucking trust you. You're going to wait until I am fucked up and then you are going to try to take advantage of me! Go!" Everyone awkwardly looked at Alexander. His outburst made everyone feel uneasy about his presence.

"I would never do that and you know it! You know me! I can't believe you would even suggest it." Rhian held back tears as he stood up to leave. He didn't want to abandon Alexander because he knew that he might do something stupid, but he couldn't stay there after what he had just said. He was heartbroken that Alexander's opinion of him was so atrocious. He walked away without saying another word.

"You're not in love with me. You're just in lust with me but you can't fuck me… pervert!" Rhian ran up the stairs with tears in his eyes. He bumped into John who saw his distress and hugged him without saying a word. Rhian cried into John's shoulder, finding comfort in his embrace. John offered to walk with him wherever he was headed.

Alexander had dropped the acid in his eye but still hadn't felt the effects. He began to open up to Matt about the problems he was having with Rhian.

"Dude, why did you yell at him like that? That kid would never try to hurt you."

"I just don't trust him anymore… He kissed me and then the other night… We almost… had sex."

"So what?"

"I'm not gay!"

"Alexander, it isn't nineteen fifty anymore! You love him and you know it… why are you running from it? He obviously loves you back. I would give anything to have someone look at me the way he looks at you."

"I can't love him like that…. I'm straight."

"Dude, I'm straight but if I had someone, girl or guy, look at me and care about me as much as Rhian cares about you, I wouldn't even think twice about it. You are in love with him. Stop fighting it before you lose him forever… I know him well enough to say that a person like him is not easy to find. Trust me, you don't want to let this one get away." Matt's statement was shockingly honest.

"I need another beer if I'm going to keep talking about this."

"Just be careful not to get lost. The acid should start working its magic soon." Alexander was so preoccupied with thoughts of Rhian that he didn't hear what Matt said. As he reached the top of the stairs, he began to feel warm so he went outside for some fresh air. Alexander walked into the night with no direction planned. He was following the song of the siren in his head. The siren's song led him to the garden. He was completely silent throughout his journey, yet he didn't notice that his phone ring several times and continued uninterrupted. It was after hours so the building was locked and the rooftop garden was not accessible, but a few months before they had discovered the emergency ladder hidden behind one of the walls that faced another part of the building. There was a short wall that he would have to jump over but it wasn't a challenge. He quickly climbed up to the top but when he got there he could no longer hear the song of the siren so he sat down.

A black figure was standing in front of him, who was now seated and staring into his hands. He slowly looked up to see who it was.

"Hello, Alexander."

"Hi… Who are you?"

"I'm death. I've come to take you with me." The figure wore a black cloak, which covered the face, Alexander wasn't sure who it was but he was intrigued. He had lost track of time and wasn't aware that he was still tripping on the acid. He hadn't taken much but it was clearly enough to cause this hallucination.

"What does your face look like?" He was still in disbelief and remained calm for the moment. The cloaked figure didn't respond but suddenly two red eyes appeared from inside the hood and they shined intensely. The sight frightened Alexander and he backed away while staring into the red eyes. He knew the presence in front of him was a sinister one. He pulled out his phone and tried to flash its light at the figure thinking that perhaps light would make it disappear but his phone didn't turn on. He sat in horror as the figure leaned in to say something. The red eyes weren't glowing anymore but the mere presence of this figure was still frightening.

"I am here to take you with me… fly away with me." The figure pointed at the ledge. Alexander would have to jump. "I am your angel, here to make it all better for you." Alexander was petrified now paralyzed with fear. He closed his eyes and put his arms over his head in an attempt at getting a grip of reality. As he sat there trying to figure out what was real and what wasn't, he thought about Rhian and how he had been so terrible to him. He thought about how things would be better if he were dead. All of the anger and hate that he ever felt seemed to focus on himself in that moment. He opened his eyes and looked down as if considering the offer. He had never before been so dispirited but he could now understand why Rhian was upset when he criticized the young people who committed suicide. For one brief but impactful moment he understood.

"Will it hurt?"

"It will feel like you are flying. You'll be free as a bird." Alexander looked down at his phone, which was now working. There was a text from Rhian. *Are you ok? Please let me know that you are alright. I'm worried.* He became overwhelmed with guilt because he had been so horrible to him and yet he still cared so much about him. He decided that it was best for both of them if he didn't come back. He started to type a message out.

"I just want to say goodbye…" Alexander said to the figure. *I'm sorry for everything I did to you. I won't be able to hurt you anymore. Goodbye.* Alexander began to cry hysterically as he looked down at his phone. Not twenty seconds had gone by till his phone began to ring; it was Rhian.

"Don't answer that. You will only hurt him more if you talk to him now." The figure spoke with authority.

"Hello." Alexander answered with a somber tone.

"Where are you?"

"I'm sorry for everything... It will all be over soon." He spoke with a low note but with resolve. It was apparent in his voice that he had been crying.

"Alexander where are you? I will not lose you."

"Where do you think I am?"

"The garden?"

"Yeah."

"I am on my way. Don't move. Please, just stay put. I can't lose you! Forget about what happened between us. If I ever meant anything to you, even if it was just as a friend, use that to wait for me." Alexander hung up without saying another word so Rhian knew that he had to hurry. He and John quickly got into his car and Rhian drove as fast as he could, running several stop signs and even a few lights.

"Do it now before he comes! I am taking you tonight, so either you do it or I will!" The figure again spoke, this time with a roar. Alexander heard the screeching of car tires and heard Rhian call out his name. He looked back up at the cloaked figure with fear. Alexander was lying on the floor in the fetal position. "I don't want to die! I don't want to die! Help me Rhian! He wants to take me with him! He wants me to kill myself! Please help!"

The figure was yelling at Alexander with a voice like thunder. "You are a waste of life! The world would be better off without you!"

"I'm not a waste of life! I'm not horrible! Shut up! Stop talking!" Alexander remained in the fetal position against the wall until he had heard Rhian's voice. He changed his position and lied face down on the cold cement floor. Rhian quickly climbed the ladder onto the rooftop.

"No you aren't a waste of life and you're not horrible!"

"He keeps yelling at me. He wants to take me with him! Please Rhian don't let him take me!" Alexander was in a panic.

"It's not real, Alexander! He isn't here!" Rhian said to him as he ran over to him and lied down next to him. Alexander began to hit his head on the ground.

"Make it stop!" Rhian cradled his head to prevent him from hitting his head again. He held on to him tightly and began whispering in his ear as he ran his fingers through Alexander's hair to soothe him.

"It's going to be ok. I'm here now and he can't hurt you. Everything will be ok, I promise."

"I don't want to die!" Alexander continued repeating those words as he began sobbing.

"It's ok Alexander, I'm here and I'm not going to let anything bad happen to you. I'll always be here. I'm not going to let anything happen to you. I love you…" Rhian repeated those words for several minutes while gently stroking Alexander's hair. After a few minutes Alexander calmed down enough to realize that it was all a hallucination. He was breathing heavily and shivering uncontrollably. He had left the party without his jacket and although it wasn't freezing cold, it was cold enough that he should have worn something more than a t-shirt. Rhian could see how cold he was so he took off his jacket without giving it a second thought. He felt the cold against his skin but he knew he had to help Alexander warm up. Once Alexander had warmed up a bit and was able to talk, Rhian decided it was time to help him down the stairs.

"I'm going to go down the ladder with you but I will be holding you the whole way down ok?"
"Ok." Rhian climbed over the edge and onto the ladder. Alexander followed. The boys climbed down at the same time with Alexander on the inside and Rhian wrapped around him but holding onto the ladder serving as a safety in case he got the idea to jump. They finally made it to the ground where John was waiting in worry. The three made their

way back to the car. Rhian drove them back to his place but stopped to pick up a hot drink for Alexander to help him warm up. He had been really cold from being out for so long in the cold.

"I'm getting a hot chocolate, what do you want?"

"I'll have one as well." John said.

"I'll have a coffee if that's ok…"

Rhian was still in shock about the entire ordeal and spoke softly. He handed him the coffee as they drove back to his place. When they arrived, Rhian brought him back to his room and laid him down on his bed. He lay down next to him as they had done before but this time Rhian was so upset that he couldn't sleep. He was also worried that he might get up or that something might happen to him as a result of the drug so he stayed awake and made sure he was ok. He took his pulse throughout the night and made sure he was covered up and warm. Between checking up on Alexander and trying to relax, Rhian spent the better part of the rest of the night thinking about what had happened. He was so angry but he was also relieved that Alexander was ok. After a few hours he finally fell asleep.

Alexander woke up alone in Rhian's bed as he had many times in the recent past. He thought to himself how he could make things as painless as possible for both of them and decided to remove himself from Rhian's life by telling him that he didn't want to be friends with him. Of course he knew Rhian wouldn't understand and would try to stop him but there was no other way to deal with it. For his sake he had to push him away.

"I don't think we should be friends." He looked down at his feet with his face angled as if he were looking behind Rhian's left shoulder. Rhian reached up and touched Alexander's face with his left hand gently. He turned Alexander's blank expression, which by this point was turning into a sad expression, to face him. He locked eyes. Rhian's eyes begging for answers and Alexander's eyes saddened by what he had just suggested. Rhian was overtaken with anger and dropped his hand from Alexander's face, then slapped him.

Rhian was fuming but he couldn't hold back the tears. Alexander was shocked by what had just happened because Rhian had never actually physically hit him. Come to think of it the two were never rough when it came to their horseplay. Alexander was taken back but all he could do was stare down at Rhian who was looking at him with an instinctive ferocity he recognized as a defensive reaction.

"What do you mean you think we shouldn't be friends? You told me you would never abandon me and then you led me on, then you treated me like I somehow ruined your life or something when I was the only one telling you that you could amount to anything. I have never tried to tear you down and now you are saying that I have somehow caused your life to fall apart and that I am to blame for you trying to kill yourself. I apologize for being a bad influence on you a few times and yes perhaps I have done some stupid things, but be honest with yourself. You were the one who tried the drugs. You were the one who would sneak into my room and sleep next to me. You were the one who would refuse to talk to me and you were the one who messed things up for yourself. It wasn't me it was you!"

"I guess I'll go now." He said quietly as he walked away. The way he saw it, he had screwed everything up beyond repair and he was lucky that Rhian was a good enough person to come save him.

"Fuck you Alexander! Fuck you! You can't just break me and walk away."

"Rhian I'm sorry for everything… but" Alexander began, expecting Rhian to back down as usual and listen to him.

"No… No you're not… you know you're not either. You have been doing this for too long. I'm not playing your games anymore. I wanted you. All of you but you can't seem to grasp that. I know you have told yourself over and over again that I am crazy and that I am just infatuated with you but the truth is… You're in such denial that you will never see what I see." He said calming down a bit. "Look, Alexander, it isn't about you being gay, bi, or straight… It is about you being in love with a soul."

"How do you even know you are in love with me? I don't think you're in love with me… I think you think you find me physically attractive."

"I know I love you because you are the light that pierces through the shadows of my world. You are the only one who can make me smile even through the darkest of times. When life feels like it's falling apart for me, no matter how mad I am at you the thought of you can make my pain and fear disappear. I know that I love you because I find myself wondering what I could do to make your day better at almost every moment of the day. I want to please you, more than anyone I've ever met before. You are so much more to me than just a friend. Our chemistry is something that nothing else in my life has ever come close to. But there is no way to fully explain it because it's more than just the things you do or the way you make me feel. It is the way we are together. You make me a better person. I can feel when you are angry or happy or sad. I find myself waking up happy at the thought of being around you because you are so amazing to me. I feel as though our souls are intertwined and wherever I am you are with me. When we touch even if by accident, I get this electrifying pulse that excites me and comforts me and gives me hope for a bright tomorrow. Alexander, you mean more to me than you will ever know. I know I love you because for me, you are the life that keeps me going day after day."

"Wow…"

"I believe we were made for each other, like soul mates and we found each other for a reason. I know this is all really confusing but I promise you it will be all right. There is nothing wrong with you, there never was. You are just in love… with me Alexander, and you want to be with me but you're being stubborn and refusing to see it…" Rhian now took a pause to let the effect of his words sink in. He started again with a bit more passion. "But I can't wait for you to be ok anymore. You have really hurt me and although I forgive you for it and will always forgive you, I can't keep doing this for my own sake. I am done. I'm gone. I feel like I am on the brink of losing my mind because of all the confusing things you have done. You know your actions really do hurt me and yet you still continue. Why? Why can't you just let me go instead of pulling me along like you have been?"

Alexander was dumbfounded. He was embarrassed that Rhian had actually called him out on his stupid actions and afraid that he was going to lose Rhian. But the thing that was most prominent in Alexander's mind was that he was confused because deep down he knew Rhian was right. He felt things that he didn't want to think about and instead pushed those feelings away, writing them off as *I'm straight so I can't love him like that.* But he also knew that there was something stronger and deeper to their relationship that even in his most well thought-out explanations couldn't decipher what was wrong because he couldn't accept a different train of thought. He didn't know how to deal with any of it so he preferred not to deal with it at all.

"I don't think like that… I'm sorry Rhian… I love you but I don't see things like that… We are just different…" He said making one last attempt at his denial.

"Bull Shit! Bull Shit! If that were at all true then you wouldn't continue hurting me just to get the love and attention you want. You wouldn't try to upset me just so that we could have our make-up time and my life could be all about you. You are addicted to my love and me and you are in denial of it. I am done here. Have a wonderful break." with that Rhian began to walk away. Alexander reached out and grabbed Rhian's arm to prevent him from walking away.

Rhian shot him a look of anger. Alexander pulled him in and held him with both hands, then pulled him in and kissed him passionately. Rhian became overwhelmed by the action. He wasn't prepared for this kind of reaction. But of course all thoughts were quickly fading as he kissed back.

Again Alexander felt the feeling he had felt after the first time they kissed. It was an intense feeling of pleasure stemming from the contact between their lips. It was like the immediate release of a built up pressure causing a sudden relaxation. As they kissed Alexander could feel his entire body tingle with excitement. He didn't want the feeling to end.

"What are you doing?" Rhian asked softly, trying to retain his sense of self-control.

"I… I liked kissing you… a lot… I tried to kiss other people after it and it was nothing like this…" Alexander said leaning in for another kiss.

Rhian was frozen with complete shock. "Was that why you hooked up with John?"

"Hooked up? I didn't hook up with him…"

"But I saw you kissing him."

"Wait, how?"

"I was sleeping on the couch and woke up when I heard someone at the door. I looked out the window and saw you two making out. I figured you two were going to sleep together."

"Wow... No, I kissed him because... I needed to know if he made me feel what you did with that kiss... I even kissed a random girl to try the same thing. Both felt the same to me but when you kissed me... there was something different about it... I don't know how to explain it..."

"Really?"

"Yeah... the kiss changed me..."

"You see it too... Don't you? It's love Alexander... It's love...."

"But I... I... am not gay... I mean I like women... so... why now... why am I gay now...? I still like women... I don't understand why YOU make me feel like this. I mean when you told me your feelings I actually thought about it what it would be like to be gay. I told myself that I wasn't afraid because I thought about it and the idea of it didn't appeal to me. I thought that if I were to be gay I would be completely gay and not bi or curious or anything like that. I was so confident that I would either know for sure that I was gay or know for sure that I was straight. So when I looked into being gay and felt nothing I was convinced that I was straight... no offense but the idea of getting it on with a dude hadn't turned me on until you kissed me."

"It's because you can feel the connection that we share. It's our love..."

"But I don't understand. How could that be possible, I didn't think men turn me on? If I'm not gay?"

"Like I said before, it isn't about you being gay, straight, bi or any other flavor of the rainbow. I didn't fall in love with you because I think you are physically beautiful, which you are." Alexander flashed a coy smile. "I fell in love with the person that you are inside. You really are the whole package and I think you fail to see that sometimes but it doesn't matter because I do." Rhian was speaking directly to his soul.

He was looking directly into his eyes to make sure he finally understood. "You are in love with the person I am and now that you can see it you can also feel it." He said as he looked down and noticed that Alexander was very aroused. His attention shifted downward. Alexander hadn't noticed what was going on in his own pants until he noticed Rhian's eyes locked on his crotch. He looked down and was startled. He was *not* gay but all of the talk and kissing excited him. He and Rhian looked up at the same time. Rhian blushed with embarrassment.

"Well I guess this disproves my last statement doesn't it..." He said with a lighthearted laugh.

"Not necessarily..." Rhian replied quietly. He couldn't form a coherent response in his own mind because he was unsuccessfully trying to avoid what was going on in Alexander's pants, and now in his own.

"Fine, I'm gay... whatever just fuck me..."

"I doubt you're ready for. Besides, you couldn't handle this." Rhian flirted. Deep down inside he knew that he should say no but he could feel the sexual tension rising.

"If I'm going to be gay I'm not going to be a half-a-gay. I'm going to be a committed gay."

"That's not exactly how it works, stud." By now, Rhian figured that the moment was over and Alexander would avoid him just like he had before. Rhian was waiting for the turning point.

"Rhian, what I'm saying is that if I'm going to lose my masculinity by being with a guy, no offense, I might as well do it right." Rhian was amazed at how ignorant his last statement sounded.

"If you are referring to *bottoming* as being the ultimate form of emasculation then you are way off base..." He was now offended by the implication. Of course, he should have known this considering that Alexander treated him like a girlfriend.

"I'm sorry, I didn't mean it like that. I'm just really nervous! Please be patient with me." Alexander looked away out of frustration before going on. "You always talk about how good it feels and how so many straight men will 'unfortunately never know the pleasures.' I want to know what that's like. I mean in theory being the man... I mean 'topping,' whether it's a male or female that is bottoming doesn't make much of a difference. But as a guy, 'bottoming' is a completely different experience. It requires a lot of trust... and I trust you..." Rhian couldn't believe that Alexander was actually serious about being physical with him. He thought Alexander was just playing with his mind again and was ready to walk away broken hearted, again.

"Alexander... are you really asking me to have sex with you? Why now? What changed?"

"I don't really know why now or what changed if anything... All I know is that I am very turned on by kissing you and all of this talk makes me want to touch you..." He closed the gap between them. "...be close to you..." He put his hand up to Rhian's cheek. "I want to feel connected to you..." Alexander planted a soft kiss on Rhian's lips. "Rhian, I want you... all of you..."

"You know, even bottoming doesn't make you gay..." Rhian's logical side tried to take over in the conversation. Perhaps it was his mind trying to defend his heart. If they were indeed about to have sex he could write it off as meaningless because Alexander was still straight and he wasn't a woman. "A woman can wear a strap on and make you feel what I can..." He pulled away to allow himself a second to breathe. "But it's not in the sex... It's in the connection that two people share."

"Shut up and make love to me…" His words barely a whisper as he planted another kiss on Rhian's lips and he was again enflamed with passion "I love you and I know you love me."

That was all Rhian needed to take control of the situation. He kept his focus on Alexander's beautiful body. "You'll enjoy it; I'll make sure you do because I'll go as slow as you want me to. I will take care of you but you are going to have to let me take control. It's not like when you have sex with a girl so tell me if you don't like something… though I doubt you won't enjoy it all." He said with a satisfied smirk. Alexander remained silent and completely still, unable to look away because the thought of finally having sex, though different than he had expected, was very arousing. He stared at Rhian with a look of fear mixed with passion and desire. Until now he had held on to Rhian with both hands on his lower back but after Rhian began to take control he released him.

Rhian grabbed Alexander's face, kissing him passionately once again. The action caused Alexander to melt in his firm grip. He had given Rhian full control, something he had never done before with anyone. He moaned softly as Rhian's lips withdrew from his and moved down to his more sensitive neck. Alexander felt a tingle run down his spine, a combination of pleasure and excitement. His moaning served as the encouragement that Rhian needed to continue exploring his body. He kissed harder with each kiss, suckling at the sensitive flesh gently at first and then harder as he put more motion into his actions. Rhian was determined to make this experience as erotic and pleasurable for Alexander as he could.

Using both hands, Rhian began to tease him by lightly grazing the exposed skin on his arms and neck. He gently touched his neck, dragging his fingers over his shirt down the length of his back all the way down to the lower back causing him to straighten up his back. He now moved his lips to Alexander's ear using his tongue to lightly tease his ear lobe, sucking on it and using his lips to increase the pressure on it lightly. Alexander shivered and became tense. "Relax, it's me. I'm not going to hurt you… just enjoy it. It's all for you." Rhian felt him relax his shoulders again and continued by running his tongue on the outline of his ear. This again sent shivers up Alexander's back but he didn't tense up this time. He remained relaxed. Rhian moved him over towards the bed now and sat him down with a firm push downward on his left shoulder. Alexander followed his direction looking up at Rhian, waiting for his next move, his next instruction. Rhian moved over to his left ear now and repeated his actions. This time he lightly nibbled his earlobe.

Rhian slowly and sensually unbuttoned his shirt one button at a time. He then removed it carefully as he turned his attention to Alexander's shirt. He grabbed the bottom of his t-shirt and pulled it over his head with a swift motion and threw it on the ground. Rhian had seen Alexander's bare muscular chest before but there was something very different about seeing it this time. He had never seen him so exposed, so intimately. He had seen him walking around the apartment but this was the first time he was exposed for Rhian. He continued to undress him, this time removing his pants with care. He wanted to visually capture every contour of the sight of Alexander's body. As his gaze passed Alexander's erection, he gave a suggestive smile.

Rhian could tell that Alexander was really enjoying what he was doing so he continued to tease his skin by brushing his fingers up the length of his thighs. Alexander moaned loudly when Rhian grabbed both of his thighs with his hands and firmly trailed upwards making sure to touch every inch of his skin on his way up towards his face. Once he reached Alexander's face, Rhian made eye contact with him again and closed the gap between them as he placed his lips back on

Alexander's. By this point both boys were so lost in their arousal that they didn't care to silence their primal gasping and moaning. Alexander could feel Rhian's erection rubbing against his bare skin, which was a new feeling for him but he continued to give in to Rhian's burning passion.

Rhian had left Alexander's boxers on until he could see the wetness that had stained the fabric. He slowly pulled down the boxers, revealing the head of his cock. Rhian prided himself on his oral skills; something Alexander had heard him brag about before. "Suck it..." Alexander said with a low groan. Rhian didn't wait for a second invitation. He began sucking on Alexander's cock using his tongue to add stimulation and to make sure not to lose the physical contact throughout. From the moment Rhian began going down on him, his legs had tensed up and his toes curled. As Rhian took Alexander's length down his throat Alexander moaned even louder than before. He flinched and even lifted his feet of the ground from the bursts of pleasure he was feeling. Rhian continued this for several minutes making sure to take Alexander close to the edge but not far enough to push him over. Once Rhian felt that Alexander was relaxed he stood up and pushed on his torso leading him onto his back. He obeyed Rhian's nonverbal cue and took a deep breath. He knew things were about to change for him but aside from mystery of what he was about to experience, he felt at peace. There was a level of closeness that he had never felt with anyone else before and he felt ready to consummate it.

Rhian took out a condom and a bottle of lubricant that he had in the drawer. He dripped some of the lubricant onto his exposed manhood before unrolling the condom over it. Once he had successfully prepared himself he dripped a little bit of it onto Alexander. Alexander shivered and flinched at the unfamiliar sensation as Rhian used his warm finger to spread the cool lube properly. Rhian made sure to coat his cock with enough lubricant before lining up to enter him.

"Please be gentle… I've never done this before."

"Like I told you, trust me… How has everything felt till now?"

"Really good…"

Rhian returned his attention to what he was doing. The room was very silent filled with anxiety in anticipation of what was to come and a sexual tension that could be cut with a dull knife. The room was noticeably warmer now than when they first began. Alexander gripped the bed with both hands, bracing himself. "Relax…" Rhian stated with authority. He began to push himself into Alexander, entering him slowly. Rhian had closed his eyes in ecstasy and let out a loud sigh, "Wow, you're really tight…" He continued, slowly and gently until the entire length of his cock was completely inside of Alexander. He opened his eyes to see Alexander's squinting as if he was in pain. He didn't want to hurt him so he didn't pull out right away. He held his position as still as could, waiting for Alexander to relax. After a few moments he could see Alexander open his eyes. The look on his face was that of uncertainty and fear of what he was doing. He was clearly still nervous and not allowing himself to enjoy everything. Rhian realized that this was a monumental change for him and displayed an immense amount of trust. He planted a gentle kiss on Alexander's lips to comfort him. When he felt sure that Alexander was relaxed enough he began to slowly pull out just far enough for Alexander to let out a loud moan. He was breathing heavily as Rhian continued thrusting in and out slowly at first and then eventually much faster. They lost track of their surroundings, forgetting about time and the level of noise they were making.

"Oh my god! Oh my god! Keep going, that feels so good!" Alexander shouted in ecstasy. Rhian was thrusting into Alexander over and over again watching and appreciating Alexander's beautiful body as it glistened from the dim light that reflected off of his sweat-covered skin. He kissed his neck, tasting its saltiness and adding to the pleasure Alexander was feeling. The realization that this wasn't just sex for the two but rather a moment of pure intimacy that they were sharing, had given Alexander a feeling that he hadn't felt before, not just because he was being pleasured differently but because a force greater than anything he had ever felt before had penetrated him to his very core. Rhian stared into Alexander's beautiful eyes as Alexander stared back into his. This was when it finally made sense to Alexander, amidst all of the pleasure, that Rhian was his and he was Rhian's. He had only dreamed of feeling so connected, passionate, and consumed. He truly was feeling love and he understood what it meant to make love.

After losing himself for a while in the ecstasy of making love, Rhian was reaching his climax. "I'm getting close to coming… I want you to cum with me."

"Ok…" Alexander began to masturbate himself and after only a few strokes realized he wouldn't be long either. He stroked while Rhian continued to thrust until he let out a loud moan. "Oh! Oh! I'm coming! I'm coming!" This made Rhian thrust even faster, forcing him over the edge. He gave one last deep thrust, putting pressure on Alexander's prostate, which he had been stimulating the entire time, and increased the pleasure to a new level as he came like never before. Alexander had never experienced such a powerful orgasm before. He was in shock but in a state of complete euphoria. His body shook with excitement and he couldn't move a muscle other than to breath, which he was still having trouble doing.

Alexander closed his eyes as he tried to grasp what had happened. This was all new to him so he was overwhelmed with the sensations of the experience. Rhian collapsed onto him and then rolled onto the bed. He lay next to him also at a loss for words and breath. Alexander was entranced, still captivated by Rhian's intense sexual passion. The two lay in the bed breathing heavily, recovering from what was the most amazing experience that either one had ever had. They were both sweating from the heat in the room. The windows were fogged as an indication of what had just transpired. Both were lying speechless with their fingers intertwined. Rhian had his leg partially over Alexander's.

"Wow… That was…. wow…" Was all Alexander could say.

"How do you feel?" Rhian asked turning to his side and placing his hand on Alexander's chest stroking his bare moist skin.

"I feel great… I didn't know you could do that…" He responded with a wide-eyed gaze directed at the ceiling.

Rhian laughed out loud. "Well, now you know. That was the most amazing feeling I've ever felt. You are beautiful Alexander."

The reality of what had just happened hadn't quite set in for Alexander until Rhian called him 'beautiful,' then it started to set in. Alexander told girls that they were beautiful, not the other way around. He suddenly felt as if he was no longer a man. He felt awkward and turned to the side. "I'm tired man… I'm just going to go to bed… Goodnight."

Before Rhian could say anything Alexander had turned over. "Ok… goodnight… I love you." but there was no response. Rhian turned over to his side and tried to fall asleep. Alexander's strange behavior wasn't unfamiliar anymore but he understood that his was all new to him and perhaps he wouldn't welcome it as openly right away. Sleep came quickly for both boys after using up all of the energy that they had. Alexander awoke some time in the middle of the night to Rhian curled up in his arms. He stared for a second feeling a bit confused, then it hit him that they had just had sex. He was uneasy about the sight, and yet he felt an odd sense of comfort. He was relieved that he had some form of closure about his feelings for Rhian, but now he was faced with a big decision. Or at least that's what he thought. He quietly removed his arm from under Rhian and got out of bed.

He made his way to the bathroom to avoid waking Rhian up. He walked in and closed the door, making sure to lock it. Alexander looked at himself in the mirror noticing that he looked drowsy so he turned on the water before scooping some of it up and splashing it on his face. He took a deep breath as a reaction to the cold water shocking his warm skin to wake him up from his lulled state of sleepiness. After drying off his face with a towel, he was fully awake and knew it would take a while for him to go back to bed so he sat down on the couch in the living room. He picked up his basketball, which was on the floor near his backpack, lied down and began to toss the ball up in the air pretending to be shooting baskets.

"Well, you are officially a homo…" He said to himself quietly, throwing his ball up in the air. "What are you doing Alexander? What is going on with you? Who are you?" Alexander felt bad for saying the 'h-word' out loud. He had worked hard at not being homophobic for Rhian's sake. He wasn't homophobic; he had just grown up in an environment where the language was. He wasn't sure what to think about what had happened because the only thing he wanted to do was run away.

He didn't feel any different than the day before. Nothing had changed; he was still the same person yet he was now calling himself a 'homo' as if he was some kind of freak. "Alexander?" Rhian softly called out from the room; he was still obviously half asleep. "Are you ok?"

"Yeah, I'm fine… Go back to bed…" He calmly replied

"Ok, I love you... goodnight..." Rhian replied before falling back asleep.

"Yeah... Goodnight...." Alexander called out with uncertainty in his voice. He lay there for a few more minutes

"I love you too," he whispered to himself taking in the magnitude of what he was saying. He still couldn't wrap his mind around everything. He repeated the phrase several times to himself "I love you too... I love you too... I love you too... Rhi... Rhian... I love you too Rhian... I love you too Rhian!" he forced himself to shout. Rhian stirred a bit but was already asleep and continued sleeping undisturbed by Alexander. "I'm sorry Rhian.... I don't love you... I don't love you Rhian..." He quietly said swallowing hard. He knew that was a lie, but he didn't want to be different. He didn't want to be gay. He wanted to be straight. *I like girls. That's something I know for sure. I could find a girl to be with and I could still be Rhian's friend. Of course he would take some time to get over it but he's my best friend. He would have to understand.* It made perfect sense to Alexander. He was resolved that he would find himself a nice girl to settle down with and Rhian would be happy for him. He fell asleep on the couch with the ball in his hands. He awoke the next morning to the smell of eggs, bacon, and coffee. He could hear something frying. He looked around and saw Rhian in the kitchen making breakfast. Rhian was wearing a goofy looking chef's hat that he had bought him as a gag gift a few months before.

"Hey you, good morning! I've made you breakfast. How many pancakes do you want?"

Alexander was still waking up but was also a bit stunned at the scene in the apartment.

"Um... I'm not really hungry..." he said sounding frustrated with Rhian.

"Oh come on Alexander I worked…"

"I said I'm not hungry!" Alexander yelled out of frustration.

"Ok I'm sorry, I can make you something else…" Rhian said, now confused and a bit startled.

"I didn't ask you to cook me breakfast! I didn't ask you to take care of me and I didn't ask you to fall in love with me! You've done more than enough for me! You aren't my girlfriend you fucking fag!" Alexander shouted angrily. He couldn't believe what he had just yelled. He was looking down at the ground unable to speak.

"Rhian… I'm so…" He quietly began.

"Don't come near me!" Rhian yelled with tears in his eyes as he turned around ready to defend himself. "I can't do this anymore. Just stay the hell away from me!"

"Rhian I didn't mean to…" He pulled Rhian in an embrace but Rhian pushed him away. Alexander tried again.

"Leave me alone!" Rhian pulled away but backed into the wall. He tried to get away but Alexander squeezed his arm to prevent him from leaving.

"Rhian, I'm sorry!"

"Let me go!" Rhian yanked his arm away hitting his wrist on a nearby chair. He let out a cry from the pain. "Don't ever touch me like that again!"

"Rhian I didn't mean to."

"It's always going to be the same thing with you isn't it? You say something or do something to hurt me and I'm just supposed to forgive you and pretend that it didn't happen because you didn't *mean* it or you just aren't ready to *accept* it. I won't wait for you anymore. There won't be a next time. You're right. I'm not your *girlfriend*… I'm just a *fucking fag*. Now get out!"

Alexander didn't question Rhian's demand. He knew it was fair. He drove off, disappearing for a few hours.

Chapter 10

KA

LU

MN

IA

"Call the police Sebastian!" Leena ran to the bloody shape that lay motionless near the door of Rhian's apartment. As she reached him, she realized it *was* Rhian lying there covered in blood almost unrecognizable only identified by the bracelet he always wore; the bracelet that matched Alexander's, which Alexander had stopped wearing a while ago. Rhian's clothes were ripped to shreds but the most disturbing part of the crime became apparent when Leena noticed the word "Fag" had been carved into his thigh. She became hysterical, as she cradled her brother who lay dying.

"I don't think he is breathing! Send an ambulance as quickly as possible." Sebastian cried out to the operator. It was after a few seconds that the initial shock had worn off and he realized that he and Leena were alone and the people that did this to Rhian might still be around. He jolted up before choosing a barren tree branch as his potential weapon of defense against any remaining attackers. He stood over Leena ready to protect but once he heard the police sirens he tossed the branch to avoid being considered a suspect.

"Please don't leave me! Please stay with me!" Leena howled over and over again. Sebastian had never seen her like this. "I'll take you away. I'll take you to Cali and we can start over there. I'll protect you from him. Just please don't go!" Rhian remained unresponsive.

Leena was still in shock. The world around her was moving slowly. It was like she was in a bad dream. The police officer had asked her what had happened but she couldn't respond.

"He called us. He had a really bad falling out with his roommate. He said he needed to talk. We didn't get the message until fifteen minutes ago. When we arrived, we found him on the ground." Leena shook as she watched Rhian being taken away on the stretcher.

"So he had an argument with his roommate? Where is his roommate? Do you know him well?"

"I don't know. I assume that he went home after the fight."

"Home?"

"Back to his parents' house. We are on winter break now."

"Ma'am, you should come with me. I know he is your friend but he is in good hands and you don't need to see this." The kind officer obliged.

"You don't understand. He doesn't have anyone. I'm like his sister."

"I understand but you have to let them do their jobs. Please come with me so I can finish up my report." She looked back to him for only a moment and then did as the officer asked.

The paramedics worked as quickly as they could. No one knew how long he had been unconscious but they estimated it to be about ten minutes. They managed to resuscitate his heart but they knew they had to hurry and get him to the hospital if they were going to save his life. One of the paramedics noticed the carving on Rhian's thigh and he carefully took a picture of it before covering it up with a sheet.

"Do you have reason to believe that his roommate could have done this?"

"Alexander..?" Leena's eyes grew wide as she saw him approach the scene. For the first time in a long time she only saw red. She ran up to him and slapped him across the face.

"What's going on?" Alexander asked trying to protect his face.

"What did you do? What did you do!?" She yelled uncontrollably while pounding on his chest.

"What do you mean? Where is Rhian?" He looked over and saw him lying in the stretcher just as the doors on the ambulance shut. "Where are they taking him?" Alexander shouted.

"Sir, do you live in apartment 11?" The police officer asked Alexander.

"Yes… What's going on?" He could feel his heart drop.

"I need to ask you some questions. Where were you when your roommate was attacked?"

"Rhian was attacked?"

"Yes. Now answer the question. Where have you been for the past hour?"

"I was driving around town. We got into an argument and he told me to leave."

"I hope for your sake that you aren't lying."

"I would never hurt him!"

"Sir, you need to relax or else we can continue this at the station."

"I think I prefer to stay here." Just as he finished speaking another officer approached the questioning officer and whispered in his ear.

"You have the right to remain silent. Anything you say can and will be used…" Leena and Sebastian let out a collective gasp.

Alexander looked up at Leena's face. *Monster!*

Rhian was in a coma, lying helplessly fragile on the bed. Overwhelmed by the sight, Leena began to sob uncontrollably as she stepped back in horror. After the initial shock had worn off, she approached the bedside cautiously and gently picked up Rhian's hand bringing it up to her lips with a soft kiss.

"You have to be ok." She whispered behind tears of agony. She closed her eyes for a moment but was startled when the heart rate monitor, whose cadence was cut short, sang the familiar constant note of fatality. Rhian's heart had stopped. Leena released Rhian's hand as she looked around for a nurse. Within seconds a team of nurses came rushing in. Everything felt unreal and she froze. The nurses forced her out of the room but she was still looking at him as she saw the doctors trying to revive him.

"No… Not like this…"

"Ma'am, you can sit in the waiting room but I suggest you go home and get some sleep. He'll most likely be sent to the OR and it could be hours before you hear back. Go home and get some rest."

"I'll wait, thank you." The nurse sighed as she walked away.

Seeing the heart rate monitor flat line reminded her of the night she lost her mother. Leena was only six-years-old but she could clearly remember how everything played out. Her mother was very sick and was in and out of the hospitals. They regularly traveled the country in search of a doctor who could help her but all the money in the world wouldn't have made a difference. Leena couldn't remember a day when her mom was alive that didn't revolve around her illness. For Leena, the hardest part of her mother's disease was watching her suffer without remedy.

Leena hated hospitals. She hated going to the doctor unless she was forced to. It was one of the reasons why she exercised regularly and ate a specific diet. She didn't want to die the death that her mom did. She watched her slowly die for the majority of her childhood. While it was a painful experience to lose her, Leena now appreciated that her mom didn't have to suffer anymore. But she had plenty of time to get over that. Rhian was on the edge of life and his future wasn't looking too bright. She wasn't ready to give up but she could feel the familiar shadow of despair over her. She walked away from the room with clenched fists. She wasn't going to fall apart.

After sleeping for a few hours Leena woke up in a panic. She made her way to the nurse station but she didn't recognize any of the nurses on duty. There must have been a shift change because there was no sign of the nurse from the night before.

"Excuse me, a patient by the name Rhian Pierce came in last night and I wanted to know if he was back from OR."

"I'm sorry miss but unfortunately if you aren't related I can't give you any information." Leena became irritated. She regretted ever letting herself fall asleep. Perhaps if she would have stayed awake she would have known what happened to Rhian.

"I know that it's your job to protect patient information but I am telling you that Rhian is like my brother, I just want to know if he is ok. Please." Her sincerity pulled at the strings of the nurse's heart but she wasn't prepared to break the rules for someone she didn't know.

"I can't give you any information about the patient. All I can say is that your friend is no longer with us. His parent's wouldn't allow me to say anything else about the circumstances. I'm sorry.

Chapter 11

"You're free to go." The officer removed the handcuffs from Alexander's wrists.

"How long was I here? Did you find the one who did it?"

"Just get the hell out of here and be glad the charges were dropped."

"He's fine… He's probably at home. He is probably waiting for me to come home. I need to go. I need to see him!" Alexander reassured himself as he took off running as quickly as possible. He pounded on the apartment door with both fists.

"Where are you? Where the hell did you go? I know you are still here!" Alexander almost tore down the door as he demanded Rhian's presence. His tear-filled red eyes were burdened with sorrow as he frantically searched for any trace of Rhian.

"You can't leave me! You can't end it like this! You have to be here! You promised that you wouldn't give up on me! You promised that you wouldn't leave me! Where are you now? I came back! I came back…" Alexander cried out in utter despair, his face turning red as the blood rushed to his face and his veins became full. He punched open the door to Rhian's room, which they had shared, and made his way in. In that moment he needed Rhian more than ever, but all he had was a room full of reminders that he was gone.

"You promised me! You weren't supposed to go! It should have been me! It should have been me…" He picked up one of Rhian's sweatshirts and brought it up to his face carefully caressing his cheek with it. The soft fabric was comforting. He could still smell Rhian's cologne on it, which sent him into a spiral of memories, from the first time they met to the time they first kissed, to the amazing night they made love.

Unfortunately for him this moment of complete euphoria was short lived by the appalling reality of what had happened. Rhian was no longer in his life. Taken just as swiftly as he had come into his life, he was gone and no amount of dreaming or belated acceptance would change that. He finally pulled the sweatshirt away and opened his eyes looking around the empty room. He lied down on the bed gripping the sweatshirt tightly. As soon as his head rested against the pillow he felt something underneath it. He reached underneath and pulled out a picture. It was the first picture the two boys had taken together. Alexander smiled through the tears as he remembered that Rhian was so adamant about finding the perfect background for them to take the picture. They had settled on a mural that depicted the school's history. It really was a great picture but what stood out, as always, was the joy in both of their faces. There was a carefree happiness that they both possessed, which brought a moment of joy to Alexander. He flipped the picture over and saw that Rhian had written something on the back.

Alexander,

You are the soul I love with every fiber of my being. You are my One and Only. I will always be yours.

Love,
Rhian

"You were my *One and Only*."

Sobriety is terrifying when you've grown accustomed to the comfort brought on by the loss of control to a bottle. It is quite a traumatic experience to wake up to the problems of life after escaping through the bottle, but the biggest trauma is the feeling of loneliness when the people you love are nowhere to be found and all that remains are the empty bottles that serve as reminders of the loss. The fear of loneliness may cause people to do very strange things, but the willingness to give up security at the risk of loneliness can truly break a spirit.

It was about eleven in the morning, the carpet was warm from the rays of sunlight that had been pouring in all morning unnoticed by the occupant in the room. Life was in full swing for everyone except Alexander who was sitting on the couch clinging to a bottle of whiskey like it was his last meal. Based on his appearance, that may have been the case. His shirt was stained with liquor and what might have been vomit. The apartment was in disarray and smelled worse than a bar at last call. There was a heaviness that lingered in the air, which was intensified by the sight of disaster in the room. Alexander had been living at the mercy of the bottle, cut off from the world around him since the day at the hospital two weeks ago. His eyes glazed with drunkenness only masked the deep sadness that he felt inside.

Consumed by the image of Rhian lying on the hospital bed, Alexander imagined what it was like for Rhian to be there without anyone by his side as he took his final breath. *What if he opened his eyes for one last time and there was no one. What if I could have been there?* He thought to himself. He felt guilty for leaving Rhian alone in the apartment. He felt guilty because Rhian was always so good to him. But he felt most guilty for taking so long to realize what he should have known all along. *Maybe if I hadn't been so stubborn Rhian wouldn't have been in the apartment that morning. He might have been with me. He might still be… alive.* He wanted nothing more in that moment than to be looking into his enchanting eyes, feeling the comfort of his bright smile.

Clouded by grief, Alexander's mind shifted its focus to the fact that he would never be able to see Rhian again. Most of his sorrow was related to the guilt he felt for the way he damaged his relationship with Rhian and how he hurt him. But he hadn't considered the obvious reality that Rhian was gone for good. It wasn't like a vacation that he would come back from eventually or relocation. Rhian wasn't going to come back. There would be no more anger about whether or not Alexander was in love with him. There was no waking up to the love of Rhian's illuminating spirit. Love had never touched Alexander to such consequence that the loss of such would leave him in desolation. Losing Rhian shocked him to the core, shredding every bit of his worn spirit. There was no sign of a better tomorrow because the promising future he had finally accepted was now gone.

Leena was reading in the café trying to distract herself when she came across an interesting fact that she knew Rhian would appreciate. It had only been a couple of weeks since he was taken from her but she hadn't been able to think anything else. She canceled her winter plans in order to mourn her loss. She was still scarred and didn't see it getting any better. She pulled out her phone and opened up the most recent text messages. It was sent a few days ago to Alexander but he hadn't responded. The message read; *I miss him...* Seeing it brought tears to her eyes and she knew she couldn't go on like this. She had to deal with what happened.

In the first few days following the accident Leena made every attempt possible to find out where Rhian was going to be buried while also trying to find out what happened to Alexander. She called the university to find out who had notified them of his passing but they weren't able to give any information. She went back to the hospital to talk to some of the nurses but it was as if he had disappeared. She remembered that the nurse had mentioned his family but his parent's weren't returning her calls. In a desperate attempt to find out any bit of information, she contacted the police officer that had comforted her that day. He was only able to confirm that he had been at the hospital but was no longer there. The information was unclear and there was no certainty about where the body had been taken for burial. She also learned that the charges against Alexander were dropped. The officer wouldn't tell her why but it was definitely suspicious for them to drop the charges when there was no other suspect in custody. Knowing that the charges were dropped wasn't enough for Leena because deep down inside she still felt that Alexander was responsible. Even if it wasn't he who attacked Rhian, he left him alone and gave the attacker the chance to do it. She avoided him for a few days after he was released in order to give herself time to let go of her anger. She needed a distraction.

Finding Rhian's body didn't change the fact that he was gone. She knew that. It didn't do her any good to continue searching for answers to questions that perpetuated the feelings of sadness. She decided to put her talents to good use and gather the others for a memorial service in memory of Rhian. She put her books away and took out her notebook in order to properly plan the event. She made her lists and began to delegate tasks. She called each one of their friends to check up on them and show her support. It was her way of coping with it. She pretended to be strong for the others and she was almost able to believe that she was strong enough to herself. Everyone was onboard with the idea, everyone except Alexander who responded with a simple *ok* message. She was hoping that he would show up but she wasn't going to hold her breath.

It was the night of the gathering and Alexander had spent most of the day drinking. He was aware that Leena wanted him there but he didn't want to show up. He had lost his phone somewhere in the mess of the apartment. He figured he could claim that he forgot because he couldn't find his phone. It didn't matter what excuse he used he wasn't going that night. A loud knock at the door startled him from his mindless state. He wasn't expecting company and considered not answering but he figured that whoever was at the door could hear the television.

"Leena… What are you doing here?"

"Are you kidding me? Get dressed. You're coming with me!" As she stepped into the apartment the smell stopped her in her tracks. "On second thought, go take a shower and then get dressed. I'll pick something out for you to wear while you're showering."

"Leena, I'm not going."

"What do you mean you're not going?"

"I can't go!" Leena stared at him waiting for an explanation.

"Why not sweetie?" She calmly asked after an uncomfortable pause in the conversation.

"It's my fault, Leena! He is gone because of me! I never got to tell him how I really feel about him. I never got to be with him."

"Honey, it's not your fault. Sometimes things just happen and there isn't anything we can do to change that. He loved you and he knew you loved him. There is no doubt about that. You should come with me, everyone is at my place and they would love to see you. You've been locked up in here for too long."

"I feel safe. I keep telling myself that if I wait long enough he might soon come through the door and I'll be able to tell him how I feel." He was clearly disillusioned but Leena couldn't tell him that.

"Come with me. I think you need to see the others. Everything will be ok." Leena put her feelings of sadness aside long enough to calm Alexander down but she herself was on the verge of tears. As Alexander showered she looked around the apartment and began to feel overwhelmed by the flood of memories. She stepped out for a few minutes to get a breath of fresh air before going back in and helping Alexander get dressed. He was ready in a few minutes and they left Alexander's safety zone.

"There you are." She adjusted the collar to his button up shirt as they got out of her car. "You look so handsome. Rhian wouldn't be able to keep his eyes off of you."

"Leena, I can't do this… Take me back!" He said in a panic.

"Sweetheart we are here and you need to see your friends. I know it's hard but they all loved him too. You can stay with me the whole time. I won't leave your side. I promise." She grabbed his hand and smiled at him.

They made their way into the apartment where everyone sitting around talking. Alexander's scruffy face and blood-reddened eyes suggested that he had seen better days. Most of them stared at him silently until Sebastian broke the awkward silence.

"Hey bud!" He came up to him and gave him a hug. Everyone else followed, warmly welcoming Alexander back to the family.

Only Leena could make a wake fabulous and still appropriate. She had decorated her place with large candid portraits of Rhian in various phases of his personality. It was incredible how Leena could put this thing together on such short notice and make it feel like they were truly honoring their friend. She loved Rhian so much but she had been moping not mourning. Tonight was about mourning and moving forward. She intended on commemorating him so that she could move on with her life and remember more than the image of his bloody body on the ground.

Leena had hired a caterer for the group of friends. Although she knew how to cook, she wasn't prepared to make food for so many people. She wanted to make the night all about Rhian so she had the caterer make soul food for them in memory of their friend. Everyone ate in silence that evening, though the food was fantastic, it reminded them of their friend, which cast a shadow on the meal. She had spent a good deal of money on the food so she noticed when it didn't seem like anyone was hungry. Seeing that everyone was still moping, Leena decided to change things up by sharing her thoughts.

"Thank you all for coming tonight, I know it's not exactly an official service but as most of you know, we weren't able to find out any details about Rhian's funeral and I wanted to make sure we had a chance to pay our respects so I'm glad you all came…" She paused for a moment to look at everyone. "He loved each and every one of us in a special way and I know he would have been so happy to see all of you here. Um… Rhian was more than just a friend to me. He was like the brother I always dreamed of having. He knew how to cheer me up if I was having a bad day and make me smile again. I remember the first time I met him we were running and the jerk was trying to outrun me but ended up tripping on a rock. I had to make sure he was ok but I was cracking up inside." She said with a soft laugh. "I didn't know at the time but I had met my best friend that day. He would always brought out the best in me and was able to make anyone around him smile no matter how bad life seemed. If there is such a thing as an angel, I believe that he was one and I'm so glad that he touched my life." With that she began to cry in front of everyone for the first time. John walked over to her and put his arm around her then hugged her and held her while she cried into his shoulder.

Sebastian stood up to take over. "So, Rhian was an amazing person as we all know. I remember the first time I met him, he and Leena had come into the restaurant when I was still just a waiter. I remember thinking to myself, 'those two look like spoiled college students' because I was used to kids coming in and being rude. I was having a terrible week because I was short on money that week but when they left, he left me a $15 tip. I was shocked and tried to give it back because I thought he had made a mistake but he hadn't." He stopped for a moment so that he wouldn't lose his composure while speaking. He couldn't fight the tears that began to fall but he continued as best as he could. "He cared about all of us. We didn't have to tell him we needed him because he was already there and ready to help. He would always take care of my girl while I had to work so that I could afford to make the rent. He was a genuinely good person. I'm going to miss you Rhian… I love you buddy." He sat down quietly. By now everyone was in tears except for Alexander, who was sitting in the corner of the room looking down at the ground avoiding eye contact with anyone. Sophie stood up next to speak.

"What I loved about Rhian was his ability to enjoy any occasion, no matter how miserable it was. I don't think he would want us sitting here feeling sad. He would be trying to teach Sebastian how to twerk, giving Leena a lap dance, or making fun of me for my accent. I remember this picture here." She pointed to the picture of Leena, Rhian and herself laughing and covered in face paint. "We were painting a *Happy Birthday* banner and he came up and painted my face, then Leena's and then we got him back. We ended up ruining our shirts but it was so much fun!" Sophie continued to tell story after story about Rhian and her times with him at work. Everyone was in better spirits now as they all shared their own experiences with him. Several hours later they were still sharing stories. It was a good time for everyone, exactly what Rhian would have wanted, everyone except for Alexander.

Alexander stood up and walked out of the room. No one had noticed that he was gone except for Leena, who followed him into the kitchen. "What are you doing?"

"Oh, I didn't realize you were here. I am just getting some water."

"You look like you are miles away. Are you still feeling bad?"

"Of course I am. All of these memories just make it hurt even more. Talking about him isn't going to bring him back."

"He isn't coming back, Alexander… I know it's hard but you have to start moving on with your life. Part of moving on is facing the reality. I wanted us to get together because I didn't want to keep feeling like there were things left unsaid. This is our way of saying goodbye. You need to do it too, for your own sake."

"I'm not ready to let go."

"You don't have to let go sweetie, but you do have to live your life."

"I don't know if I can anymore…" Alexander broke down for the first time. Leena opened her arms and embraced him tightly as he began to cry. His tears were not just tears of sadness; they were tears of regret. "I should have been a better person to him. I shouldn't have pushed him away for so long… I can't speak in front of all of them. They probably all think I'm the reason he isn't here anymore."

"Sweetie, no one blames you for anything. Things happen sometimes and they all know it. I think you need to share with them. It'll be good for you and for them. Come on sweetie." Leena held his hand, giving him the much-needed reassurance that he wasn't alone, as they walked back into the other room. The people were laughing at a story John was telling that he and Rhian shared.

"…Rhian was more than just a cool guy, he was a best friend to each and every one of us. There was a love he had for us that was just different. He never gave up, never showed animosity, never wished anything but good to us and I know I didn't deserve him in my life." He sat down. It seemed like everyone had said what they wanted to say until they became painfully aware of the fact that Alexander hadn't. While they hadn't noticed him leaving the room, they were attentive to the fact that he still hadn't spoken. No one felt any hostility towards him; quite the opposite, they wanted to make sure that he would be ok. Everyone breathed a sigh of relief when he stood up and looked around nervously at the faces in front of him.

"I uh…" He took a deep breath and closed his eyes as he looked whispered a prayer, *I know you can hear me so please help me with this. I need strength to speak right now. Be my guardian angel and hold my hand.* Just as he finished his short prayer Leena firmly grabbed his hand, which gave him the courage he needed to begin speaking. "There are no words to describe the hurt I feel in my heart. Rhian meant more to me than I could ever explain… He did so much for me that I never deserved. There is no excuse for my bad behavior in the past few months, I know most of you watched Rhian hurt because of that and for that I am truly sorry. I am sorry that you had to see your friend suffer, I am sorry that I was so distant from all of you, but most of all I am sorry to you Rhian, for not being the man you needed me to be." He said as he looked down at the friendship bracelet that he had been wearing. "Rhian was always so caring, loving, and amazing to me no matter how I treated him. He was always there for me, for all of us." He stopped just as the tears began to flow from his eyes. "He was always there for me." He repeated as his voice began to quake. "He gave all of himself to others, always making sure that those around him were happy when he was there. He loved everyone without prejudice, even those who no one wanted to be around. He gave his time, energy, and love away without ever expecting it back. Rhian always gave the impression that he was strong and confident. He never wanted his friends to feel like he wasn't strong enough to be there for them. I remember watching the many tears he cried over his parent's and then wake up and face life as if nothing were wrong. He was so strong and so confident that I really admired him. He never let me down. He was always real and though I could see that he sometimes thought that he wasn't good enough, the truth was that he was more than good enough. Rhian, you were one of a kind and there is no way for me to ever fully express what you meant to me. I love you. Goodbye."

Leena was touched by Alexander's tears and telling words. She spent the rest of the night sitting with Alexander, again holding his hand for comfort. It wasn't clear if she was trying to comfort him or if she was trying to find comfort in him. Leena drove Alexander home after the gathering and walked him in.

"Please promise me that you are going to go back to a normal life."

"I don't know how I'm going to do that."

"I know it feels like surrounding yourself with all of his things is the only way life seems to make sense but you have to realize that it's not good to surround yourself with the sadness. I can help you gather his things and clean up the place if you'd like. We can donate the things that are still useful. I think that's what he would have wanted."

"No! I can still feel him. If you take his things away I won't feel him anymore. I don't want to be left here alone… I don't want to be alone…"

"You are not alone sweetie… you have me and your other friends."

"I didn't have to talk to him… He already knew when something was wrong, and what it was. He read me like a book. No one else has ever been able to do that. I feel like I lost a part of myself, a part that I will never get back. I didn't just lose him that night; I lost a part of myself that only he could bring out. I laughed the loudest because of him. I've smiled the most because of him. I will never feel the same way again without. I can't be happy again."

"Rhian would want you to be happy and find another person to love you and to make you feel the way he did."

"It's not that I'm afraid I won't find another love or that I won't be able to love someone like I loved him. I'm afraid that I will never be the same person that I was. He wanted me to always be my best and I wasn't able to see what he could see. I don't think anyone will be able to see in me what he did. Leena, I will never live to be what he wanted me to be."

"You only have to be who you want to be. He saw your potential because he didn't expect anything from you but saw your strengths and encouraged you to use them. Be yourself and you will be who Rhian wanted you to be. I don't think he would want you to stay locked up and feeling sorry for yourself. He would want you to go out and be with friends. He loved being around people and he would want you to do the same. He would want you to *live, love, and laugh* just like he would always say."

Alexander sighed and sat down for a moment to think about what Leena had said. She waited for a response but he remained silent. Suddenly he stood up and walked toward the mess on the floor and began cleaning it up. Leena realized that it would be better to not try and push him so she helped him clean. The two cleaned the apartment together the entire night without saying a word. Once they had finished Alexander grabbed one of Rhian's shirts and his stuffed bear that he would still sleep with when he was upset and took them to his room.

"Are you going to be ok if I leave you alone?"

"I'm not alone. I have Mr. Teddy and I know Rhian is with me." Alexander responded with a sad smile. "I'll be alright. Thank you." He hugged her goodbye and walked her to her car.

"Why did you leave us so soon?" Leena spoke to the pictures she had put up on the walls of her apartment. "I know it wasn't your choice but I really wish you wouldn't have left. I am trying to be strong but it's really hard to without you here to keep me strong. It's so strange what Alexander said about how you somehow gave us the confidence to do things because you were so confident in us. I know you would tell me that everything was going to be alright and that I needed to look towards the future, but I never pictured the future without my best friend. You were an angel in life so I know you will still continue to be my angel, dear. I love you and I'll miss you." Leena pulled down the pictures of Rhian and put them on her table. It was time to sleep and let everything settle in her heart and mind. Life had to go on.

Chapter 12

"I told you! We should have never let him leave home. "

"There is nothing we can do about it now, Theresa."

"You're right… I wish it wouldn't have come to this but Pastor told us something like this would happen if he didn't change."

"Just be quiet." Mr. and Mrs. Pierce were bickering in the emergency room. While they were upset about their son's condition, it seemed that they were more concerned with who was right about letting him go away to college. Her true sentiments were hidden behind the usual *holier-than-thou* attitude, made obvious by the raised eyebrows and a chin that followed upwards. She hid her pain well as she continued to argue with her husband about the most irrelevant disturbances around her and complain about every discomfort she felt, while they waited for the doctor.

"This room is so cold! You would think that they would keep it warm for the patients."

"I'm sure there is a reason for that…"

"And there are no windows in here. How is anyone supposed to get better without light?"

"Maybe some patients would be sensitive to light, dear…" He sarcastically added. She was not amused.

"Well, I guess that's true. I'm sorry; I am just really upset by all of this."

"I know, honey. I am too but we just have to trust that everything will be ok."

"I guess." She leaned in to give her son a kiss on the cheek at the same time there was a knock on the door. "I wish he would have just listened to me. I told him that God would cast his judgment but he wouldn't listen to me."

"Well he is stubborn. He gets it from you. There is a balance to everything. When you wrong the Almighty, you will be punished."

"But is he really wronging anyone?"

"Of course! He chose to be gay, it's unnatural and you know that. If he loved God he would make every effort to change."

"I read somewhere that men like him turn gay at a young age. It happens when there is a disconnect from their fathers…"

"Are you suggesting that he is this way because of me?"

"No, but I am saying that something caused him to be that way. Did we push him too much to be exactly what we wanted?"

"We are his parents. We are supposed to push him to succeed."

"Success is one thing, but you always wanted him to be just like you. You told him to play football but he never wanted to. He wanted to dance and you wouldn't let him because *that was for girls.* Maybe we should have given him more freedom to be who he wanted to be. Maybe then he wouldn't have rebelled. I also read that trauma can happen at a young age, which can lead to confusions later in life. He had tendencies growing up but we didn't help him change and the book said that when that happens those tendencies become crystallized and that's part of it. You always barked at him about the way he did things that seemed feminine instead of teaching him why he should act more masculine."

"I have a gay son." A nurse who had overheard them walked into the room and added.

"You do?" Rhian's mother was now fully attentive to what the nurse was saying.

"He is the most charismatic, beautiful soul I have ever met and I'm not just saying that because I'm his mother. He genuinely loves the people in his life. He is a hard worker and volunteers to help others in his free time. When he was born, I had all of the same hopes and dreams that you did. I wanted him to change the world. I wanted him to find a wife and give me beautiful grandkids. But I, like too many parents, never stopped to think about what he wanted. It sounds so cliché but it took me a very long time to accept who he was and not who I wanted him to be. I pushed him out of my life for a very long time and told everyone that I wanted what was best for him. I really thought it was best for him. When my husband passed away, he came to the funeral. We reconnected and he invited me to visit him. I expected to walk into a wreckage of a life but when I got the courage to see what kind of life he was living I was shocked. My son was changing the world, for the better. He took after me and pursued a career in medicine. He is a very successful doctor in New York. He volunteers one month of his time every year, treating people who live in poverty. You have to accept that they are not yours. You have to understand that they are meant for a higher calling, one that you may not understand. I can't explain it to you but they are like lights in a dark world. My Steven has brought me so much joy. Seeing him happy makes me happy and I would never want to take that away from him. I knew from a young age that he was special, mothers always know…" Theresa looked down.

"…Perhaps it doesn't make sense to you, it didn't to me at first, but have you ever wondered why they make up such a small population? It's because they are special. They truly are gifts from God given to some of us because He thought we would do the best job at raising them to shine bright like stars." The nurse walked out with a compassionate demeanor.

"She has a point…" Theresa was caught on the nurse's words.

"I didn't raise a daughter. He needed more masculine friends and instead he chose to stay isolated. Now he is being punished for poor choices. Don't doubt what we know. There is a reason for everything. I'm sure he is paying for his sins. Don't excuse him. If I had it my way, he would have never had the friends that he did. They only encouraged his behavior."

"I guess you're right, although I think that Alexander was a good influence on him." She looked down at her son with sadness as she tried to convince herself that her son was the one who let her down. But she couldn't help but feel as if she had failed her son and her husband. There was a knock on the door that startled both of them and brought her back to the room. It was the doctor.

"I will be honest with you; there is no certainty that Rhian is going to make it."

"He seems fine to me." Mr. Pierce bluntly suggested.

"He is stable… for now… but we will be airlifting him to Chicago. They are better equipped to save him." The doctor's words were unsettling to Theresa who grabbed her husband's hand.

Theresa rode in the helicopter with Rhian while her husband drove the car. Before they took off she left explicit instructions with the nursing staff to withhold answers about Rhian. When they arrived to the hospital in Chicago, the doctor shook his head and whispered something to the nurse that was writing some things down. Theresa began to follow the team of nurses but was told to wait in the waiting room. After several hours Rhian was finally moved into a room.

"Mrs. Pierce, I'm afraid that Rhian is in a coma. He lost a lot of blood and his heart stopped several times. It is a miracle that he is even alive. There is no telling how long he will be comatose or what he will be like if he ever wakes up."

"What do you mean if he wakes up? He has to wake up."

"Ma'am, even if he does there is a possibility of brain damage." Theresa began to cry silently.

"He is my son and I love him no matter what kind of brain damage he has." The doctor left Theresa with her son.

"Pastor, we have received a special prayer request from the Pierce family. It seems that their son Rhian was involved in a nearly fatal accident." The man burst through the door of the pastor's office. There was a lack of urgency in his voice that might be expected for a situation like this. The pastor looked at the man and smiled.

"Thank you. Please have my car ready as I will be going to see them personally."

"Are you sure that is a good idea?"

"Of course it is." Pastor's presence was powerful. When he spoke, it was law. There was no questioning him because he was the final authority. To many, he was like a saint, always ready and willing to help. His voice could soothe the most restless of souls with its hypnotic deep lull.

Pastor walked into Rhian's room and was immediately greeted by Mr. Pierce. He stood up and extended his hand.

"Hello Pastor!"

"Hello, how is he doing?"

"Not well. We are praying that God will work a miracle." Theresa was calm, though uneasy. His presence made her feel uncomfortable. She didn't fully trust him but she knew he was there to help.

"Well I can't undo what happened to him but I can try to help you in this time of need."

"Oh Pastor, your prayers are more than enough for us." Mr. Pierce politely said.

"Mr. and Mrs. Pierce, I have decided to cover all of the medical expenses and pay off Rhian's school bill. He won't be able to attend and it isn't fair that you will be forced to pay it. He can return when he has fully recovered."

"Pastor you can't do that!" Theresa protested. "It's a lot of money and we can't accept it. This could go to people who really need it."

"Rhian is one of our children and you really need it. We are going to take care of everything. You don't have to worry about anything."

"Thank you Pastor!" Theresa was in disbelief. They had worried about paying for the loans that Rhian had taken out to go to school but the pastor was offering to pay off the debt so that Rhian could recover without a problem.

"I will just need his address at school and some of his information."

"Of course! Anything you need."

"I need the power of attorney. I want to make sure that there is no trace of him at that school."

"Why?" Theresa became defensive.

"The people who did this to him may try to find him and finish what they started."

"You think they would?"

"Theresa, these people nearly killed him. They are very dangerous and I want to make sure that he is completely safe. Lord knows what he did to make these people mad but it almost cost him his life. I don't want them to hurt him or your family."

"I guess you are right." She was uneasy about doing so but she agreed. The very next day Pastor did as promised. He paid off Rhian's school bills and had his file made confidential so that no one could inquire about him but Rhian himself and Pastor. He then went to Rhian's landlord and paid off his share of the apartment's balance. Pastor handed the landlord an extra sum of money. The landlord didn't want to accept the cash but he wasn't willing to argue with Pastor.

"Rhian Pierce lived here for a few months. He was a good tenant and left without problems. Do you understand?" Pastor instructed the landlord before walking out. With that taken care of he returned to his office for the busy day ahead.

Pastor called Theresa every day for an update on Rhian's condition. As the days passed, Pastor was more and more certain that Rhian wasn't going to come back. After two weeks he unexpectedly seemed to lose interest in the Pierce family. Theresa didn't mind because his endless interest in the details of their lives made him an overbearing presence and she needed a break. Unfortunately for her, there was no one else she could talk to because Pastor had warned that another attack might be possible if Rhian was found. She didn't want to lose her son twice so silence was the only possible answer.

With New Year's Eve on the hospital staff's mind, the nurse that had been taking care of Rhian was anxiously awaiting the end of her shift so that she could join her family for dinner. She wasn't prepared to walk in and find that Rhian was awake. She immediately called the doctor to have Rhian examined. He wasn't speaking but he was able to move. Shortly after, his parents arrived. His mother cried for the first time since his attack. She was overwhelmed with the excitement of a second chance. She was reminded of the first day that they brought him home from the hospital.

"Honey? How are you feeling? What do you remember?" Theresa's voice was soft and kind. Rhian stared at her for a moment with panic. It was obvious that he remembered something but he didn't say a word.

"Can you talk?" Mr. Pierce bluntly asked.

"Yes." Rhian responded carefully.

"Do you remember what happened to you?"

"I… I don't really remember anything… I know that you are my mom and dad… And that Cabbage died."

"Cabbage was his dog. He died a few years ago." Theresa explained.

"It's possible that he doesn't remember much right now but he may regain his memory after some time."

"What do you mean *may*?"

"In rare cases, patients have been known to experience temporary amnesia. He may not remember the accident or events leading up to the accident. Unfortunately this is a very unpredictable situation because if he is suffering from retrograde amnesia there is no telling when or even if he'll ever regain those memories. The best recommendation would be to get him back into his old routine so that he has a better chance of regaining his memory." The doctor walked out of the room followed closely by Theresa who had more to discuss.

"Doctor, is it possible that he may never regain those memories? What if we don't take him back to his old routine? Would that decrease his chances of recovery?"

"I highly discourage you from trying to prevent his progress."

"Of course we don't want to prevent his progress! It's just that we weren't on speaking terms when he was attacked."

"Attacked? His file said he was in a car accident… Either way, he needs to recover in a familiar environment.

"Thank you, Doctor." Theresa went back into the room to be with her family.

Rhian was soon discharged from the hospital and back home with his mom and dad. He looked very uncomfortable throughout the entire drive but his parents didn't say much. He went to bed as soon as they arrived. His room looked exactly the same as it always had.

"Theresa this is our second chance. This is what we wanted. If he can't remember anything that happened recently, maybe we can fix him." Theresa looked at her husband in disbelief for what he was suggesting, but she couldn't disagree. It was their second chance to raise him the right way. Maybe this was God's way of telling them that they were right and that they had another chance to do it right this time. In the back of her mind, the nurse's words replayed and she also considered that perhaps it was a second chance to help become the light he was destined to be but she quickly banished those thoughts. She loved her son but she also loved her husband and she feared that defiance might put a strain on her marriage.

Theresa felt bad for Rhian because she knew the hell he went through in the past and she didn't want him to face the same situation. She knew that her husband would do his best to keep Rhian from remembering his past so she hoped that there was a way for them not to lose him again.

"I think we should call Alexander. They were friends and Rhian seemed to respond really well to him… I know it's a stretch but maybe he can help us." She knew that Alexander was the perfect compromise. Rhian's father would gladly welcome the masculine Alexander who could make his recovery possible. "If he regains his memory he isn't going to trust us. I'd rather have someone who could be a good influence on him in his life than to let him go back to the others. But if he doesn't ever remember then Alexander could still serve as a positive influence."

"I don't think he will be willing to help. He was one of Rhian's closest friends and he didn't seem to be much help before."

"I'm sure he would be willing to help. If he really cares about his friend, he will want what is best for him."

"I guess you're right. But Pastor said that we shouldn't talk to anyone from that place. They still haven't caught the people who did this to him. Are you sure it's safe reach out?"

"I think we should invite him to stay with us for a short while. We have to explain to him that he can't tell anyone else that he is coming."

"I don't really understand the purpose for having him here or involving anyone other than ourselves but if you think it's a good idea… Well, I don't really have a choice, do I?"

"Not really, Dear." Theresa kissed her husband on the cheek as she left the room to check up on Rhian.

Alexander was awakened by the sound of his phone ringing. The phone displayed an unfamiliar number. He contemplated ignoring the call but his curiosity got the better of him.

"Hello?"

"Hi, Alexander… This is Theresa… Rhian's mom." Alexander's heart dropped. He was furious and confused. He wanted to demand some answers from her. He wanted to tell her how awful it was for them to exclude Rhian's extended family from the funeral plans. He wanted to say all kinds of terrible things so that she could understand how terrible it was to lose him that way and to not hear a word about it but before he could say anything she interrupted his thoughts.

"I know you probably have all kinds of ideas about Rhian's whereabouts." Sighed. "We thought it would be better for him to be home."

"Home is where the heart is."

"Well that's true but his heart was always here with us. I know this is probably a lot to handle but we would like for you to come visit him."

"Where is he buried?"

"Alexander I want you to understand something, my husband and I never wanted Rhian to become gay. We did everything we could for him but bad influences tend to find their way into his life regardless. You were the only friend that made us feel like you were a great influence on our son. My boy needed more friends like you while he was growing up so that he would have grown up like other normal boys… Like yourself." Alexander realized that she was referring to the fact that they believed that Alexander was straight according to them. Rhian's mom continued, "We aren't too pleased with his other friends, at school I mean, so we only wish that you would come. This invitation is for you and only you so I ask that you respect our wishes." Alexander figured that he could find out where he was buried and bring the others at a later time. He just wanted to end the conversation as quickly as possible before he became too angry over the phone.

"So where is he buried so I can see him?"
"Alexander… Rhian isn't buried anywhere… Rhian is alive."

Alexander was still in shock when he ended the call with Theresa. He wanted to tell the others that Rhian was alive but Theresa had warned him that the attackers were never caught so it was still dangerous to share his location. He wanted so badly to call Leena and tell her the good news but it was best to validate that he was indeed still alive. He couldn't believe that the man he cared so deeply about was only a few hours away. He made the drive to the Pierce house later that night.

When he pulled into the driveway he closed his eyes. He could still see Rhian's lifeless body lying on the ground as the officers arrested him. He could remember the feeling of uncertainty he felt in the cell as he waited for answers. He remembered the conversation with Leena as she told him that Rhian was gone. The heartbreak he had felt over the last few weeks was focused on that one moment and it was overwhelming. He opened his eyes and took a deep breath as he prepared himself to enter the home. Alexander was afraid that it was all just a lie that perhaps Rhian's parents were lying. But they had no reason to lie to him. Either way he wouldn't believe it until he saw Rhian. He wanted to believe but he couldn't without proof.

As he walked up to the door one heavy thought entered his mind. *What if Rhian doesn't want to see me? What if Rhian hadn't asked for me because he was very mad?* It was surreal. There were a million questions and he would soon have them answered. *I don't know if I can handle seeing him… and I can't pretend to be happy in front of those people after everything they did to him. I can't do this!* He thought about turning around and driving away. *I have to do this… for him!* He knocked at the door with a strong fist. He saw Rhian's mother come to the door with a smile on her face.

"Hello dear! Come on in!" She politely invited.

"Thanks…"

"Are you hungry? I must made dinner so I hope you're hungry."

"I'm not hungry… I want to see Rhian."

"In time honey. We want to talk to you before you see him."

"I didn't come here to talk to you. I came to see him."

"Alexander, there are some things we have to explain to you before you see him. I understand that you are upset with us for not telling you that he was still alive but we couldn't risk it. In fact, I'm risking a lot by inviting you here but I know that I can trust you. I also know that Rhian would want you here."

"What do you mean risk?" Alexander asked with shrugged brow.

"The people who attacked Rhian were never caught. The police ruled that he was just at the wrong place at the wrong time. From my understanding it all happened in his apartment. I don't know what my son was involved in but I am still afraid of what they might do if they find him. It was obvious that someone wanted him dead."

"The police officer that we talked to said that the case was closed and that there weren't any details that they could disclose. As far as we knew, Rhian had vanished without a trace. The only reason we couldn't file a missing person's report was because the police had already closed the case."

"We didn't want anyone to know his location because we didn't want them to find him. I know it was hard but I had to protect him. Please understand that it wasn't personal." Alexander remained silent.

"Look, I understand that it was for his own good but it was horrible not knowing. At least now I'll be able to offer the others peace of mind."

"No. You can't tell anyone that he is here. Like I said, the attackers may still be looking for him."

"I can't lie to them."

"I'm not asking you to lie. I thought that you might consider staying… to help Rhian recover."

"You want me to stay… here? With you and Mr. Pierce?"

"Yes. It would be a huge help if you could. You could stay in the guest room and we would pay for your meals. It would be cheaper for us than paying for a nurse. It would only be for a few weeks. I know it is asking a lot but you are his best friend and I know he trusts you. He doesn't remember anything before the accident and Mr. Pierce and I want to use this as a second chance. We made a mistake when we pushed him away but we don't want to do that again. We want to make things right."

"You aren't planning on telling him anything… are you?"

"We would prefer to let God decide if and when Rhian remembers. All we can hope for is that he will forgive us for what we did."

"So you will be accepting of him no matter who he is with? Even if it is with another man?"

"He won't be with a man. Rhian was just confused. I'm certain he will find a nice girl to be with." Alexander realized that she hadn't changed. She planned on lying to her son in order to get him to follow their wishes. It was crazy and it was wrong. He couldn't hide the intensifying rage that was moments away from erupting. But amidst his fogged judgment a beam of clarity burst through and he realized that if he ever wanted to see Rhian again he would have to agree to whatever Theresa asked of him. Her words were almost convincing except that he knew the truth. But she was still able to reassure him that there was no other option for him. This was going to be a hard secret to keep but if he agreed to stay but this way he could be with Rhian.

"I am still in school…" Theresa realized she had won and that it was now time to negotiate.

"How are you paying for school and where are you living?" Alexander froze. He couldn't tell her that he was Rhian's roommate. There could be no suspicion about his relationship with Rhian or the fact that he could have possibly prevented the attack had he not been trying to run away from Rhian.

"My parents are paying for the tuition and I took out some loans for my rent."

"So you don't work?"

"No ma'am."

"We would need your help for a few weeks. Do you think you could just come here on the days you don't have class?"

"I might be able to do that but I don't have the money to pay for the gas."

"We could pay for that. It's not a problem. I don't want to lose him again and I feel like your influence would be a good one." Theresa sincerity was welcomed after the seemingly rehearsed business exchange she had just made with him.

"I can be here as many as four times per week and as long as you pay for the gas and my meals while I'm here I will help you." Alexander kept his hard demeanor to prevent her from reading his excitement. This was as good as it was going to get for him, at least for now. He figured that after some time, when Rhian was recovered they would eventually leave the Pierce home and return to their apartment together.

Theresa led Alexander through the dimly lit hallway towards the kitchen. Along the walls were pictures of Rhian and what seemed like other family members displayed proudly. Rhian never talked about having any siblings or other family that he was close to but the pictures suggested that he didn't grow up alone. It was interesting to Alexander that they had the pictures up at all. He figured that they would have taken them down and tried to forget about their son after they had kicked him out. But it was quite contrary to his expectations. The display of memories on the wall reinforced what Theresa had said about not losing him again. He imagined them turning into cold, heartless people and abandoning their son but that wasn't the whole story. In a way he began to feel sorry for Rhian's parents because he realized that they couldn't understand him and they probably never would. It didn't excuse their behavior but it did give him an idea of the bigger picture. There was a lot he didn't understand about their situation but he would soon learn more.

They sat in the kitchen with Mr. Pierce who had a stern look on his face.

"Alexander, I liked you. I still do. But I want to make sure that we are on the same page. I don't like the way my son was influenced to continue in his godless lifestyle. I am hoping that we can come to an understanding about the direction of my son's life. We want certain things for him and we would like you to help him get there." Alexander began to feel very uncomfortable because he wasn't sure where the conversation was going. He didn't want to be asked about the nature of their relationship because he wouldn't know what to say. Rhian's dad continued, "As his best friend we would hope that you would want what's best for him the way we want what's best for him." Alexander wanted to stand up to him by telling him about the many sleepless nights Rhian endured because of their decisions or about the time Rhian spent in the camp that nearly killed him. He wanted Mr. Pierce to understand that in his opinion he cared about Rhian a lot more than they did. But he refrained.

"Of course I want what's best for him…" *What's best for him is to be as far away from you two as possible.* He thought, biting the inside of his cheek to keep the words from spilling out.

"Alexander, he lost part of his memory. We aren't sure how much but we want to use this as an opportunity to bring him back into our lives and lead him down the right road."

"He doesn't remember that he left home and didn't want to come back." Theresa interjected as Alexander's blood began to boil. *You have to control yourself… for him. He is alone and the only people he has are these two lunatics. You have to be there for him.* He wanted to get up and walk out but he couldn't bring himself to do it. Theresa's talk had prepared him for this one with Mr. Pierce. "So we want to fix the broken relationship that we had. But we don't want him to be confused again. He went through so much hardship because of it and we want to keep him from remembering that lifestyle. We aren't bad people, we just want what's best for our son so please respect our wishes and we will allow you to be a part of his life." *I should call the police. I should call Leena and the rest of his real family to come rescue him.* But alas the sad reality was that he couldn't financially handle the burden of taking Rhian away. There was no realistic way for him and his friends to take care of Rhian. In that moment, he realized that the best place for Rhian to be was in the comfort of the place he used to call home.

"I understand that you are just trying to do what is best for your son. How can I help?" He clenched his fists under the table as tightly as possible as those words bitterly came out of his mouth burning him like poison. He felt nauseous for making a deal with the Devil.

"We appreciate your cooperation. We knew you would see it our way."

"He is sleeping in his room. I can take you to see him if you'd like, but first eat some dinner." They ate in silence exchanging occasional glances and very few words. Alexander was very uncomfortable but he wasn't going to risk losing his chance at helping Rhian over feelings of anger. The discomfort of the environment seemed to play a major role in why he was able to go along with their insane plan. He felt judged without even doing anything. It was as if Mr. Pierce was watching him eat his food and wondering why he wasn't eating the *Christian way.* He was self-conscious about his every movement for fear of what Mr. Pierce might say. *Should I be more polite? Is being polite too feminine? Can I smile or is it inappropriate?* All of these questions ran through his mind throughout the dinner because Mr. Pierce was a particular guy but he also knew that they were very religious. Once they were done eating Theresa showed Alexander to Rhian's room. Alexander breathed a sigh of relief because was finally allowed to see Rhian but he was also able to escape Mr. Pierce's overwhelming presence.

"He is still sleeping, do you want to wait for him to wake up?" Theresa asked as she held open the door.

"I'll wait with him."

"Ok, suit yourself." she responded.

Alexander found a chair near Rhian's bed and sat down. The familiar sound of his breathing tempted Alexander to lie down next to him. He reached out and ran his fingers through Rhian's hair. Rhian stirred and took in a deep breath as he softly opened his eyes. Alexander backed into his chair in anticipation. He feared anger. He feared rejection. But mostly, he feared being a lost memory. Rhian slowly turned his head toward Alexander. The only light in the room was a dim lamp on the nightstand. It was difficult for Rhian to see the person in the chair clearly. He stared attentively for a few moments before finally breaking the deafening silence.

"Hi?" The uncertainty lay heavy in his inflection.

"Hi, Rhian. How are you feeling?" Alexander was hopeful that his voice might trigger something in his mind and bring back the memories of *them*.

"I'm awake… So I guess I'm feeling good." Alexander chuckled at the predictability of Rhian's playful nature.

"I'm glad to see you." He directed his bashful smile at Rhian.

"Ok. Who are you?" Alexander's smile faded quickly at the realization that Rhian didn't know him anymore. He clenched his teeth and took a deep breathe then recomposed himself.

"It's me… Alexander…"

"From church?"

"No… I'm your best friend…" He paused for brief second. "But it's ok if you don't remember because you will soon." Alexander's hope beamed from within.

"Ok, well best friend, could you get me some water please?"

"Sure, do you want ice?" Alexander remembered that he always had ice in his drinks and responded at the same time as Rhian. "Of course you do."

"Of course I do." They looked at each other and Rhian cracked a smile. Alexander spent the night talking to Rhian about how they had met and the times that they had shared together in college leaving out the fact that he was gay, their relationship and the way it played out before the attack. Without those ugly memories, all that remained were the good times they had shared. It was these memories that reminded Alexander how he had fallen for Rhian. He kept him smiling and laughing the entire night as he shared stories of their adventures together.

Seeing Rhian smile again was exactly what Alexander needed to commit to his recovery. Alexander kept his promise to Theresa, visiting for several days per week and spending quality time with Rhian. While it seemed to be working for him, he didn't realize that his grades began to suffer. He chose to ignore that he was no longer doing as well as before because he knew he was smart and he could make it up in the finals. Trying to balance between Rhian and school kept Alexander out of the loop with his other friends. They noticed that he stopped coming around and was never available.

"Alexander!" Leena yelled out to the familiar figure walking ahead of her. He had his earphones in so he couldn't hear her but she wasn't going to let him get away without an explanation. She reached out and tugged firmly on his arm.

"Oh, hey!" He said with excitement.

"Hey yourself! Where have you been?" She examined him closely. She looked for signs of self-inflicted abuse but he maintained a peaceful demeanor.

"I'm sorry Leena… I've been really busy."

"I noticed. I came by the apartment the other night and you weren't there."

"Yeah… I went home."

"Is everything alright?"

"Everything is fine. Like I said I've just been very busy."

"I'll accept that for now because you do seem at peace but I expect dinner with you soon. I want to know all of the details of what's been going on. I love you doll!" She kissed him on the cheek and they parted ways. Alexander was relieved that she didn't press him because he wasn't sure how long he would be able to lie to her.

It was now late spring and Alexander was almost done with his semester. More importantly, he had spent so much time with Rhian that he felt closer to him again. Alexander noticed that Rhian seemed to feel the same way about him. They shared a level of comfort that matched the way they were before. Things were as close to perfect as could be for the circumstances. He also noticed that Rhian closed up when his parents were around. It wasn't obvious to them, but to Alexander it was obvious.

"Please eat Rhian." Alexander pleaded with him.

"I'm not hungry."

"You haven't eaten all day."

"I haven't been hungry today."

"I know my cooking isn't the best but it's better than cereal." Rhian was irritated.

"Fine." He took a bite of the food and smiled. "Ok this is really good."

"See I told you." Alexander shot back a big smile. "What's going on? Why have you been so quiet lately? Are you ok?"

"As ok as a person who lost a few years of his memory can be…"

"I know it's hard but someday it will come back. I believe with all my heart that you will return to nor… your memory will come back."

"Why are you here?"

"What do you mean? Your parents are both working and someone had to stay with you."

"Do you work?"

"Yes… I am here working to help you recover?"

"That's not a job."

"There are at home nurses."

"You're not a nurse."

"Well, no… But I am your best friend and I care about you. I want you to get better."

"But how long are you going to stay? Don't you have a life of your own?" Alexander was taken back by the question. His life had revolved solely around Rhian and he didn't do things for himself anymore.

"Well I like spending time with you… You are my best friend."

"I know… but I don't remember you… doesn't that bother you? Don't get me wrong I'm really glad that you're here… I'm really alone when you're not. But I haven't done anything to deserve you in my life.

It's like you are taking care of someone who just met you and you're not even getting paid. Isn't that kind of crazy?"

"You may not remember me, but I remember you. We shared many great experiences."

"Were you my boyfriend?" Alexander was caught off guard by the question. He couldn't lie to Rhian but the truth was that they were never officially together. Alexander was never actually his *boyfriend*. Hesitant to reveal the truth, Alexander remained silently in his thoughts. Rhian could tell that Alexander was keeping something from him but before Rhian could ask, Alexander had an answer.

"No, I wasn't. The reason I'm here all the time is because…You rescued me. In your previous life, you saved me from a bad situation."

"How bad was it?"

"It was… Life or death." Alexander reminisced.

"I almost killed myself but you managed to save me from myself." Rhian raised his hand and hit Alexander in the back of the head.

"Why would you do that?" He asked angrily.

"I made some bad choices one night. I was immature."

"How were you going to do it?"

"I was on top of a building and about to jump but luckily for me you showed up just in time you calmed me down and got me off of the building. I was so scared, but when you showed up everything was alright."

"So we are close…"

"Yes we were… are very close."

"What aren't you telling me?"

"What do you mean?"

"You are hiding something… I can almost feel it." Rhian could read Alexander better than anyone else. He knew Rhian was close enough to him before to feel what he was feeling, but was it possible that they still had that deep connection? Or is it possible that they had somehow rebuilt what was lost prior to the attack. "I may not remember you but I sure as hell can tell that there is something wrong. I don't really understand it but it's like there is a weight on your mind and it drains you."

"There are things that I did that I'm not proud of… I can't undo them but they still haunt me."

"It does you no good to worry about something you can't change. You have to live with the consequences of your actions but the key is that you get to live. You can't stop your life nor can you ignore what happened. Cry if you have to. Punch something if you need to. It's ok to feel. It's not ok to stop moving forward. Never forget, never regret." Alexander took a deep breath. Hearing Rhian say this was like receiving forgiveness. Even if Rhian remembered what happened between them, he would forgive him. Alexander was truly at peace for the first time in a long time.

"You're right." Alexander smiled with relief.

"There's that smile."

"What smile?"

"The perfect one."

"Thanks." He snickered lightheartedly to avoid continuing the exchange of compliments. Rhian waited for something more than just a giggle.

"You love me don't you? And I love you? You can see how I do can't you?" Alexander's eyes grew wide with surprise. How was he going to respond to that? Should he lie? Should he be honest? Just as he inhaled to respond, his phone rang. Theresa was calling to check up on the boys. Alexander took the call in the other room to escape the tension.

"Yeah, we are eating lunch now but I wanted your permission to take him to the city for a walk and some hot chocolate."

"I don't see a problem with that. Have fun!" Theresa agreed cheerfully.

"Alright, I'll have him back by dinner." Alexander walked back into the room where Rhian had settled onto the couch. He thought about telling him the truth. He thought about asking him to run away with him. He thought about their dream of San Diego. All it would take is three words. I love you. But he couldn't bear to break his heart again. He couldn't tell him the truth about his parents. He had suffered so much without them and he knew how much they meant to Rhian. He couldn't take it all away.

"Get ready, we are going out."

"Where?"

"It's a surprise."

"Alright, I love surprises." He said with a smile. He was excited to be getting out of the house. Rhian quickly threw on a pair of shorts and his favorite green t-shirt. Alexander was waiting in the car for him.

"Buckle up!"

"Yes sir! Where are we going?"

"I told you, it's a surprise."

"Well I'm curious. I guess I'll just have to trust you."

"I guess so." Alexander reassured with a smile. As they journeyed to the city, they played a playlist from Alexander's music player. Rhian was listening closely to each of the songs.

"Where did you get all of this good music?"

"What do you mean?"

"These songs are great! I love them all. They are all of my favorites or new favorites."

"Of course you do. You created the playlist."

"Really? I have good taste in music." Rhian happily patted the dash to the beat of the song.

"The doctors said that it would be better for you to do things that you used to in order to help your memory. That's why I played the music and that's why I'm taking you to Chicago."

"Really?" Rhian was more excited than before. His excitement made Alexander's heart melt. After a while they arrived in front of a place with a dark, boring façade.

"What is this place?"

"You'll see." They walked into a colorful room full of happy faces and the smell of sugar permeating the air. It was a cupcake parlor. Rhian gazed at the array of delicious cupcakes. They all looked so good that he couldn't decide which one he wanted.

"I'll have the Red Velvet and he'll have the Cookie." Alexander interrupted Rhian's thoughts about cupcakes.

"Which one is that?"

"You'll see." Alexander enjoyed Rhian's trademark wide-eyed intrigue. He pulled out his wallet and paid the cashier.

"You're paying for them too? You are too nice Alexander. Too nice."

"You love cupcakes more than anyone else I know. We've been here in the past. You loved this place. They sat at the lakefront and watched the people walk by as they enjoyed their cupcakes.

"Can I try some of yours Alexander?"

"I got the Red Velvet because it is really good, but it is your other favorite cupcake so I figured you could taste it." He handed it to Rhian and watched his face light up again as he tasted it for the first time.

"Wow! That's really good!"

"I told you!" They laughed as they talked and Alexander told Rhian about some of the things that they would do together. Rhian and Alexander were in their own world. They finished their treats and walked back to the car. The boys found their way to the Magnificent Mile. They went into several high-end stores. Rhian saw the prices of the items in most of the stores and just laughed.

"Quit making fun. It's not the price you are paying for, it's the artistic vision."

"Well sorry! I wasn't making fun, I was just noticing how expensive everything is."

"I used to do the same thing. Then you explained to me that the price of fashion is not in the designer's name but rather in the artistic expression that is found in the clothes. To most, they are just simple garments made to cover yourself from the elements, and while that is true, *fashion is the outward expression of the inner person.*"

"That's deep. Well come on let's go try things on." Alexander watched as Rhian tried on several articles of clothing. Of course all of them made Rhian look really good. *I've never checked out a man like this before. I have never been so aware of what his butt looks like or the way his shirt accents his shape. He really is a beautiful person inside and out.* A thought he used to fear was now something that made him feel secure in his love for Rhian. The boys went from shop to shop trying things on, watching other people look around and try to determine whether or not they had money or not. They had a great time forgetting the old memories and making new ones.

"I have another surprise for you."

"Are you serious? Today has been more than I could have ever asked for. You are amazing."

"Well we have one more place to go."

"Where is that?"

"A concert."

"What kind of concert."

"You really like electronic dance music. There is a festival that I know you wanted to go to last year but couldn't. I'm taking you tonight. You're favorite DJ is performing."

"That sounds exciting! Alexander I couldn't thank you enough for everything."

"You deserve to have a great time." The boys made it to the concert just as the sun began to set. There were thousands of people crowding the area in front of the stage but the speakers were set up along the length of the field. They stood near the back of the crowd, just in case the crowd got too wild. Rhian clung to Alexander's arm throughout the performance so that he didn't lose him. As the night progressed the boys found their way closer and closer to the front of the crowd. They shouted and sang along with the words of the songs, jumping up and down with the rest of the crowd. The energy of the crowd was intoxicating and amidst the chaotic motion and sensory overload, Alexander found himself in a complete moment of bliss. He felt his heart beat in sync with Rhian's. All of the joy in Rhian's heart was shining through and Alexander was in tune to it. It was in that moment that he felt the safest. Perhaps it was the high of energy from the crowd or the sheer happiness he felt from being with Rhian. By the end of the show, the two boys were beaming with excitement. As they walked speechlessly to the car, Rhian held on to Alexander's arm, leaning his head against it intimately.

"Alexander, you've told me about the good times we shared, but weren't there any bad ones? You mentioned that I rescued you… What happened?"

"You don't want to hear about that."

"It sounds like we are very close friends and we really care about each other so yes, yes I do."

"I hope it doesn't shock you too much. I was at a party and…"

"Was I with you?" The question was suggestive.

"You were there. We took a drug, but you didn't do it. You left. I took the stuff and when I noticed you were gone I went looking for you. As luck would have it I didn't start tripping until I left the party. I got lost in my trip and ended up on the roof of a building that we used to hang out at. I saw what looked like the Death. He kept trying to persuade me to kill myself. I wanted to do it. I wanted to stop hurting…. the people around me. It was selfish, it was stupid, but I was in a very bad place. When you called me and asked where I was, I knew I couldn't do it. I couldn't make you find me like that. You came right away and saved me. I never felt so safe." He realized that things might become awkward.

"Wow… so I kept you from hurting yourself… but why would you want to hurt yourself like that? What could have been so terrible for you to want to take your life?"

"That's something that would be better left unsaid. At least until you remember. Things were kind of rocky between us at the time."

"Things were rocky at the time of the accident… weren't they?"

"Yeah…"

"So why are you here?"

"Because I promised that I would be there for you if you needed me." Rhian smiled.

"Thank you. For everything." The boys returned to the Pierce residence and Rhian had to sneak in. Alexander decided to go back to campus that night. As he drove, he considered how far he and Rhian had come. He wondered what he could do to make Rhian fall in love with him again. His phone rang but he was so deep in thought that he answered without checking to see who it was.

"Hello?" Alexander finally answered Leena's call.

"Alexander?" It was Leena. He cringed when he recognized her voice. He had been avoiding her since the day he bumped into her. It wasn't that he didn't want anything to do with her, he just wasn't sure how to keep himself from telling her the truth about Rhian.

"How are you?"

"How am I? How about, *I'm sorry for disappearing and not calling.* Where the hell have you been?" She was furious.

"Leena… He's alive!"

"What are you talking about?"

"Rhian is alive! His parent's took him away before we could see him and they didn't tell us!"

"Fuck you Alexander, I put up with your craziness before he died but I'm not letting you mess with my head like you did with his! This isn't funny! Now stop!"

"Leena, I wouldn't joke with you like that. They hadn't caught his attackers so they couldn't tell anyone where he went. It's really messed up but you have to believe me." He fidgeted with his phone for a minute. "I sent you a picture that we took today. Look at the date on the sign behind us."

"Oh my god! I need to see him!" She was confused and didn't know whether to be happy, angry, or sad. Alexander told her everything that had happened. He explained that Rhian's parents wanted to keep his location hidden for a little while longer.

"They don't trust anyone."

"So you are telling me that I can't see him. That's unacceptable…"

"I know it sounds crazy."

"Because it is. He was attacked here at school. If someone is looking for him it will be here. I don't see why I can't go visit."

"I think they know something we don't."

"What do you mean?"

"I think he might have been attacked because of something they did."

"Then he isn't safe there either."

"Probably not. But he's been safe so far. Whatever the case may be Rhian would be safer away from all of this. I plan on taking him away at some point soon. I have to earn his trust enough before I do. The last thing he remembers before the accident was his dog dying. That was a few months before they sent him away to the camp. He still trusts his parents."

"This is beyond complicated. Why are you with him then?"

"I have no idea. They told me it was because I was a good influence on him and I could help be there for him in case he remembered. They don't want to lose him again but they also think he can be straight if he is around me long enough. That's at least what his mom told me."

"Wait, so you are taking care of him? They have no idea of your history… do they? And of course neither does he?"

"Yeah, I guess that's how karma works, eh?

"Is that where you have been all semester?"

"Yes."

"Alexander, please be careful. I know you feel bad about the way things ended between you two but you can't lose yourself because you feel guilty." Though she was in shock about Rhian, she was also concerned about Alexander. Although the picture was proof, it wasn't real to her yet. The only thing that was real was Alexander's mysterious behavior.

"I'll be alright."

"Please call me when you have a minute and we can sit down and talk in person. I can't have this conversation over the phone. Also, please don't disappear like that on me again."

"I'll call you soon."

Leena spent the rest of the night staring at the picture. She tried to find the flaw that would discredit its authenticity but she couldn't find it. She began to cry when she realized that what Alexander was saying might actually be true. Overwhelmed with emotion she pulled out her phone and typed out a long message to Rhian. She saved the message on her phone and put it away.

That night, Alexander lied down to sleep. As he drifted away from consciousness he could hear the sound of children laughing all around him. He was spinning on a merry-go-round and a little boy was running alongside as he spun it while Alexander held on. He could see that the boy was having the time of his life. There was a strong presence of happiness that surrounded the two of them. When the merry-go-round finally stopped he got off and walked towards the sound of a little girl laughing. She was beautiful, sitting on a swing being pushed by Rhian. He knew in his heart that these were their children.

Rhian's smile was different in this scene. He always had a beautiful brilliant smile, but now there was something more. Fulfillment perhaps, but it was more than obvious that Rhian was in a state of complete happiness. As Alexander walked up to him he put his hand on Rhian's shoulder and Rhian turned with a big smile and planted a kiss on his lips. Alexander felt electrified and alive.

"Come on Daddy! I want to go down the slide!" The little boy yelled out as he pulled him by the hand.

"I want to go down the slide too Daddy!" The little girl was right behind them. Rhian walked over to a nearby table where they had placed a basket. He began to set the table as Alexander played with the children. He called them over once everything was ready and they all sat down for their meal.

The dream changed and he was at a party. It was his daughter's wedding. She looked beautiful next to her handsome groom. Again the smiles on her face and Rhian's were inspiring. It brought on a feeling of complete security and happiness to everyone around them. He could tell that the people in the party were more than just friends; they were family. He was wrapped in a blanket of love and joy.

In the blink of an eye Alexander was brought to the beach where he could see the sun setting. He was holding Rhian's hand and they were both old. The serenity that he felt was euphoric. It was more than just a dream it was his destiny.

The morning brought with it a renewed sense of optimism for Alexander that day. He wondered what Rhian saw when he had thought of a future together and if it was anything like what he had dreamed. He was determined to be with Rhian. *He may not remember be, but if he was able make me fall in love with him then perhaps I can do the same.*

"Hello?" Alexander was awakened from his deep sleep by the ringing phone.

"Alexander?"

"Yeah…" He cleared his throat in an attempt to convince the caller that he wasn't sleeping.

"It's Mr. Pierce."

"Oh hey, how are you?"

"I'm well. Where did you take Rhian yesterday?"

"I took him to Chicago."

"You promised to have him home by dinner."

"I'm sorry, sir. We lost track of time and Rhian was having such a good time."

"Alexander, I think Rhian is at a point in his recovery where he doesn't need to have you there all the time. It would be best if you kept some distance from him for a while. It isn't personal but I don't want him to become dependent on anyone but God."

"I don't understand. Is this because we got back late?"

"It's because Rhian is a grown man and he doesn't need another grown man taking care of him. He may not remember everything but he is recovered enough to go out and get a job. He needs to get a job and most importantly get back into the church. Whatever you and my son had going is over." Alexander felt very uncomfortable. Did he know about them? Did he know that they shared more than just a friendship?

"Mr. Pierce, I don't know what to say… I thought everything was alright. I just wanted to help."

"I appreciate everything that you have done for us but it's time for him to move on. It's not good for you either. How were your grades this past semester?"

"I failed a class. I have to retake it this summer."

"Maybe it's time for you to focus on yourself." He couldn't argue with sound logic and without Rhian around to cloud his judgment, Alexander could clearly see that he was right.

"Can I still come visit?"

"Yes, after a few months." With such an indeterminate timeframe, he felt uneasy about it but he couldn't say no. Mr. Pierce wasn't going to change his mind.

"I will keep my distance, if that's what you want. But I would like permission to maintain an open line of communication if Rhian desires to contact me."

"That's fine. I can agree to that." The conversation ended shortly after they came to agreeable terms. Alexander stared down at his phone considering the outcome of his obedience. Rhian hadn't replaced his phone since the attack so he relied on using someone else's phone. Rhian was right… I can't live like this. It's all been a lie because he doesn't know the truth. I need to tell him the truth. I need to go there and rescue him.

Alexander arrived at the Pierce's later that evening. He had spent the entirety of the car ride choosing his words carefully. He couldn't wait to see the look on Mr. Pierce's smug face when he told Rhian the truth. He couldn't let them get away with it. He pulled into the driveway almost taking out the mailbox. Walking up to the door he could see the family in the living room. Mr. Pierce was handing Rhian a small box. He stopped to watch what they were doing. Rhian had a big smile on his face as he unwrapped a cell phone. Rhian hugged his father and kissed his mother on the cheek. He seemed ecstatic over the simple gift.

Rhian hugged his parents and smiled with excitement probably the way he used to before he was sent to the camp. Alexander realized that he would be stealing this happiness away from him if he told the truth. As much as he thought it needed to be said, he didn't want to kill Rhian's spirit the way his parents had done before. He couldn't sacrifice Rhian's happiness for his own. While he was considering all of this his phone rang, it was from an unknown number.

"Hello?" Alexander solemnly responded.

"Alexander, it's me Rhian! I just got a phone!"

"That's great, *buddy*!" He hated using the word buddy with Rhian because he was so much more than that. He also knew that Rhian cringed when he called him his buddy.

"I know! Now you'll never get rid of me." His smile could be heard through the phone.

"Rhian, I am not going to be coming to visit you for a while."

"Why not?" Rhian's mood suddenly changed.

"Because… I have a very busy schedule between school and work."

"I thought you didn't have a job?"

"I do now."

"Oh. Did I do something wrong?"

"No! Of course not… It's not you. It's me."

"I don't understand." Rhian was confused

"I'm sorry." Alexander calmly hung up without further explanation. He couldn't tell Rhian the truth. He wanted to tell Rhian to come outside. He wanted to take him for a ride, tell him the truth and never return. But the sad reality was that Rhian was finally happy and all of those nights they spent talking about his broken relationship with his family were no longer meaningful. He had the relationship he wanted with his parents. They weren't like before, or so it seemed, and Rhian wasn't in any danger anymore. It was time to let go.

Alexander drove in silence to the city. He had one destination in mind, Navy Pier. It was where he fell for Chicago and where he promised himself that he would someday make a life there. He found himself questioning his own future, wondering how he could go on creating a bright future without Rhian.

He walked to the end of the pier where the sound of the waves crashing against the rocks was the only thing that could be heard. He closed his eyes and took a deep breath of warm air embracing the feeling of the wind as it caressed his face. He reminisced further about his plans with Rhian to move to San Diego after a short pit stop in Chicago because they both loved city life and joked about moving there to grow old together. He started to laugh as he pictured a future with Rhian. He could see them both throwing snowballs at each other during winter and then going to get hot chocolate afterwards. He began to live the dream he had about their shared future and felt a strong desire to let himself get lost in the fantasy. But he was brought back to reality by the distant sound of an ambulance. When he opened his eyes he could only see the water in front of him. He looked down at the bracelet once more before pulling it off and launching it into the water. *Maybe someday we will be together and he will be happier than ever.*

Chapter 13

"You don't smile like you used to… Why aren't you bubbly anymore? I miss that Alexander." Leena protested the melancholy mood.

"Sorry, I've just got a lot on my mind."

"You miss him, don't you?"

"Yes. Is it so wrong?"

"Absolutely not! But you made a decision and now you have to deal with the consequences."

"I want to see him, but it will only make it harder on me later on."

"There is nothing that anyone can do for him. If he lost his memory for good then he will have to find his way back to you but if he regains it then he will definitely find his way back. Either way you can't fix it, you just have to live your life and pray." Leena didn't believe in God, but she knew that Alexander did. While it was as good to suggest prayer as it would be to suggest growing wings and flying, it worked for Alexander.

"You're right. I know all that, yet I still can't let it go."

"You don't have to let go of anything, you just have to move on and live *your* life. Control what you can control and the rest will work itself out. In the meantime, enjoy margaritas." She took a drink of her colorful margarita and winked at him from behind her turquoise Wayfarers.

"I guess you're right. Let's go get into some trouble." He had relaxed and his mood had improved.

"Pool?"

"Pool!" Alexander exclaimed. Ever since he stopped going to visit Rhian, he had spent more time with Leena. They liked to do things that would likely get them into trouble if they were discovered. One of their new traditions was to sneak into a hotel and go swimming in the pool. This time it wasn't just the two of them. They invited most of their friends and extended an invitation to anyone in Leena's building who was there for summer school. Leena brought her portable speaker so that they could have a party on the go. Armed with a few bottles of liquor and daring spirits the group of friends partied at the pool that night for several hours.

A game of water polo had begun and everyone lost track of time. Alexander was completely invested in the game and failed to notice a girl who had been checking him out. The game ended and Alexander's team lost. Of course it wasn't fair that the team that won had members of the school's water polo team. Alexander made his way to one of the lounge chairs with a drink in hand. The girl who had been eyeing him made her way over to the chair next to him.

"Great game."

"Thanks." He took a drink from his beer. He wasn't really interested in conversation. Just as she was going to ask him another question, the lights around the pool were turned off.

"Everybody out!" The hotel manager angrily shouted. The group quickly evacuated the pool area and left the hotel. Leena invited everyone over but most of the others went home.

Alexander didn't see the girl again that night. The group of friends decided to get together again later that week for a movie night that turned into another party. They began to play naked beer pong. Leena had invited a boy she met in class that night and by the end of the night she had disappeared into her bedroom with him. She wasn't the type to have one-night stands, or at least not recently. As everyone got more and more drunk and the games continued people started to pair off. Curiously enough Alexander paired up with the girl who was checking him out at the pool. He felt a bit self-conscious since he was naked and so was she but he didn't let it bother him too much and found a quiet spot to talk to her.

"So what's your story?" This girl was very forward.

"What do you mean? "

"Do you have a girlfriend? Boyfriend?"

"I'm single… why do you ask?"

"I'm just making sure you aren't already taken. There is something special about you." She said as she placed her hand on his shoulder and pulled him in for a kiss. She was aggressive, which Alexander seemed to like, but he didn't want a meaningless kiss. He didn't want to just connect for a few minutes and then never talk to her again. His mind was now preoccupied with thoughts that he didn't want to think about.

"I can't do this."

"I knew you were gay…"

"No, it's not that… I just can't…"

"What's wrong?" She seemed genuine.

"There is someone else." He smiled at her and walked away. He didn't see the girl again.

The attack that Rhian suffered took more than just his memory. By taking him back to his pre-camp high school memories, it took away the identity he forged from bad experiences in his recent past. He was far removed from the boy that believed his honesty would save him. He wasn't stronger because of the camp, he wasn't more resourceful because of his parents kicking him out, and he wasn't heartbroken because of Alexander. In an ironic twist, Rhian was reborn back into the nightmare he so desperately wanted to wake up from.

"Hello Theresa, how are you?" A rather large woman wearing a mismatched outfit and too much perfume approached Theresa and

Rhian as they walked into the church for the first time since the attack. For Rhian it had been years since he had been there. He was taken back by the size of the building itself. So much glamour for such a humble occasion it was blasphemy. She was the fourth person to approach them in the five minutes since they parked the car.

"I'm well. Thank you."

"It's such a pleasure to see you back. And is this the dear prodigal returning home? Oh, Rhian it's wonderful that you are back home where you belong." Rhian felt sick to his stomach.

"Thanks." She smiled as if expecting more. When Rhian didn't pursue further discussion she promptly began to walk away.

"Enjoy the service." She added without looking back. Rhian watched her greet several others as she walked the halls. He looked at Theresa for answers but she simply shrugged and they laughed off the strange behavior. The service was just as Rhian remembered; shouting, praising a church member for going above and beyond their Christian duty, a series of loaded statements that suggested nonconformity was a damnation, and finally an emotionally draining alter call in which those who didn't stand or walk the aisle were called rebellious. What normally drove Rhian to tears and forced him to walk the aisle to pray was no longer there. It was gone and he didn't feel the least bit guilty about it.

After the service was over the Pierce family decided to have family lunch at a local restaurant. As luck would have it there were several people from the church gathered around a large table. Sure enough the pastor was sitting at the head of the table with a big smile on his face. The man was rarely seen without his signature smile on. They did their best to go unnoticed until the pastor realized it was them. He got up and walked over to their table.

"Hello family! How are you this afternoon?"

"We are doing well Pastor, how are you?" Mr. Pierce answered. He understood that the question was directed to the man of the house. After all this was the Man of God and when the Man of God spoke, it wasn't to the woman, it was to the Man of the House. Rhian watched his mother tense up. Pastor made her feel very uncomfortable.

"I am surrounded by members of my congregation. I feel like a shepherd with his flock so I would say I'm right at home." Too many words for Rhian to care.

"So you think they are sheep too?" Rhian's snarky tone caught Pastor off guard but he didn't let it show.

"How has your recovery been Rhian? Has your memory returned?" His stare was intense and Rhian could see why he made Theresa uncomfortable. It was almost threatening.

"I'm fully recovered but my memory has yet to check in."

"That's alright. It gives you more space to make new memories. How about you swing by my office after the night service."

"Well, I don't think we were planning on going to the night service. Perhaps next week." This was a clear act of defiance. No one turned down an invitation from Pastor to visit him in his office, especially if Pastor initiated the conversation. Mr. Pierce seemed horrified by his son's blatant disrespect towards Pastor. He was about to cut in but Pastor beat him to the punch.

"I'll tell you what, are you looking for a job? I think I have something that might be perfect for you. I hear you are very intelligent. I need someone on my team that has an incredibly detailed memory and is good with numbers."

"Are you sure you want the kid with memory loss to work on things requiring a good memory?"

"This job wouldn't require you to remember the past few years. Just give me a call if you decide you need a job. I'm always willing to help one my sons out."

"Thank you. I will keep it in mind."

"Enjoy your meal. I will see you soon." Pastor announced to the family while looking at Rhian. It seemed like he was challenging him but Rhian didn't budge. His parents seemed outraged by his behavior. Theresa couldn't believe that her son was so publicly disrespectful towards the Man of God. Mr. Pierce didn't say another word to him for the rest of the meal. Rhian could see the people from the table that Pastor was sitting at. He saw them whispering while staring at him. He could see their judgments directed at him from across the room. As they walked out Pastor wished them well. The others around the table simply raised their brows and their chins in protest of their presence while they whispered maliciously.

Integrating back into church life meant Rhian had to attempt to connect with the other young people. While he tried to be friendly with them most acted stuck up and rude. At the last youth activity he tried to join in on a group discussion about social media but when he sat down the group of people stopped talking and eventually walked away. He didn't fit in but they seemed to go out of their way to exclude him. He had resorted to sitting alone and watching the other young people enjoy themselves. This world, while it was the last he remembered, felt wrong. It felt different. He felt out of place because he was nothing like them. He saw the world through very optimistic eyes; they saw it as a place to fear. For the people from the church, normal was a life void of enjoyment and committed to a cause that they didn't fully understand. But that was life for them, they didn't fight it, they didn't question it because they didn't want God's judgment upon them. Everyone did his or her part and there were no questions.

Rhian had been a part of this system all of his life starting out in the church's school from a young age all the way until he graduated. He could see the brainwashing and fear. It was frightening how the diabolically manipulative men in authority managed to make people like Rhian believe they were all alone. If you had any doubt in the cause, you were like a cancer that needed to be removed. It was quite genius how they succeeded in selling an idea that wasn't real. They sold the possibility of doing something that had never been done before; something that mattered. It was instilled in the youth that if they dedicated themselves, wholly to the cause, they would be able to make a difference in the world and could someday be recognized the way their pastor was. It was possible to become a celebrity by simply doing what was asked of you better than those around you. Like anyone else, the people craved more than just a life of senseless obedience. The opportunity to reach a status of social relevance and the ability to leave a legacy was the perfect prize. Rhian used to believe in it, until he was taken to the camp.

After returning from the camp Rhian realized that the church specialized in creating addicts. People addicted to the idea of god, the importance of self-sacrifice, and the high they received from being *humble*. It was an impressive feat that the church had accomplished, keeping its addicts faithfully returning day after day, sacrificing precious time living a lie, and following faithfully, ignoring what they didn't understand. It was a vicious game not meant for the weak. But the most impressive accomplishment was the wall the church created. It was a wall that couldn't be broken, forged from the stories of failed attempts at crossing it. The wall, while not a real visible structure, ran through an area that included several towns because the church had been in existence for many years and through time its influence had spread to a radius of about thirty miles in all directions. The people would move around from time to time but they never moved past the wall. Most of the time they would have to ask permission from the leaders of the church just to take a vacation. There were countless former members who had left the church for a better life, only to end up broken and in shambles. They would be picked up back into the church, *rehabilitated*, and then made to be an example. Of course these stories were of people who lost every form of support when they left and found themselves consumed by the pleasures that led to their eventful destruction because they were never taught moderation.

"Come on boy, go talk to the girl!" The man with short dark hair said to Rhian as he stared off into space. Staring at nothing and thinking about everything had become his new hobby since Alexander stopped coming to visit him. Who he had been and who he was now were two different people. Alexander painted a happy life for him but there was a lot he wouldn't talk about. The pushy man with cropped hair continued staring at him as Rhian realized that he wouldn't let it go and he would have to go up and talk to someone.

"What? Oh, ok." Rhian did his best to sound enthusiastic. It was a terrible idea for him to be there. The purpose of the activity was for the single young adults to mingle at a fast food place. To Rhian it seemed more like taking children to a playground or monkeys in a zoo. It was loud, obnoxious, and a waste of time. *Why don't any of these people have manners? And why am I even here? These people don't like me and I don't really like them… I should have stayed home.* He thought to himself as he walked in the direction of a girl who was starting right at him. He stopped at the table where there were three girls giggling stupidly, which usually bothered him but there was something about the girl that was staring at him that intrigued him.

"Um, hi, I'm Rhian. What's your name?"

"Who are you talking to weirdo?" One of the girls at the table shot a look of disgust.

"I'm talking to her so if you would please refrain from budding in that would be great." Rhian shot back with a raised eyebrow as he pointed to the girl who had stared at him. She wore a bright red bow to contrast her stunning black hair and brilliant blue eyes.

"Well she doesn't want to talk to a freak like you!"

"Jess… will you relax?" The girl interjected.

"Fine. But he's trouble… Don't say I didn't warn you…" Jess was displeased.

"Hi Rhian, it's nice to meet you. I'm Jerri. Jerri Lynn."

"You are beautiful Jeri Lynn. Would you like to have lunch with me sometime?" *Where did this confidence come from?*

"How about now? That is the purpose of this meet and greet isn't it?" she coolly suggested. They found a table near the back, away from all the others.

"So tell me about yourself Jerri. What do you like to do?"

"Well I like to sing, play the piano, and sow." *How typical.* Rhian thought

"Wow! I love the piano… Perhaps you could teach me how to play."

"Maybe, what about you? What do you do for fun?" Rhian remained silent for a moment, remembering that the only thing he had done for fun in the last few months was hang around Alexander in the city.

"I like to watch television, read, and listen to music."

"You hesitated… Are you lying?"

"My hesitation comes from a lack of experiences. I've been cooped up in my house for the past few months and I'm barely starting to get out."

"Why is that?"

"I was… involved in an accident. The doctors said I lost part of my memory so I'm not really sure what to talk about beside the last few months."

"That was you?"

"What do you mean?"

"They announced that one of the members of our church needed prayer. They wouldn't say why just that you weren't doing too well. I guess you're better now."

"I guess so." Rhian was curious.

"This is great then!"

"What's great?"

"You get a second chance to be whoever you want to be and do whatever you want to do." She seemed overly enthusiastic. "Tell me Rhian, what do you want to do?"

"I want to fly."

"Then let's fly!" She hopped up and quickly walked out the back door with Rhian stumbling to keep up. Her youthful excitement fascinated him and though he wasn't too keen on going to the activities, she was interesting. She led him to a nearby highway overpass. She climbed up next to the guardrail. The sound of cars speeding by was loud and powerful. She lied down on the ground and closed her eyes. Rhian lied down opposite to her with his head touching hers.

"What are we doing?"

"Shhh, just feel it." She said.

"Feel what?"

"The rumble of the road. You can't see them, you can only hear them for an instant but you can feel them long after they are gone. It's not flying but if you close your eyes it can be. Just focus." Rhian did as instructed. He could feel the ground shake as the cars passed by. It was exciting. It was liberating. He was free and he liked the feeling. Suddenly he felt a pair of soft lips on his. Without opening his eyes he instinctively put his hands to her face, caressing her soft skin. The sensory overload was euphoric and he lost himself in the moment. He became very aware of her soft skin and the sweet scent of her perfume. As they opened their eyes he experienced a powerful yet familiar feeling.

They returned to the restaurant to join the group. No one had noticed that they had ever left. When they came back Jerri's friends were sitting at separate tables talking to boys that had approached them. When she and Rhian returned to the restaurant her friends made their way over to their table and brought along their dates. They had a good time as they talked and got to know each other. Rhian hit it off with the guys and surprisingly with Jerri's friends. After the activity was over his parents picked him up.

While sitting in the cramped back seat of his father's car he pulled his phone out and began to dial Alexander's number. He wanted to talk to his friend about the amazing girl that he had just met but there was a part of him that wanted to see if Alexander would be jealous. They hadn't spoken to each other since the night Alexander told him he wouldn't be coming to visit. Perhaps this was a way to get him to come back. Albeit an immature act, he truly missed his friend and wanted him back in his life. In the meantime, he told his parents all about Jerri, leaving out the kiss and the fact that they left the activity. He saw how happy it had made them and he knew this was something he wanted to pursue.

"Alexander she's incredible. She is beautiful, smart, fun and she intrigues me! I think I've been bitten by the love bug!"

"Wow… That's great… What's her name?" Alexander did his best to sound genuine.

"Jerri Lynn. I didn't think that going to these activities was a good idea but I am glad I did. I can't wait to go next week."

"That's good Rhian. I'm happy for you." Alexander didn't seem as excited as Rhian had hoped but he figured Alexander was just having a bad day.

"How are you?"

"Oh, I'm alright. I've been working hard and staying busy as usual."

"That's good." Their conversation went on for a few minutes before Alexander had to go.

"Rhian, if you need anything let me know ok? I love you, *buddy*." There it was again, the word *buddy* as if they were just good ol' pals.

"Likewise."

As fall approached, Rhian continued attending the activities and growing closer to Jerri and her friends. While his new life was very different from his old one, he was enjoying all of the experiences that he was having. He kept in touch with the guys from the activity and they got him involved in hunting. He also began taking horseback riding lessons with Jerri who owned a horse properly named Horse. Every day was like a new adventure with her. He really enjoyed spending time with her because even though he could feel himself living behind the wall of oppressive religion, he was happy with her by his side. He felt like the attack had stifled his ability to enjoy his life but Jerri was the perfect remedy.

Rhian called Pastor shortly after meeting Jerri and decided to take him up on his offer for a job. He was tired of sitting at home and waiting for the weekly activity. He was also sick of relying on his parents for money to do things. He wanted to take Jerri out on a date with his own money. Pastor assigned Rhian to the church's accounting department. He wasn't aware that there was such a thing in the church but it made sense being that the church was so big. In fact, he never realized how much money passed through the church. He really enjoyed seeing his work make a difference. He was in charge of assigning funds to different departments in the church. He was able to decide which departments were deserving of their funding and which departments needed some adjustments. It didn't require him to spend forty hours per week at the church but it kept him busy enough. It was also the perfect opportunity to see Jerri because she worked as a secretary in another office. He saw her several times per day and he was happy with that.

With life in a good balance, Rhian had to wonder why things had ever been so tumultuous before. Alexander was unclear about his struggle but it was hard to believe that things could have ever been anything but good. Nevertheless, he had to question whether the stability was real or just a farce aimed at keeping him from the truth. It was time to make the effort and rekindle the friendship he had with Alexander that had turned to simple exchanges of small talk.

"Hey." Rhian called his friend.

"Hey…" Alexander sounded guarded.

"So I was thinking that it would be nice to see you. I haven't really talked to you much or seen you since…"

"I know."

"Well what do you say? Will you come visit?"

"Sure. I'd like to."

"*Sure. I'd like to*, you're coming? Or *Sure I'd like to catch up sometime in the distant future but I don't actually plan to?*"

"I will come see you." He was a bit more relaxed now.

"I want you to meet Jerri." There was a brief pause.

"Ok. I can do that."

"You two are going to hit it off. I know it."

"Yeah, I'm sure we will."

"Let's plan for dinner this Friday at my parents' place."

"Ok, sounds good."

"Perfect. I'll see you then!"

"See you then."

Alexander nervously waited for the weekend expecting it to be an awkward occasion. He arrived at the Pierce home fairly early. Mr. Pierce greeted him at the door.

"Hello Alexander." He extended his hand out to greet the young man.

"Hello Mr. Pierce."

"I trust that you have been taking care of yourself."

"Yes sir."

"Come on in." Rhian ran up to him with a big hug. He was clearly excited to see his friend.

"How are you?"

"I'm doing well. How about you?"

"I'm great. Happy to see you."

"Likewise." Alexander awkwardly smiled at Rhian who seemed to be waiting for him to continue explaining. The momentary silence was uncomfortable so Rhian continued.

"The food is almost ready. Jerri is teaching my mom how to cook." He chuckled, happily changing the subject.

"You better watch it Rhian! I have a knife." Theresa called out with the knife in hand. She waved it around to validate her empty threat. "Hi Alexander, it's good to see you." She added before turning to finish what she was doing. She wasn't as enthusiastic as Rhian was to see him.

"Alexander… This is Jerri." Rhian proudly announced. She turned around and flashed him a warm smile. This girl had a glow to her or perhaps it was just her straight white teeth and bright red lipstick.

"It's a pleasure to finally meet you Alexander. I've heard so much about you." She seemed like a genuinely sweet girl to him. *Great… I don't stand a chance.* He thought to himself.

"The pleasure is all mine." Jerri's aura was intoxicating. It made the room light up, and brightened his mood. Alexander was also stricken, but not with love for Jerri. She was like no other girl he had ever met before. He knew he had lost Rhian.

The dinner was delicious and the family had a chemistry that Alexander hadn't seen before. He remembered how things went when he visited with Leena and how it was nothing like this. *They are only treating him like this because he is dating her. Yeah she is wonderful, I'm sure, but I wonder if he is really as happy as he seems. Of course he is! What are you thinking, just look at him. He is smiling and being himself entirely. He isn't pretending to be happy. He is happy… I can't give him this. Maybe I was wrong. Maybe we were never meant to be.* Alexander was lost in thought and didn't realize he had locked eyes with Rhian.

"Penny for your thoughts?" Jerri said to him, as the table grew silent.

"I was just trying to remember the last time I had a good home cooked meal this delicious. I can make a mean grilled cheese, but this is home-style at its finest." *What does that even mean?* He wrestled with his thoughts.

"Well thank you for the compliment." Jerri replied.

After dinner Rhian, Jerri, and Alexander played a board game and chatted over desert. Alexander learned a bit more about Jerri's background and vice versa. Even thought it was awkward, Alexander really enjoyed her company. Jerri was very amicable towards Alexander. It was as if the three had known each other for years. There was a bitter sweetness to the occasion as Alexander was able to affirm that Jerri was indeed good enough for Rhian but more importantly that she made him happy.

It got late and Jerri had to go, but Rhian invited Alexander to stay.

"It's a long boring drive and it's late. Just stay. It'll give us a chance to bond."

"I don't know… I really do have to get back."

"Are you working in the morning? Do you have school?"

"No."

"Then there isn't a problem. Just tonight. Please, I miss you and I want to talk to you."

"I guess I can stay." Alexander was clearly hesitant. He seemed uncomfortable but as long as Rhian was asking, he couldn't say no.

"So tell me, how have you really been?" Rhian inquired.

"I have been…"

"*Good,* yes I know you said that already but what does that really mean? I can see that you aren't really comfortable and I know something is on your mind so tell me, what is it?"

"How are you doing? Because the truth is that I am alright as long as you are alright." I worry about you. I worry about you every day and I need to know that you are safe and that you really are happy." Rhian didn't expect that response.

"Well, to be honest I think my life is starting to work out, for once. I finally am getting along with my parents and I feel more comfortable with the people in my life. Of course, Jerri has a lot to do with that."

"So you think things with your parents are going better than when you were in high school?"

"Well considering that was where my memory went back to, yes. What aren't you telling me?"

"So you are content." He dodged the question.

"I am where and what I'm supposed to be." That confused Alexander.

"I am sorry that I took off without explanation…"

"I'm sure you had your reasons. Besides, you weren't forced to be here. But I'm very thankful for the time we shared. I think about that concert every day. I can't thank you enough for breaking me out of my bubble."

"Rhian we share a very close friend. I'm sure she would like to see you."

"What's her name?"

"Leena. She loves you like a little brother and she misses you. We talk about you all the time."

"Why am I barely hearing about her?"

"Because…" *I wanted to spend time with you all by myself.* "…she was studying abroad but she will be back in the States shortly. Would you like to meet her?"

"Absolutely! Tell me all about her!" Rhian accepted the reason and excitedly began asking questions about his soon-to-be *new* friend. The boys eventually fell asleep on the floor. They had lied down to continue their conversation as they both fell asleep. Later that night Alexander woke up confused about where he was. He felt the familiar warmth of Rhian's body along the length of his. He realized that their fingers were intertwined and the whole thing seemed like a cliché. It warmed his heart but the feeling quickly faded when he remembered that he was just a few feet away from Rhian's parents. The longing he had for Rhian was overwhelming; bringing him back to the first day he lost him. He left without making a noise figuring he could call Rhian and apologize for his swift departure.

That night signified an end to the idea that would be at peace with losing Rhian. He would never be able to let go and no matter how hard he would try to forget about him, he would always be in love with him. He resolved in his mind to accept things the way they were and to move on. As much as he wanted to be with Rhian, he knew how happy he was with his new life with Jerri and his parents' support. Alexander spent a lot of time convincing himself that this was the right decision. Whenever he felt a desire to be with him, he would think about the look on Rhian's face during the dinner with Jerri. Though his love for Rhian grew with each passing day his appreciation for Rhian's happiness did too. Sacrificing his feelings was something he had to do but he never lost hope that someday things might be different.

One Year Later

It was now December again. One year had passed by since Rhian's attack and so much had changed. After leaving the Pierce home in the early summer, Alexander dedicated himself to his schoolwork in order to make up for the bad semester he had while taking care of

Rhian. He had a heavy course load for the fall and springs semesters but he would still be able to graduate on time.

After shifting his focus towards graduating, Alexander became very anxious to finish school and start his new life. He wanted to move to the city and reinvent himself but he still had to finish school. He had distanced himself from Rhian but he had also gotten closer to the others so it was very exciting to know that they would all be graduating together.

Rhian and Alexander spoke once every few weeks, just to keep the line of communication open, but both were very guarded about their private matters. One would ask how the other one was doing and they would chat about the events of their lives but neither would get into much detail. After the night he had ran out, he didn't make an effort to reintroduce Leena into Rhian's life. It was mostly a selfish act because he knew that having Leena in Rhian's life meant that he wouldn't be able to get over him. One morning during their usual calls Rhian sounded more excited than usual.

"You're in a good mood today. How are you?"

"Alexander, I have some exciting news to tell you."

"What's that? Did you win the lottery?" He snickered.

"No! I wish. Actually, you can kind of say that I am winning the lottery… Jerri and I are getting married in March." He paused for a moment to let that sink in. "I know I don't remember our past but I know you care about me and I care about you so I was wondering if you would be my best man." Alexander was speechless. "Are you still there?"

"Yeah… Um…" Facing the reality was hard enough but now he was going to have to watch his hope die in person. He wanted Rhian to be happy but the last thing he wanted was to be there when he committed his life to Jerri. *No. I can't because I'm in love with you. I want to be with you and I know she makes you happy but so do I. I would dare to say that I make you happier than she does but you don't remember that.* "…Sure. I mean I'd be honored to!" He said altered his sad mood.

"You don't sound too convinced…"

"Well, I am just a bit surprised… Don't get me wrong, I think Jerri is great and she seems to make you happy but how long have you known her? And you're getting married in a few months?"

"I know it seems crazy… but she connects with me like I've never connected with anyone before… except for you of course." This made Alexander think for a moment. *What did he mean by that?* Rhian continued. "I like being around her and she makes me happy. I know you are just being a good friend by being honest with me but trust me; I am making the right decision. I just know it." Rhian almost sounded star struck.

"Ok well like I said, I will do it."

"Thank you so much! I love you, Alexander."

"I love you too. Goodbye."

Alexander was blindsided by the news of Rhian's engagement. Leena, who had joined him for coffee could see the distress in his eyes. She felt sorry for him but she didn't fully understand him either.

"What's wrong? What happened? Why do you look so sad?"

"I'm fine."

"You are not fine!"

"He's getting married…"

"What?"

"Yeah, he is in love with Jerri and he wants to marry her. He asked me to be his best man, how could I say no? Leena it's killing me! I'm so jealous and I'm pissed off at myself. I've never felt like this for a girl so why do I feel like this about him? I should have never let him go."

"Then go tell him!"

"I can't do that to him. I can't hurt him like that. He is happy and I don't want to take that away from him."

"That boy loved you and I'm sure he still does. And you love him. He may not remember… but you two are soulmates. You are meant to be together and you know it. He was happiest when he was the light in your life."

"Leena, I can't." He was irritated with himself more than with her persistence.

"You can do whatever you want to do, but don't lie to yourself. You are being a coward and it's that simple." She stopped trying to convince him as they sat in silence for a few moments. Without saying much more they cut their coffee date short.

Chapter 14

"Rhian, this is Leena. She is one of my best friends." When Rhian made eye contact with her he froze as the feeling of familiarity intensified.

"Have we met before?"

"Yes, we have. We are… were very good friends before…"

"Why haven't I seen you before now?" Alexander was quickly becoming uncomfortable. He cut in before Leena could answer.

"Because she was studying abroad… in France." Alexander named the first country that popped into his mind. Leena looked at him with a half-smile and a furrowed brow.

"Well, I'll let you tell the story then." She challenged. Rhian laughed at Alexander's nervousness.

"How was France?"

"Oh it was tres magnifique! Although I wish I could have spent more time exploring the countryside."

"You'll have to tell me more about it later. I have to go find my bride. I will see you two at the table. I can't wait for you to meet Jerri, Leena."

"We'll see you inside." She flashed her perfectly rehearsed smile. "You told him I was in France?"

"I'm sorry I didn't know what else to say."

"What about the truth?"

"I couldn't. They told me I couldn't tell him the truth. They said that the person who attacked him wasn't caught and if I told people where he was they might come looking for him."

"No one is looking for him! It was a wrong place wrong time scenario. That's why they haven't caught anyone. It was a burglary gone wrong and that was it."

"You don't know that."

"No, but I would rather not think that my friend was involved in something that could get him killed. Besides, you know Rhian as much as I do, does it really seem like he would do anything to get himself killed like that?"

"I guess not. I'm sorry Leena… I wanted to spend time with him… alone and I was afraid that if I brought you up to see him that he would want to spend more time with you and I wouldn't be able win him back."

"How did that plan work out for you, *best man*?" He lowered his head in defeat. "I forgive you. I understand why, but be honest with yourself. Is this what you want?"

"We are not discussing this here."

"I don't want you to make a mistake."

"If we were meant to be it will happen."

"Not if you don't act. There is no such thing as luck, you either go after the things you want in life with every fiber of your being or you pretend to be happy with what you have because it's safe and it won't hurt you like the risk of failure. But if you lie to yourself and pretend you will hurt others because while you are pretending to be happy, there is someone else out there hoping that you are brave enough to be honest but they will never feel true happiness because you were too afraid." She walked away from him so that he could think about what she had said.

She found Rhian in the back sitting next to the girl Leena assumed to be the bride.

"Leena, this is Jerri. Jerri, Leena."

"Hello, it's a pleasure to meet you." Jerri was her usual sweet self. Leena was taken back by how friendly the girl was.

"The pleasure is all mine."

"Where did Alexander go?"

"He had to run to the restroom." They continued making small talk while they waited for the food to be served. Alexander soon joined them and acted like everything was fine. Any sign of rancor was gone. He was as pleasant as he could be. After some initial conversation Jerri got up to use the rest room. Leena waited for her to be out of the room to get up and follow.

"What are you doing?" Alexander tried to keep her from leaving.

"Relax I'm just doing my job." Leena made her way to out.

"Girls and their shared bathroom breaks." Rhian brought Alexander's attention back to him.

"Yeah..."

"They can't do anything alone. That's why they need us guys." *Who is this Rhian? He sounds so much like these church people.* Alexander chuckled awkwardly at the slightly sexist remark.

Leena found Jerri in the bathroom making sure the details of her presentation were perfect. She scanned the length of her dress inspecting every inch for lint.

"Are you nervous?" Leena startled Jerri.

"Oh! Leena I didn't see you there."

"It's ok. Are you nervous about the wedding? I would be. Alexander told me that you two have only known each other since August."

"I guess it will be a year soon." She was reminiscent.

"I am only asking because I wouldn't want you to feel like you were making a mistake. I love Rhian like a brother and I want to know that you two aren't rushing into things."

"You know, I was just thinking about how I always pictured myself as being a nervous wreck right before my wedding. It makes sense. But I'm not the least bit worried. I know you are just looking out for him but I can assure you that we are not rushing into anything. We talk about this all the time and we both agree that while it's crazy to think that we are getting married so young and after only knowing each other for such a short time, we are certain about this. I love him very much and he loves me. I've never been more certain about anything in my life. I am very lucky to have such a wonderful man in my life and I will cherish that forever." Talking about Rhian made her seem like she was flying in the clouds. Leena could tell that she really was in love with him.

"I'm very glad we got to meet each other."

"I am too. It is nice to put a face to the name."

"You knew about me?"

"Of course!"

"So you know about his past?"

"Yeah! Alexander told me all about the things you all used to do in college. I guess you all are still in college. I don't think I could have hung out with you while you did some of the things you all do but from what he has told me you are a wonderful girl. Rhian was lucky to have been friends with you. I truly hope that we too can be friends." Leena was very uneasy about what Jerri had said. How much of Rhian's past did Alexander share with them? It couldn't have been much because she was still marrying him.

"Jerri, there is something I have to tell you. I can't let you marry him without telling you the truth..." This was her one and only chance to do the right thing and if Alexander wasn't going to do it she would.

"You love him... don't you?" There was no malice in her voice. She was genuinely inquiring.

"I love him like a brother... That's not it. He has a bit of a history that I don't think Alexander told you about..."

"Is this about him being gay?" Leena was speechless. She was shocked that Jerri already knew.

"Yes…"

"The night I met him, my friends told me that he was gay and that he was in a relationship with a man, but that after being in a coma he couldn't remember that he was gay…"

"That's ridiculous…"

"It's good to hear that you think that."

"No, I mean that someone could think he would forget that he liked men. Rhian didn't fall in love with someone for their gender. He fell in love with the person. Evidently you made him feel what the man he forgot about made him feel."

"Well he must not have cared much about Rhian if he didn't come after him." Leena's blood began to boil because she saw how much it hurt Alexander to let him go. But she also knew that he believed in what he was doing. She had to respect his wishes.

"Jerri, it's a lot more complicated than that. The point is that he loves you and that you love him. If you think that this is right and you love each other then you should be together. Just promise me that if he does remember his past that you will be patient with him and let him figure out what he wants."

"Thank you for your honesty, Leena. I believe with all my heart that we were meant to be together and that we are doing the right thing. It means a lot to me that we have your blessing. I promise that if he remembers I will give him all the time he needs to figure things out." The girls left the bathroom together and rejoined the boys at the table. They continued the evening without any more revelations.

"She really is perfect." Leena told Alexander on their drive to the Pierce house. They would stay the night there.

"I told you! I can't compete with that. Look how happy they look."

"I know… She knows…"

"Knows what?" Alexander lingered on her last statement.

"That he loved a man…"

"You told her about us?" He was furious.

"Calm down… I didn't tell her that you were the man."

"What did she say?"

"She knew his story the night they met. I'm pretty sure she is counting on him not remembering."

"I guess we all are."

The ceremony was in Rhian's home church, which was decorated extravagantly with flower vases on every flat surface. There were baskets of colorful flowers, hung from the ceiling that adorned the aisle. The altar was lined with flowers, which surrounded the wedding party. A bouquet of white roses was placed in front of each of the windows. The string quartet performed a beautiful Canon in D. The ceremony began and the wedding party came out. The flower girl cautiously released the flower petals from her hands evenly distributing them to both sides of the aisle. The people unanimously let out a gasp when Jerri made her grand entrance. She looked beautiful. All eyes except for Alexander's were on her.

Alexander was lost in thought, trying to work up the courage to say *I object* when the time came. Yes it was a tradition to ask if there are any objections but perhaps if he could work up the courage he might be rewarded for his efforts. The ceremony ended as quickly as it had begun and Alexander daydreamed throughout the majority of it. Before he had his chance to *object*, Rhian was already kissing the bride and they were taking pictures. He missed his chance. When everyone was dismissed to go to the reception he found his way outside as quickly as possible. He made it out to the where the dumpster in the ally was before violently throwing up. Poor Alexander never threw up but this time there was no stopping it. Rhian came out to look for him.

"Are you ok?"

"I'm fine."

"You are throwing up. You're not fine. What's wrong?"

"I'm just feeling a bit sick." He looked up and locked eyes for a brief second. Their connection was clearly still strong. Rhian knew that Alexander was heartsick.

"Look, I know we had to be close before everything happened." He walked him over to the edge of the building and sat down next to him. Alexander joined him on the ground a few feet away from the puddle of vomit. "I promise that I will never forget you or grow distant from you. You will always be my best friend no matter what happens. I know that this is probably a bit strange for you because you haven't seen this life that I have made but I promise you that I am happy. I love you Alexander and I will always appreciate everything that you have done for me."

"Rhian, you and I were… special. I will always care about you more than you'll ever know and I really will always be here for you if you need anything." He looked down for a second.

"Is that all you have to say?"

"Yeah…"

"Ok, then let's go back inside for the rest of the party."

"Rhian…"

"Yes?"

"I…"

"When you look at me it's not like you look at friend. If you were going to tell me that you are in love with me I would ask that you keep it to yourself. I don't have a problem with those feelings at all but I am married now. If you had any objections they should have been handled before I committed my life to her. It's too late for that now. I made a promise and I intend on keeping it. I love you." Alexander didn't say a word. Just then Jerri came out looking for them.

"There you are! Come on boys we have a reception to attend." She was cheerful.

"Coming Mrs. Rhian Pierce." Rhian emphasized the *Mrs.* to get his point across to Alexander. He quietly followed the couple back inside.

Alexander was asked to give a speech during the reception. He told some stories of their time together in college and then concluded with, "Rhian is a special person and after meeting her I can definitely say that Jerry is too. He lights up a room whenever he walks in and so does she. Together their smiles will brighten anyone's mood. I miss hanging out with you like we did back in college because no one else knows me as well as you do. I sincerely wish nothing but the best that life has for you two. If you ever need anything, you can count on me. I love you both." Rhian hugged Alexander tightly followed by Jerri.

When it was all over, Rhian and his new bride were headed off to their honeymoon while Alexander and Leena headed back to school. He was jealous that Rhian had finally found happiness in Jerri and it was painful to think that he had lost him again. They drove home in silence that night.

"Are you going to be ok?" Leena asked as he dropped her off at her apartment.

"I'll be fine…"

"Call me if you need me." He politely smiled in response and drove off. Shortly after, he arrived at his apartment where he searched through his closet like he had lost something very important. He dug out a bag that contained a sweatshirt. It was Rhian's sweatshirt that he had held on to for over a year now.

"I think about the last few moments I shared with you, the real you, every single day. I wish I could take back what I did… but I can't. I have to live in torment for losing you because I made the mistake but I can't make you pay for it. I will not be responsible for holding you back. I was too afraid to face reality and that is my burden to bear; I would rather carry it and know that you are happy than to keep you from having everything you ever wanted. I will survive and with enough time I will be ok because you taught me how to enjoy the life I have." Alexander lied down in his bed clutching Rhian's sweatshirt hoping that there was still a trace of his scent lingering but it had completely faded. His tears ran silently until he fell asleep. The nightmare was over and so was the dream.

Chapter 15

Rhian and Jerri spent seven days on the honeymoon of their dreams. Jerri's parents paid for the wedding but Rhian's parents paid for the honeymoon. It was Theresa's dream to see her little boy on his wedding day with his beautiful bride get into the limo and head off to the honeymoon that she and her husband never had. While there were bumps in the road, she knew that someday she would get her wish. After all of the trouble that they had gone through with Rhian's rebellion and his absence in their lives it allowed her to make peace with the past.

Their time in Hawaii was like a dream come true for Rhian who never imagined that he would actually be this happy with a woman from his church. Their first night together was very awkward for the both of them. Rhian had no idea what he was doing but he was determined to make it a night to remember. Jerri was very nervous because it was her first time being physical with a man. To that point she had only kissed a boy. This was a completely different experience. The first night all they did was cuddled and talked about their plans for the future. Rhian was becoming frustrated with his nervous bride. He massaged her neck and began running his hands over the bare skin on her breasts but she pushed him away and chastised him refusing to go any further.

On the third night of their honeymoon she was finally open to physical expression of love. The inexperienced Rhian did his best to be gentile with her and pay close attention to what she was feeling. He kissed her neck gently then continued with growing intensity and passion. He was immediately turned on by the sound of her soft moans. He took pleasure in the feeling of her burying her nails into his back. He took in the sight of her beauty with enthusiasm, greedily focusing on the curves of her thighs and the fullness of her breasts. He lustfully appreciated her bare skin with the palms of his hands, gripping and rubbing her the way he thought he would like. She moaned even louder than before, which only further encouraged him. He kissed her deeply then suddenly broke the kiss and began moving down her body towards her navel. As he continued downward she convulsed slightly and pushed his head away in protest.

"What are you doing?"

"I want to please you…" Rhian answered with a devilish smile.

"Are we allowed to do that?" Jerri sounded worried.

"What are you talking about?"

"I thought we weren't allowed to perform oral… that's what one of the teachers told me a few years ago… She said that we were only supposed to use that for intercourse and for reproduction… I don't want to break the rules…"

"Jerri, I don't think it's against anyone's rules for me to pleasure my wife. Besides, what I do in my bedroom is none of their business…" Rhian sounded frustrated.

"I don't know if I'm ready for that."

"Ok…" She had killed the mood. Rhian went to sleep frustrated and confused that night. The very next morning he woke up to Jerri performing oral on him. He didn't want it to stop so he encouraged her by using his hand to guide her motions. After he had enough of the foreplay he gently guided her onto her back where she would become his. It seemed to come more naturally to him than to her. She winced in anticipation of the pain. While her anxiety made him slightly uncomfortable he knew it was now or never.

"Are you ready?"

"I am. As ready as I'll ever be." He slowly began to enter her. She yelled out and dug her nails into his back. He continued slowly inching his way inside until he had fully entered her. He remained unmoving so that she could adjust to his girth. As her anxiety faded so did the tension in her body. He slowly began thrusting in and out until she was able to take all of him. The pain didn't go away but it became dull and was soon overpowered by pleasure. She was very vocal about what she was experiencing. Rhian took this as encouragement and continued to thrust faster and with more force. She was soon in a world of complete ecstasy. They remained in bed for most of the morning recovering from their strenuous activity.

They returned home soon after both with a glow on their face.

"Rhian I just realized that we never made plans for after the wedding. Where are we going to live? Maybe we should stay with my parents for a few weeks and then we can consider getting an apartment."

"That's a good idea. I think we can make that work."

"It would only be temporary while we find a place of our own. Where are we?" She curiously looked out the window at the unfamiliar area.

"I have a surprise for you."

"What is it?"

"You'll see." They stopped in front of a cute two-story green house. She looked at him with a raised brow.

"Whose house is this?"

"It's yours my love." Rhian said with a big smile.

"Are you serious?" She exclaimed in disbelief.

"Yes, I am. I've been saving for this since the day I met you. I was able to put a down payment." Jerri was excited that her life was turning out exactly as she had always dreamed it would. She was in love, newly married and about to start building a home with the man of her dreams.

It was now September and Rhian and Jerri were settled into their new home and returned to normal life. The honeymoon phase had faded quicker than expected for Rhian who was worried about succumbing to the monotony of life and becoming a drone like the other church members. In the past he had always been on the move but ever since the attack his jittery nature had pacified. Big risks weren't a part of who he was anymore. While his marriage seemed rushed to many, it was a calculated risk that yielded the security he needed. He believed that if he could settle down with a woman that he actually loved those demons from his past couldn't hurt him anymore. He could justify the pain and fear he grew up with as being all a part of God's Will.

"Have a good day, husband." Jerri said with a smile as she kissed him on the cheek while he got ready for word.

"Thank you." He was polite with her as usual and kissed her on the cheek as he headed out the door. On his way to work he considered calling Alexander to see how he was doing. The awkward conversation after the wedding had kept him from calling as often as he used to. Rhian figured they needed some space. He hadn't called him all summer and fall was now here. It seemed like a lifetime ago since they spent the day in the city together. So much had changed since then.

"Hey Alexander? How are you?" Rhian sounded somewhat disconnected with forced friendliness. He wanted to ask Alexander so many questions but it wasn't the time.

"I'm alright, just working on a group project. Whoever said teamwork is more efficient obviously never worked with a team." They both laughed. "So how are you? How's Jerri?"

"She's fine, we both are. Things are quite peachy..." Rhian never used the term *peachy*. Alexander assumed he was being sarcastic. He could tell that Rhian was forcing a smile through the phone.

"That's good to hear." He was hesitant to ask why he was forcing a smile. "I am doing really well in school, surprisingly."

"Why do you say that?"

"Well I have been very anxious and stressed lately and as a result I haven't been sleeping as well as I used to. But I'm still pulling off high grades in all of my classes. My GPA is higher than it's ever been."

"That's very impressive! Good for you!"

"Yeah, it's definitely already opened up several opportunities for me. I have several job offers in different parts of the country but I'm not sure about any one of them yet.

"Well it's great that life seems to be working out for you. I'm sure there are people who have yet to be offered a position."

"That's true. Well I am torn because I have been offered positions in New York, Chicago, and… San Diego." They both remained silent. Rhian knew that Alexander had an affinity for San Diego but there was something even more special about it than just a nice place to live. It symbolized so much more for him and Rhian was aware that it was probably now a bittersweet thought.

"Well New York sounds like quite an adventure. But it is very expensive."

"Yes. Yes it is."

"As for San Diego… Well anything in California is more expensive but it was the dream." There was disappointment in his voice.

"Yes… It was." Alexander was confused. He never told Rhian that they had planned to go there together after graduation. Rhian had figured out that he was in love with him by his body language. Alexander talked a lot about San Diego during Rhian's recovery. It was possible that Rhian put two and two together.

"But Chicago is where your dreams can come true. It is the perfect compromise. It's near the water for summer and has the big city feel like New York. It's not either one but it is Chicago. Perhaps that's the pit stop that you need to make before going out to San Diego." It was like Rhian knew that they had talked about this in the past. Alexander had a love for San Diego; it was where he wanted to grow old. But Chicago felt like home and he wanted to grow there before going out to the West Coast.

"You have a good point."

"And of course, you are a short drive from me so I could visit you whenever I wanted." Alexander felt his heart skip a beat at the thought that they might someday be together. But before his heart could wander too far he was reminded of Rhian's marriage.

"I have to go. Have a good day."

"Ok. You t…" He hung up before Rhian could finish answering. "I guess he had something more important to take care of." He stated to himself.

Rhian and Jerri spent the holidays with Jerri's parents, while Rhian's parents decided to take a vacation. Alexander had managed to get out of family events since Rhian's accident. He made up excuses claiming to have a lot of schoolwork even during the break. But it was the Christmas before his final semester and his course load wasn't as big as it was in the past. He wasn't going to get out of visiting his parents. He had seen them every few months but not long enough for them to ask him what was going on. He would have to answer for his strange behavior. There was no easy way to explain what had happened between him and Rhian. In fact, he didn't tell them about the arrest or what he had done to help Rhian recover. All they knew was that Rhian was involved in an accident and that he wasn't living with him anymore.

"Mom, the food is delicious. I'm gay." They were sitting at dinner with several other family members.

"No you're not. Shut up and finish your food. Oh, and thank you for the compliment."

"Mom, I'm serious! Dad are you going to say anything?"

"You're right… the food is delicious." The other family members ate in silence.

"Dad! You're really not going to say anything?" He was becoming upset at the lack of reaction.

"Alexander, your mother is right. You're not gay."

"I'm in love with Rhian. That's why I've been so distant." They both looked at him and tilted their heads at the same time with confused looks on their faces.

"Of course you are! The way you two look at each other… I knew from the moment you brought him home."

"You knew?"

"Yes. And you're not gay. You love a man but that's just how love is." His dad reaffirmed.

"Your generation is so obsessed with labels and validation for everything you do. You want to belong so you throw a label on it and want others to *accept* it like it's any of their business. You love him that makes you human. Stop trying to make it more theatrical than it needs to be." Everyone remained silent for another moment before one of the other family members began to laugh. Then the entire table burst into laughter. The hardest part of the holiday was over. Or at least he thought it was. As the day continued he began to realize that telling his parents was both liberating but also upsetting. He fought his feelings for so long partly because of his fear of their reaction. He was adopted.

What if they got mad? What if they wanted to get rid of him? Yes it was stupid to think that after all of the years they had been a family something like this could still interfere but Alexander was still worried. He approached his parents later that evening.

"Can I talk to you two?"

"Of course, dear."

"It's about Rhian."

"What about him?" His father inquired.

"I lost him… Well it's complicated."

"If you love him, be with him. That's not very complicated."

"He's married now… to a girl from his church?"

"But I thought he was gay?"

"What happened to labels?" Alexander's mother gave her husband a look of disapproval.

"You're right I'm sorry. Continue."

"Well he is happily married and I didn't want to come between him and his wife."

"Then you are too late."

"I know but something tells me that if I wait long enough he might come to me."

"You are holding on to something that isn't real anymore. While you spend your life thinking about what could have been with him, he is getting closer and closer to his wife and further and further from your fantasy. I'm sorry for being harsh but that's just the case. It's too late to change the past but we are the owners of our future. Own your mistakes and keep moving forward. You can't predict what amazing things life has in store for you."

Alexander spent the rest of his Christmas break thinking about his dad's words. He was jealous that with every day that Rhian got closer to Jerri he grew further apart from him.

"Hey…" Rhian sounded disheartened.

"Hey… How are you?"

"I'm… great." There was the rehearsed good mood.

"I'm not."

"What's wrong?" Rhian was genuinely concerned.

"I miss you…"

"Alexander… Please don't do this."

"I mean, I miss the way you were before the accident. I miss having my best friend here to talk to when I need him."

"You still have me…"

"It's not the same. You don't remember me nor how we got close. I need that. I need you to understand things that you can't."

"Whatever you are going through right now will work out. Don't stress yourself out more than necessary because it's not good for you. I'm sorry if you feel that you can't fully rely on me. I get it but I wish you could because I want you to be happy and I can tell that you aren't right now." They remained silent just listening to the other breathe.

"I am graduating in a few months. I want you there. You supported me when I needed you and I wouldn't be here if it weren't for you."

"Of course I'll come I'm so proud of you!" His mood was bright.

"Thanks! It is on the second Saturday in May. Do you think Jerri would come as well?"

"No, she will be out of town that weekend visiting family." Rhian was lying.

"Well that's alright. I'm just happy that you will be there."

"Of course. I look forward to seeing you walk that day." He paused for a moment before continuing, "Alexander…"

"Yeah?"

"I'm very proud of you. I love you, my friend." The word *friend* burned because he knew it was Rhian's way of reminding him that they were just friends and that's all they would be.

"Thanks… I'll talk to you later."

"Alright. I'll see you." The conversation was short but impactful to both. Alexander was reminded of his broken dream. Rhian was refreshed just by talking to Alexander. He didn't understand why Alexander had such a soothing effect on him. Rhian was troubled by his thoughts after the conversation but he didn't have anyone to talk to. He needed an outlet for all of the pent up emotions that he had repressed. He wasn't particularly close to anyone besides Jerri but he did keep in contact with the guys from the first night he met Jerri. He knew their beliefs and that they wouldn't understand what he was feeling. He was alone.

Three Months Later

It was now late March, Rhian had kept his feelings bottled up and had again maintained his distance from Alexander. He was in his office one morning when he came across a blog that discussed similar things to what he was going through. The blog was titled: *I love him and her*. The blogger was a self-proclaimed successful young entrepreneur with a loving wife and two children. He grew up with a very close friend who followed him around everywhere. The two were inseparable but as life went on they lost contact for a few years. It seemed that fate had a different plan for them because after college they reconnected at an event many miles away from home. They hit it off and began hanging out often. Both are married and still remain very close but the blogger has grown to feel more for his friend than before. He talked about how his feelings were new to him because he had never been curious about men but he found himself very attracted to his friend. He went into detail about the things that he noticed about him but what caught Rhian's attention was when he talked about his love for his friend. *I love my wife there is no doubt of that. But I also really love him. I fought my feelings for him until the day I accepted that you could love another human being regardless of gender and it was ok.*

Rhian continued reading the comments that people had posted. It seemed that there were a lot of people who understood what he was feeling. There were a few who thought differently and didn't understand. They claimed that some of these people were crazy because *straight is straight and gay is gay* but Rhian didn't see things that way. He started to write out his own story with a few changes for anonymity.

My name is Tom. I am a 24-year-old married man with a very loving wife. We met after I suffered a terrible accident in which I lost part of my memory. I don't remember the sequence of events leading up the time of the accident, all I have are memories constructed by the stories that were told to me by my best friend. I don't know if I was more attracted to men or women before the accident but I know that I find both attractive now.

During my recovery I was living with my parents and was taken care of by my best friend, we'll call him Guy. Guy took very good care of me making sure I was always comfortable and that my recovery went well. The strange thing is that I don't remember him at all. I only know who he was during my recovery. At first I thought that he was just there to keep me out of trouble but the more time I spent with him the more I started to realize that he genuinely cared about me. One day he took me to see some of the spots that I used to love to hang out at. I think he was trying to get me to remember him. Those places were great and all but being with him, spending time with him, getting to know him was what made me feel more than friendship for him. I always thought he was very attractive but after that day I saw more.

Not too long after that day Guy left my life to pursue some of his personal dreams. He was in love with me. He never told me but I knew it. The truth was that I fell in love with him too, but I kept it to myself because I was afraid losing what we had. I met my wife after he left, but I never stopped thinking about him. On the day of my wedding he was going to tell me how he felt but I stopped him. I told him that any feelings should have been dealt with before I made the commitment to my wife. I love her and would never want to hurt her. But no matter how much I try to pretend that my life is completely perfect, I feel as though I am missing something. I want to be friends with him but I don't know how to be a friend without wanting something more...

The Graduation

"Alright Honey! I'm heading out."

"Ok love. It's too bad that there weren't enough tickets for me to go but it's great that he considers you important enough to invite you. Have a safe trip." Rhian felt guilty for lying to her but the damage had already been done and he couldn't tell her the truth now. Besides, what would he even say? 'I wasn't sure if I made the right choice in marrying you and I wanted to spend some time alone with Alexander.' Yeah, that would go over perfectly. No, he had to keep it to himself. He kissed Jerri goodbye and was out the door.

When he arrived, Rhian followed the mass of people who seemed to all be going in the same direction. He knew this place like the details of a dream in the fleeting moments after waking up. He became hyperaware of his surroundings and felt as if he was being watched. With his anxiety rising he tried to find the auditorium as quickly as possible. Once inside he politely asked an usher for help finding his seat.

"You're going to go straight down this aisle and your seat will be on the left, it's near the front."

"Thank you." He found his seat and settled in. There were still plenty of open seats available around him probably because he arrived almost an hour early. He looked down at his phone as if expecting a message. He stared at the background, which was set to a picture of Jerri in Hawaii. He felt guilty for not inviting Jerri but the truth was that he didn't want her there. He wanted to be there for Alexander.

He was lost in his phone when he noticed that there was a man staring at him. He looked up at the man who was about his age that seemed startled by his presence.

"I'm sorry sir, am I in your way?"

"I, um… no you're fine. I believe my seat is down this row. Excuse me." He was obviously upset but Rhian didn't give it much thought. He continued to play around with his phone as more and more people filled the seats. After a few minutes the row he was in was full. He was being stared at by the people a few seats away from him. He tried to avoid eye-contact for fear of the awkwardness.

"Hello Rhian." A woman greeted him followed by a man that was likely her husband.

"How are you son?" The man extended his hand to shake Rhian's.

"I'm doing well. How are you?"

"Excited to see our son graduate. We are Alexander's parents."

"That explains the familiarity. I was…"

"We know sweetie. You don't have to explain." She smiled at him and took her seat next to him.

Everyone's attention was turned to the stage so the people sitting next to him had finally stopped whispering but he could almost feel their eyes burning through him. He didn't let it get to him and instead paid attention to what the speaker was saying. The rest of the ceremony went on and when it came time for the names to be called out he was very excited to cheer when Alexander's name was called. He heard Leena's name called out and a smile crept across his face as he clapped loudly and cheered with the people next to him. When he heard Alexander's name he jumped up and cheered again joined by the same people next to him. He knew they were looking at him again but refrained from acknowledging them. He didn't want to steal the attention from Leena and Alexander because he could simply talk to them later on.

As the ceremony came to a close Rhian was struck with a terrible migraine. He closed his eyes and kept his head down.

"Are you ok?" Alexander's mother was concerned.

"I'll be fine. I just have a bad headache. I think I need some fresh air." He got up and stumbled out of the aisle and towards the door. He was clearly not doing well. Just as he made it out the door the graduates were dismissed and the ceremony ended. Alexander's mother was concerned but the aisles almost immediately became crowded with people. Alexander approached them and noticed that Rhian wasn't there.

"Where is Rhian?"

"He had to step out. I think he has a headache. He took off before I could really help him."

"Congratulations buddy! We are all proud of you!" Sebastian shouted.

"Thanks... I'll be right back. I have to find Rhian."

"No problem. We'll meet you out there." Alexander managed to push his way through the crowd and out the door. He scanned the surrounding area for any sign of Rhian. Off to the side of the building, away from the crowds he could see him leaning against the wall.

"Rhian, what's wrong?" Alexander sounded panicked.

"Nothing, my head hurts. Congratulations. I'm very proud of you." He was struggling to speak.

"Thanks… You need to lie down. Let's get you to my apartment."

"I just need a minute." Leena came out of the building followed by all of their friends who were clearly still in shock about Rhian's presence. Rhian immediately put on his best smile for them even though his head was hurting him.

"We need a picture!" Sophie announced. They all crowded in as Rhian tried to hide in the background.

"Rhian you come up front!" Leena demanded. Rhian sheepishly obeyed.

"Everyone say cheese!" Alexander's mom ordered as she took the picture. The camera flashed once and then again. The second flash must have triggered something in Rhian's brain because he passed out and landed on the ground unexpectedly. He fainted and wasn't waking up.

"Call an ambulance!" Alexander demanded. He dropped down and put his hands on Rhian's face "Come on, wake up!" He was beyond worried.

"Relax Alexander. He probably just passed out from the heat. It's hot out here. Leena tried to calm him down. She knew how worked up he could get. He ignored her and cradled Rhian's head until he stirred and regained consciousness.

"What happened?"

"You fainted. We need to get you to a hospital."

"I'm fine. I just need to lie down for a few minutes. And water. I need water. I'm really thirsty." He looked over and saw Sophie, Sebastian, and the others staring at him and he began hyperventilating. "I think I'm having another migraine… this one is bad!" He began to tear up from the pain. "Can we go somewhere I can lie down? Please." Rhian begged. Alexander picked him up and carried him to Leena's apartment, which was only a few blocks away. They took him into one of the rooms and Alexander closed all of shades as and had everyone wait outside. He could hear Rhian breathing heavily from the pain.

"Alexander, those people out there? They don't just know me… I am supposed to know and care about them aren't I?"

"Well you used to…just lay down and relax. Cover your eyes." He handed Rhian a small towel to cover his eyes with.

"Oh! It hurts so bad." Rhian suddenly tossed the towel on the floor and sat up in the bed with a look of horror. "Take me to the rooftop garden…"

"Rhian you are in pain."

"Take me now!"

"Are you sure?"

"Yes. I need to see it. I need to know it's real." They snuck out the back door to avoid answering questions. Alexander led the way in silence. They climbed up the stairs and upon arrival Rhian was back on the ground in pain. He closed his eyes and when he opened them he looked over at Alexander in disbelief.

"You… you…" Rhian was wide-eyed and scurried away from Alexander while sitting on the floor. "Why didn't you say anything?" Rhian began to cry. "All this time you knew, but you didn't say anything… Why did you let it get to this? You were my best friend and so much more… I trusted you!"

"Rhian, you need to calm down…" Alexander tried to put his hand on Rhian's shoulder but he backed away.

"Don't touch me! Answer my question!"

"I didn't have a choice…"

"You always have a choice."

"You were happy and I wasn't going to cause you to be sad. You had your parents back and I know that means the world to you even if you won't admit it. I love you. I will always love you."

"I don't believe you…" Rhian was cowering on the ground. Alexander stared at Rhian helplessly and got down on his level. He locked eyes with him, leaned in, and kissed him on the lips. The kiss felt like an eternity to the boys but only lasted a few brief moments. Alexander kissed him passionately and Rhian kissed back. When he pulled away, Alexander smiled at him but Rhian was now more upset. "Why did you do that? I'm married Alexander!"

"What? But you love me…"

"But I married her… and I love her too. You didn't want me… and you didn't try to get me back…"

"I spent months helping you recover. I thought you knew I was in love with you."

"I can't do this right now! I have to apologize to the others."

"Rhian please don't leave…"

"Alexander, please don't do this, especially not here." Rhian took off down the stairs on his way back to Leena's leaving Alexander and his apology in the garden. He barged into the apartment with an uncontrollable eagerness that startled Leena and the others who were still waiting for him and Alexander to emerge from the room. Alexander had refused to let anyone in and no one saw the two sneak out. There was a moment of silence in which Rhian's expression told them all that he was back. He ran up to Leena and fiercely embraced as the tears ran down his face. He was back.

"I'm so sorry. I remember now!" He cried. She held on to him tightly.

"It's ok sweetie, it wasn't your fault. I know."

"I have missed so much! I will never leave you all like that again! You are my family and family has to stay together."

"Of course. Are you feeling alright?"

"I'm much better now!" Sophie and the other girls stood up and hugged him tightly.

"Don't ever leave us like that."

"I promise I won't." John and Sebastian got up and followed in welcoming him back. "So, tell me what I've missed?"

"Not much… A few parties, maybe a vacation or two, oh, and I'm engaged." Sebastian proudly announced.

"You are? That's fantastic!"

"She is wonderful. I met her about a year ago. She is very special and Lilly adores her."

"That's great! How *is* Lilly? I bet she is getting big!"

"Well she missed her uncle Rhian…" The room grew quiet. "But she is doing well. She is very smart no doubt thanks to you and all of your help when she was younger. She loved it when you read to her and now she is reading way above her age level."

"That's good to hear." They spent the rest of the afternoon catching Rhian up on their lives. Alexander didn't returned from the garden, not that anyone had noticed. But after the others had their heartwarming reunion with Rhian they left.

"Leena, when was this picture taken?"

"Which one?"

"This one, he said pointing to a picture that was in a beautiful frame on the table.

"Ah, that one… That picture was taken on the day of your *memorial service.*"

"My what?"

"We thought you had died… After the attack."

"You did?"

"Rhian, you disappeared at the hospital. The last thing I remember happening was seeing you go into cardiac arrest. We waited all day for you but the doctor never came out. We fell asleep and when woke up… We heard you died. We were told that the family didn't want any information released about you. I think they were afraid that you were involved in something that would cause your attackers to come looking for you. We tried to find out anything we could but there was no trace of what had happened. It was like you never existed." Rhian remained silent.

"I don't understand."

"None of us did… Where is he?"

"Who? You mean the guy who lied to me?"

"He didn't lie to you Rhian. He was trying to protect you. At least that's what he thought he was doing. I don't fully understand his reasons either but I know he did it because he thought he was doing the right thing. His heart was in the right place but when it comes to you, he doesn't seem to think with his head anymore."

"I feel betrayed."

"He loves you, the way you used to dream about him loving you." Rhian let out a disparaging sigh.

"The dream is now a nightmare."

"What happened? When did you remember everything?"

"When I regained consciousness after the picture I began to have flashbacks. Then, when I was in the room I began to remember the garden. I told him to take me. We got up there and I immediately remembered the night he wanted to kill himself. It was awful. I relived the entire experience and then I began to feel every emotional up and down all at once. It was too much. I couldn't look at him. I felt sick to my stomach."

"It was a lot to take in at once. Anyone would have reacted the same way. But I really think you should talk to him. He had a very hard time without you. I don't think he is over you. He had hope that you would remember him and when he saw that you did remember he was probably experiencing a rush of emotions of his own. He hadn't seen you, this you, in over two years and to be honest I don't think he's really been alive since then."

"I guess I could talk to him… But I don't even know where to start."

"Go over there and say what you feel. You owe it to each other to have a face-to-face talk." Rhian hugged Leena as he headed out the door.

"I will call you later. He offered to let me stay at his place but I doubt that's going to happen so I'll probably be back."

"I won't wait up." She winked at him. He smiled but shook his head in disapproval.

Rhian knocked at the hideous green door. He could hear movement on the other side. Alexander opened the door with apologetic eyes.

"Rhian I didn't mean to hurt you. I wanted to tell you but I was afraid of losing you again and then I saw how happy you were. All I want is for you to be happy. You hadn't been so content since we first became friends. They took your smile away but you found it again and I couldn't live with myself if I was the reason you lost it again."

"They were looking for the map."

"What are you talking about?"

"The day I was attacked. I know who did it and why. They wanted my map."

"Which map?"

"The map to White Horse Ranch."

"You had a map?" Alexander shouted. "Why would you hold on to that?"

"Because after I told you about what had happened there, I promised myself that I would get justice for the girl. I was able to reconstruct a map of where I was taken and I found the place. I couldn't risk telling you. I didn't want to involve you. I didn't want you to get hurt."

"I want to protect you."

"You can't. I have to continue living my life the way it is. No one can know that I regained my memory."

"Rhian, I love you and I'm not going to let anything happen to you. Rhian grabbed Alexander's arms, pulled him close and planted a fiery kiss on his lips. Alexander didn't protest Rhian's advance. Alexander didn't wait for Rhian to take control of the situation. He domineeringly took the lead and picked up Rhian without breaking their kiss. He grasped Rhian's buttocks roughly massaging him through his jeans with his palms as Rhian kept his legs wrapped around Alexander's body. He carried him to his room where he tossed him onto the bed. He removed all of Rhian's clothes without hesitation and then proceeded to remove his own.

Their kissing turned into an oral exploration of Rhian's body. Alexander paid special attention to his most sensitive areas. Rhian was completely lost in the fantasy come true. Once Rhian had almost reached his climax Alexander stopped his exploration and prepared himself to make love to him. He could see Rhian's mouth open wide as he slowly entered him. Rhian bit down on the pillow as a reaction to Alexander's girth but it wasn't long before they were both enjoying their love. Alexander became more turned on when he looked down and realized Rhian was moaning with pleasure and digging his fingers into his back as encouragement. Rhian was in pure ecstasy as he could feel Alexander thrusting, stimulating his prostate unlike ever before. Rhian's toes curled, as he was pushed closer and closer to his climax. Alexander was lost in the feeling of making love to Rhian. He was rough with Rhian, picking him up and changing positions with newlywed excitement. That night they fell asleep in each other's arms.

"What have you done?" Rhian was woken up by the sound of Jerri's voice asking him. He was dazed but conscious. He realized the voice was in his head but it was his conscience trying to remind him of his wife. Rhian suddenly felt dirty for what had happened and the guilt took over. He gathered his clothes on his way out of the room making sure to close the door carefully. Without wasting a single moment he got dressed and was out the door. He needed to see Jerri. He needed to know that everything was ok. But he didn't want to think about the consequences right now. He just needed to get away and forget about what he did. He silently wept on the ride back

"That must have been some graduation…" Jerri stated as Rhian walked into their bedroom. "Are you ok?"

"Yeah I'm fine just really tired. I'm sorry it's so late. There was a party and he wanted me to stay and meet some of his other friends." Rhian momentarily escaped his guilt by covering his face with his palms. The room was dark but Jerri could clearly tell that there was something wrong.

"It's not a problem, dear… I understand." She turned over and went back to sleep. That night Rhian stayed up until the sun came up. Jerri let him sleep in the next morning and decided to go to church without him. She didn't want to but to skip church wasn't an option.

The doorbell rang several times before Rhian finally woke up. He was still not fully awake as he made his way towards the front door. There was no sign of Jerri so he figured that she was already gone for the day. He unlocked the door and turned the knob without checking to see who it was. He always checked before opening the door but he was still very unaware of his surroundings.

"Can I help…?" Rhian stopped mid-sentence and released the doorknob when he saw the familiar face in front of him.

"Long time no see." Rhian slowly retreated in fear but before he knew what hit him the intruder kicked him in the chest, knocking him down on the ground.

The doorbell rang again. Rhian had spaced out and imagined the intruder but his heart was now pounding and he was terrified of opening the door. It felt so real to him. He cautiously opened the door just enough to peek out. Rhian became wide-eyed when he saw Alexander standing right in front of his door.

"Rhian, can we please talk?"

"Go away. I don't want to talk to you right now."

"Rhian, please. It's me. You know who I am. Just let me in." He pushed on the door with very little force, which was enough to petrify Rhian. He briskly backed away and tripped on his own feet as he backed away from the door.

"Please just leave. Please leave me alone. I don't want to see you. Please!" Rhian was frantic.

"Rhian, what's wrong? I've never seen you like this with me." Alexander dropped to his level to comfort him. He raised his hand to caress Rhian's face but he closed his eyes, cringed, and curled up defensively.

"Please. Just go." Rhian broke out into defenseless tears as a result of the daydream. Suddenly Alexander saw himself as malevolent in Rhian's eyes. He immediately felt sick to his stomach because he never thought of himself as a monster, but in the reflection of Rhian's fear he realized that his actions had shattered the trust they shared and damaged Rhian, again. Alexander became his own personal demon.

"I'm sorry. I love you." He returned somberly.

"Don't come back for me." Alexander tensed his jaw but instead of saying another word he got up and left. There was nothing more he could do.

Chapter 16

"How are you and Jerri Lynn doing?" Pastor asked.

"We are doing very well, Sir." Rhian didn't like the idea of meeting with him once a week just to talk about his personal life. But that was the requirement for Pastor's immediate staff. He wanted to make sure the people around him were taken care of.

"That's good to hear. Tell me, have you considered children?"

"With all due respect we haven't been together that long. I'm not sure I'm ready for the responsibility just yet. I want to save up enough money to afford kids."

"So you have thought about it."

"In a way. I want two or three. But I want them to have the best that life has to offer. If we wait a few years I will be able to work and save up so that I can send them to great schools and hopefully to a great college someday." Rhian knew that it wasn't what Pastor wanted to hear but it was honesty. To his surprise Pastor smiled and nodded in agreement.

"I understand. Well if there is anything I could do to help you attain that goal let me know. I want what's best for all of my members."

"Actually, there is something I would like."

"What's that?"

"Well, I should have told you but I have applied for several other jobs recently." Pastor's smile didn't fade. "I am very grateful for the opportunity you gave me but I feel like it's time for me to move on to something different. I received an offer and I am very excited for the opportunity. I wanted to ask for your blessing to take it."

"Rhian, of course you have my blessing. I was hoping that you would move on to bigger and better things."

"You were?"

"Yes! I gave you this job so that you could get on your feet. I am happy that you are moving on with your life. It's better that way, you and *Jerri*." His emphasis on Jerri's name made him feel uncomfortable. "You are a remarkable young man and you're going to do great things. Besides, we all have to take certain stepping-stones on our route to success." The smile on his face suddenly faded. "Now, I do expect a higher tithe from you."

"Of course. Much is expected." Pastor again smiled. This time Rhian saw the empty shell for what it was. The uneasiness was his que to leave.

"I'm proud of you, son." Rhian shook his hand and departed.

Rhian's new job was a much-needed change. His job at the church wasn't interesting anymore and after the night with Alexander he lived in constant fear of being discovered. It was time for an alternative. The new job did pay more but it required him to commute farther, which was what he wanted. It meant less time with Jerri and more time by himself. The guilt had been eating away at him since the night he spent with Alexander but he didn't dare talk to anyone about it. Jerri began to notice the change in his mood and the way he distanced himself from her. She did her best to keep his attention. She made it her mission to keep a clean home and to always have a warm meal ready for him when he arrived home. She did her *wifely* duties just like she had been taught to do but it didn't seem to matter.

"You should call Alexander and go on a fishing trip or maybe hunting." Jerri was clearing the table after breakfast. It was the only time she really got to spend with Rhian since he got his new job.

"What are you talking about?" He was thrown off by her suggestion.

"Well, you haven't seen him since the graduation. Besides, he's your best friend and you need friends."

"You don't go out with friends." He challenged.

"That's because I'm busy making sure the house is clean and you are taken care of." She let out her frustration.

"I'm sorry, I didn't mean to sound so rude. I've been stressed out with work."

"What's wrong? I know there is something on your mind. You can talk to me."

"I'm fine. There is nothing wrong."

"I'm your wife. I know when something is wrong with my husband."

"Jerri, I'm fine. Just drop it." He raised his voice.

"I'm sorry. I just want you to be happy." She left the room. "Have a great day at work."

"I love you." He heard the door to the bathroom slam.

The weeks began to pass and he grew distant from her. There was no sign of their situation getting any better. In fact, they hadn't been as physically romantic since he came back from the graduation. Jerri made every attempt to capture his attention but it went unnoticed. She had never been to an adult store before but after a few weeks of feeling undesired she had resorted to new ideas. Embarrassed by what she was doing, Jerri found a sexy costume that she thought he might find appealing and purchased it in a hurry. She stuffed the black bag under the passenger seat in her car and drove home paranoid that someone she knew might see her. She arrived she went into the room hid it in the closet.

Several hours later she had finished cleaning the house and decided that she would try on her new outfit. As she examined herself in the mirror, she felt dirty for wearing it and worse for using Rhian's money to buy it. But along with the feeling of guilt she also felt sexy, a feeling that she hadn't been able to explore until now. She saw herself as beautiful in the outfit and while she couldn't show that side of herself off to anyone, she enjoyed the few moments she had with it. She lost track of time in front the mirror and was startled when Rhian arrived home.

"Jerri?" Rhian looked around the kitchen for any sign of his wife, finding it strange that she wasn't already there with a perfectly set table waiting. He heard shuffling in the bedroom. Jerri scurried to cover up with a bathrobe.

"Hi." She emerged with excitement. She hadn't decided if she would show him her new purchase.

"You haven't made dinner?"

"No… I'm sorry I was busy cleaning and I got a headache so I lied down and…"

"It's ok. How about I cook tonight?"

"That would be wonderful." Jerri was pleasantly surprised.

"Would you be alright with breakfast for dinner?"

"That would be alright with me." She smiled and kissed him on the lips. She quickly went into the bedroom and changed into more appropriate clothes. After dinner Rhian decided that he would spend some time painting. He had started working on a portrait of he and Jerri on their honeymoon but he stopped working on it. She was excited to see his motivation return. She let him work while she read a book. Suddenly, while they were sitting in silence Rhian threw one of his brushes at the easel.

"Rhian, sweetie, what's wrong?"

"Nothing… I'm just having trouble with this painting."

"It looks beautiful honey!"

"Thanks… But it's still not complete."

"What's missing?"

"I'm not sure…"

"Maybe we should add a little one…"

"What do you mean?"

"Well we haven't talked about when we wanted to start a family… Maybe it's time we talked about it." He felt his heart drop.

"Well… I haven't really thought about it… I mean I guess we should talk about it."

"I thought with the new job paying you more that you would want to start a family soon…"

"I… I hadn't really thought about it that way. I figured I'd start saving for our future."

"Isn't that our future? Don't you want children?"

"I do… I just… Are we ready for that?"

"Is anyone ever really ready for that?"

"You have a point… Well maybe we should start trying…" Rhian regretted his words but he had said it. He didn't know what else to say so he turned around and continued mixing his paints pretending to actually continue painting. Jerri waited for a bit more of a response but when she didn't get anything she crossed her arms and walked away. She was a good woman. She was definitely good to Rhian and she never pushed him to tell her what was wrong, but even she had her limits.

"What do I have to do to get you to talk to me? Tell me what to do to make you happy because I just don't know what I can do!" Rhian stopped painting.

"What are you talking about?"

"I can see that you are miserable. What am I doing wrong? Tell me what to do and I will do it. I just want us to be happy!"

"You aren't doing anything wrong."

"Then why are you treating me like I am holding you back?"

"I want to go dancing!" Rhian admitted. Jerri looked at him with concern.

"Dancing… We don't dance… We shouldn't be in that kind of environment Rhian… My parent's would have a fit if they found out we went dancing."

"You want to know what you can do? Dance with me. I am sick of feeling like I have to follow some rules that don't even make sense to me. I love you and I want to dance with you. You are my wife and I should be able to enjoy dancing with you." Jerri was horrified by the idea since she had never been dancing. Like Rhian, she grew up in a very conservative home. Women were in the home while the man worked. She didn't wear pants because they were for men. It was a stretch for her to wear sweatpants at night, much less to go out dancing. But she was determined to get her husband back and if this was what she had to do then she would do it.

"Alright… I'll go put something nice on… for you. I love you." She sounded disappointed but it was more than likely just nerves.

"I love you too dear." He said with a huge smile. This was the first time in a long time that Rhian would be able to dance his troubles away. He was more than happy to go. They quickly got ready and headed out for their night of dancing.

They arrived in the city and parked their car near the club. As they approached the place the music became louder. They waited in line for a few minutes before they were allowed in. Once inside the dark rooms of the club Rhian fearlessly entered and made his way directly to the bar. He was completely unaware of the fact that many of the guys on the dance floor were checking his wife out. Jerri felt very uncomfortable but when she realized that Rhian was ordering a drink she pulled on his arm.

"What are you doing?"

"Relax dear. We need something to loosen us up."

"Are you insane? We drove here!"

"It'll be alright. We will only have one. We can share if you would like." He said with a cool smile. She couldn't resist him and gave in.

"Just one." Rhian finished ordering their drink then turned back to her and kissed her on the cheek. She looked up at him and smiled. She was excited and nervous at the thought of drinking alcohol. This was a day of so many firsts but deep down she was excited. Besides, she wasn't going to ruin this for him. She wanted to see him happy again and if it was the only way for him to find his happiness again, then she would gladly let him have a good night. Rhian took a sip of the drink.

"This is really good." He said. "I haven't had one of these since I was back in school…" It immediately occurred to him that Jerri was still unaware of the return of his memory. He hoped that she wouldn't ask but Jerri wasn't stupid.

"I thought you didn't drink in high school?"

"Well I… I drank once, but it wasn't much. Here try some, it's a pina colada, like the song."

"Sounds delightful?" Jerri said with a laugh joined by Rhian who was ready to dance. Jerri took a sip and immediately withdrew making a sour face.

"What do you think?"

"That was awful!"

"I asked him to make it good. I guess he did." He laughed again. She looked at him and nodded her head. It was much easier for her to accept this side of him than she had anticipated. She wasn't sure what to expect but he made her feel safe and everything seemed to be going well. She took the drink from his hand and took more of it, this time taking two sips from it. She pulled him over to the dance floor and put her arms around him.

"Tell me what to do."

"Just move your body like me." He moved slowly at first and gradually increased his pace to match the rhythm of the music. Once they were on beat, he didn't have to instruct her anymore because she caught on. She followed the music and a few of the other girls in the room as she danced with him. She was having a lot of fun laughing at herself for how silly she thought she looked. But she didn't care what she looked like because she was there with Rhian and she was having a great time.

"Do you mind if I go get myself another drink?" Rhian asked.

"I do mind. You said that you would only drink one."

"Alright." He was disappointed but she was right. They continued to dance but Rhian was kind of annoyed. Nonetheless he didn't let it ruin his night and he continued to dance. Jerri had never heard some of the songs that they played in the club but she wasn't a huge fan. In fact she started the night feeling as excited as Rhian but only a short while she was sick of the loud music and didn't feel well.

"Can we go soon?"

"But it's still really early…"

"I don't feel well and I don't really like this environment… it's too much for me."

"Ok…" Rhian was now frustrated with her. He was having a good time and thought that she was too, but her sudden change in mood suggested otherwise. They left the club not long after arriving. The drive home was very quiet with the sound of the road serving as the only distraction from the deafening silence. When they arrived home Jerri went straight to bed while Rhian just sat alone in the living room.

He opened the only message on his phone. Alexander had sent it the morning after the graduation. All it said was *Hi* but it was powerful enough to make him melt. Along with the feelings of desire that came with it were feelings the feelings of intense guilt that had been weighing down on him for weeks. He hadn't been able to delete it but he couldn't respond to it especially after Alexander showed up and Rhian had such a negative reaction. He hoped that eventually that night would stop haunting him but there was still no sign of peace for his restless heart. He fell asleep on the couch that night.

The next morning they Rhian and Jerri tiptoed around each other, avoiding anything related to the previous night. Rhian left for work as soon as breakfast was over and kept himself busy all day. The last thing he wanted to do was to think about Jerri or Alexander. When he arrived home Jerri seemed more than happy to see him. She kissed him as soon as he walked through the door.

"What are you doing?" He asked playfully.

"I missed you." She said with a seductive smile. She began to undress him but he wasn't too keen on the idea.

"Not right now… I need to take a shower and relax."

"Rhian, what's wrong? No man turns down sex but lately you don't seem to want me near you… And last night I didn't know who you were?"

"Jerri I really don't want to talk about it."

"I'm your wife, you should be able to tell me anything." She had remained strong for as long as she could but she couldn't take it anymore and began to cry. "Don't you trust me? I've been trying to be the best wife I can to make you happy and help you relieve stress but you don't seem to notice me or anything I do for you."

"I remember."

"Well it would be nice to know that you remember I'm your wife every once in a while."

"No I mean my memory came back…" She was paralyzed by the revelation. The thought of his memory hadn't crossed her mind since Leena had talked to her. Her fears were coming true.

"When did it happen?"

"At the graduation ceremony."

"Why did it take you so long to tell me?"

"Because… it complicates things."

"How does it complicate things?"

"You love me right Jerri?"

"Of course."

"And you will stand by me no matter what right?"

"Rhian, you're scaring me."

"It's Alexander."

"What about him? Rhian please don't be so obscure. Just tell me!"

"Before I ever met you… before I lost my memory, I was in love with someone else."

"Ok…"

"It was Alexander, I fell in love with him while I was in school. He always said he was straight but he always had a special place in his heart for me. He pushed me away when he didn't know how to deal with his feelings. The morning before the attack we got into a fight."

"Was he the one who attacked you?"

"No. It's not important what we argued about but the point was that after that morning I was done with him. I wasn't going to give him another chance."

"What's the problem?"

"The night of the graduation… I slept with him and I haven't been able to stop thinking about him since. I love you but I am in love with him."

"I need to go…"

"Jerri, please don't go. I love you and I want to be with you. I made you a promise."

"I understand that but I need some time. Please."

"How much time?"

"I don't know! You need time too. You need to think about what you just told me because you've obviously been avoiding it." She walked out as quickly as she could. Rhian sat in the living room thinking about his circumstances until he fell asleep on the couch in his lonely home. He was awakened by the sound of a phone ringing. It was Theresa.

"Rhian why is your wife sleeping in my house? What happened? She won't say what's wrong but she keeps telling me to talk to you."

"Mom, I don't want to talk about it…"

"I'm your mother Rhian… you can talk to me about anything." She said trying to reassure him.

"Anything?"

"Yes dear, anything!" She was being pushy.

"Ok, let's talk about how you and dad abandoned me. Let's talk about how you and dad sequestered me and kept me from my friends, the only family I had. Let's talk about how you manipulated Alexander to lie to me so that you could keep me from being myself!"

"We were only doing what was best for you. You are happy now aren't you? You have everything you ever wanted. A wife and soon a family."

"No! I am not better, I am worse. I am in love with a man who I can't be with because I am committed to a woman I love and who loves me with all her heart."

"We should have told you the truth from the beginning."

"It's too late for that now. I have to make sure that my wife is ok. Tell her that I will pick her up in an hour. I don't want her around you or dad."

"We only want what's best for you. We are your parents and we love you."

"You are unbelievable. You have tried to change me for years. You pushed me away when you realized that I wasn't going to change. If you love me then you have a strange way of showing it. Mom, I trusted you… and dad! Because I had to… Because I loved and respected you both as my parents but you used that. You used that to try to change me because you felt uncomfortable with having a son who loved men and women. You can't begin to understand the betrayal I feel right now."

"It was all for your own good."

"It was for *your* own good. You lied so that you wouldn't have to tell people that you have a gay son."

"Your wife just left. She is on her way home."

"Goodbye mother."

"Rhian, I never stopped loving you or thinking about you. I will always be your mother and I will always love you. Before you jump to conclusions I need you to look in your dresser. I hid a small box there that I doubt you have found." Rhian hung up before he lost control of his emotions. He waited until he heard Jerri walk in through the door. She sat down next to him and held his hand.

"Rhian, I had heard about your past. That night when I met you, my friends told me that you were gay but had lost your memory. They said that you had been kicked out of your house because you were gay and that you had met someone but they never knew who it was. The truth is that I didn't think it would happen. I didn't think you would remember. I asked your mom but she assured me that you wouldn't remember. We all assumed that you would never remember your old life. I made a promise to Leena."

"What kind of promise."

"I love you with all of my heart and I promised that if you ever regained your memory and it was true that there was someone else, I would let you go."

"I don't believe this! I don't believe all of you! Why doesn't anyone consider that I might want to live my own life? I didn't ask for any of this. I didn't want things to be this way." He pulled his hand away from hers.

"I know it's a lot to take in and I'm sorry but we only wanted what was best."

"How about you all let me decide what is best for me?" Rhian was furious and the two sat there silently. "Look, I know this isn't easy for you either but we are married. I made that promise to be with you for life and that is what I think is best."

"I love you."

"I love you too." They held each other in silence.

"Everything will be fine, my love. Let's go to bed and deal with this in the morning." They went to bed that night with heavy hearts.

Jerri didn't fully understand Rhian's way of seeing the world but she could relate enough to accept his ideas. This was different. There was no way for her to relate to him. It was at that moment when he said that he 'didn't ask for any of this' that she really understood him. He was feeling the same way that she was feeling. She wanted so badly for things to work out for their marriage but it didn't seem like that was going to happen. She felt trapped by a situation that she couldn't change because it was out of her control, the way Rhian felt trapped by a situation that he couldn't change because he arrived there by means that were out of his control.

She could see the hurt in Rhian's eyes. He loved Alexander with all his heart and longed to be with him. She knew that he loved her too but she knew that what he felt for her didn't compare to what he felt for Alexander. Rhian didn't see her as his soul mate. No matter how badly she wanted to make it work she couldn't force Rhian to commit his entire being to her. Jerri knew that he could eventually let her go, but he would never let go of Alexander and *that* would keep him from being happy. She loved him but she also loved herself enough to make the choice she never thought she would have to make.

Rhian awoke the next morning to an empty bed and a letter that rested neatly on the pillow next to him. He stared at the letter and prayed it wasn't what he thought it was. He put the letter in his dresser and got ready for work. He went downstairs and grabbed some cereal before going into work. After coming home from work he went into his room and grabbed the letter. To him it represented more than just words on paper. Thoughts raced through his mind as he considered opening it up. But he didn't. He put the letter away and began sobbing like a child because Jerri wasn't there. He hoped that the letter was a simple note to let him know that she had gone out of town and would be back. He hoped it was simply encouragement and that she would eventually come to bed with him. But she didn't. She never again came back to that house.

Chapter 17

One year, to the day, after Jerri left, Rhian finally broke from his routine. He had woken up every morning, gone to work, come back from work and took care of himself without shedding a single tear. Rhian was living in a bubble all by himself, refusing to reach out to any of his friends. As he was driving home that day he saw a family walking down the street. There were two dads and three kids. He slowed his car down and stopped, watching the family stroll by him without a care in the world. That moment reminded him of the dream he had several years ago. His heart suddenly felt lighter. He made his way home and into his sock drawer. Hidden underneath his black socks was the letter from Jerri that he never read. He opened it:

Rhian,

There are few things in life that have made me feel as happy as you have made me. You are the love of my life and the most amazing person that I have ever met. You taught me so much about life that I never knew. I have never loved anyone as much as I love you and it is because of this that I am making the difficult decision to let you go. I am giving you the freedom to follow through with the dreams you had because you are too special to keep cooped up in a life that was not meant for you. I understand that you couldn't control what happened but I can control this and I am so sorry that I wasn't honest with you about what I knew when I first met you. If I could take away the terrible feelings that you went through I would do so in a heartbeat but I can't do that. I hope that you find your happiness and share it with the world. I can only pray that you will someday forgive me for leaving but I also pray that you will understand that I did this for me and not because I thought it was best for you. I know where your heart lies and it is not

Rhian wiped the tear in his eye. He wasn't trapped anymore and he hadn't been since she left him. But regardless of the facts, the letter absolved him of any guilt he had for wanting to be with Alexander. He turned his attention to the box and looked at it wondering what was inside. Inside was a bracelet with the words *Best Friends* inscribed on it.

"Hello?" Alexander's voice was low and raspy.

"Hey, how are you?"

"I'm alright… How are you?"

"I'm doing well… That's a lie. I'm terrible. I hate my life." Rhian sounded like he was upset.

"Relax Rhian; I'm sure it'll be alright."

"Why? Why did you let this happen to me? You don't let life hurt the people you love if you can protect them. So why?"

"Rhian, do you remember how bad it was when you lost the relationship with your parents? Do you remember randomly leaving class and calling me because you were having a melt down? Do you remember the hurt that caused you?"

"Yes."

"I do too! I saw it all. I held you through all of it. And I should have continued holding you instead of causing you the hurt I put you through but I didn't, and that's something that I will have to live with but I was not going to let you relive all of that and have to deal with recovery alone."

"But I would have gone with you?"

"Be realistic! I couldn't take care of you like they did. I didn't have the resources. I wish I did and if I could go back and do it over I would be honest with you from the beginning. But I can't. Before the attack you had lost your smile for a while and that was something that hurt me. So when I saw you smiling with your parents like you used to with me I realized that I couldn't take it away from you. I couldn't hurt you like that again." Rhian remained silent for a few seconds.

"But I haven't smiled in months and I'm still hurting…"

"I know and I'm sorry. I didn't expect it to ever get to this point. I always thought that I would learn to let go and that you would never remember me."

"I wish I would've never met you!"

One Year Later

Rhian sat quietly in front of his Theresa at the dinner table. Awkward silent dinner with his parents had become the norm. This wasn't the loving relationship that he had shared with his parents when Jerri was around.

"Honey, don't you think you've been in mourning long enough? Jerri has been gone for two years and you have yet to get rid of your stuff. I know I'm supposed to tell you to fight for her but I love you too much to encourage that. It's time you go out and find yourself a girl that deserves a good man like you."

"I don't want to talk about it, Mom…"

"I'm just trying to cheer you up sweetie… I hate seeing you like this."

"Do you understand that I can't change who I am? Do you understand that I have always been this way and I will always be? I love Jerri, but I am completely in love with my soul mate… Alexander."

Mrs. Pierce bit her bottom lip. This was the first time that Rhian had given a name and a face to his same-sex interest. The most insulting part about it was the fact that it was someone that they had welcomed into their home. They trusted him! But Theresa wasn't that naïve.

"Yes…" She finally responded after an awkward silence.

"Rhian, we didn't understand… I honestly don't really fully understand it…" His father added.

"But how can you know he is your soul mate." The question was simple. It shouldn't have required time or thought to answer. But since the attack Rhian hadn't thought about the answer. He paused for a moment, as his mind was flooded with thoughts of the dream he had so long ago, the night Alexander rescued him from his jump off the pier, the kiss, and of course Alexander's willingness to sacrifice his own happiness for Rhian's. He took a deep breath, closed his eyes, envisioned Alexander's strong hand holding his, and looked at them with the brightest smile.

"You know the comforting feeling you get under the summer sun that surrounds you more intimately than a blanket as it warms every cell in your body? Or the moment you succeed at something you never thought possible? Do you know the feeling you get when you discover that your prayers have been answered? Do you know the moment where your heart breaks at the thought of losing the thing you care about most in your life? That is Alexander. He is the comfort that warms me. He is the reason I smile. He is the one I could never live without and when I am with him I feel like I am on the verge of touching God." They remained silent as they took in what he was saying.

"Go to him." His mother finally responded as she looked down at his feet. "I should have said that a long time ago." She looked over at her husband waiting for his response. She was afraid of what might come from her brave outburst. When he made eye contact with her she looked away. It suddenly occurred to Rhian that the box with the bracelet hadn't magically appeared in his dresser. He looked up at her.

"You knew?" He said with an almost inaudible whisper. She flashed a smile at him before looking back down.

"Go and don't come back…" Rhian's heart sank from the sting of the words he had heard once before. He looked at his father for validation that he indeed was kicking his son out again. Even after everything that had happened to him and how strong he had become, rejection from his father was still a major fear of his. Perhaps that was why he never tried to push his parents away again. But as he was coming to his own conclusions Rhian's father continued. "Don't come back until you've touched God."

Chapter 18

Alexander didn't waste any time after graduation. He moved to Chicago only a few weeks after the ceremony and began a new job in one of the beautiful high rise buildings in the downtown. His office had a south-facing city and lake view. He loved his new fast-paced life because it was everything he ever wanted. Few things can compare to summertime in the city, when the Magnificent Mile is bustling with activity and North Avenue beach is full of people playing volleyball. The lake comes to life with sailboats, speedboats, and the sounds of children taking their first plunge into the open waters. This was a new chapter in Alexander's life that he had anticipated for a long time. The opportunity to go to San Diego had come up but in the end he wasn't ready to leave the Midwest yet.

His love for the city transformed after a few short days when he finally moved there. His first summer was one of the best he had ever had. He made new friends and was able to attend Lalapalooza. Every weekend he had a new adventure planned filled with exciting events and new people. Though his new home kept him quite busy, there wasn't a day that he didn't think about Rhian. He had come a long way in a short amount of time, achieving many personal goals. He was living the life he had always dreamed of and was proud of himself. Alexander showed great promise at work impressing his coworkers and his boss.

It had been two years since Alexander had graduated. He had only kept in contact with a few of his friends from school. He called Sebastian and Leena frequently and spoke with some of the others through video chat.

"Hey stranger!" Leena's familiar voice was on the other end of the phone call.

"Hey Leena, how are you?"

"I'm doing very well. What are you up to?"

"I'm currently about to go to lunch. I have an hour break so I was going to go to the park."

"Fabulous! Because I'm in the city to have lunch with you."

"What?"

"Yeah, baby! Meet me near the bean! I'll see you in ten!"

"Ok."

He was ecstatic to see her again since the last time they were together was Christmas. On the elevator ride down he reminisced about the wonderful times they had in college. He made the walk from his building to Cloud Gate (or the Bean as the tourists called it) in no time. He looked around for her familiar face but couldn't find her anywhere. He continued in the direction of the lake towards the art piece but there was something strange. It was completely silent. The area was never quiet, especially at that time. Suddenly, the familiar voice of Elvis Presley began singing *Can't Help Falling In Love*. He approached the structure cautiously and when he arrived underneath Rhian came out from behind, getting down on one knee.

"Alexander Thomas, you are one of the most incredibly frustrating human beings I have ever met. You have taken me on one of the most challenging journeys that I have ever embarked on. You have made me feel terrible things. Things that no other person has ever made me feel. I have never cried more tears over anyone than I have over you. Through everything I realized one very important thing; I don't regret a single moment of it. The pain I felt was overshadowed by the amazing things you did for me. You showed me what it was like to be loved. Through all of the problems that we faced, I never lost hope even though I may have been in denial. You never gave up on me and you always believed in me and for that I could never thank you enough. What you and I have is something that I could never live without. You are truly one of the most amazing human beings I have ever met and I

love you with all my heart. Alexander Thomas, will you marry me?"
This was exactly how Rhian wanted this moment to be, except he
wanted to be the one asked.

Alexander remained speechless as a million and a half thoughts
ran through his head. He looked Rhian in the eyes still in shock. He was
glowing, or at least Alexander thought so. He was never more certain
about anything in his life. He had gone through enough with Rhian and
wasn't prepared to handle another minute of it. He pulled Rhian up to
his feet with urgency. Rhian's immediate heartbreak was
overwhelming. He felt humiliated in that moment. He had put himself
out on the line in the middle of the city and here was Alexander again
making a fool out of him, about to reject him. He took a deep breath but
just as he exhaled Alexander got down on one knee.

"Rhian Alexander Pierce, *you* are the most amazing human
being that *I* have ever met. You have also taken me on a wild and
unexpected journey. You have made me experience things I never knew
were possible. When I first met you I was immediately drawn to the
way you just shined but as time went on I fell more and more in love
with the soul that was able to see the things in me that I couldn't. You
believed in me when I couldn't believe. Rhian Alexander Pierce, you
are not only a painter of pictures but also a painter of life. I never lost
hope that you would someday come back to me. It was always you and
it will always be you and only you. Will you do me the incredible honor
of spending the rest of your life as my husband?" He pulled out a small
box containing a ring.

"Yes! Yes and a thousand times yes!"

"Excuse me sir, I was told to give this to you." The unfamiliar
man approached handing Rhian a manila folder labeled *663*. He glanced
at the contents and saw a picture of his thigh with the word *fag* carved

in, blood dripping from the letter *f*. He closed the folder and looked up at the man for answers. "She wanted me to tell you that she was happy for you." He began to walk away but turned around. "She also said congratulations, Pastor closed your case. You have a clean slate." He looked over but only caught a glimpse of the familiar figure as she disappeared into the crowd. Rhian was free. And there beneath the silver city reflection began the rest of their love story.